Suddenly, she ... marriage; it wa... wrong man you brought misery to yourself and him; you lost all chance of the happiness that you and some other man might have known.

"I think I should go now," she said. "If I'm missed, there may be another fuss and I don't think I could bear any more today. Thank you for listening to all my troubles."

Hot, hasty words beat their way to the surface of Hadstock's mind. Don't go back; stay here with me; I love you. . . . But with the taste of them on his tongue he knew that he could never speak them. He knew what it meant to be poor, having been rich, and what descent in the social scale meant; he could visualize the search for work, the search for a home, the scandal, the friendlessness, the placelessness.

He would, at that moment, gladly have lain down and died if his death could have benefitted her, even a little, but such drama, he thought satirically, was denied him, like so many other things. . . .

Afternoon of an Autocrat

NORAH LOFTS

FAWCETT CREST • NEW YORK

A Fawcett Crest Book
Published by Ballantine Books
Copyright © 1956 by Norah Lofts

Library of Congress Catalog Card Number: 56-7946

ISBN 0-449-20139-2

This edition published by arrangement with Doubleday Company, Inc.

Manufactured in the United States of America

First Ballantine Books Edition: December 1985

PART I

AFTERNOON OF AN AUTOCRAT

CHAPTER 1

ON THE THIRD SATURDAY AFTERNOON OF OCTOBER, IN THE year 1795, Sir Charles Augustus Shelmadine set out on what—though he naturally had no notion of it—was to be his last ride.

Stubbornly old-fashioned, he still ate his dinner at midday and made of the meal, as of everything else he undertook, a thoroughly good job. The first pig killing season had just taken place and the walnuts were at their best, though the crop was poor this year; he had dined well, and as he proposed, this evening, to entertain some friends for cards and supper, that meal, usually a frugal affair of two or three courses, would be supplemented by as many again, so if he were to do justice to his own table some exercise was desirable.

As recently as eighteen months ago he would have made his round of the village on foot, but he had lately come to the conclusion that walking provoked his gout. Moreover, today he intended to make a visit to the cobbler's, which was across the Stone Bridge on the other side of the Waste; his new boots, ordered three weeks ago, had not yet been delivered, and it was clear that Amos Greenway needed a prod. So at half past two his stout grey horse was brought to the door, and with some assistance from the mounting block, and some from the

3

groom, he heaved himself into the saddle and set off along the
avenue. It was a fine autumn day, golden and mellow with
sunshine and with just that hint of chill in the air which was
conducive to appetite. The chestnut leaves were sharp yellow
and bright amber, the hawthorns crimson and bronze; the old
man took, in the weather and the scene, a pleasure undimin-
ished by the repetition of more than seventy years.

As he neared the gate Bessie Jarvey, the lodgekeeper's wife,
broke off her work in the potato patch and hurried clumsily to
throw open the gate for him. In the family way again, he
noticed; he'd thought so last time he saw her, now he was sure.
That would be seven youngsters, all under working age; how
they fitted into the Lodge, which consisted of two octagonal
rooms, one on each side of the gateway, was a puzzle; a puzzle
to which there was no solution for it was obviously impossible
to add to either room without spoiling the perfect symmetry of
the entrance. And in any case, he remembered, Jarvey's father
had reared ten children there, all fine healthy brats too.

"Potatoes done well this year, Bessie; better-looking than
mine," he said, looking down at her as she bobbed, holding
the gate wide.

She received the compliment with a smile, closed the gate,
and went back to her digging. Sir Charles, on the patch of
smoothly raked, weedless gravel which divided his gates from
the highway, halted for a moment and looked out over the scene
which never failed to give him pleasure. The Manor gates stood
at the lowest point of the village, just where the main road and
what was known as the Lower Road, and the river, all ran
together. From this point the land sloped gently upwards, so
that looking straight ahead of him, he could see the green of
the common pasture, the vast expanse of the two common
fields, and beyond them the blazing autumn glory of the trees
of Layer Wood, which stretched on all the way to Nettleton.
When he turned his head to the left he could see all along the
main road, which ran straight up the slope, past the church and
the Rectory and the inn and the main part of the village, until
it turned at the Stone Bridge and disappeared over the Waste.
It was all beautiful, all pleasing.

He was—he thought—no sentimentalist, and he would have
repudiated the word "love" as a description of the emotion he
felt for Clevely village; yet the passionate interest, the posses-
siveness, the complacent approval with which he regarded it
came near to justifying the term. Here and there, of course,

there were things—and people—that went wrong from time to time, but that was what he was here for—to put things right; and, above all, to see that nothing changed for the worse. He knew villages whose squires failed in their duty and went running off to London, or Bath, or even, until lately, to the Continent, and naturally in such villages most scandalous things happened, most pernicious ideas took root. And he knew other villages where squires on the spot encouraged and even initiated most revolutionary changes—they dared to call them progress. There'd be no such doings in Clevely, not as long as . . .

"Come up, Bob," he said to the horse; they bore it left and trotted briskly through the village, past the flat-faced Rectory where the reddened creeper glowed in the sun, past the ancient church with its round Saxon tower, in whose shade so many Shelmadines took their last rest amongst so many Cloptons and Greenways and Jarveys and Fullers under *their* unmarked mounds.

As he neared the inn he slackened pace. He was no Puritan and would have been the last to deny that any man who had done a sound day's work had the right to as much sound liquor as he could pay for, but no one—that is no villager—who wasn't a loafer and a rogue would be drinking at this time of day. Almost as though expecting this visit of inspection the little inn stood with both doors open, so that at a glance Sir Charles could see into the taproom with its sanded floor and barrels and the room which had, until an occasional coach started coming through, been Mrs. Sam Jarvey's parlour; they called it the Coffee Room now, though what they drank there he wondered, not coffee, he hoped, for Mrs. Sam had never made a decent cup of coffee in all her ten years' service at the Manor. Both rooms were empty, no labourer, no superior person was drinking this afternoon. Sir Charles nodded to himself; that was as it should be. In the orchard at the side of the inn Sam Jarvey was gathering . . . what? Damsons, by God; late, much, much too late!

The forge was next, just at the corner where Berry Lane led off to Flocky Hall Farm. Strong 'Un, the smith, the third of his line whom Sir Charles had known by that name, was busy fixing a new rim to the wheel of Matt Ashpole's cart—and not before it was needed. As usual, Sir Charles paused to have a word with the smith, who remarked that what was needed was not a new rim but a new wheel. The remark made Sir Charles smile, not because it was witty but because it was in tradition;

all workmen always, when called upon to make a repair, said that what was needed was a replacement—too simple to see that if replacement could be made at will, they'd be hard put to it to find a job.

He turned left into Berry Lane, so named because it was lined with bramble bushes on which blackberries grew in profusion. Despite the picking which had gone on lately there were multitudes left and the air was heavy with their warm black scent. Nobody was picking today, and that too was as it should be; blackberry picking ended on the thirtieth of September. Sir Charles did not precisely believe, as many villagers did, that on that date the Devil flew over, claiming what berries were left as his own and cursing any who dared to take one, but he liked every traditional date to be recognized and honoured.

His mood darkened a little as he went along the lane. He would have liked to ride along, straight past Fuller's and up to Flocky Hall, as he had been used to do in old Abram's day. He had been very fond of Abram Clopton, a yeoman farmer of the real old breed whose family had been at Flocky Hall as long as Shelmadines had been at the Manor. Three tall Cloptons, bearing their bows, had gone with a Shelmadine to Crécy—that was no legend but sober truth, for all four of them had died and had been brought home, at Shelmadine expense, and buried together in the church. Most of the dead brought back from that campaign had been buried at Dunwich and been taken out to sea again when half that town was washed away. From that time on, until fifteen years ago, when old Abram died, the tie between the two families had been sound and close; but things were different now. Young Fred Clopton was progressive—a thing Sir Charles could in no way abide. He admitted—being nothing if not fair-minded—that Fred had a perfect right to do as he chose on his own land; let him grow his turnips and his clover; let him marl his land and winter-feed his cattle and sell fresh beef all through winter, and talk about the "Clopton herd" and market off his squealing little calves one by one at fabulous price as though they were some kind of jewel. All well and good. But to flaunt his success and his money, to buy his wife a pianoforte, to send his two red-faced little wenches to Baildon Female Academy, and to go smashing off to market in a high gig with yellow wheels, that was a different thing altogether, because it made other men envious and discontented, made them mutter about *enclosures*! Flocky Hall was enclosed, three hundred and five acres, all fenced, but it had

been like that ever since the monks at Baildon Abbey had started
sheep farming centuries ago; and it wasn't being enclosed that
made Fred Clopton successful, it was his luck, and his industry
and the steady accumulation of wealth from centuries of thrifty,
hard-working forbears. Damn it, Sir Charles could prove that
that was true, for there were two other enclosed farms at Clevely;
Bridge Farm, two hundred and ten acres, which had been part
of the estate but which had been sold off in 1721, when things
went wrong, and now belonged to a damned Dissenter named
Shipton, who certainly wasn't making a fortune; and Wood
Farm, three hundred and twenty acres, still a Shelmadine property which Sir Charles had let, in a weak foolish moment, to
a retired army officer named Rout, who'd lost an arm at the
Battle of Bunker Hill and had a desire to live in the country
and farm. He wasn't making a fortune either; always behind
with his rent. Discontented fellows who grumbled about the
open fields and longed for enclosure never looked at Shipton,
or Rout, they only saw Clopton.

He had now arrived at Fuller's farmhouse, a pretty, half-
timbered building with a small orchard between it and the lane
and a small yard behind it. Fuller was, after Rout, the largest
of his tenant farmers; he leased one hundred and ten acres,
fifty-five in each of the great fields, and his tenancy gave him
rights to the common pasture as well. He was a good farmer,
hard-working and punctual with his rent, but once or twice
lately he had made a remark derogatory to the open-field system; and if he made one such today, Sir Charles had decided,
he would give him notice, his lease being renewable next Lady
Day.

As it happened, there was no need for a remark; the first
thing that met the Squire's eyes as he turned into the yard was
a cart loaded with turnips, standing with upended shafts by the
pigsty; and the second was the fantastic, crazy, incomprehen-
sible thing which Fuller had done to the kitchen. Sir Charles
had always admired Mrs. Fuller's kitchen with its floor of buff
and pink and primrose-coloured pamments, its wide hearth with
the spits and the brick oven at the side, its big black dresser
set with bits of brassware and pewter plates and mugs. In earlier
days, when he walked, or could dismount and mount again
without a thought, he had often accepted Mrs. Fuller's invitation to step inside and drink a glass of her home-brewed ale,
or cowslip wine, and eat a piece of her best plum cake; more

recently she had brought these offerings to him on a tray and he had accepted them, graciously, out of custom.

Today he stared at a desecrated shrine. The kitchen had been stripped; its floor lay knee-deep in straw; across the far end where the dresser had stood beside the door which led to the inner part of the house there was a brand-new manger, and the madman, Fuller, was standing in the manger, fixing over it a great wide slatted rack which jutted out and covered almost half the ceiling space. He was hammering so vigorously that he had not heard Sir Charles arrive and at the words, "What the devil are you about, Fuller?" he gave a start and almost swallowed the nails that he was holding between his teeth. Then he spat them into his hand, jumped down from the manger, and came stumbling through the straw, a big-boned, gangling fellow, deceptively mild of eye and manner. He raised the hand which held the hammer to the lank, sweat-damp hair that lay in a bull-pow on his forehead.

"Good day, sir. I'm sorry, didn't hear you come."

"I asked what the devil you are about, Fuller." He knew that the answer would be displeasing, since it involved change, so the question might as well be brusque.

"Well," Fuller said deliberately, "I'm fixing up a place for my beasts. This year I aim to coddle one or two of my best through the winter." He jiggled the nails in his left hand but his light blue eyes, the colour of a speedwell, did not waver from their deliberate stare.

"I had a good hay yield and Fred Clopton had more turnips than he wanted, so he sold me a load and I reckoned I'd try this here winter feeding."

"And that demanded that you turn your kitchen into a byre?"

"What else could I do? Pigs need the sty, horses need the stable; mustn't build on my hired acres—you pointed that out yourself, sir, last time I mentioned the matter. Where else can I put my beasts?"

"That," said Sir Charles, "is the question, Fuller. When *every* farmer gets these crazy notions and must keep his beasts through the winter, where will they all go? In a year or so the whole country'd be packed full of bullocks like Baildon Market at Michaelmas. You never thought of that, did you? No! None of you fellows can ever see beyond your noses, and your noses are all snouting out quick profits and nothing else."

Something sparkled in Fuller's pale eyes as he formed, in his mind, the answer to the accusation and the refusal of the argument; but he knew his landlord: Sir Charles could be impervious to reason, but open, occasionally, to appeal. So the farmer said mildly:

"I only wanted to hev a try, sir. For one thing, I'd hev my muck; thass all good wheat straw I've put down, and by winter's end I'd hev a good heap of muck. My top end of Layer Field is hungry for muck."

"Your piece of that field, like everybody else's, gets its fair share of dunging when the cattle turn in there after harvest, Fuller. You're just being selfish, trying to get ahead yourself at the expense of everybody else."

Fuller shook back the limp lock of hair, and there was in the quick jerky gesture something resembling that of a horse, fly-tormented.

"Who'm I hurting, sir? Who'll be a penny the worse for my trying to do things better fashion?"

"I shall," said the Squire promptly. Nodding towards the erstwhile kitchen, he asked with a glint of humour, "You don't imagine that you are improving my property, do you? Turning the trimmest little kitchen in Suffolk into a byre. And there's another thing! What about your poor missus, where's she going to bake and brew. In the parlour?"

"For the time being. She was agin it at first, but I talked her round and she's willing for me to hev a try."

"Well, I ain't. So you can clear all that nonsensical rubbish out, my good man. I shall be by on Tuesday and I shall want to see that kitchen just as I always have seen it."

"Ah," said Fuller, now provoked past caution, "thass just it! Same as things was in the beginning so they must be for evermore, amen. Thass why Clevely lag behind so; thass why us who would get on hev to be hobbled to the old ways that even them old monks knew was backward in their time when they put a fence round Flocky."

Sir Charles let go the rein and planted his plump hands on his knees, sitting forward as though in a chair. The red colour deepened in his face and invaded the whites of his eyes.

"That'll do," he said sharply. "I can tell which way the wind blows. You're hankering after enclosure like all the other selfish cantankerous fools. I happen to remember when Greston was enclosed; Mr. Montague, the Parson, and half a dozen farmers did very well out of it, and forty decent poor men were thrown on the parish. That is not going to happen here!"

The enclosure of the neighbouring village of Greston—

which had been mismanaged—was his stock argument against the innovation which he detested; and he used it so much, always quoting the forty poor decent men who had become paupers, that unwittingly and unintentionally he was building himself a posthumous reputation as the poor man's friend.

"Forty idle fellows at Greston what had just kept going grubbing half a crop out of gardens and keeping a few half-starved beasts on the common lost their rights and now go out to work by the day for wages," retorted Fuller hotly. "And whether that be a bad or a good thing is a matter of opinion."

"Then here's something that ain't. Your notice, Fuller. I shall not renew with you next Lady Day!"

The farmer's thin face took on a grey dirty look as it whitened under the lingering summer tan, but his eyes did not meeken or waver.

"All right then," he said, "sack me! Sack all but the lazy and the lickspittles! It'll come just the same. You can't hold back the tide!"

Good-humoured again now that he had shot his bolt, Sir Charles said, "I never thought of trying. But I *can* keep fellows like you from putting pigs in bedchambers! I shall be by on Tuesday. Good day, Fuller. Come up, Bobbie."

He rode briskly out of the yard and turned back towards the main road. The interview had ruffled him a little, but only a little; he'd half known that there was going to be trouble with Fuller; now it had come and the way he had dealt with it would put a stop to all that nonsense. It was a relief to have it over and done with; and, besides, he had got his way.

Fuller—who had not got his way, had got, in fact, notice instead—stood for a moment breathing as though he had been running, and then turned, stumbled back through the straw, and leaned against the manger while sobs racked his stringy body and a few difficult tears brimmed his eyes and lost themselves in the harsh lines of his face. He wouldn't easily find another farm to hire—the French war and the corn prices which offered such opportunities to men who *could* go ahead had at the same time put a premium on any sort of land. In the far North and West, they said, the ploughs were out on heaths and moorlands that had never felt the touch of the share before. Sod and blast the stubborn old devil, Fuller thought. He gave himself a shake, brushed his horny hand over his eyes, and jumped back into the manger. Ignoring the threat of Tuesday's inspection, he went on hammering at the rack as though nothing

had happened. The turnips had to be stored somewhere...
Tuesday's row couldn't be worse than this; you couldn't be
sacked twice.

Sir Charles clattered over the Stone Bridge, an ancient struc-
ture only just wide enough to take wheeled traffic, but built
with nooks in its walls to allow foot passengers to step back
into safety. Immediately upon its other side he was riding alongside a high wall built of the same pleasant red brick as his own
house and lodge cottage. The wall and the house which it
encircled had been built at the same time as the Manor, and
by the same hands, for the house had been, until fifty years
ago, the Dower House of the family. Sir Charles' father, like
many of his neighbours, had come a cropper at the time of the
South Sea Bubble and in 1721 had been obliged to sell the
Dower House, Bridge Farm, and several hundred acres of land.
The experience had taught him nothing, he had remained a
gambler, both in investments and at cards, until the end of his
life; but it had had its effect upon Charles, who had never
invested a penny in any stock or share, and had made it an
inflexible rule to rise from table the moment he had lost two
guineas. This habit, once the subject of disgusted comment
amongst his "deep-playing" neighbours, had, as he grew to be
old, come to be regarded as one more endearing eccentricity,
and when anyone in the six parishes said that something had
cost or was worth "a Shelmadine" everyone knew that it meant
two guineas.

The high wall was broken at one point by a pair of wrought-
iron gates, similar in pattern though of less impressive size
than those of the Manor, and when he reached them Sir Charles
slowed down and sat for a moment staring at the neglected
moss-grown drive which cut through the tangled, overgrown
laurels and lilacs of the shrubbery and past the ill-shaven lawn
to the house, whose canopied door and window sills and shutters were all in sad need of paint. He was depressed by what
he saw. Still, it was no business of his. The Dower House had
been sold to a seafaring man, a Captain Parsons, who was
reputed to have made a fortune in the slave trade. He had one
daughter, and a good many young men from families, like the
Shelmadines, recently impoverished, had made a bid for her
hand. Charles Shelmadine himself had "taken a shot at her,"
was in fact dancing with her at a ball in the Assembly Rooms
at Baildon, with old Captain Parsons beaming his approval,
when he fell in love, at first sight, across the width of the

ballroom with the beautiful, crazy creature whom he had married and with whom he had spent three enchanting, terrible years. The shames, the shocks, the anxieties, the delights and ecstasies of that brief married life, and its appalling end, would have left a mark on many men to the end of their days, but Charles Shelmadine had possessed then the rudiments of the art, which in later years he perfected, of shutting out of his mind anything unpleasant about which he could not take positive action. In quite a short time he was able to think that it was a blessing that Felicity had died before his attempts to indulge her whims and demands had ruined the estate all over again. As it was, she had, in bearing the son in whom he had so much delighted, sown the seed for a bitter harvest.

Now as he halted by the gate of the Dower House, all these memories merely brushed the fringe of his mind, which was focussed upon the question of whether or not to call upon Miss Amelia this afternoon. It had, until recently, been his habit to call once, at least, in a month; often he paid an extra visit. She had never married, despite her many chances; like others with her advantages she had been very choosy and hard to please. With the passing of time she had grown domineering and sharp of tongue, but Sir Charles had derived considerable pleasure from his visits to her; she listened intelligently and sympathetically, and he had once or twice found himself telling her things which he had never told anyone else; and she understood the value of money as few women did. Lately she seemed to have grown miserly; for the last three years the house and grounds had deteriorated and when, on a recent visit he had exercised the privilege of an old friend and tried to bring the talk round to her personal financial problems, she had been very evasive, so much so that she sounded vague and rambling. And she had offered him, instead of the Madeira which he expected in that house and considered his due, some very inferior Marsala—without a word of apology.

No, he would not visit her this afternoon. The rumpus with Fuller was quite enough. When he had administered the well-merited prod to Greenway, he'd ride on and visit the little hunchback, Jacky Fenn, and hear how he was getting on with his fiddle playing. That would put him in perfect good humour again.

"Come up, Bobbie," he said, and they jogged along to the end of the red wall.

At this point the highway made a boundary between Clevely

and the neighbouring parish of Minsham All Saints; the latter had been enclosed further back than even Sir Charles could remember, and now, on his left hand as he rode, the hawthorn hedges were high enough to shut out the views; but on the right hand there was view enough, for on that side of the road lay Clevely Waste, a vast open space of commonland, uncultivated save for the little patches of garden and orchard lying near the hovels which fringed its edge nearest the highway. Here lived those of the Clevely villagers who enjoyed rights on the Waste but had no share in the open fields or common pasture. Here lived the self-employed, the odd-jobbers, and the merely idle.

In appearance the cottages presented a sharp contrast to those in the main part of the village, where Sir Charles was very particular about the white-washing of walls and the mending of thatch. Like all other landlords he was often forced to choose between doing indoor or outdoor repair, and invariably he did the latter, giving as his reason that one must keep property weatherproof. The owners of the Waste cottages seemed not to mind about the weather; one or two of the structures were fairly soundly built, but most of them looked as though, long ago, they had grown from the soil and were gradually sinking back into it. Many of them, according to legend, had been built in bygone times under an ancient licence known as "Squatters' Rights" by which any man was entitled to his freehold if he could, between dusk and dawn, rear four walls, slap on a roof, and have smoke rising from a chimney in the morning. They gave evidence of their hasty and makeshift origin. Sir Charles, since he felt no responsibility for them, did not find even the most tumble-down of them offensive to the eye; they crouched low and fitted in with the background of nibbled grass and gorse and bracken and stunted hawthorns which was the Waste. And in the same way, he thought, their inhabitants fitted in with the pattern of village life.

Fuller just showed his pigheaded ignorance when he spoke of all Waste dwellers as idle fellows. In many ways they were useful and sometimes they were industrious; Amos Greenway, though he frittered away a good deal of time, still made and mended boots and shoes and clogs and all kinds of harness; Matt Ashpole went twice a week into Baildon with his bony old horse and ramshackle cart and was available for any odd carrying job and did a bit of dealing as well; Bert Sadler dug all the graves; old Widow Hayward took in washing, acted as midwife at one end of life and layer-out at the other, and had somehow managed to rear three sturdy sons who had all gone soldiering: Matt Juby was idle and a drunkard to boot, and Spitty Palfrey was much the same, but neither of them ever refused a casual job, mole- and ratcatching, emptying privies, work at hay and harvest time. Somebody had to do these things and it was foolish to say that enclosure, by forcing them into regular work, would benefit the village; it was simply because they still had their Waste and could support themselves for part of the year with their geese and goats and pigs and scrawny cows that they were available when they were needed.

The cobbler's cottage stood at the far end of the strung-out line, and it was one of the more solidly built ones. In time past it had been cared for, with flowers beside the door, a step white with hearthstone, and a neat potato patch at the side. Even now recent neglect had not quite reduced it to the general level. Julie Greenway had been a very superior sort of woman when she married Amos, daughter of a small yeoman farmer at Notley, and herself apprenticed to the dressmaking. An old unmarried aunt of Sir Charles had lived at the Manor until her death and Julie Greenway had made all her dresses, and once she had come to do a fitting and had heard that a dairymaid was ill and had offered to make the butter, saying that it would be a treat to get her hands on a churn once more. Damn good butter it was too. If Julie had married a farmer she'd have been another Mrs. Fuller, or another Mrs. Clopton—Mrs. Abram, of course, not Mrs. Fred with all that pianoforte nonsense! But it had been easy—twenty-three years ago—to see why she married the cobbler, a good-looking, merry, devil-may-care young scamp he'd been before the Methodists got hold of him.

At that time had Amos been one of his tenants, Sir Charles would have given him notice; next to, if not equally with, progressive farming the Squire abhorred Dissent. But the cobbler was a freeholder, so Sir Charles had shown his complete disapproval in the one way open to him, he took away his custom. Whether Amos noticed was doubtful; Sir Charles did, for it seemed that no cobbler in any nearby village could make a decent pair of boots and even when he transferred his custom to Baildon he never attained a really easy fit. And then, one evening, Amos Greenway, trudging home through Layer Wood from one of his Methodist meetings, had seen a light, a flickering blaze, and gone towards it to find a lonely keeper's cottage all aflame. The keeper was out doing his duty, and his wife, with a child in her arms, was at the foot-square bedroom window screaming into the lonely night. Amos had yelled, "Push him through! I'll catch him," and had done so. Then laying the child aside he had fought his way in and dragged out the woman.

Next day, when the news reached him, Sir Charles had walked straight to the cobbler's cottage and said, "I hate Dissent, as you know, but I honour a brave man, Greenway. My custom is yours in future."

Amos, all blistered and hairless and plastered with old Widow Hayward's herb poultices, had said simply, "It will be welcome, sir." Then he added something about having often preached about brands snatched from the burning and now knowing what they felt like.

Since then Sir Charles' boots had fitted better, but there was no denying that Greenway became more and more dilatory as time went on and Methodism encroached upon his time. Once he had left his work, which included stitching a stirrup leather for his Squire, and gone sixty miles to hear John Wesley preach, walking every step of the way. Now he was late with this last job, and Sir Charles intended to take no excuses.

Between the road and the cottage wall was a little bed of marigolds, almost past flowering. The door to the room which Amos used for his work was half open and just inside a large cat, almost the colour of the marigolds, lay basking in the last of the sun's warmth. Sir Charles leaned sideways and rapped smartly on the door with the handle of his crop. The cat sprang up in an offended manner and backed into the flower bed, where it stood glaring at him with its yellow eyes and moving its tail from side to side.

The door opened wide, revealing not the angular figure and dreamy countenance of the cobbler, but the small neat figure of a girl, who made her bob, and then looked up at him with a timid, wavering smile.

He prided himself upon knowing the name, as well as the history, of every living soul in Clevely, and liked to prove it by using the names freely, surprising young people, particularly when he caught them up to mischief, by saying, "You're Samuel *Thomas* Jarvey, ain't you? Samuel *John* is the one with bowlegs." It irked him this afternoon that he had to wait a perceptible moment before bringing the girl's name to mind. It was out of the Bible, he remembered that much, but not a girl's name at all. Something ridiculous like Jordan or Galilee! Ah, he had it.

"Good day, Damascus. Y'father about?"

"No, sir, I'm sorry. He's over to Nettleton."

"Well, I hope he finished off my boots before he went galloping about the countryside. Methodist business again, I'll be bound."

He spoke sternly and was not surprised or displeased to see an expression of acute distress come into the girl's face. He was, however, surprised when, after a second during which it looked as though her eyes might jump out of her head, she said quietly:

"Oh yes, sir, he finished them and he was going to deliver them either on his way there or back."

"Ah, that's all right then," said Sir Charles, softening immediately. "You're busy," he added, looking at the broom in her hand.

"I try to clear up a bit when I get home, sir. Mother can't do much nowadays."

"Rheumatics bad again? Pity, great pity!" He was always downcast by any evidence of age or infirmity but in this case he felt an almost personal concern. He had been very partial to the busy, capable little dressmaker, and had been sorry to see how, soon after Amos took up with the Methodists and began to neglect his trade, her looks and her spirits had seemed to decline; and later, when she had grown stooped and lame and twisted, he had been sorry again.

"Have you tried nettle tea?" he asked kindly. "I swallowed gallons of it when my gout was bad, and to my mind it did more good than all the doctor's brew! You put a good bunch of young nettles into a crock, pour boiling water over, let it stand, and then strain it off." He remembered that in its natural state nettle tea had a flat, nauseating flavour which he had disguised by the addition of lemon juice; he remembered too that lemons were not easy to come by and pretty expensive. "Then you add the juice of a lemon, just to make it tasty. I'll send you one or two along. You make a good jorum of that and tell her I hope it'll do the trick."

"Thank you, sir. That would be very kind."

All the time he had been speaking, looking down at the girl who stood looking up at him, he had been aware of a small, nagging feeling of annoyance. He had a very weak spot for young female creatures, particularly when they were neat, fairly comely, and respectful; he was not averse from pulling a stray curl, chucking a wench under the chin, or administering a little pat on the rump; at Christmas and the Harvest Horkey he was free with his kisses, an old man's privilege. Now, having been stern and then kindly to this young female who was neat, not uncomely, and very civil, he felt that the little encounter should be rounded off with some fatherly gesture, yet he could not bring himself to make it. There was an irritating primness about her, that was it. The way all the pretty, would-be-curly hair was dragged back from the centre parting and clamped into those hard-looking plaits on the nape of her neck, leaving her brow so naked and so much too big for the small face; the ugly high neck of the print dress; prim, repellent. A pity. But there was something more, something more seriously wrong; and suddenly he knew what it was. Those eyes—they weren't the colour any human eyes should be; damn it, they were nearly yellow, were in fact almost the colour of the cat's, not quite yellow, a cloudy, greenish amber. Most unusual and most disturbing.

As he stared the cat made a delicate, graceful bound through the air and landed on the girl's shoulder, thrusting its soft head under her chin, and curving its sinuous body so that its plumy tail went behind her head. Now, with the ugly collar, the unbecoming slaty colour of the print dress hidden, and with the prim expression melting into affection, she was almost beautiful. Sir Charles was happily able to give her a little pat on the shoulder not occupied by the cat and to say with his full geniality:

"Good day, m'dear."

"Good afternoon, sir," she said.

The Greenways' bit of garden lay to the side of the house; a potato patch, some gooseberry and currant bushes, and a fruit tree or two. The potato patch was thick with weeds and Sir Charles remembered that it was always Julie who in the past had been seen at work there; if this year she had been too much disabled to raise a crop they'd feel the pinch during the winter. And a little hunger might do Amos no harm; bring him to his senses a bit.

Where the garden ended he turned right to follow the foot-and-bridle path which ran between the Waste and Layer Wood and then on between Layer Field and the wood.

Damascus Greenway, whose name had been shortened to Damask so long ago that the full name on Sir Charles' lips had sounded unfamiliar, set the cat down on the step, went in and closed the door, propped the broom in a corner and stood still, spasmodically clasping and unclasping her hands. She had just told a deliberate lie, and told it for worldly profit, the very worst kind of lie!

There they stood on the workbench; a pair of top boots finished save for the fixing of the yellowy-brown cuffs which would complete them. The tops lay near, awaiting the thirty minutes or so of steady stitching needed to round off a good job. And *why* hadn't she been honest and said that they weren't quite ready, but that they would be finished and delivered by nightfall? That was all she had to say; that was what Father would have said. And instead she'd gone and told a lie. And it wasn't as though she didn't know better; she knew exactly what every lie did; it knocked another nail in the Cross upon which Jesus had died; it added another spike to the Crown of Thorns. She'd done that, Damask Greenway, who lived Him . . . and she'd done it simply to prevent Sir Charles saying that Father neglected his work for his Methodism.

Now she stood, and the voices began. The grave, grieved voice of God saying that man shall not live by bread alone; saying betrayal, thirty pieces of silver; saying he who denies me I will deny; saying a lie, Damask Greenway, a tribute to Satan, who is called the Father of Lies; saying another nail, another thorn.

And the voice of the Devil, who could, if he wished, make himself so clearly heard, so plausible, saying how sensible not to offend Sir Charles, how clever to hide Father's lapse, with winter coming on and all the potatoes to buy this year and Mother not able to take in any sewing.

Often she wondered whether other people, other Methodists, members of Nettleton Chapel, heard these conflicting voices saying, so clearly, such contradictory things. She thought not. Everybody else seemed so *sure*. Father, for instance, if he had been home, would have said, "I'm sorry, sir, they're not done, but if you're in a hurry I'll sit down and finish them off, it'll take half an hour."

("And *you'd* have said that," said the Devil, "if you could have done the job; you couldn't, so you did the next best thing.")

She felt dizzy and a little sick; so many voices! She knew the remedy. "Take it to the Lord in prayer," as they said in the prayer meetings.

She knelt down by the bench and dropped her head on her

folded hands, within two inches of the shining toes of the boots
which had caused all the trouble.

("Not the boots," said the Devil, "your father leaving the
boots unfinished was the cause of the trouble. Be honest with
me, at least!")

She began to pray, addressing God as though He were Sir
Charles Shelmadine, only infinitely more touchy when offended,
infinitely more kind when pleased, and infinitely more powerful
at all times.

She was really very much muddled about God and Jesus
... it was Jesus who had called her to come to Him in that
barn on the June night when she was fourteen, it was Jesus
who loved her and whom she loved and who was hurt by her
sins; but loving Jesus had somehow committed her to the task
of pleasing God, who was quite different, who could never be
hurt, only angered or pleased. There were even moments when
she did not think God had been fair to Jesus, sending Him down
here to earth to suffer and be crucified, just because men, whom
God had made, "in His own image," or so they said, hadn't
turned out the way God wanted them. Once she had tried to
talk to Amos about this matter and he had said, "But, child,
they're all one; the Trinity, Father, Son and Holy Ghost." And
any further question on her part had been silenced by the realisation that she had no idea of the Holy Ghost at all. Jesus,
patient, loving, suffering, she knew; and God, strict, jealous
but capable, properly approached, of being benevolent; that
was all.

So now she knelt and asked, from the depths of her heart,
forgiveness for the lie that she had told; she begged for forgiveness so urgently that sweat broke out on her forehead and
between her shoulder blades, and her hands were slippery with
it. Oh God, *don't* let that extra nail, that extra thorn hurt *Him*
who never did a sin at all! Forgive me, punish me, I told the
lie.

(A plaintive, real human voice from the kitchen called,
"Damask, ain't you about finished in there?" and she called
back, "In just a minute, Mother.")

And she waited. Presently God spoke. With the utmost
clarity He told her that she could work out her own salvation
and punishment. She was to wait until Amos came home and
finished off the boots. Then she was to deliver them to the
Manor. By that time she would be late and must take the Lower
Road to Muchanger—the haunted road. So she would show,

in one act, the sincerity of her repentance and her faith in God, who would protect her. It was all as clear and simple as any order she had ever received in her place of servitude. She got up from her knees, immensely relieved and determined to ignore something which had begun to move, coldly and creepily, somewhere just behind her apron band. Hastily she finished the tidying of the workroom and went back into the kitchen, where her mother, with a shawl over her shoulders, huddled by the fire, clumsily and slowly peeling the potatoes for the evening meal. Once a month Saturday was for the Greenways a feast day. Damask was free on that day from twelve o'clock, and by missing the servants' midday dinner at Muchanger she could be home by one o'clock or soon after, buying sixpenny-worth of pudding beef on the way. The pudding could be on the boil by two o'clock at latest and ready to eat by six. She could then share the feast, wash the plates, and be back at Muchanger by eight. And there was enough pudding left to be heated up and eaten on Monday and Tuesday of the following week.

"You do look muddled," Mrs. Greenway said. "Come now and hev a sit down and a bit of a chat. Did I hear a knock on the door?"

"Sir Charles, come for his boots. I promised he should have them tonight. Father'll just have to finish them off before he has his supper and I'll take them up."

Mrs. Greenway did not comment upon this. There had been a time, nearly four years ago it had ended, when she and her daughter had been on one side, Amos on the other. They'd never gone against him, or defied him . . . but there it was, they'd been together and he'd been alone. Then there'd been that revivalist meeting at Summerfield with a Mr. Whitwell preaching, and all of a sudden Damask had gone over to the other side. Mrs. Greenway had been very lonely ever since. Religious fervour, she thought, was very much like some sort of disease; some people caught it, some didn't, no matter how much they were exposed to it. She never had. Loyalty to Amos had carried her to hundreds of meetings, she had sat through innumerable sermons, knelt through innumerable prayers, and never experienced any change. She had conformed to pattern, never did any work on Sunday, wore plain clothes, attended chapel as long as she could walk to Nettleton, never said a bad word, but her heart was not in it. She would look round at her neighbours, Matt Juby and Matt Ashpole, and naturally be glad

that Amos was not as they were, drunken ne'er-do-wells, but
wasn't there, she wondered, a middle way, the way of her
family, where a girl could wear a pretty dress and curl her hair
... and a man tend his business and make a good living and
be proud of it?

And wouldn't it have been better if Amos had made enough
money—as he was well able to do—to let Damask go and be
apprenticed, as she herself had been, to the dressmaking instead
of going to work in the kitchen at Muchanger? She had once
ventured to say as much to Amos just at the time when Damask
was of an age to begin work, and he had looked at her with
astonishment. "What can it matter?" he asked. "So long as she
lead a good life, what do it matter where?"

"Well, service is a hard life, and Damask ain't very big.
And she's dainty-handed; she'd do well at Miss Jackson's."

"She'd hev more templations, living in the town, and be
more prone to get vain and giddy. I shall get over to Muchanger,
time she start, and fix so she hev one Sunday every month, so
as to attend chapel."

Now, looking at her daughter's hands, still slender and
shapely, but rough and reddened from hard work, Mrs. Greenway gave a little secret sigh; and looking at scraped-back hair
whose prettiness had once been her pride, she sighed again.
Then she rebuked herself, and thought what a good girl Damask
was, and compared her with Matt Ashpole's ripstitch of a
daughter, Sally. And then she asked herself again that old tire-
some question, was there no middle way?

Meanwhile Sir Charles had found ample justification for his
ride beside the Waste. It was not the first time by many; once
he had found a stranger, a Nettleton man, slyly taking fuel
there quite illegally; another time he had been just in time to
save Shad Jarvey's donkey from drowning in the pond, and a
fine mess he'd made of himself, dragging it out of the mud;
and on more summer evenings than he could be bothered to
count he had come across couples engaged in illicit love-making
in the one-would-have-thought-unpromising and unsuitable
shelter of the gorse bushes which edged the Waste. The opportunity of preventing the begetting of bastards was not likely to
offer itself this afternoon in October daylight, June evenings
were the dangerous times; still, one never knew, young people
were quite unaccountable.

He did find, however, two of Matt Juby's snub-nosed, ill-
clad brats amusing themselves by throwing stones at two teth-

ered cows, Bert Sadler's with the broken horn and Jim Gaunt's with the defective quarter. He bellowed at them in a voice which could have been, and probably was, heard in Nettleton:

"Stop that, you young devils, and come here to me."

They came cringing, and he gave them, not a talk upon kindness to dumb creatures, which he would not have known how to deliver, but a stern lecture about the ill-effects upon the milk yield of cows thus made unduly active; and to impress the lecture on their memories, he followed it with two good stinging cuts with his crop upon each ragged behind. That, he reflected, riding on, was the way to keep order, constant vigilance, prompt rebuke. Given a free hand, he knew himself capable of keeping all England in order, and the Continent too, if it came to that. Disgraceful the way the Continent had been going on lately. Not that it had ever been properly run—and here he had the evidence of his own eyes; for he, in his youth, had made the Grand Tour. And he had summed it up in a verse of doggerel which had been his only excursion into the world of creative art. He had written it in a letter to his father, and also in the visitors' book of the inn, just near the St. Gothard Pass, where he had spent the night and entertained the spirit of poetry for a brief moment. It ran thus:

In France I ate well, but paid dear for my meat:
In Germany there was nothing but calves' flesh to eat:
In Italy the inns are bad and the people are beasts:
But the Swiss, honest Swiss charge fair for their feasts.

It might not be verse of the highest standard, but it summed up tersely and accurately young Charles Shelmadine's reaction to "foreign parts"; it also emphasised his difference from his father, who had enjoyed every mile of his tour, and often harked back to it with wistfulness.

Nothing else demanded immediate action. He noted with approval that the geese were doing well, and his mind slid forward to Christmas. He reared no geese of his own, but he always bought half a dozen, spreading his custom justly among his tenants. He observed with interest that Shad Jarvey's donkey was still alive and able to forage; the beast must be of incredible age. He marked, with disapproval, the fact that Matt Juby's cow still had husk. Only a fortnight ago he had drawn Matt's attention to the fact and offered him the necessary linseed and horehound to make it a draught, and a long-necked bottle with

which to administer it; but the loplolly fellow had evidently
done nothing. It was typical of Juby to allow his boys to stone
other people's cows on one part of the Waste while his own
coughed itself to a skeleton on another. If Juby wished to share
in the Christmas dole he'd have to mend his ways.

The Waste ended in a thicket of gorse and bramble and
bracken beyond which lay a grass-covered ridge called the
Dyke, which ran in a ruler-straight line between the riverbank
and the ride which ran through Layer Wood. The Rector, who
was something of an antiquarian, believed it to be part of a
Roman road which had run direct between Colchester and the
sea. He had been talking for twenty years of doing some digging
to test this theory, but he had never had time; he never would
have. The Dyke's interest for Sir Charles was that it made a
firm boundary between the Waste and the cultivated land and
also served as a windbreak, since the fields lay directly to the
south of it.

Between the end of the Dyke and the opening where the
ride which he intended to take ran into Layer Wood, he halted
and looked out across the two great open fields. They lacked
interest at this season. The one nearest the wood, known as
Layer field, had just enjoyed its fallow year and all but a few
of its many sections had been ploughed during the last few
weeks so that the frost, when it came, could do its part in
making the soil friable. The other, slightly larger field, called
Old Tom, had been left with the stubble on it, after harvest,
and the village livestock had been turned into it, to lick up the
fallen grains of corn, to nibble the greenstuff which sprang up
through the stubble, to knead with their hoofs and manure with
their dung the soil which would this year lie fallow. They were
gone now; most of them to the butcher, thus fulfilling the year's
pattern. Stock beasts, the cows, and a bull or two were kept
alive through the winter, the rest went into the brine vat. That
made the Squire remember Fuller . . . and turning his darkening
glance, he looked out over Old Tom. There in the level afternoon light the even furrows lay, acres and acres of them, each
man's sections divided from his neighbours' by a narrow
unploughed baulk. One side of each furrow shone pale violet
in the light, the other was chocolate-coloured. And they wanted
to alter all this. People who called themselves "progressive,"
all sorts of people, from Members of Parliament down to dung-
booted fellows like Fuller, they wanted to do away with the
big, beautiful open fields, to chop them into little piddling

pieces, fenced round and given over to pernicious ruinous experiments—no fallow year, for example. These so-called progressive fellows wanted to grow clover or turnips or some such nonsense instead of resting a field that was wearied from a corn crop. It might make money for them for a year or two, as it had for Fred Clopton, but at what a price! The spoilation of the good soil which had been tilled in the sound, tried old way ever since Domesday Book. Sir Charles knew that that was true, for somewhere in the cluttered records in his library, he had a copy of the particulars of Clevely as it had existed then; it was on sheepskin, and the writing was illegible, but the map was amazingly accurate and the two great fields, the common pasture by the river, were just as they were today. All those hundreds of years the fields had given a harvest, rested a year, been sown again, and nobody was going to tell him that a system that wasn't good could have lasted so long!

Fuller's words came back to his mind, "You can't hold back the tide." It was the threat of change, not the insolence of the remark, which rankled. As a rule, he ignored the thought of his own mortality as firmly as he ignored anything else which displeased or discomfited him; but he knew, of course, that one day, like everyone else, he must die. What then? How would Clevely fare when he was no longer there? He would have given a great deal to have been able to say, "My son will uphold the good old traditions." Instead he had been obliged to face the glaring, appalling fact that unless he were prevented, Richard would fall upon Clevely with the ferocity of a tiger upon a lamb . . .

Nowadays he seldom thought of his son, save at moments like these when he was thinking of Clevely's future. There was nothing to be gained by cherishing sentiment or regret about something that was over and done with, and which could not be helped. God knew he had tried, been patient, indulgent, tolerant to the point of folly, always bearing in mind that Richard was Felicity's son as well as his own.

Staring out over the peaceful fields, he allowed himself to look back over his years as a father and found himself in no way to blame, unless overkindness were blameworthy. He'd loved the boy; they'd had seventeen very happy years together; then Richard had gone wrong. Completely wrong, bad to the very marrow of his bones. One failing, one vice would have been different, if he'd been merely drunken, merely a wild gambler, merely lecherous, merely spendthrift; but he was all four, and more; there wasn't a vice or folly or an insane extravagance which Richard hadn't taken to with the avid ease of a suckling taking its mother's milk. When Sir Charles looked back upon what he had borne between Richard's seventeenth and thirtieth year he was amazed at his own forbearing. Debts and scandals, promises made just to be broken, insolence, ingratitude, and worst of all, that frightening feeling that there was actually something lacking in the boy, that there was nothing there to get hold of, to appeal to, to reason with. It was like having to deal with an imp out of Hell.

He'd gone on, for thirteen long years, thinking it *couldn't* last; Richard must come to his senses; gone on blaming bad company, loose women, changing times; gone on making conditions, "I'll pay this time if you give me your word never to see this Mrs. Davison again"; "We'll forget all this if you'll swear to keep away from Angelina's"; and knowing all the time that the imp was laughing at him, making its own plans for his defeat and mockery.

There could be, of course, only one end; and it had come just on ten years ago, when he had said, "I've done with you. Go to the devil your own gait. If you show your face here again the servants have orders to deal with you as they would any other intruder."

He had never regretted it. Like many another fearfully postponed act it had hurt less than he had expected. He could now think of Richard as though he were dead. And the handsome, merry, high-spirited boy whom he had loved *was* dead; some strange evil thing had come and devoured him and taken possession of his body and made use of his name. Sir Charles would not own that thing as his son.

So Clevely had no heir apparent; Richard would inherit the title and would become Lord of Manor, which nowadays meant little beyond some say in the rights of the Waste. The estate was not entailed and Sir Charles had his own ideas for its disposal. Sir Richard, when the time came, could come home to England and build himself a hovel next door to Amos Greenway's and live like Matt Juby for all Sir Charles cared. And if Fuller and others like him were looking forward to enclosure at Clevely as soon as Sir Charles was gathered to his fathers they were in for a surprise. One day—not tomorrow or even next week, naturally—but one day, all in good time, he was going to send for old Turnbull of Baildon and make a good water-tight will; everything he owned, down to his gold watch and chain, was going to be left to the Baildon Guildhall Feoffees, that august body of guardians who administered several trusts bequeathed by a man named Jankym Reed, who had died rich and heirless in the year 1540. Nothing in the care of the Feoffees ever changed, even the bequest which provided for thirty red-hot pennies to be thrown amongst thirty poor boys every Christmas Eve, was solemnly and faithfully administered. They would keep Clevely exactly as Sir Charles had kept it, an everlasting memorial to good sense and tradition. The income which he now enjoyed could be used towards reducing rents in bad seasons, for maintaining the property in better order than he had been able to afford to do, and to help individual deserving men who had fallen on evil days through no fault of their own. He had it all worked out; it would be no more than an hour's work for old Turnbull to write it down with the appropriate number of "aforesaids" and "whereases."

As always, his mind came comfortably to rest upon this thought and his face was calm again as he turned into the green, moss-carpeted, tree-shaded ride which led through Layer Wood. He was on his way to the loneliest place in the district, a keeper's cottage even more remote than the one concerned with Amos Greenway's deed of heroism. It was not his cottage, nor was its occupant his keeper, Fenn was a Mortiboys man, and his interest in the boy he was about to visit was the result of sheer benevolence.

Three years before, at the enormous Harvest Horkey which he gave every year on the day after the last load of corn was safely in, and to which everybody in Clevely was bidden, he had seen a small, pale-faced, hunch-backed boy standing with his mouth a little open and his eyes fixed on the men who were playing the fiddle for the dancing.

He'd gone over to him and said, "I don't know you, boy. What's your name?"

The boy had jumped, as most boys did when suddenly accosted by Sir Charles, but his face remained tranquil and his large dark eyes had met the Squire's frankly.

"No, sir, I'm staying with my uncle at the forge; but he said it would be all right for me to come. My name is Jacky Fenn."

"You're welcome; all welcome today. You enjoying the music?"

"Oh yes, sir, thank you."

"Be a fiddler yourself, one day, eh?" Not that there was

much likelihood, not long for this world if Sir Charles were any judge; he'd seen that look on a child before.

"I'd love it more than anything in the world, sir. But you have to have a fiddle, don't you?"

There was something immensely engaging in his frank look and lack of shyness and shuffling.

"I suppose you do. And fiddles cost money, don't they? Any idea how much?"

"I think about two guineas, sir."

"Two guineas! Bless my soul! That's a lot of money, ain't it?"

"Yes, sir, a very great deal of money." He let out his breath like a sigh and his eyes went back to the fiddlers.

"Had all you want to eat? That's right. Enjoy yourself, Jacky Fenn."

Next time he went into Baildon, Sir Charles sought and, after some initial difficulty, found a man who had two fiddles for sale. One, a very cheap new shoddy bit of work, was thirty shillings, the other, old and beautiful with some mother-of-pearl about it and inlay on its belly, was ten guineas. Sir Charles bought the old one, and having by now found out from Strong 'Un where his nephew lived, rode over to present it. He had also learned that the boy's mother was dead, had died young of the lung rot, and that Jacky kept house for his father, not being strong enough to work outside.

So he would be much alone in that remote place, Sir Charles thought, and the fiddle would be nice company for him.

"There you are," he said to the astonished, speechless child. "You learn to play and one day I'll come and hear you. I'm very fond of a good tune, a good *old* tune, mark you. I've spoken to Jim Lantern about you and he's coming over one evening soon to show you the way of it."

He had then ridden away before Jacky could say a word.

During the intervening three years he had called at the cottage five or six times; the boy had quickly mastered the instrument and could now fairly make it sing, as Sir Charles said; but it was more and more evident that the boy's time for playing the fiddle or doing anything else was very short. And that was sad; still, in Heaven he would have a harp and a good straight back to boot; and there was no use being sickly and sentimental about such things.

Jacky himself opened the door and gave the old man a look of doglike adoration before he reached inside for the fiddle and the muffler which always made Sir Charles think of Joseph's coat of many colours in the Bible; the muffler had been knitted out of hundreds of odds and ends of wool and was like a rather dingy rainbow.

"Well, how are you, my boy? And how's the fiddling?"

"I've got three new songs for you today, sir. Three new *old* songs, I mean, sir."

"That's the style. Fire away."

Half leaning against the jamb of the door, the child genius—he was nothing less—played "Once in the Month of May," "Edgar's Sad Wooing," and "Jack on the Green." The rein lay slack on the grey horse's neck and Sir Charles' plump red hands lay slack on the rein. The last rays of the sun withdrew from the treetops and the swift October dusk began to flood through the woods. The wind was rising, carrying the bittersweet wail of the fiddle music into the distant thickets. The old Squire's broad face, highly coloured and solid from seven decades of good feeding and drinking and excellent health, and the boy's, pinched and pale from thirteen years of suffering and poverty, wore, for a little while, the same look of peaceful pleasure. Then the last note shrilled out triumphantly, lingered, and died. Jacky lowered his bow and stood, panting a little from exertion, and Sir Charles roused himself.

"As bonny a music as I ever listened to," he said heartily, "and it's a comfort to know that when old Lantern goes to his long home, you'll know all the good old tunes to play at the horkeys and weddings. When that day comes we'll rig you up a little donkey cart. Well, you go in now, it's turning cold. Going to be a wild night."

With some difficulty, for his breeches were a tight fit across his thick thigh, he pushed his plump hand into his pocket, fingered for, and found a half guinea.

"I shall be along again," he said as he withdrew his hand. "Here y'are!" He pushed the neat shining coin into the boy's little claw. "Nay, nay. I'm only paying for my pleasure. Good day, Jacky."

Fumbling at another pocket, he pulled out his watch, snapped open its case, and stared at its face. It was later than he had thought, and he was a good way from home. Best cut through by the Lady's Ride and on to the Lower Road. He'd intended to look in at Wood Farm, where the on-the-face-of-it-friendly visit would tend to remind Captain Rout that Michaelmas was rent day and three weeks past; but he could do that just as well tomorrow.

"Come up, Bobbie," he said. "Best foot forrard now!"

The grey horse, knowing that each step now led towards home, set off briskly; nevertheless, it was full dark when they emerged from the wood and turned into Lower Road. And there it happened, whatever it was.

Dark tales were told by winter fires concerning the Lower Road near Lady's Ride. Away back in the time of the Civil War it had been the scene of the last desperate gallop of Lady Alice Rowhedge, who had been convicted of witchcraft. There were very few people in the six parishes who did not at least *half* believe that on certain nights, when the wind was high, she and the great black stallion which had obeyed her like a dog rode this way again.

It was, of course, a windy night; and possibly a branch had fallen, startling the sober grey horse and making it throw its rider.

At Wood Farm the Routs heard the clatter of its hoofs and Captain Rout popped back into the corner cupboard the bottle of brandy he had just taken out and opened, very skilfully with his one hand, holding the bottle between his knees; and Mrs. Rout put on her most piteous hard-done-by, all-at-sea expression. But the horse did not slacken pace and after a moment they looked at one another and breathed again.

"In the deuce of a hurry tonight," said Captain Rout, and went to the cupboard again. A man so handicapped, whose career had been cut short, whose future was decidedly unpromising, needed all the consolation he could give himself.

At Bridge Farm, Shipton the Dissenter, just back from the meeting at Nettleton which had also drawn Amos Greenway away from his duties, was belatedly feeding his pigs; he was nearly two hours late and the pigs believed that death by starvation was imminent; they were squealing so loudly that he could hear nothing else. Mrs. Shipton was deafened by the din too as she prepared in the kitchen a hot meal, the Saturday ritual to make up for not cooking on the Sabbath day.

The grey horse clattered over the wooden bridge just as Fuller, lantern in hand, was collecting the four bullocks which he meant to stall-feed through the winter from the common pasture. It was late, for he had finished his rack and heaved the turnips into it, and he could have left the beasts out until morning. But the urge to see the job truly completed, to see his bullocks in the straw, with their noses in the manger had been irresistible. As Bobbie's hoofs rang hollowly at the bridge, Fuller said into a bullock's unresponsive ear, "There he go, pigheaded old sod! Riding like the devil; pity he don't break his bloody neck!"

The grey horse halted by the gate. Bessie Jarvey, who had just sat down for the first time that day, said, "You go, Jim?" without any great confidence. However, Jim grunted and rose, not willingly, but with dispatch. Sir Charles did not like to be kept waiting and Jarvey remembered the time when Bessie had been abed with her fifth and he himself had been in the privy and half a minute's delay had been unavoidable. Sir Charles had said, "You getting old and slow, Jim? Or is all this night work sapping your strength?"

So tonight briskly he swung back one half of the heavy gate, briskly he put his hand to his forelock and said:

"Good evening, sir," before, in the darkness, he was aware of the empty saddle. He said later that it made him feel no end of a fool. He also said that he noticed how profusely the horse was sweating; a bit more than you'd expect it to even after a sharp gallop, the night being so chilly.

Bobbie, according to custom and drawn by his stable, went smartly through the gate and was out of reach along the avenue before Jarvey had fully taken stock of the situation and realised that he must do something. He must get up to the house, and tell Sir Edward Follesmark and the Rector; they were there, he knew Bessie had let them in just before she sat down. They'd know what to do. "Bugger Bobbie, going by me like that," he muttered, "now I must tramp it. I could have rode."

They found Sir Charles sprawled in the road, halfway between the opening of the Lady's Ride and the gateway of Wood Farm. The way his head lolled indicated that his neck was broken. Fuller was obscurely relieved to think that this must have happened before he confided in the bullock, choosing to forget that all through the late afternoon he had been wishing ill to his landlord. They took Rout's gate from the post and used it as a stretcher upon which to carry the body home. They mentioned Richard in muted voices; they remembered many things; they speculated about the future.

Only one thing was sure. The old man, now dead, had in his fashion "kept the faith and finished the course." Nothing would ever be the same again.

CHAPTER 2

ON THE AFTERNOON OF THE THIRD SATURDAY OF OCTOBER IN
the year 1795, but making due allowance for the longitudinal
variation in time which those who mastered the subject at school
will understand and those who did not be content to ignore,
Mrs. Richard Shelmadine set out on what she knew would be
her last ride through the city of Kllapore.

The Rajah had sent the message in the morning; it was
couched in the usual arrogant terms; His Highness would be
prepared to take leave of them on this day, an hour before
sunset.

Richard had described exactly the various horrible things
which he was prepared to see happen to the Rajah, and to
himself, before he intended to comply with this command; and
so long as he confined his courses to English, Linda had made
no protest; when he changed, with that astonishing facility of
his, and began a tirade in the native language of the grave-
faced servant who stood awaiting an answer, she said, "Richard, *please*. Ask the man to wait outside. I have thought of
something . . ." He did as she asked, not because he was amen-
able to her wishes, but he had a well-founded respect for her
quick-wittedness; many a time during their wandering exiled

31

years she had found a way to turn to their advantage an unpromising situation.

As soon as they were alone, she said:

"No one could expect *you* to go. But perhaps I should. He
rather likes me, you know. He might *give* me something."

Something more like a snarl than a grin crossed Richard's
face.

"I've noticed His Highness's partiality! If I'd had any sense
I should have let you negotiate. Still it is a notion. Being
impotent as a mule, he can't give you what he would *like* to—
so you may come back with one of the bright buttons with which
he decorates his fat belly!"

She gave a little laugh, one of the tinkling, mirthless, brittle
laughs which she learned long ago to be the best way of parrying
the thrusts which aimed to hurt.

"One of the emerald set! Well, that would be very acceptable."

"Go then, and get away with all you can. All I ask is that
you make no civil excuses for me. Tell him I didn't come
because I couldn't trust myself not to kick his teeth in."

As often before, having won her point, she was ashamed
of the duplicity which had gained her the victory. But to have
spoken truthfully, to have said, "One of us should go; Surunda
has been very kind to us; and though he decided against making
the concessions he never led you to expect anything else," that
would merely have resulted in Richard's ordering her not to
go.

A half-remembered Biblical phrase drifted through her mind,
something about being wily as a serpent and harmless as a
dove; it brought with it the memory of English Sunday evenings, with the scent of hay and honeysuckle drifting in at the
open door, of sunset brightening the stained glass of the windows and her father's voice thrown back from the sounding
board of the high pulpit. But these were things better forgotten;
the days of the dove were over, it had been sacrificed long
ago; even the serpent had found survival difficult enough of
late.

She dressed for the visit with scrupulous care utterly divorced
from vanity. She had never been very pretty, just young and
fresh and lively-looking; and five years in India had ruined
what looks she'd ever had; the smooth pink-tinted oval cheeks
were bleached to the yellowish ivory of elder flower, and there
were hollows in them, and at the temples and about the eyes.

Her hair, once the prettiest thing about her, shiningly golden and very curly, had also bleached and faded to a dullish primrose colour and was almost as straight as an Indian woman's. And she was so thin that her neck was stringy. Cousin Maud had been right when she had warned her that India was no place for a white woman. "In a year you'll be a scarecrow and in two you'll be dead," she had said. Well, it was five years and a few months, and tomorrow she would be on her way back to Fort St. George and within a fortnight, with any luck, on her way back to England. The assignment to Kilapore had been Richard's last chance; the Company had finished with him now. And though there were white men, quite a number of them who had come out to work for the Company and then been dismissed, or had left it to launch out on their own and, many of them, made a living and, some of them, a fortune, Richard was not of their stamp. It took energy and enterprise and industry and ruthlessness to make a way in India, and of these qualities Richard possessed only ruthlessness.

She put on the lavender-coloured silk dress which, earlier in the day, as soon as the servant had gone off with the message, she had taken out and shaken. It was the last of four similar dresses presented to her as a parting present by Cousin Maud, whose generosity had exceeded her knowledge of what was suitable wear in India. She had known enough to say that India was no place for a white woman, but she had not known that it was equally no place for stiff silk, tightly waisted dresses with heavy panniers. Linda had soon removed the panniers and let out the seams of all four gowns. The silk had rotted and split—in India one sweated, there was no other word for it, sweated like a coach horse; and in the rainy season mould grew on one's dresses and shoes overnight. When the rose-pink, the blue-green, the yellow, and the lavender gowns had all shown signs of immediate dissolution, Linda had selected the lavender one, the most modest and practical-coloured of the four, and laid it away. When the others fell to pieces, she had bought lengths of cheap flimsy cotton stuff in the bazaars and made herself some loose cool garments of curious style, a cross between the "morning" prints she had worn at home, before she went to London to act as Cousin Maud's companion and amanuensis, and the clothes worn by Indian women.

The dress gave one or two ominous little creaks as she lifted it over her head and more as she strained back her arms to manage the fastening; but as the long gleaming folds fell to her feet and the lace-lined sleeves covered her sharp elbows she knew a moment of rehabilitation. It was a dignified dress, a proper English dress, and she regretted that the amethyst necklace, Cousin Maud's wedding present, had had to be sold. It would have done much to conceal the painful scragginess of her neck and collarbones. Poor Maud—she had herself made an amazingly advantageous marriage and in dear little Linda's capture of Richard Shelmadine, such a charming man, and heir to a baronetcy, she had seen her old worldly success repeated, with additions; for Maud's own husband had been elderly, middle-class, invalidish, and—to say the least of it—grumpy. Richard Shelmadine was only thirty, just the right age for an innocent, unworldly girl of eighteen, and though he was wild, had indeed quite a *bad* reputation, everyone knew that a reformed rake made the best husband. Maud had done, had given everything that could possibly make the match start off well.

(There'd been that stormy interview at Clevely. Sir Charles had said, "This is the last time, Richard. You marry and settle down or I'm finished with you!" And the perverse devil which ruled all Richard's actions had, two months later, derived the greatest satisfaction from composing a letter which said, "According to instructions, sir, I have chosen my bride. She is the daughter of a poor parson; she has a dowry of five hundred pounds, the gift of her cousin who is the widow of a man who sold tallow candles with great profit; she is plain of face, rustic of manner but has the ability to make me laugh, and I can make her cry." It was the last six words which had proved to Sir Charles that there was no hope.)

The hat which matched the lavender dress was a genuine leghorn straw, wide of brim and becoming; but it had changed colour; much exposure to strong sunshine had darkened the straw and faded the amethyst ribbon almost to grey. Still, it hid a great deal of the straight bleached hair and in its shadow the hollows were less noticeable. As she pulled on her lace mittens, very carefully, for they too had grown brittle, Linda was satisfied that she looked, not attractive, but at her best.

The curtained, wheeled, scarlet-lacquered, silver-decked, cushioned litter which was provided for the use of those at the Rajah's harem who found it necessary from time to time to visit one of the various holy places in the district called for her exactly fifteen minutes and one hour before sunset. Indian timekeeping had always been, and remained, a mystery to her. (Richard had once said, "It is your inquisitive, puppy-nosing-into-everything attitude that I find so engaging.") She had been interested to know that Surunda Ghotal, Rajah of Kilapore, a man whose wealth just could not be counted, owned no watch, no clock. Once when she was thinking about the future she had thought, If I could borrow a little money to start with and could find someone who could make watches and clocks cheaply and quickly, because it wouldn't matter if they didn't last, I could make a small fortune in India. She had had a vision of herself, with a pack like a pedlar's, selling off the cheap timepieces. Indians, particularly those who were coming more and more every day into touch with the East India Company, couldn't go on, surely, reckoning time by whatever means they used.

Still, the litter was punctual; it took exactly fifteen minutes, timed by Richard's watch, to cross the city from their horrid little hired house to the palace. She looked into the room where Richard lay, sprawled almost naked upon the bed, with an empty brandy bottle on the floor beside him, before she went out and climbed into the litter. The driver cracked his whip, the necklace of small golden bells which hung from the horses' necks set up their jingling, and she was off on her last ride through the city.

Today, meek as any member of the harem, she did not lift the curtains, which were just light enough not to be oppressive, just opaque enough to defeat curious eyes. During her first, and her second, and her third ride in this very litter, she had lifted the curtains and peered out, making her observations and her comparisons and her comments. Now she knew it all; knew how the people, so many people in the overcrowded streets, made way for the litter and averted their eyes as they dragged their goats, and their children, and their overburdened donkeys, and their old people out of the way; knew how the driver used his whip on those who were slow. Once she had looked out and thought, Suppose *one*, just one of those golden bells came loose and fell in the dust and somebody picked it up, how many bowls of rice could he buy? And had realised that if golden bells were freely broadcast they would lose all value, would buy no rice at all. Today she kept the curtains in place and rode unseeing past the crowds and the dreadful-looking beggars and through the dust and filth. She had finished with Kilapore.

She knew by the way the air freshened when the litter passed into the palace precincts, a little above the city, refreshed by fountains, set with trees. Presently with the fierce jerk which all Indian drivers considered stylish the litter stopped, a waiting servant drew back the curtains, and Linda, after settling her hat which the jolt had tilted to a more than fashionably rakish angle, stepped out.

She remembered how impressive the palace had seemed the first time she saw it, which was at night, lit by the flare of many torches; and how amusing it had seemed on her second visit, in daylight. It was a vast rambling building which looked as though many successive owners had added to it and taken pains to see that each addition was individual and different. There was a central part, approached by a flight of marble steps and façaded with pillars, which was of pink plaster and which resembled an iced cake; there was a round tower made of purplish-red brick and a square one of grey stone topped with a silver dome; there was an outjutting wing entirely of wood, and everywhere there were balconies and cornices and buttresses and archways and shutters of varying materials and colours. Symbolic of India, perhaps, she thought, as she mounted the steps, passed on, as it were, from one to another of the white-clad servants who stood at intervals on either side and who raised their hands to their heads as she drew level with them and then slightly turned; symbolic of India, huge, sprawling, overdecorated, conforming to no pattern, full of contrasts, and yet mounting up to something magnificent by virtue of very size. Magnificent and on the verge of rot; there was symbolism, too, in the shutters which sagged from their hinges, the balconies which would collapse if ventured upon. Piece by piece India was collapsing, falling into the hands of the East India Company. Surunda Ghotal's palace would hold together a little longer, and so would Kilapore, but they were doomed. She rather hoped that Kilapore would keep its independence just long enough, that the collapse would come after Surunda Ghotal's death, not before. Yet why she should feel sentimental about him she did not know . . . a few careless kindnesses which cost him nothing but the moment's attention needed for the giving of an order, should she be grateful to the point of sentiment for those? And could she blind herself to the fact that one of these half-crazed, hysteric, greed-frenzied potentates who started off by administering violent rebuffs and then listened to arguments and gave in would have been, in the end, of more value to her and to Richard than this grave, courteous old man who had received them so kindly, listened so attentively to all the arguments, asked for time to consider, and then refused to give any concessions at all?

The servant on the uppermost step passed her on no farther; instead he turned and led her through the now familiar but still uncharted labyrinth of the interior of the palace, through high walls where her heels rang on the tiled floor, through narrow dim passages, through curtained archways, upstairs, downstairs. Finally a doorway gave upon a place which she had never seen before, a small enclosed space which denied absolutely the haphazard nature of the rest of the palace and its precincts, a little place of pure and formal beauty. It was walled all round with white marble, solid blocks to about shoulder height and above that a two-foot-deep fringe of carving so delicate and intricate that it looked like petrified lace. From the point where she stood, and where the servant had halted and turned his hand palm upwards pointing straight ahead, ran a path paved with the same white marble. On either side, between path and wall, was a space of bright green grass such as she had not seen since she came to India; and in each piece of green lawn, perfectly matched, were three fountains in play, the spray catching the light in broken rainbows. Set along each side of the path, in perfect symmetry, were small flowering trees, and at its end was a little marble summer house, traced over, but not embowered, with climbing roses. The whole space was artificially, mathematically precise, but it was beautiful, with the measured, disciplined beauty of a sonnet. She stood for a moment taking in the cool delight, the green, the white, the fountains' graces, the little trees, so strictly shaped and each standing in its ring of fallen petals, then she looked towards the place where Surunda Ghotal sat, half reclining upon his couch in the summer house, his infirm leg propped out straight before him. In his youth, leading a punitive expedition against the rebellious polygar, he had been wounded in the thigh and the wound had never healed; there were times when, close to him, you could smell the festering, rotten-sweet-stench of it. Possibly because of his enforced inaction he had grown very stout, and the drugs upon which he relied to relieve the constant nag of the pain had made his hair sparse and dry, the whites of his eyes saffron-coloured, his lips and finger tips a smoky purple. He was, at forty-eight years old, a very ugly old man; just as Linda Shelmadine, at twenty-eight years of age, was a plain, prematurely aged woman. It was not admiration for one another's physical attributes which made the link between them, it was something more subtle, the recognition of the other's intelligence, and a shared measure of what Richard had called "inquisitive puppy-nosing-into-everything" quality.

Until the arrival of the Shelmadines in Kilapore, Surunda Ghotal had never seen a European woman, but he had heard about them from three independent sources. A member of his harem—and he had collected his women much as he had collected the items of his huge menagerie—had once, as a child, been very sick, and had been nursed by Portuguese nuns in a convent at Goa. To the best of her ability, years after, she had described them to her lord and master. Then, some years before the English East India Company had seen in Kilapore a possible field for exploitation, the French East India Company had sent one of its agents to spy out the land—just as lately Richard Shelmadine had been sent—and the Frenchman had shown Surunda Ghotal the little painted miniature of his mistress which he carried with him; and that woman had looked to be an entirely different breed of creature from the women whom the concubine described. Finally there was the evidence of his own eldest son, Jasma, whom he sent in the year 1794 into Fort St. George to live incognito, with orders to get himself some job which would bring him into close contact with the English, and to learn the language. "Moved I more easily I would go myself," Surunda had said. "I observe that they move with the inevitability of the locust swarms and in your time, if not in mine, they will arrive in Kilapore. It will then be to our advantage to know what is said since it is evident from what has happened in other places that hired interpreters have a foot, as they have tongue, in either camp. You will live," said Surunda Ghotal, with his little secret smile, "miserably, being unknown and in a state of servitude, therefore you will learn swiftly, in order to escape. And you will then return and teach me."

The scheme had worked well; anxiety to return to Kilapore combined with the Indian facility to acquire at least a superficial knowledge of any subject quickly, had soon put a term to Jasma's exile. The long sessions during which he endeavoured to impart what he had learned to his father were agony to them both, since it was unnatural for a son to instruct his father, and impossible for him to correct him. Nevertheless, by the time Richard Shelmadine, entrusted with the task of negotiating with the Rajah solely on account of his knowledge of Hindustani, arrived in Kilapore, Surunda Ghotal had acquired enough English to make himself understood by Linda Shelmadine, and in the end was able to regard his efforts as well worth while. She never knew that his demand for her to visit him, his very courteous reception of her had been prompted by sheer curiosity; and she never guessed that behind his good manners, on that first occasion, an enormous amazement lay hidden. Jasma, amongst a thousand other observations, had given his report of those few intrepid European women who had ventured out with their menfolk to Fort St. George. He said that they feared the sun always, and frogs sometimes, but were otherwise extremely bold; they took no interest in their surroundings but lived like trapped birds in a cage, awaiting the day of release; and, like birds, had two voices, the loud one in which they gave orders, the soft one with which they addressed their mates. Surunda's concubine from Goa had been impressed by, and anxious to emphasise, the complete sexlessness, the unselfishness, the otherworldliness, and peculiar physical appearance of the Western women she knew, while the visiting Frenchman had, quite justly, emphasised precisely the opposite qualities in his particular specimen, so it was with the nearest thing to excitement possible to his sluggish nature that Surunda had heard of the arrival of an Englishwoman as far inland as Kilapore. At last his curiosity was to be satisfied.

He was disappointed with her; she fitted in with none of the descriptions he had been given, nor did she immediately strike any impression of her own; just a female creature, not beautiful, not even peculiar. He would probably have dismissed her from his mind after the first ten minutes had Richard been in a better mood—or had she been more obedient to the orders Richard had given her before they set out.

"God knows," Richard had said, "why he asked you to the palace at all. Damned insolence, no doubt. They never let *their* women show their faces outside their own quarters. And you'd better keep well in the background. Speak when you're spoken to, not otherwise."

He had judged it advisable to present himself in a state of complete sobriety and the strain of that unaccustomed condition was showing before ever they set out. It grew fiercer with every minute of the long-drawn-out interview. For the first half hour the Rajah asked all the questions, moving in circumambulatory fashion towards his real objective—the exact reason for Richard's presence in Kilapore, the terms and conditions of the concessions the Company wished to acquire. Then, for twenty minutes, Richard, who knew what he was talking about, and was anxious to make a success of his mission, held the floor, while the Rajah seemed to pay slight attention and in the end said, "There would be much to think; sixty days of think in this head, in heads of old wise men to advise."

It was then at the beginning of the season of greatest heat and the prospect of spending two months far inland did nothing to calm Richard's nerves, which were screaming for the brandy oblivion they had been denied all day. He had said what was required of him, and said it well, let him now be dismissed.

"Now you shall tell me much thing," Surunda Ghotal said, and proceeded to ask all the questions, stupid little questions which his curiosity dictated and which were, to his mind, of much more urgent moment than the ones he had asked earlier about the East India Company and its advances to him. Any man but Richard Shelmadine would have realised instantly that here, by a stroke of good luck, was handed to him the key to Surunda's interest and friendship at least, but the arrogant perverse devil who ruled Richard was bored, impatient, and affronted. There were things which a gentleman down on his luck must do just to keep bread in his mouth and a roof over his head, but Richard Shelmadine had fulfilled his obligations when he had made his twenty-minute speech—in this fat old heathen's own language, which was more then most men could do. His answers grew shorter and brusquer; he said, "I don't know," or, "It would be impossible to explain," so often that Linda blushed with embarrassment and began first to supplement Richard's grudging answers and then to take upon herself the responsibility of making the first response to the endless questions. The Rajah seemed surprised, even a trifle ill at ease for a moment, and Richard turned upon her his nastiest, most mocking grin. When the moment had passed, Surunda focused his whole attention upon her, and during the next half hour she did her best to give him whatever he wanted—a description of Windsor Castle; an explanation of what was a newspaper and how it circulated; a dissertation upon the jury system. Jasma had brought back with him from Fort St. George two or three copies of *The Times* and *The Spectator*, all well over a year old by the time they reached Surunda's hands, and they had been his English textbooks, which, as he had mastered the language in which they were written, had also provoked his curiosity by their references to strange things. It was wonderful to find that this Englishwoman, so dull to look at, so disappointing, was in reality the thing he had often wished for—

someone better informed than Jasma and willing to answer questions.

He would gladly have talked to her for hours, but he was aware at last of the Englishman's mounting impatience, so he said, "Many, many thing I have to ask. The Christianity, of that I would hear; as also of party politic and of Turnpike Road. Sixty days will be time if you will be kind to tell me. One thing there is to ask now."

Richard gave an audible sigh.

"In your house there are servants?"

"Here, in Kilapore you mean, Your Highness?"

"In Kilapore, yes. Servants are obtain for you?"

"Yes. They were—I think—hired with the house."

"That is not good. Tomorrow I shall send one to rule them. He is a man of . . . It is the knowing how to do . . . *experience*." He produced the word triumphantly. "One who went, with my son, to Fort St. George and learned in the house of Mr. Mack-in-tosh. Very stern. He shall rule and none shall rob you."

"Thank you," Linda said earnestly. She cherished the hope that in the house of Mr. Mackintosh the stern man might have acquired a little English; then she could give orders without bothering Richard.

With an effort which brought a look of abstraction to his face the Rajah sought for some formula of dismissal and finally found it.

"Sir and Lady," he said, "I beg your leave to retire your selves."

On the way back to the hired house Richard said, "You prolonged that ordeal by at least an hour."

"I know," she said meekly. "But we wanted to please him, and I thought that your long speech had tired you." It had become second nature to her by this time to avoid trouble by placing the most favourable interpretation upon Richard's actions whenever possible. Criticism merely led to quarrels.

"I could make that speech in my sleep! I just could not be bothered to answer his damned silly questions. I'd told him all that he needed to know—and he could hardly be civilly attentive to what *did* concern him. He's stupid, like all the rest of the apes, and anxious to exhibit his two words of English, and to show his power. Making us sweat it out here for two months while he makes up his mind when he knows damned well what his answer will be."

"And what will it be?"

"He'll concede. If he hadn't decided he would have asked a few questions about terms and conditions instead of about Windsor Castle and newspapers."

Before she spoke again she hesitated, reluctant to offer a contrary opinion and so worsen Richard's mood; but perhaps he should be warned, perhaps it was her duty to mention what she had noticed.

"I couldn't follow, of course, what you were saying, but I kept my eye on him, and he did seem, as you say, fidgety and inattentive. He was listening though, and every time you mentioned Bholobad his hands clenched."

"Avarice, my pretty one. Bholobad is the Company's ace of trumps in these negotiations; the place where the Rajah has doubled his income in three years' trade with the Company."

But she had placed her construction upon Surunda Ghotal's reaction to the word and when, at the end of sixty days, the Rajah's answer had been a point-blank refusal to trade on any terms at all, she had not been surprised. Bholobad might be the place where the Rajah's income had doubled, but she remembered, and so did Surunda, no doubt, that the Rajah who enjoyed the enhanced income was not the same one who had ruled the state and received the Company's first emissary. The course of events had followed a pattern by now well established; concessions were granted; the Company moved in; some trivial dispute was fanned into a brief bloody civil war, and when that was over the Company's own chosen candidate was on the throne. He might enjoy more income than his predecessor, but he had no power at all.

During the two months of his pretended indecision Surunda had shown several signs of favour to his uninvited guests; he had sent them gifts of fruit and vegetables from the palace gardens, put a litter at their service so that in the brief, less scorchingly hot hour of the late afternoon they could take drives and gain from the moving air at least the illusion of freshness; he had invited them to bathe in the palace pools.

Yes, he had been kind; and for that reason she had now come to take a courteous leave of him. He had completed Richard's ruin, but he had done it unintentionally.

Seeing her arrive alone, Surunda Ghotal nodded knowingly to himself; then as she drew near he smiled.

"Good afternoon, Meesis Shel-ma-dine. Pleased to sit."

He indicated a second couch, set at some distance from his own.

"My husband asks you to excuse him. He has many things to arrange. We leave early tomorrow morning."

"Ah, he is angry to me. I am understanding. And you? You also are angry to me?"

"No. I am sorry, naturally. If my husband had succeeded in persuading you . . ." But there was no point in completing that sentence. Richard, in the end, had used every bit of persuasive power; had even changed tactics and used charm; all to no purpose. It was over. "You did as you thought best," she said.

"And was I not wise?"

"That is difficult to say, Your Highness. Sometimes as I look about I am bound to think that in the end the Company will rule all India. At least you have put off the day when they move into Kilapore and"—her lips moved in a small smile—"if you use all the time you have gained as energetically as you have used this last two months, when the struggle comes you will be in strong position."

"What are you meaning of the last two months?"

"On our drives in the afternoons, I have noticed the two new forts, one on the road to Chilpuddy, the other on the road to Dorhea; they have risen so fast I think the men must work all through the night. And many soldiers have arrived from somewhere."

"Your eyes are keen," he said approvingly. "Yes. They have said to me, using sweet words, 'Give us Kilapore to do with as we did with Bholobad,' and I have said, 'No.' One day they will say to me, 'Now we will take Kilapore as we took Bengal,' and on that day I shall say, 'Attempt it.' But it is not of such things we should speak on this last day. Pleased to refresh yourself."

She looked at the little table near the couch; it bore a tall, slender silver flagon and a thin beaker of porcelain, and three small dishes piled with the highly flavoured, violently coloured sweetmeats which all Indians loved. She had tasted similar ones on a former visit and been nauseated by their over-sweetness, so today she merely poured herself a beakerful of the slightly acidulated, effervescent liquid which in the palace served in place of wine. She was grateful for its coolness.

"So tomorrow you go. That is sad, for me, very sad. Where do you go?"

"First to Fort St. George, of course. And then, as soon as possible, back to England."

"So? Meester Shel-ma-dine, he works no more for the great East India Company?"

She said steadily, "We have been in India for five years. There are things in England which need my husband's attention."

The quaking feeling of sickness which always assailed her when she was forced to think of the future made even the cool bubbling liquid nauseating. She set down the beaker and pressed her handkerchief to her lips. England, which should have meant such different things, stood for a return to the shifts and debts, the sordid lodgings, the dubious means of survival which had been their lot before some influence had been exerted to find Richard a place in the Company's service.

"You have been very kind to answer such many questions." Surunda Ghotal's voice broke in on her dismal thoughts.

"And you have been very kind to us. Most especially I thank you for lending Mee Lal to rule my household; it has made everything very easy for me."

"I now wish to make you little gift. For gratitude. And for memory. There is a word . . ."

"A keepsake," she said. Involuntarily her eyes went to his tunic; today he was wearing the one with the emerald buttons, each of the four matched stones as big round as a guinea and set in a circle of diamonds. All very well for Richard to laugh— the gift of one such button would make all the difference. She thrust the thought away and said, with truth:

"I have no need of a keepsake to remember you, Your Highness. I shall always recall our conversations with pleasure and your kindness with gratitude."

"And I shall remember all things you teach me." He leaned forward as much as his bulk and outstretched leg allowed and regarded her steadily for a moment. "One thing," he said, "you are teaching me is from you to me alone. Other people may have told me what is Turnpike, but this thing is from you to me alone. In history of India, here and there I am hearing of women, one or two, very few, Ranee or Begum with young son, maybe, one or two with husband, very clever, come to great power and ruling most well. *Always* to hear this I am laughing. In my palace are many women and always when a new one comes—now no longer for me—but in past time, always I am asking myself, Is this one to be like those of whom in history I am hearing? And it is not so. Not once. Never. And still I am laughing because of the stories. You are under-

standing me? I wish you to know that now I am not laughing.
In days to come when I am hearing of women so clever I am
saying to myself, Ah, there is woman with mind like Meesis
Shel-ma-dine, with mind to understand and eye to see and
tongue to say wisely. And for this reason, as well as for memory,
I make you now this gift. Please to come with me."

Tales of the legendary, fabulous wealth of the Indian potentates were commonplace in Company circles; tales of chests
full of gold, of rubies as large as pullets' eggs, of great diamonds that were blinding to look at. Such tales were lent
substance by known facts; the state elephant of the Rajah of
Bholobad, for instance, on really great occasions had worn four
anklets, each four inches wide, crusted with emeralds and sapphires. As Surunda reached for the heavy gold-topped staff
which he used for his rare essays in walking, Linda permitted
herself to hope. It was just possible that he was now about to
lead her to his treasure room and give her a "keepsake" that
would make Richard laugh in quite another key.

As Surunda took his first shuffling steps across the pavilion,
she thought of something else; something she had often wanted
to say to him, but had never quite dared.

"Your Highness, there are two doctors in Fort St. George;
one, Dr. Adams, is very clever. He would come to see you, I
am certain, and he might do something to make you less lame.
May I ask when ... ?"

"No, no," he said testily. "My doctors do well; I am living
these many years."

Well, she thought, at least he is consistent; he will have no
business with the English and asks no favours. India for Indians,
and Indian doctors for Indian legs wounded by Indian spears.

Outside the pavilion they turned sharply and stood before
a gate set in the marble wall. Surunda opened it and said:

"There are stairs; go with care."

She recognised the place; it was the vast courtyard in which
he kept his menagerie and it joined, at one point, the even
larger court in which his elephants were stabled. Why was he
bringing her here this afternoon? Perhaps, she thought, only
half mockingly, he intended to give her an elephant! Such a
grotesque keepsake would be, somehow, in character. And one
could have worse gifts. An elephant could carry all their baggage down to the coast, and would fetch a good price at the
fort.

Surunda closed the gate and descended the stairs slowly,

painfully. As he moved draggingly towards the first cage—the one which held the black-maned Nubian lion—she recalled that on the first occasion when he showed her his beasts he had been carried in a small litter, like a sedan chair. Thinking of this and the size of the yard, she said, as she would have said to any man, elderly or infirm:

"Would you like to take my arm? I'm really very strong."

"No, no," he said in the same testy voice, but this time the refusal was accompanied by a glance of . . . could it be? . . . disgust. She remembered that never once had he touched her, never shaken her hand, never shared a couch. Probably there was some law against it. Memories of childhood flashed back again, all those things in Leviticus, "he shall be unclean for seven days."

"I am managing," Surunda said less crossly. "I am slow, but there is light yet and when the light goes there are torches."

They passed the lion; and the long-necked, spotted giraffe; and the elephant that was here and not in the other courtyard because it had been born an albino; two striped wild horses from Africa; a reindeer which had been ailing on her previous visit and was now moribund, and an English hound dog with melancholy eyes.

The cages were much better built and cleaner than the hovels in which most of Surunda's subjects lived, the courtyard immeasurably better kept than any of the city streets, but the unmistakable, acrid odour of captivity was all about, a miasma of sadness. She thought of the Rajah's women, collected, held captive in much the same way. Then she shrugged the thought aside. Why should I pity them? Am I free, who chose my own gaoler?

They came on to the archway which led to the elephant stables; they passed on. So it is not to be an elephant. Have I lost my sense of direction and are we in reality taking a short cut to some part of the palace? Perhaps a pullet-egg ruby after all.

Beyond the arch the bird cages lay. Surunda, panting from exertion, had not breath for speech and passed the birds as he had passed the animals, almost without a glance. Linda, from a mixture of politeness and interest, looked for the second time at the tall ostriches, the birds of Paradise, the hummingbirds brilliant and fragile as flowers, the lone, duck-billed platypus. She too was silent lest any comment should evoke a response for which breath would be grudged. But before the cage of the tiny birds which looked like blossoms, she said, "How beautiful!"

"Wait. Until now you are seeing nothing."

In front of the last cage he paused, moved the stick forward, and leaned on it with both hands.

"The golden pheasants of China," he said simply.

There were two of them; and even upon eyes so lately dazzled by the hummingbirds their beauty struck with a pang. About the disposition of their green and white, red and blue, yellow and bronze feathers there was a suggestion of deliberate artifice, as though upon the instinctive skill and prodigality of nature a more mature and cunning design had been imposed. By comparison the other birds were gaudy, the work of a happy haphazard child; these were from a master hand; and it seemed that they knew it, for in addition to their complete beauty there was a regal dignity, a matchless grace.

Now she knew why he had brought her here; to show her his newest and loveliest acquisition. She said, without the care with which she ordinarily chose her words with him:

"They are the loveliest things I have ever seen in all my life."

"I am glad," he said. "They are for you."

They had arrived only two days earlier. He had wanted them for years, just as he had wanted one of the tiny dogs with feathered tails which were also Chinese. It was very difficult indeed to get anything out of China. *All* China was closed to *all* trade, just as he had closed Kilapore to the Company's trade. Nothing ever came out of China by legal means. Some silk, some porcelain was smuggled out, because peasants so hungry and merchants so avaricious could lay hands on silk and porcelain; but the golden pheasants were to be found only in the gardens of the wealthy, and the little dogs were strictly the preserve of royalty; Surunda had wished, but he had never hoped, to own a specimen of either rarity. Almost four years earlier he had done one of his minor polygars a great favour and when repayment was mentioned he had brushed it aside, airily, saying, "One day you may give me a Chinese pheasant, or one of the dogs of Pekin," which was tantamount to saying, "One day you shall give me the moon or a slice of a rainbow."

Yet, two days ago they had arrived, beautiful and dignified, in a cage of wickerwork, with nothing to show that almost four years, a sum of money equivalent to two thousand English pounds, and the lives of five men had been expensed upon their transportation from one place to another. And because they were new, and so beautiful, they were, of all his countless possessions, the things which Surunda held dearest on the afternoon when Linda Shelmadine came to say good-bye to him. And for that reason he must give them to her.

Earlier in the day he had, with an eye to choosing a "gift for memory," taken stock of his treasures. He had opened, and then dived into, several chests, the contents of some well known to him, others which he had forgotten, if he had ever seen them; sapphires bluer than the sky; emeralds green as young corn; diamonds, pearls. He had tumbled them back, dissatisfied. He had given too many jewels to too many other women, even to dancing girls who had relieved an hour's tedium. A jewel was far too ordinary a gift to mark the end of a friendship so rare. And with that thought came the knowledge of exactly what was the apt, the suitable, in fact the only gift.

Now, looking at the beautiful birds, he was satisfied with the rightness of the gesture. It did not occur to him to reflect that by tomorrow or by next day the Chinese pheasants would have lost their novelty and therefore their charm for him. Nor did he wonder whether a pair of largish birds, however rare and beautiful, was, in a practical sense, exactly the right gift for a woman about to set out on a journey of several thousands of miles. Even the look of blank dismay on Linda's face did not enlighten him; he took it for astonishment at his munificence. She had a vision of the pheasants in their wicker basket on top of the jolting ox wagon which would carry their luggage to the coast; she knew in anticipation the difficulty of finding a place to put them while they waited to take passage; and finally the picture of their arrival in London drifted before her inward eye—a drizzling day at the docks, the hackney coach in which they set off to look for a cheap lodging! We want accommodation for a married couple, and two rare pheasants. . . .

She felt the spasm of half-hysterical laughter in her throat. She took a small piece of the inner side of her cheek between her teeth and bit it hard. One emerald button that would never be missed . . . oh, the irony of it! When she could trust her voice, she said:

"It is most kind, most generous of you . . . and in keeping with the way in which you have always behaved to me, but I could not take anything so valuable, so rare. I thank you from my heart for wishing to give me such a present, but I cannot accept it. For one thing you could never replace them."

"That is why," he said simply. And the words revealed the full value of the offered gift. She recognised the element of self-sacrifice . . . She thought rashly, I don't care what Richard says; somehow I will take them back and I'll send them to his father at Clevely. He may not wish to receive me, or Richard, but he could not resist such a gift. They'll be safe there.

She turned to Surunda and tried to express not only her gratitude for the gift, but her awareness of the subtle honour it conferred. He cut her short before she had completed her first sentence.

"I am glad that they please you," he said. He beckoned to one of the watchful, unobtrusive servants and said a few words.

"They will be ready. It grows dark. We go this way."

He opened another door and she saw ahead of her a long passage, already lighted by torches, each held by a servant immobile and expressionless as a statue. Fitting her step to the Rajah's slow, limping pace, she passed along the length of it, prey to an emotion unfamiliar and without a name. It was like dying, this feeling of "nevermore." Surunda Ghotal would remain here, with his great possessions, warding off the encroachments of the Company, growing old, dying. And she would go on to whatever the future held for her. They would never, in this world, meet again.

The passage led straight back to the high wide hall which lay just behind the door at the top of the marble steps by which she had entered the palace less than an hour ago. She expected that here he would take leave of her; but he hobbled forward, through the doorway and down, awkwardly, clumsily down the flight of marble steps upon which he had never set foot since the day when he had started out upon the expedition which had resulted in his disablement. As he had said, the pheasants were ready; the wide wicker cage strapped into position beside the driver of the litter. The sudden dusk had fallen and more torches lighted the scene. At the foot of the steps the Rajah paused.

"It is now," he said.

She could not speak. Her eyes were dry, but there were tears at the back of them; her lips moved, but from the painful constriction of her throat no sound would come. All she could do was to reach out with her mittened hand. Surunda Ghotal moved his stick from his right hand to his left and reached out his hand. Linda took it and they stood so for a moment.

Then he said, "Go in peace."

She tried to say, "You also," but no words came, and she turned and hurried to the litter as though seeking shelter.

The Rajah stood and watched as the horses, under the whip-lash, plunged forward. The men who had been hovering came forward with his chair and he sat down heavily and allowed himself to be carried up the steps. At the top the torchlight fell on his face and anyone bold enough to look at him would have seen that his eyes and the heavy discoloured pouches below them were damp; but nobody saw; it would have been highly unwise to be witness to a moment of weakness in so stern and terrible a man.

"Well, and what glittering prize did that bit of bum-sucking gain for you, my pretty?"

"A pair of very rare, very valuable pheasants."

Richard's laugh, thin and high and sneering, rang out, jangling her nerves until it was difficult not to cry, "Stop it," and scream.

"Serve you bloody well right," Richard said. "And what do you propose to do with this loot? Have a feast of the Passover?"

There'd been a time when she could have said simply, "Oh, but you wouldn't *kill* them," and that would have been his cue and the birds' death sentence.

"Such a meal is hardly for the likes of us," she said lightly. "They're worth their weight in gold. They're Chinese, the only ones ever to be seen outside China. Plainly destined for Windsor, or Chatsworth—five hundred pounds the pair!"

As always, the mention of money arrested his attention.

"So valuable?" he asked incredulously, and roused himself to go out and look at the birds.

"Now I wonder why His Fatness should give them to you," he said.

She knew the answer. "Because he is so rich that when he wanted to give a present that would cost him something he was like a pauper; he could only give me the one thing he valued at the moment." But that was not a thing one could say to Richard.

She said, "Part of the general lack of reality. He'd have no idea what trouble . . ." Inspiration visited her. "Or perhaps he had! Perhaps he wanted to give you trouble."

That was enough.

"Ha-ha!" Richard said. "I shall make no trouble of it. No trouble at all, and possibly a profit."

She knew then that the pheasants were safe. Another small victory at the price of another enormous betrayal. She turned away, sickened by the thought of what she had become.

PART II

SUNSET OF
A PHILANDERER

CHAPTER 3

At first Damask thought that, after all, God meant to let her off lightly. Amos came home almost an hour before he was expected.

He wore an unfamiliar look, more unfamiliar than could be accounted for by the fact that he was wearing his chapel suit; his face was smooth and lightened with joy.

"I bring great tidings," he said, as soon as he was inside the kitchen. "It was decided, this afternoon, to build a chapel in Clevely."

Neither his wife nor his daughter was capable, at that moment, of fully sharing his joy. To Mrs. Greenway, now more or less house-bound, a chapel at Clevely and a chapel at Nettleton five miles away were much the same; and Damask was preoccupied with the matter of the Squire's unfinished boots. She knew this to be unworthy, however, and tried to force herself to enthusiasm. "Where is it to stand, Father?" she asked.

"On Abel Shipton's little back meadow, the one they call the Flat Iron; he've promised the narrer end where Mrs. Shipton hev kept her ducks. You know," Amos said, glowing with honest self-abasement, "I've wronged Abel Shipton in my mind many a time! Over and over again when a chapel in Clevely hev been mentioned I've thought him lukewarm in the Lord's

cause not to offer a morsel of ground, he being the only one
that could, no other Methodist being his own landlord. However, today he did so and there'll be a chapel in Clevely at
last!"

It had been his dream for many years. The chapel at Nettleton served the six parishes and was large enough to accommodate all its members, so that at first sight there might not
appear to be a crying need for one at Clevely: but when Amos
thought of the six villages he could see one lighted and five in
darkness. He would look around on Sunday evenings and
count—ten souls from Nettleton, four from nearby Minsham,
three, two, one or none from more distant places, himself and
Abel Shipton the only representatives of Clevely. Five miles
was a long way to walk for old people, or children, or those
who were not yet fully persuaded. He was certain that if he
could build a chapel in Clevely he could make converts; if he
could kindle the light people would gather around it.

"Who's going to pay for it?" Julie asked. She was trying,
in her turn, to take interest and it was not her fault that the
question had just a tinge of sharp practicality.

"All of us," said Amos eagerly. "Me and one or two more'll
do the work and every one of us at the meeting today made a
solemn promise to give all we could towards the cost of the
stuff. We reckoned we'd get the timber cheap, anyway, Judson
being a member of the chapel at Baildon and being in that line
of business." He broke off and then added, in a different,
dreamier voice, "'A light to lighten the Gentiles,' thass what
that chapel'll be."

Julie looked about the sparsely furnished, comfortless kitchen
and wondered a little drearily how Amos expected to pay his
contribution towards the chapel building, they lived near enough
to the bone already; what further sacrifice could be demanded?

"Father," Damask broke in on Amos' dream, "Squire came
by this afternoon and was put out at not finding his boots ready.
I promised to..." Oh dear, that was another lie almost! "If
you'd work on them now I'd take them on my way home. The
pudding won't be ready for another half hour."

"The Manor ain't on your way home, child," Julie said.

"It is if I go by the Lower Road."

And there, Julie thought, quite humbly, lay the difference
between the really religious people like Amos and Damask and
those who only paid lip service, like herself. *She* would not

dare to walk that road after dark, she did not much relish the thought of Damask's doing so.

"All right, I'll get on," Amos said. He would much have preferred to stay in the kitchen and go on talking about the new chapel; but he now had the best of reasons for working hard and keeping his customers. In the workroom, donning his leather apron, he realised that since the job was merely simple stitching he could carry it into the kitchen and talk as he worked; and this he did, oblivious to the waning of Julie's interest and the agonised glance which Damask cast him every time he halted his needle to give full value to a remark, or ceased work to stare into space.

"Father, do get *on*," she said at last. "The pudding is ready to dish."

The later she was the less chance of any other person being abroad on that road and calling a human, heartening "Good night." The later she was the deeper would be the darkness, the greater the risk of something not friendly, not human. . . .

She rattled the plates as she took them from the shelf, ostentatiously and noisily grated some salt from the block, lifted the lid of the saucepan so that the good scent of the pudding might titillate Amos' nostrils, but it was not in him to scamp a job even when pressed for time. When at last he placed the final firm stitch, cut off the waxed thread, and tucked the end under, it was well past the ordinary supper hour. Damask almost snatched at the boots and began to bundle them into one of the canvas squares used for the delivery of such important orders. That done, she dished the pudding hurriedly and put on her cloak.

"But you ain't had your supper," Julie said plaintively. "You can't go off like that, missing your dinner as you do these Saturdays. You'll turn faint or something."

"I rather wanted you to do a bit of figuring out for me," Amos said, "about this here timber. I don't reckon so easy as you do, Damask; started too late."

He had been quite illiterate up to the time of his conversion; then he had learned to read in order to study the Bible, and had proceeded to learn how to write in order to make notes for his sermons when he became a preacher. He wrote, curiously enough, a very good scholarly hand. Damask had acquired her smattering of education early in life through the Nettleton Sunday School, which she had attended every Sunday afternoon until she went out to work. The Sunday school had been the hobby of an old schoolmaster who believed that Methodism was the remedy for all the spiritual ills of the world and universal literacy the remedy of every other kind. It was useless, he held, to tell children the Bible stories, of which if they remembered anything at all, only garbled versions would remain in mind; they must learn to read for themselves. So on Sunday afternoons, after a brisk prayer and a loud hymn to work off what surplus energy remained after a long walk and an attendance at morning service, the young Methodists of the six villages settled down to learn their letters. Most of them made little progress, some fell asleep; the old man devoted his attention to the few who wanted to learn. Of these one or two even reached the stage of learning grammar.

"Our Lord," the old man would say, "spent his earthly life as a poor humble man, but He didn't say 'I ain't' and 'I worn't' and nor need you!"

The grammar was a high fence at which most of even the eager learners fell; those few who reached the other side were taught the rudiments of arithmetic. Damask was one of the few. The old man, delighting in her teachability, often regretted that she was not a boy, capable of becoming a proper scholar.

"I'll help you with that next time I'm home," she said to Amos now.

"You sure you can't stop for just a mouthful?" Julie asked, beginning to cut into the crust of the pudding. Hunger watered in Damask's mouth as the brown gravy oozed and the rich scent escaped. Then she thought of the Lower Road and shook her head.

"Oh dear. And I was counting on us heving a cup of tea together after."

"Ah!" Amos exclaimed, as though a question had been answered. "I been figuring out where we could make spare a bit. Tea! No more tea in this house till that chapel stand four-square in the Lord's sight!"

"But that 'on't save much," Julie said in a small voice. "We use so little. What I got in the tin now was bought back in August." She loved her cup of tea, made an event, a treat, of each rare brewing and used the leaves three times over.

"Then we'll save on cheese too," Amos said. "Not a bit of cheese will I touch from this day on."

Both Julie and Damask knew that his main meal on four days of the week was a hunk of bread and cheese; they stared at him, Julie's faded blue eyes with awed dismay, Damask's amber ones with awed respect. A truly good man—and his daughter was a liar! That brought her back to a consciousness of her circumstances. She went over and kissed Julie.

"Good-bye, Mother. I'll see you next month."

By her father she paused but did not kiss him. "Good night, Father. I'll see you tomorrow week at chapel."

"Good-bye, Damask; thank you for all you've done for me today," Julie said, and sadly put some pudding on a plate.

"Good night, Damask," said Amos, drawing his chair to the table. "I'll see you unless Stevens is still ill; if he is I might hev to take his pulpit over at Summerfield."

Summerfield, she thought, opening the door on the dark, windy night. Summerfield, magic word, her talisman against fear. For it was at Summerfield, on a June night, that Jesus had called Damask Greenway and she had answered the call.

She was fourteen, and at the end of the month was going to start work and that was one reason why Amos had insisted on her going to the weeknight meeting that was to be held at Summerfield by a famous preacher named Whitwell. Damask nearly missed it because during the week, cleaning the workroom she had dropped a heavy last on her foot and a nail on one toe had turned black and was coming off. She couldn't walk to Summerfield; and Mrs. Greenway had half hoped that they could stay home together, and make gooseberry jam, and have a cup of tea and gossip more freely than they could do in Amos' presence. Mother and daughter were very close to one another at that time.

"But once she gets to work, she'll never be free for a midweek meeting; and this Mr. Whitwell is famous. On the Norwich circuit last month he brought over three hundred sinners to repentance."

"Well, Damask ain't much of a sinner," Mrs. Greenway said.

"We're all sinners," said Amos sternly, "and I should like to see her cast her burden at the mercy seat afore she go out to face the world. I know what I'll do. I'll borrow Shad's donkey."

"That'll mean starting a full hour sooner than we need," said Mrs. Greenway. The remarkable state of preservation of Shad's ancient animal was due to its lifelong refusal to be hurried.

"Ah well, your father's a good man," said Mrs. Greenway, seeing her cosy evening doomed and seeking comfort where she could. "When I look round at some ... Mrs. Juby hev a terrible black eye again today. We can't complain, I s'pose."

Damask had gone sulkily. Apart from Sunday school, where sheer boredom had brightened her wits until every lesson was fascinating, she found everything in connexion with chapel tedious in the extreme. Yet Amos had been right; the meeting was the turning point of her life.

The barn was crowded; not only had the faithful rallied from all quarters, there was a good number of people who had come in search of entertainment. Revivalist meetings offered much amusement, with women falling down in hysterics and scream- ing and tearing their hair, and men rushing to the front and blurting out that they were great sinners and often giving most intimate details of their misdoings. The commonest sin was wenching, then sharp dealing, then drunkenness.

Amos had prudently brought a stool which he placed near the door of the barn, so that as Damask sat there the scent of cut hay, of honeysuckle, and wild roses drifted in and touched her before it became sullied by the odour of human breath, human sweat, and the ale reek which hung about some of the unregenerate. She was still sulky, and until John Whitwell climbed up into the improvised pulpit and began to talk, she would rather have been at home making gooseberry jam, with a cup of tea to look forward to.

Whitwell spoke very simply and said nothing that was new to such a regular chapel-goer as Damask; what was new was his burning belief and his power to convey it. He believed in God who loved the world and offered even to the worst of men a chance to repent and enjoy eternal life in Heaven; he believed that the Devil tempted men to sin, to resist God, and waited gloatingly for the chance to torture them in Hell throughout all eternity.

He was fluent, and passionately sincere, and he possessed good looks above the average and some rudimentary hypnotic power. When at the end of his discourse he threw his arms wide and, with the last level rays of sunshine falling on his smooth yellow hair, earnest face, and beautiful eyes, cried, "My brothers, my sisters, make the choice tonight, for tonight your soul might be required of you. Eternal joy or eternal pain. That is the choice. And here is Jesus, opening His crucified arms to you, calling you to come and cast yourselves upon His infinite mercy; come while there is time," fifty-five people moved forward, and quite a few of them were those who had come too see the fun.

Damask went too, of course. She was fourteen, and it was June and she was under a spell. So confused that to the end of her days Jesus of Nazareth would wear John Whitwell's face, speak with his voice. Dust moved in the barn as the penitents shuffled forward, and the sun shimmered in the dust and there was a halo about that yellow head. She went forward and offered her heart, to Amos' supreme joy.

The next four years, save for an occasional lapse into sin and a consequent troubling of conscience, were happy ones. Her heart was in safe keeping. She was happier than Juliet, who at the same age gave her heart to Romeo; happier than Sally Ashpole, who at the same age gave what she thought was her heart and what was certainly her virginity to one of Widow Hayward's soldier sons; happier than all the uncounted girls who at the same age gave their hearts to governesses and fellow schoolgirls and other fallible human creatures. Jesus never repudiated her love, never exploited it, never changed. He was always there, always loving, even when, or perhaps especially when, she hurt Him by sinning. And she had no doubt, on this evening, as she stepped out into the windy dark that He would be with her on the Lower Road.

She cherished a half hope that at the Lodge, Jarvey would open the gate for her and say that he had an errand up to the house and would carry the boots with him. Or would that be cheating? Now and then it was difficult to decide whether a chance accident was a sign of God's favour or a particularly cunning wile of the Devil. Tonight no such decision was called for; the eldest of the Jarvey boys admitted her and scuttled back into shelter like a rabbit. The wind was full in her face as she trudged up the avenue, and by the time she reached the back door of the manor she was completely out of breath. The yard between the house and the stables lay deserted, unusually quiet, and it was a long time before anyone answered the door to her. She was obliged to ring the bell three times, and when someone came it was not one of the maids, it was the stout, regal housekeeper, Mrs. Hart, who did not ordinarily answer doors. She looked as though she had been crying and just stood there without speaking.

"Good evening," Damask said, "I've brought the boots. I promised Sir Charles this afternoon..."

To her astonishment Mrs. Hart made no move to take the

parcel; she lifted her black silk apron and held it to her face, beginning to cry again, wildly.

"His boots!" she sobbed. "He'll not need them. Poor dear man, he'll never wear boots again!"

"Why . . . is he ill?" Damask faltered.

"He's dead! Brought home not ten minutes since, on a gate, his neck broke."

And who then would pay for the boots? All that leather of the best quality, all those hours of Amos' labour. Oh what a pity that they hadn't been finished earlier, finished and paid for! That was her first thought and she was immediately ashamed of it.

"Oh dear," she said. "What happened?"

Like most mourners, Mrs. Hart, though she would have been impervious to comfort, found the invitation to tell a dramatic tale a palliative to her grief.

"What happened? Ah, that nobody can say." She lowered her apron. "His horse came back, about six o'clock, all in a muck sweat and the saddle empty. So then Sir Edward he rid the highway with a coupla men and Parson took Bobbie, just as he was, all of a tremble, and went with a couple more along Lower Road and Mr. Hatton went off to Berry Lane—you never saw such a to-do. And then, like I told you, they found him, poor dear, dead, with his neck broke, and brought him home on a gate. The best master that ever breathed, he was, for all he was so particular."

"Where did they find him?"

"In the Lower Road, just by the Lady's Ride."

Genuinely grief-stricken as she was, something professional, automatic still functioned perfectly in the housekeeper's mind. All girls were stupid, it took five minutes and at least one repetition to get the simplest thing into their minds. She always acted on that assumption and now, in one more instance, she realised how right she was. Damask Greenway hadn't so much as blinked at the first telling of the broken neck, the sudden tragic death—but now, just about five minutes later, she went all pale and gave a great gasp.

"Come to think of it," said Mrs. Hart, "you'd be one of the last people to see him alive, wouldn't you? That'll be something to remember." She mopped her face again. "Did you notice aught . . . anything to show why he should have a dizzy spell and fall off his horse?"

"No . . . no. He seemed . . . quite ordinary." (And I told him a lie!)

"Ah, so I said." Mrs. Hart sounded immensely satisfied. "There's more in this than meets the eye. It'd take something more than a falling branch to make old Bobbie rear and shy. And the state he was in! I allust did say that I wouldn't venture along that road after dark, no, not for a thousand . . ."

"Mrs. Hart, what shall I do with the boots?" How rude, to interrupt like that!

"Not for a thousand pounds," said Mrs. Hart firmly. "The boots? I'm sure I don't know."

"Shall I leave them?"

"I don't know," Mrs. Hart said coldly. "And this is no time to be bothering with such things."

Boots, boots, interrupting her just as she was telling how she had always felt about that dreadful road! Damask Greenway needed to be put in her place; Mrs. Hart did it, closing the door firmly.

It was not the first time, it was far from the first time that Damask had suspected that there was something queer, something quite out of the ordinary about her mind. Most people had minds which dealt with one thought, and then another, one at a time. Hers very often dealt with two, even three, all at the same time. She was thinking now, as the door shut in her face, that it was lucky that Mrs. Hart hadn't taken the boots. Father could perhaps sell them as they were, or alter them to fit somebody else, or, if the worst came to the worst, use the leather again. They wouldn't be the dead loss that they might have been had Mrs. Hart taken them and put them down somewhere to be forgotten. And at the same time another part of her mind was thinking about the Lower Road . . . thinking such terrible, terrifying thoughts that no other mind could have held them and any other thought at the same time; thinking that God really did intend to punish her for that lie, to test her faith to the uttermost. And at the same time yet a third part of her mind was capable of standing back and observing what a very strange mind Damask Greenway had to be able to think of all these things together. The whirl of so much thinking made her dizzy. There was the familiar moment of blackness during which all the thoughts fought together. Then everything cleared and one thought came uppermost—the thought of the Lower Road. As she retraced her steps along the avenue, Satan offered her a new and very subtle temptation. Time was of no account now, he said; it didn't matter how late she got back to Muchanger, nobody would scold when they heard the news she brought. Also—he said—by going back by the main road she would pass her home again, and could tell the news there and get rid of the boots.

She argued that she wasn't really going by way of the Lower Road to save time; she was going to punish herself.

Ah yes, Satan retorted, but when she had made her plan she hadn't known that something else horrible was going to happen on that very stretch of road; nor had she known that she would have to carry the boots all the way to Muchanger.

But God had known, she replied; God knew everything; and if He intended her to be this much more severely punished, it would be very wrong to try to wriggle out of it.

By doing the sensible thing?

All too often the apparently sensible thing was the wrong thing—like telling the lie this afternoon!

Then, just as she reached the gateway she thought of Jesus carrying the heavy Cross—the Cross to which she had added another nail—all the way up the slopes to Golgotha. And the other nail would stay there until God had forgiven her; and she couldn't be forgiven until she had proved her penitence.

Without further parley or hesitation she turned towards the wooden bridge and stepped out briskly.

It was very dark, but all her journeys back to Muchanger in winter were made in the dark, and the blackness itself did not alarm her. Immediately beyond the bridge one lighted window from Bridge Farm cast a cheering ray and soon after that had fallen away behind her she could catch a glimpse of another lighted window at Wood Farm. After that the darkness thickened where Layer Wood loomed up and the wind changed its tone; it boomed and howled through the trees and the tormented branches creaked and clashed.

Now she was coming to the bad part. Every story that she had ever heard about this stretch of road rushed back to add its modicum of terror; she could hear again the very voices which had told the tales, culminating in Mrs. Hart's saying that she wouldn't walk this way for a thousand pounds.

Nor would she, Damask Greenway! She was here for the only reason powerful enough to make her take the risk.

The Twenty-third Psalm was an excellent thing to remember when one was frightened. She remembered it. "Yea, though I walk through the valley of the shadow of death, I will fear no evil: for thou art with me; thy rod and thy staff they comfort me."

Satan made himself heard again: You'd be more comforted if someone came along and walked with you, wouldn't you? Even Matt Juby and he a bit tipsy! It'd take more than a falling branch to make Bobbie rear and shy—wasn't that what Mrs. Hart said? And what about that night when Widow Hayward . . .

Get thee behind me, Satan!

She started the psalm again. "I will fear no evil, no evil, no evil . . ." What a dreadful word "evil" was just by itself when you came to think about it!

But she was getting along; nearly to the place where the Lady's Ride—and that was an ominous name too—opened out into the road. It must have been just about here that Sir Charles . . . Don't think about that. Nothing has happened yet; and perhaps it is all superstition after all; a good Methodist shouldn't be superstitious. And perhaps she was to be spared the worst. Perhaps the terror which she had inflicted on herself was to be her punishment. "The wicked flee when no man pursueth."

But it isn't man you're afraid of, is it, Damask?

It was then that she heard the sound of hoofs, coming quickly, coming towards her.

Her heart gave a great jolt and then seemed to stop. She stood, paralysed with terror, stock-still in the middle of the road.

Nobody not already half demented by fear could possibly have mistaken the hoofbeats of the Fuller's old cart horse for those of a spirited stallion, even though young Danny Fuller was driving hard, even though the rattle of the iron-rimmed wheels toned so exactly with the roar and moan of the wind as to be indistinguishable. But Damask was already half demented. Fear had been moving within her when she rose from her knees in the workroom and it had been rising ever since, pressing against the barriers of reason and determination and faith; now as she realised her worst fears and knew that she was not to be spared nothing, the barriers went down.

She stood in the middle of the road and closed her eyes and thought, "Deliver us from evil, deliver us from evil, evil, evil. Deliver us . . ."

She could smell the horse; she could feel its breath.

She dropped down, mercifully insensible, as the old horse checked and slithered to a halt.

There was a text: *Underneath are the everlasting arms!* And it was true. So were all the other things people said about Heaven. She'd died there in the dark and fallen, fallen through infinite space and infinite darkness and now here she was, safely held in those strong everlasting arms. She gave a great sigh of happiness and relief, and lay back in the arms more securely. It was wonderful; it was all over, the struggles against Satan and temptation and sin; all the hard work and the way the cook at Muchanger made fun of her and called her "Methody"; the long trudging miles to chapel ... all over. No more hurry, the whole of eternity, held close like this. Everything had been worth while. Presently all the glory and beauty of Heaven would be there to be enjoyed, for the moment it was enough to lie here. She snuggled closer.

Then a very human, ordinary voice said, "My God, I thought I'd killed you!" Not the voice of Jesus which had come from Mr. Whitwell's lips in the Summerfield barn. So hard on the heels of this realisation that it seemed part of it came the awareness that what her face was pressed into was some rough cloth that smelt of smoke, of cooked onions, of hay, horses, and ale.

"Wake up and speak to me," said the voice. "Are you hurt?" The voice was not very steady. Danny Fuller had had a fine shock; pounding along like that and having old Short check and swerve, and climbing down to find what looked like a dead girl in the road.

"Are you hurt?" he asked again.

Not without disappointment Damask came to full knowledge: she was still on earth; she must make an effort.

"I'm all right. She didn't touch me. And I kept my eyes shut, so I'm all right. How did you get here?" Her voice was languid and the few words seemed to demand all the strength she had left. She kept her eyes closed and still—lay limp in his embrace.

"If we didn't touch you why did you fall down? And why didn't you get to the side of the road? You must have heard us coming."

"Not you. Her! I heard her and I prayed and God heard me. He sent you."

"I think you must have had a crack on the skull," Danny said practically. The hood of her cloak had fallen back on her shoulders and he put his hand to her head, running his fingers through her hair with a touch which made a thrill of voluptuousness move over her. She shuddered a little.

"No bump that I can find," he said. He was sure of her identity now, having touched the hard bunch of plaits; no other girl wore her hair that way. "You're Damask Greenway, aren't you?" Unconsciously his manner cooled. His susceptibility to girls was the greatest trouble as well as the greatest joy of his life but his feeling for Damask was tinged with the same reserve and resentment which Sir Charles had experienced earlier in the afternoon. She was so prim and so strait-laced, and she could have been so pretty, but deliberately made herself plain and that, beside being a pity and a waste, was in some curious way a rebuke to Danny and his kind. His brown, good-looking face twitched into a mischievous grin as he said:

"I'm Danny Fuller."

That'd make her sit up! It certainly did. She opened her eyes and pulled away from him, thankful that the darkness hid the hot blush which scorched her face as she remembered how she had lain in his arms and pressed her face to his coat and thrilled to the touch of his hand in her hair. Danny Fuller, who had the worst name for running after girls of any boy in six parishes.

"I'm quite all right now, thank you," she said in the prim way he detested.

"Well, I'm glad of that. What the hell did you think you were doing, walking in the middle of the road with your eyes shut? Isn't it dark enough?"

"I was frightened," she said. "She was so near me I could feel the horse's breath on me."

"Who was?"

"Lady Alice."

He broke into laughter. "Only horse came near you tonight was my old Short! There were we spanking along and there you stood. If he didn't have better sense than you do we'd have run you down. Fancy you, of all people, believing those daft old tales!" He was pleased to find this proof of weakness and human feeling in her.

"Well, maybe it was silly." She thought for a second. "Yes it was silly . . . but all alone, in the dark . . . *And* I had another reason. Squire was found dead just here only a little while back."

"Squire? Good God! Is that really true?"

"Mrs. Hart herself told me. I went up to the house with

these . . . Oh, where are those boots?" she felt about in the darkness while Danny said slowly:

"That's wonderful; the very best thing that could happen."

"I don't see why," she said, stooping to gather up the parcel. "My father'll miss his custom; so will a lot of other people."

"There'll be a new Squire, silly. Younger and not so set in his ways. *Nobody* could be so pigheaded as the old man was. Ha-ha, now we can all go ahead and get on!"

"That's what I must do now. I was late to start with and I've still got a long way to go." She pulled the hood of her cloak into place.

"Where are you now?" Danny asked.

"The same place. Muchanger."

"Then what are you doing on this road? The Turnpike's shorter and doesn't have ghosts!"

"This is a bit shorter from the Manor end of the village; I told you, I went up with the boots. And I had another reason."

"Meeting somebody?" He wasn't yet aware that the answer to that question mattered to him; he asked it teasingly.

"No, I wasn't. That's just the sort of thing you *would* think, Danny Fuller."

"I only asked," he said, "because I thought you might get scared again . . . alone, in the dark, with all these ghosts about. Lady Alice, dead and buried hundreds of years! I *am* surprised at you."

"I'm surprised at myself. But . . . being frightened was part of it . . . part of why I was on this road, I mean. And perhaps . . . Well, I must get along now."

"I tell you what," he said, "you hop up and I'll turn round and drive you to Muchanger."

"That's very kind of you. Thank you very much but I'd rather walk."

"Why?"

She stood silently, trying to put her reason into words that would not sound too offensive.

"You aren't afraid of me, surely."

"Not *afraid*," Damask said. She added, speaking slowly, so that what she said should be precise and unmistakable, "But somebody might see us. And any girl you ever *look* at is talked about, you know that. I don't want people saying that I'm one of your jilts."

"Don't talk so daft," he said. "Who's to see us? You can't

go lugging that great parcel all the way to Muchanger and getting scared again. If you don't get in the cart, I shall turn round and drive slowly alongside, then if there was anybody to see, you would be talked about. Come on now, hop up."

She still hesitated, engaged in one of her inward debates. It was dark; she was late and the parcel was heavy. Also, in her hour of need Danny had arrived; it looked as if God had sent him. Perhaps it would be all right.

"Well, thank you very much," she said.

Danny climbed nimbly into the cart and held out his hand to help her up.

The old horse turned unwillingly and went slowly in the direction which for him was all wrong, leading as it did away from his stable, his well-earned supper. Danny did nothing to hurry him.

The seat of the cart was a plank, stretched from side to side and capable of being removed when the vehicle was needed for farm work; one half of this seat was occupied at the moment by a big linen bag full of snippets of silk and velvet which Danny had that afternoon collected from Miss Jackson, the dressmaker. Mrs. Fuller, during the long winter evenings which were her only leisure, occupied herself by making patchwork quilts which were popular in the six parishes as "bride gifts." She had a standing arrangement with her cousin the dressmaker by which all "pieces" were exchanged for a dressed fowl, a dozen eggs, a loin of pork, and a pound of butter now and again. Earlier in the afternoon, seeing Danny off to Baildon, Mrs. Fuller had said, "And take my piece bag along. And don't go chucking it in the back of the cart like you did last time. All the pieces stank of muck and the bag had to be washed. Tie it on the seat aside you."

So there it was, and there were Damask and Danny forced to sit very close to one another on the other half of the seat. And Danny was large; he had his father's big bones, not yet stripped and made angular by constant hard labour, and he was better nourished than his father had been in his youth for Mrs. Fuller was not one of those farm wives who marketed the best produce and fed her family on what was left. Early in her married life she had made that plain to Mr. Fuller when he once ventured to mention that his mother's habit had been to "make do with what's over."

"Your mother bore eight children and reared two and your father died at forty! Glory be to God, what's the use of a farm if it can't *feed* you? Before my family starve in the midst of plenty we'll leave the farm and move into town, where *I* could earn food at least." That silenced Fuller, whose wife before her marriage had kept a thriving little pastry cook's shop in Baildon and made money with her quilts besides. So Danny and his sister Susan had grown up straight and strong and handsome beyond the average, and their father, despite his hard work and what Mrs. Fuller called his "worritting nature," had already outlived his father by six years.

Sitting in such close contact, Danny and Damask were very much aware of one another. He could smell the odour of the cobbler's workroom in which her hood had hung all afternoon; he could smell soap and now and again an elusive whiff of lavender and rosemary. But he could also smell something more positive and pervasive, the ghost stink of the muck for which the cart had been used during the week. That brought something else to mind and provoked the first remark to be made during the drive.

"Father's going to try stall-feeding some beasts this winter," he said. "He took the kitchen for a byre and Mother agreed to try it if he promised to buy a gig with the first profits he made. She's been mad for a gig ever since Fred Clopton bought his."

She could find nothing to say to that; on the fringe of her mind there dwelt for a moment the certainty that it was all concerned with a worldly and therefore unworthy ambition; something her father would decry, but it seemed not to matter very much just now.

"Would you like a ride in a gig, Damask?"

"I don't know. This is really the first proper ride I've ever had in a cart even. My only other ride was in Shad's donkey rig."

The idea that a ride in the despised old farm cart could be a treat, an experience, was amazing, and touching.

"I tell you what," he said, "I'll bring the cart and drive you the whole way next time. When will you get out next? Next Saturday?"

"Oh no. I have a Saturday once a month. The others get two—they're very lenient at Muchanger—but my other day out is a Sunday, so I can go to chapel."

The last word dashed him, reminded him of her difference, her primness, the withheld prettiness which he resented. But that only lasted a moment, because he could feel her there pressed against his arm and thigh, very small, and warm, and soft, and smelling so nice and clean.

"Four weeks from now then, I'll call for you and drive you home."

"I know you mean kindly, but that wouldn't do. It wouldn't do at all."

"Why not?"

"I told you."

"Told me what?" This was the kind of conversation he was most at home with, half teasing, half probing, trying to make a girl say something out of which something else could be made.

"You *know*. You know as well as I do, Danny Fuller. You've got a bad name. You're always running after girls and taking them to the Midsummer Fair as though you meant to marry them, and then you don't."

"Well, what if I do? I like girls. I just go on looking for a girl I can keep on liking when I really know her. I never did find one, you can't blame me for that. Now just suppose, *suppose*, I said, you turned out to be that girl and then wouldn't have anything to do with me just because I'd had the sense to wait for you. Wouldn't that be a pity?"

She laughed then and he was delighted that she could laugh just like any other girl.

"I bet you say something like that to every girl you take up with! When your mother made you go to school for a year she *said* it was so you could learn to reckon, but I think you learned *disputation* too!"

"Disputation. What's that?"

"It's making an argument, not twisting exactly, but making what you say make other people see things your way. I know about it because it's something the travelling preachers do. People sometimes jump up and ask awkward questions and try to make them look silly and that's where disputation comes in."

"And are you trying to make me look silly?" he asked, seizing upon the one phrase which would allow him to drag the talk back to the desired line.

"Of course not. I'm the one who would look silly if I believed that you had been waiting for me."

"But it might be true." Something that had been working in him ever since she had confessed her fears of Lady Alice's ghost assured him that it *was* true, but then he'd thought that so many times before and he'd always been wrong, so far.

"It might *be* true," he repeated. "You might give a chap a chance to find out, Damask."

There! He knew now. Another symptom. That something special in the name, the pleasure of saying it. Phyllis, Agnes, Daisy, Rose, Joan . . . name after name had been briefly lighted and made special by the charm of the girl who owned it. Cissie, Martha, Jill, Jennie . . . name after name had darkened, waned, become just another name as the girl who owned it became just another girl. He seldom took time from his girl-chasing to remember the past or think about the future, but now for a moment he did so, and was sobered. Damn near twenty-five and no nearer being wettled than he was at eighteen. Something, anything, a look, a chance word, would set him off and he'd be hot after a wench for weeks, then suddenly out it would all go, like a blown candle, and his chief feeling would be one of relief that he'd never yet been hasty enough to marry a girl. It would be awful to wake up one morning and find yourself tied for life to a girl who had ceased to attract you. What could be worse?

He had time to think while he waited for her answer, and some excitement crept in and mingled with his thoughts. Damask wasn't like other girls; it would be a new experience to break down her primness, coax her into loosening those plaits. Every drop of his hunter's blood moved swiftly to meet a challenge which it met all too rarely. He was handsome and merry, and some deep instinct had restricted his chase to a class of girl to whom a farmer's son was a "catch"; most of them had come halfway to meet him. This was different.

Still she did not answer; and at last he said:

"Well? How about me meeting you next time you're out?"

"No. That wouldn't do," she said. "And I'd be obliged if you'd drop me here, outside the gate. If anybody saw us I should never hear the last of it."

"And would you mind? Really?"

"I should hate it. I can bear being teased about what is true but not . . . not something that isn't."

"Do you get teased?"

"A bit."

And again he knew he had been "set off," for he felt belligerent towards those who teased her. Damn it all, why shouldn't she be a Methodist? There were worse things to be! He could think of a whole host of worse things. And what if she did scrape her hair back in that unbecoming fashion; she did keep it clean; he remembered several girls who were pretty to look at from a distance but not very nice close to . . .

"I said stop. Please, Danny."

"Just as you say," he said, pleased that she had used his name. The old horse seemed to halt of his own accord, and before Danny could move, Damask had pushed past the parcel and scrambled down on the far side of the cart, so that he could not even help her.

"And I'm not to see you again—ever?"

"No. But thank you for bringing me back . . . and stopping here . . . and coming along just when you did. Good-bye."

Entranced rather than deterred by his rebuff, Danny turned the horse again and rattled away to his home, where over a belated supper table his father had just broken the news about Sir Charles' attitude towards the stall-feeding.

"So there they stand, pretty as a picture, and there they'll stand o' Tuesday when he comes nosing back. He've done his worst now and can't damage me no more till Lady Day, and then we'll all be out in the road, fat bullocks and all."

Mrs. Fuller cherished, like many other women in the village and the district, a curious, respectful, sentimental feeling for the Squire. When he praised her kitchen, or said she looked well and bonny, or accepted her cake and wine, her self-esteem warmed and expanded and something very near to worshipful love moved in her heart. It was something which she had never felt towards Steve Fuller; and when Steve, blurting out the whole miserable story, said, "He even arst how you'd manage without a kitchen, making out I was doing you a wrong," her immediate feeling was, Ah yes, he would think of that, he's a gentleman!

But all that was froth, a dreamy nothing. Her attitude towards her husband might be mainly maternal instead of the dog-looking-up-to-kind-master one which every woman in her heart longs to attain, but simply for that reason any attack on Steve was a battle cry.

"Let him come here on Tuesday," she said, "and he'll get a piece of my mind! As you say, the damage is done now and I'll tell him something he 'on't forget in a hurry. And don't you go fretting, my dear. We can manage. I hear that Claughton at Colchester is minded to retire and sell his shop. S'pose we could get hold of that! I could make a living there! And failing that, there's hundreds of places. Don't you fret. We can manage."

Danny came in, knowing that, what with his lingering in the King's Head at Baildon and then turning about and going back to Muchanger, he was dreadfully late this time. Being late when he had been out afoot was not serious, but old Short's hours, being numbered, must be accounted for.

"I brought the pieces, Mother, and a damned long time I had to wait while Miss Jackson collected them. And I've got news for *you*, Dad! Squire fell off his horse and broke his neck this evening!"

Fuller said, "Thank God for that," before he remembered what he had said to the bullock. Mrs. Fuller said, "Oh no! Poor dear man!" before she remembered what Sir Charles had said to her husband. Danny, looking from one to another of them and seeing that his lateness would pass unremarked, said cheerfully:

"I've got a feeling that everything will alter now; tonight will be a sort of turning point."

On the next evening, which was Sunday, the chapel at Nettleton gained a new attendant at the evening service. He came in at the last moment, took a seat at the back, and slipped away before anyone could speak to him. Amos was preaching that evening, and as soon as he saw the familiar face in such unfamiliar surroundings, hastily changed the subject of his discourse and preached a very earnest sermon about the joy in Heaven over one repentant sinner. He slipped from the pulpit and hurried to the door as quickly as he could and was greatly disappointed to find Danny gone; they could have walked home together and he could have continued his exhortation on more intimate terms.

Danny went home disappointed but not downcast. She had said *a* Sunday, not which one, and he would go on attending until he hit on the right one. The wasted evening, the long walk meant little. Once, long ago, at the Midsummer Fair, he'd been "set off" by a girl who was helping her father to sell his pills—guaranteed to cure everything short of a broken bone. He'd been obliged to buy a great number of pills in order to obtain a few minutes' conversation with her, and she had told him that they were going next to Bywater. An invented errand had gained him possession of the horse and cart and he'd gone to Bywater and stayed there three days. The pill vendor and his daughter had never appeared, and when Danny went home his father had beaten him with his belt, that being during the period when Steve still hoped to knock the nonsense out of him.

On the next Sunday evening, as he slipped into place, he *knew*, before ever looking round, that Damask was there; and so she was, sitting beside Amos, who had not been called to preach at Summerfield after all. Danny edged along the seat, awkwardly because his legs were too long for the space allowed, until he could see her without obviously straining his neck; and there he sat, feasting his eyes on the knot of plaits he had once thought so regrettable, and on the straight narrow shoulders and slim waist in the ugly slate coloured dress. A dispassionate observer might have considered him very lucky to have something to distract his attention from the sermon, for it was Abel Shipton's turn to preach, and his sermons were a trial to the most earnest and well-disciplined members. Not only were they painfully dull; they were delivered slowly, over-emphatically, and in a voice which was afflicted with a peculiar disability.

"Now—er, we will take for our text—er this evening—er the words—er of the Apostle—er . . ." Abel began; and Danny, who never even heard the text, was the only person present who could truly have said that he enjoyed the next forty-five minutes.

This evening Amos had no difficulty in getting hold of the newcomer; Danny was waiting outside, just where the thick candle in the hanging lantern made a little island of light in the murky black of the autumn night. While Amos gripped him by the hand and spoke the words of welcome which he had not been able to deliver last Sunday and asked Danny to wait so that they could walk home together, Damask stood silent. She knew why Danny was there; but she acted as though she had never spoken a word to him in all her life, nor ever would. Her silence passed unnoticed; everybody was shaking hands with everybody else, and saying, "Good night, God bless you," and a good many people were busy lighting their lanterns for their long trudges along lonely roads and over the field paths. Abel Shipton came and joined them and they all four set out together, lighted by Abel's lantern; but as soon as they had fallen into step Abel said:

"Oh—er, I saw Judson—er yesterday—er in Baildon—er and he said—er he'd worked out—er the timber costs—er."

Amos' attention was immediately riveted, and as soon as a bigger puddle than ordinary shone up in the lantern light, Danny seized Damask by the arm and said, "Mind the mud," and drew her aside; and after that they walked two and two.

"Well," he said, "surprised to see me?"

To say "yes" would be a lie; to say "no" would imply that she had expected him and had been thinking about him; so she said:

"I think it's wrong to go to chapel and make everybody think . . . well, things that aren't true. Father *might* have been preaching at Summerfield tonight and then how should we have looked?"

"You think a lot about how things look, don't you?" Danny said, not critically, just pursuing a line of interest.

"Well—it says in the Bible to avoid sin and *appearance* of sin: I can't remember the exact words, but I understand the meaning."

"And is walking along with me a sin?"

"You know what I mean and you know how it looks. I felt awful when Father was welcoming you in as though you'd turned from . . . well, all your old ways."

"Maybe I have. I said you should give me a chance, didn't I, Damask?"

She made no answer. He cast about in his mind for something impersonal and inoffensive to say and hit upon the topic which had eclipsed all others during the past week—Sir Charles' death and the changes expected as a result.

"When I got home the other night . . ." he began, and told her about the kitchen-turned byre and the Squire's reaction to it and the notice which now could be ignored. "Down in the Black Horse," he ended, "they were saying that the new Squire was as different from his father as chalk from cheese, just as the old man was different from his father. And Jim Jarvey, from the Lodge, said last time he opened the gate for lawyer Turnbull he told him the new Squire was in India and he'd sent a letter off with the news. People make fortunes in India; maybe he has and'll come back and build us all new byres."

"It'll be nice for your mother to have her kitchen back," said Damask primly.

They came to the crossroads where the three roads met, one running on to Clevely, one to Muchanger, and one to Strawless. In the little green triangle where they forked there was a hump, said to be the grave of a boy who had hanged himself because he was suspected of sheep-stealing, away back in ancient times. Nobody tended the grave—if grave it was, nobody was even sure of that—but everybody knew that the little mound always produced the wild flower that was in season—wild violets, primroses, cowslips, marguerite daisies, scabious, knapweed. One old story said that there was some connexion between this grave and the witch, Lady Alice of Merravay; it said that she had planted the roots of the flowers.

Here Amos always turned off on to the road to Clevely, while Damask went straight along to Muchanger. And here, as usual, Amos halted and said:

"Well, good night, Damask. Be a good girl. God bless you."

Shipton halted too, holding his lantern a little higher as though in salute; as though they expected, Danny thought, that he was going to join them and leave Damask to go on alone.

She seemed to think so too, for she walked straight ahead into the darkness, with just a "Good night, Father, good night, Mr. Shipton." None of them, fortunately, could hear how her heart, so long uneasy, had suddenly started to knock in her ears.

"Mr. Greenway, d'you mind if I walk along with Damask?"

"Why, no. But thass the long way round for you, ain't it?"

"I don't mind *that*. Good night, Mr. Greenway, good night, Mr. Shipton."

"So that—er is why—er he came to chapel—er," said Shipton a little sourly.

"Why he came," said Amos vaguely. "Well, maybe, maybe. God moves in a mysterious way, His wonders to perform."

"Danny Fuller don't—er. He move in a brash, sinful way—er, wenching and drinking. I should—er be very sorry—er to see him go off—er with my daughter."

"Ah, but you ain't got one. If you had you'd know that no harm could come to a properly brought up Christian girl, same as Damask." He was absorbed in the problem in mental arithmetic just presented to him by Shipton's account of his meeting with Judson; he was also distracted by the very terrible nervous affliction which always came upon him after ten minutes of Shipton's company—he had to struggle against imitating him; and between the two bothers he had no time or interest to spare for his daughter.

Danny caught up with Damask and took her by the elbow. "There," he said, "now we can talk properly." Fire ran all over her at his touch, but she jerked her arm free and stopped walking.

"I've said all I have to say to you, Danny Fuller," she said. "You go along with Father and Mr. Shipton and leave me be. I don't want you coming to chapel and making me look ridiculous. Nor I don't want you walking me home."

"Now, why not. Just tell me why not."

"I did tell you. And just now you said about being in the Black Horse; I don't want . . . I mean it wouldn't be suitable for me . . . with you going there."

"Well, I don't see much harm in *that*; but if *you* do, Damask, then I won't *go* in the Black Horse. Would that please you?" A great warm, weakening tide seemed to lift her, hold her helpless, threaten to sweep her away. She strove against it valiantly.

"It isn't just the inn. It's . . . it's everything. You know as well as I do; you're just pretending not to see, just to tease me."

"What else don't you like about me?"

"Well . . . swearing."

"I don't swear," he said indignantly.

"You do. I heard you say 'hell' myself."

"Bless you," he said. "D'you call that *swearing*? You should hear . . ." He broke off. "All right then, no swearing. You know I'd do anything to please you."

And that, at the moment, was true. He was schooled in the practice of pleasing in order to be pleased. He had had his first lesson long ago, during his year at the King Edward Grammar School at Baildon. There every Saturday morning an old woman was allowed to enter the courtyard and sell her toffee and meat pies and saffron cakes to such boys as were blessed with spending money. Mrs. Fuller, who had insisted upon Danny's having a year's schooling when he was thirteen, was paying his fees with her "quilt money," and allowed him fourpence a week. Accustomed to good farm food, he found the school meals meagre and for some weeks counted the hours between Saturday and Saturday. Then one morning the old woman came, accompanied by a little girl, a waifish little creature with great dark eyes in a thin, sad face. She helped to carry the basket and then stood, watching the money and the foodstuff change hands. When it was Danny's turn to be served something made him say, "Do *you* like toffee?"

"She don't know," said the old woman gruffly. "We can't

afford to eat it, we make it to sell. We ain't lucky like you young gentlemen."

He took his purchases and dropped back, waiting, whistling nonchalantly until the last customer had scampered away and the old woman drew over the basket the cloth which kept the dust and flies from her goods. Then he reached out and pushed all his fourpennyworth into the little girl's thin, dirty hand.

He knew, even then, that he was not being charitable, or generous or kind; there were plenty of boys all about who would gladly have accepted even one mouthful; he did it to make the great dark eyes smile at him. And they did. After that, so long as he was at school, he spent his fourpence on the little girl. (The old woman always took the stuff away from her as soon as they were out of the school yard; but Danny had had his smile. And on the whole the child benefited, for the old woman was suddenly granted a glimpse of the future, the hope that one day there might be some reward for bringing up an unwanted orphan grandchild—if she appealed to the gentlemen.)

"You know I'd do anything to please you," he said again, as Damask did not reply to his first protestation. "No *hell*; no *damn*. I think that's all I know, Damask. Come on, *you* tell me the other words I mustn't say."

"Now you're teasing me," she said, and tried to sound prim, but suddenly broke into laughter.

"That's better," Danny said, and laughed too and took her by the arm again. All in a moment something was established. The preliminaries were over.

CHAPTER 4

DAMASK'S FEAR OF "TALK" HAD BEEN WELL FOUNDED. BEFORE Christmas everyone knew that Danny Fuller was walking out with her, and spice was added to the gossip by the rumour that he was a reformed character. At the Christmas week market this rumour was abundantly confirmed; one of his former cronies had betted another five shillings that he would have Danny inside the King's Head before the day was out, and with such a sum at stake, exerted all his cajolery to gain his point. When he failed, he turned nasty and said, "Well, I hope it's worth it! I'm told that if you can get a Methody girl in the . . ." and went on to say something very gross and offensive. Blows were struck out there in the open street to the great delight of the whole market.

In February, Mrs. Fuller felt it safe to say, looking up from the patchwork quilt:

"I got a feeling that *this* one 'on't hev to go very far afield, Father. I allus said, didn't I, that the boy'd settle down and pick a decent girl in the end."

Fuller, with the consciousness of Lady Day being within reckoning distance now, was little disposed to rejoice about anything.

"Time enough to crow," he said, "when they're married.

And whether *that'll* be much to crow over I ain't so sure. Funny he couldn't pick up a decent girl reared to farm work and with a bit in her stocking, same as we give Susan when she married. And there's another thing—if he do wed Amos Greenway's wench and they live along of us, she needn't think she's gonna bring her Methody ways *here*. Cold Sunday dinner for the glory of God and a black look if you use a bad word! Not," he added gloomily, "that there'll be much dinner, hot *or* cold, by the look of things."

"Oh, you worrit too much," said Mrs. Fuller. "Lawyer Turnbull and Sir Edward Follesmark said, didn't they, that everything was going to jog along unchanged till Sir Richard arrived. And nobody but us knew about the notice, did they? You'll see it'll all be forgot and most like when the changes do come they'll be the ones you been hankering for all this time."

"I wish I could believe it."

"You might as well. 'Never trouble trouble till trouble troubles you'; thass what I allus say."

Amos Greenway, who never heeded gossip at any time, was particularly immune just then; his whole mind devoted to the plans for the new chapel. The timber dealer, Judson, had fallen far short of expectations and quoted an extortionate price for the needed material and Amos, depressed by this evidence of "lukewarmness in the cause" was still seeking another source of supply. He had no time or interest to fritter away on trivialities.

One day Matt Ashpole came into the workshop with a bit of harness to be mended and said:

"I hear young Fuller hev took up with your girl, serious-like."

"Oh," Amos said, vague and unconcerned as though Ashpole had mentioned a stranger. "This end's clean perished, Matt. Wouldn't hold the stitches more'n a week afore it'd break away agin."

"Well, tack it together. I might be lucky and pick up a new bit while it was holding, like. Done very well for herself, ain't she? I only wish my Sally could do as good."

"You didn't bring her up right. No man can gather figs from thistles. 'Tain't in the nature of things. All right, I'll do what I can, but don't blame me if it don't last."

Julie's attempts to talk about the affair met with no more success. She had only to ask whether Danny had been in chapel again, and off Amos would go, speculating on the possibility of persuading the young man to take an interest in the Sunday school. "It's early days yet, of course, but once I'm sure it ain't just a flash in the pan, I shall ask him. He had a bit of schooling you know; he'd be very useful."

That kind of remark exasperated Julie, but she was accustomed, by this time, to thinking her own thoughts and holding her own counsel; and one morning in March when Amos was out, she unlocked and opened the bottom drawer of the chest which stood by her bed. The musty, melancholy scent of ancient lavender came to meet her as she stooped stiffly over her treasures. First of all, taking up most of the space, was the blue silk dress in which she had been married, and a saucy little flat hat, ribboned with the same blue. Both showed signs of wear, for during her early married life, before Amos turned Methodist, she had worn them every Sunday and on many other festive occasions. She could still remember the day when Amos had said that they were "too worldly" for chapel wear. "I ain't suggesting you should chuck 'em away, Julie; the dress'd dye some sober colour and you could spare a bit out of the skirt to fill in the neck like, couldn't you? And pull the hat about a bit, more like a bonnet."

She had saved for months to buy the material for that dress and stitched it herself after long hours of toiling over other women's clothes; it was the only completely charming and satisfactory outfit she had ever owned and it was too precious to sacrifice upon the altar of Amos' Puritanism; she had folded it carefully, sprinkled it with lavender, and locked it away. It had lain there for twenty-one years.

Now she stroked the folds of the overfull skirt, the silk rasping under her work-roughened fingers, and wondered whether Amos would allow Damask to wear it for *her* wedding. Most likely not; but afterwards . . . surely Danny would not be so strict. Julie was sure in her heart that it was Damask who drew Danny to chapel. . . .

What beautiful small stitches she could make in those days; now her fingers were clumsy. And what a lovely shade of blue. Not so good a colour for Damask, with her yellow-brown eyes, as it had been for her; but the lace on the bodice had yellowed with age and would make a kind of match; it would look well enough.

She took out the small heavy parcel which had lain below the dress, unfolded the bit of linen in which it was wrapped, and looked fondly at the handsome gold watch thus displayed.

It had belonged to her grandfather and had been given to her by her grandmother. Neither Mrs. Greenway nor any other member of the family could understand why she should be chosen to be the recipient; sometimes she thought the old woman had done it to spite her three sons and seven grandsons, who all coveted it. However, hers it was, and when she was married Amos had made a neat little leather case for it and it had hung on the wall and kept time for the household. Then during the great gale in December 1789 the roof of Nettleton Chapel was blown off and funds were urgently needed for its repair. Amos had suggested selling the watch. Then Mrs. Greenway had told a lie—and one which cost her never a pang of conscience.

"No, I mustn't sell it; my gran said so. Thass to be kept in the family and passed on. If this one is a boy"—she was pregnant at the time—"he must hev it. If not it'll go to Damask. 'Tain't *mine*, really, you see. I'm only holding it to pass on."

There had been two stillbirths since Damask was born, and this pregnancy was not going well; perhaps for that reason Amos refrained from an insistence which might upset his wife. But after that Julie never felt that the watch was really safe, so one day she opened it and put a tiny splinter very delicately in a vital place. So the watch was stopped and there was no money just then for watch-mending. It went into the drawer and she hoped Amos had forgotten its existence. Not that she minded much. It was not her intention to let Damask go into the Fuller family as bare as a hedge tinker. Everybody else in the six parishes might think the cobbler's daughter had made a catch; Mrs. Greenway knew different; on *her* side of the family there were people every bit as good as the Fullers, and better. Damask might be only the daughter of a cobbler too unworldly to ply his trade and be prosperous, but if Mrs. Greenway could in any way contrive it she was going to her husband with the "three of everything" which made up a proper bridal chest. She eyed the watch ominously, wrapped it in the bit of linen, and put it in the pocket of her apron. Then she relocked the drawer, went downstairs, wrapped her shawl about her, and went hobbling across to the Ashpoles' place.

Matt was at home, taking his ease, bootless and unbuttoned before a roaring fire. A little later in the year he would be out with his ramshackle old cart and his bony old horse, buying up whatever he could find that was cheap and selling it as soon and as profitably as possible, but in winter, when the weather was bad and there was little huckstering to be done, he stayed at home, except on the days when he drove to Baildon.

Mrs. Ashpole, Julie was gratified to see, was not in the untidy, stinking room, where on a sack by Matt's feet, his lurcher bitch was on the verge of giving birth to pups.

"The missus is porely," Matt explained. "We kilt a pig last Monday and she overet herself on chitterlings. Bin sick as a dawg. But she's awright. Just lay there groaning and throwing up. Thass me owd Ripper here I'm worried about." He stretched out his foot in its filthy torn stocking and gently nudged the lurcher's flank. "Gitting a bit owd for *this* game, ain't you, gal? But then bitches on heat don't take no heed of their birth-days!"

"If there was anything I could do for Mrs. Ashpole..." Julie said, sincerely hoping there was not. "But it was really *you* I wanted to see."

"Show your good sense, too. She's nowt to look at this minnit, I can tell you." He grinned his good-natured, graceless grin. "And what can I do for Mrs. Greenway?"

"A great favour; though there'd be a bit of profit in it for you. Only you'd hev to promise me not to say a word about it to anybody."

"Want a love letter took? I'm your man, missus! Wouldn't be the first by a long chalk; I done some rum jobs in my day."

He ran his shrewd little piggy eyes over her as he spoke, inwardly savouring the irony of his suggestion. It was odd, he thought, but she hadn't worn as well as his missus, for all she had such a good husband. He and his wife had furious rows which often ended in blows and they'd brought up a large family, few of whom were anything but a nuisance, but there was some sap left in his old woman whereas poor Julie, a comely girl in her day, had shrivelled like a leaf.

"Go ahead," he said, quite kindly, "tell us the worst; no need to be shy with me."

She told him what she wanted him to do, giving as excuse for her secrecy and need to use him Amos' sensitive feelings. "Naturally he'd like to provide for his daughter, any father would; but he can't, and I wouldn't for the world hev him know I'd had to sell the watch."

"Let's hev a look at it. Whoo; thass a nice ticker. Do it go?"

"I think so." She opened it and picked out the little sliver. Amos had wound it all those years ago in the attempt to set it going and now, with just a shake, it started ticking again.

"Good as new. Why, yes, I can get rid of that all right. Mind you, I'm risking my good name to help you. 'Tain't my class of goods at all, they'll surely think I lifted it. Never mind, that'll buy all the flannel drawers your Damask'll need."

The coarseness rasped, but she smiled and thanked him.

"Hi, though," he said, "Amos is bound to see the stuff, ain't he? Where're you going to say you got it?"

"I hadn't thought as far as that," Julie admitted.

"Wimmen never think a thing to the end," Matt said, grinning, "and maybe thass a good thing. If they did the world would've ended with Adam and Eve, eh, missus?" He looked down at the dog and clicked his tongue encouragingly. "Tell you what, Amos could wring out half a crown if he really had to, I reckon? All right then. I'll get the stuff and muck it about a bit, only on the outside, and anyway it'll wash off, then I'll bring it along and arst you to buy it. Say I got it dirt-cheap because it was dirty. Ha-ha. Amos'll give me half a crown and I'll take a penny in the shilling of what I get for the watch. Fair enough?"

"Oh, thank you! That is a wonderful idea. I shall be everlastingly grateful. And you won't say a word, not even to Mrs. Ashpole."

"She's the last I ever tell anything to. Ah." He dropped to his knees beside the dog. "Thass the way, heave and shove. Soon be over now. Good owd Ripper, pod the little bastards!"

Late on Wednesday evening there was a great knocking on the Greenways' door and Amos went to answer it. Julie heard Matt Ashpole's voice say, "Hullo, owd cock! Got a bargain for *you* tonight. With your gal getting hitched I reckoned this would be worth half a crown to you."

Mrs. Greenway, with her heart beginning to beat rapidly, heard those opening words; Amos' reply, spoken more gently, escaped her; then she heard Matt start shouting abuse, and then break into a great roar of laughter. Finally the door shut. Amos came back into the kitchen empty-handed.

"Matt Ashpole, dead-drunk, trying to sell me some great quantity of cotton and flannel goods for half a crown," he said, shaking his head ruefully. "He couldn't possibly have come by them honestly and I told him so straight. I told him the receiver was as bad as the thief and he just laughed in my face."

It was a blow, and for a little while Mrs. Greenway was felled by it; but she had had blows before and lain supine and then bobbed up again. Two days later, when Amos had gone in Shad's donkey cart to buy leather at Baildon, she went across to the Ashpoles' cottage, and when Amos returned the two rolls of material were in the kitchen.

"You wronged Matt Ashpole, Amos," she said. "He was drunk, but he didn't steal this stuff. Claughton, the draper at Colchester, is giving up business; he's sold his shop to a grocer and he's got to get it all clear by Lady Day, when they move in. So the last things, soiled or faded, he was practically giving away. So . . . I thought you wouldn't mind if I snatched up the bargain. We owe Matt half a crown."

The next day was Saturday, the day when Damask came home bringing, as usual, the pudding pieces. Mrs. Greenway could hardly wait until the pudding was made and put in the saucepan before displaying her purchases.

"There's enough here for three of everything, summer and winter, which is what a girl *should* have," she said. "Then I thought you could spend your money on a lindsey woollen dress, and it ought to be a nice yellow-brown colour. Not a wedding dress, something that'll be useful for everyday best, sort of. I've got—well, if we can talk your father around—I've got your wedding dress laid away, the one I wore myself."

No outburst of girlish excitement such as she expected welcomed this speech. Damask's face went red, then white, and she looked embarrassed.

"But Mother—nothing's been said about any wedding."

"Of course not. That wouldn't be seemly. But you and Danny are walking out; and the Fullers asked you to Sunday dinner; and though you couldn't go it's just the same, it shows they agree. And it's for you and me to look ahead. You won't hev time for sewing, and I'm slow these days. Once I could stitch as quickly as I could talk, but not now."

She held out her twisted hands with the thumbs which seemed to grow more and more powerless every day, and which were doubling in under her palms as though to find shelter for their weakness. Damask looked at them with pity. It was strange, she thought, how in the last few months she had felt herself more drawn to her mother. Up to the time of her conversion she had preferred her mother to her father; she was less strict; less unworldly, and not so set against taking pleasure in anything outside the chapel. Then, when Damask's heart changed, everything changed: Amos moved into the ascendant; Julia moved to decline. Damask had sensed, as Amos had sensed long ago, that behind Julia's acceptance and compliance there

was some small reserve. She was not, as they were, whole-
hearted in the cause. Therefore, for almost five years, she had
seemed shadowy, negative. And then with just such another
sudden change everything had turned topsy-turvy again and in
the emotional confusion which had beset her since October it
had seemed to Damask that her mother was more likely to
understand her than her father was. All this unordered flow of
feeling went through her mind now as she stood looking at the
two rolls of stuff and heard her mother say, as though it was
the most natural thing in the world, that marriage should not
yet have been mentioned.

Was she wrong, too impatient, in thinking that the word
should have been spoken by now? After all, as her mother had
said, the Fullers had invited her to Sunday dinner, which was
the recognised way for parents to show their approval. None
of Danny's other girls had ever been so recognised by his
parents. She was sure of that, but she had asked him just for
the pleasure of hearing him say so, and he had given the right,
the pleasing, the reassuring answer, but in a curious way, as
though the whole subject embarrassed him. She had wondered
at the time whether it was tactless of her to mention all those
girls . . . but afterwards she had wondered whether Danny felt
that his parents had been a little hasty.

She had not been able to go to dinner and thus be, as it
were, established, because she was never free until afternoon
on her Sunday out, but she had, on the nearest Saturday, gone
to tell Mrs. Fuller and explain, and she had been given plum
cake and cowslip wine, completely harmless despite its name,
Mrs. Fuller had assured her; and she had been shown the quilt
on which Mrs. Fuller was working this winter and asked if she
liked the pattern. Even Mr. Fuller, though less warmly welcoming than Mrs. Fuller at first, had ended by being friendly and
showing her his cattle and pigs. She had really felt accepted
and respectable that afternoon; and she had expected that on
the way back to Muchanger, Danny would say something about
getting married. After all, they'd seen one another twice a
month ever since October and his family had asked her to
Sunday dinner.

Her mother's voice broke in on her thoughts.

"You are fond of him, aren't you?"

"Oh yes. I'm fond of him." What a weak, poor word to
use. She wondered what her mother would say if she used the
right ones.

"And it's plain he's head over heels in love with you. When you think what a young rip he was and look at him now ... you'd hardly believe it."

Yes, there was that too. She knew that she had power over him. If she said, "Go and jump in the river," he'd probably do it ...

Nevertheless, there was something—well, not wrong exactly, something queer about it all.

There was another trouble too; the violence of her own feeling for him. It frightened her. She believed that she would remember until the day she died the first time he kissed her, which was when he came to take her back after her November visit home; her bones had melted and she'd turned dizzy and there was nothing left on earth or in the heavens above or in the waters under the earth save the pressure of his hands on her waist and the pressure of his lips on hers and the savage hunger that they wakened. She'd pulled herself free and run into the house and up to her little attic bedroom and cried and prayed God to forgive her for feeling like that about Danny Fuller, who was, after all, only a human being. It was awful to think that she had been tempted to behave like Sally Ashpole and all the rest of them. . . .

"You'll see it'll work out right," her mother said. "I reckon Danny isn't used to keeping company with a respectable girl; it probably makes him shylike. And anyway, we got this stuff cheap; there'll be no harm in laying forward a bit whatever happens."

On the other side of the village Mrs. Fuller, chopper in hand, stood regarding what was left of half a pig after the hind leg and shoulder had been taken off to be smoked. When her mental calculations were complete, she raised the chopper and dealt two expert blows, took a knife and did a bit of trimming, and neatly scored what would be the crackling. The very best middle cut; what better could her goodwill take?

Her voice was carefully casual when she asked, "Will you be seeing Damask tonight?"

"Yes," Danny said, something wild and shy taking fright within him.

"It was only that I had a mite of pork I'd no use for, and I thought you might take it along with you. They don't rear a pig, do they? No, that'd be too sensible for Amos. They'll be glad of it then. Don't go off without it."

That was all she said, and it was well meaning and innocent

enough, but it sent Danny off scowling to wash and change
his clothes.

What a situation for him, of all people, to get himself into!
Like being stricken with the falling sickness; like running mad
in the full of the moon; like stepping into Filby Bog and sinking
in up to the neck. Up to the neck—but he'd still kept his head
out, just his head; and now even his mother was trying to shove
him under.

He had never, in all his life, been in such a muddle. He
could look back over seven years of being set on girls and see
that all his affairs had followed the same pattern, or rather the
same pattern with one variation. He'd be set off, for one reason
or another, he'd chase the girl, they'd have fun; most girls, in
the end, let him have his way with them, one or two had been
cautious—that was the variation, they did, or they didn't—
but whichever way it went the end had always been the same;
with lightning suddenness his interest had waned and the whole
thing was over.

This affair hadn't followed the pattern; it had lasted six
months and he was still mad for the girl; she was hard to please,
but he'd tried to please her, and every time he kissed her she
turned into a block of stone. And the outside world, which
hitherto had merely watched his affairs with amusement, was
now all agog, trying to be helpful; great lumps of pork! invitations to Sunday dinner! Trying to push his head under, trying
to marry him off to the one girl he'd ever known who didn't
care one bit about him. And there he was, unable to help
himself; dead-set on a girl who didn't care one bit about him
. . . and one day he'd give up the fight; he'd ask her to marry
him and she would and he'd end up the most henpecked man
since Reuben Farrow, who after a lifetime of saying "yes" and
"no" as his Martha bade him, went to rest in Clevely churchyard
under a tombstone which bore the words:

HERE LIES THE BODY OF REUBEN FARROW.
GOD MADE HIM MAN
I MADE HIM MANNERLY.

Everybody who thought at all about that epitaph thought of
Reuben as small and cold-blooded, of Martha as large and
vital. Danny Fuller knew differently; Reuben had been big,
and lusty and hot—Martha small and cold. It was always the
ice that made the fire look silly.

It shouldn't in this case! Damn it all to hell, he'd done everything he could to please her, and she hadn't been pleased. The one thing he had not done was to ask her to marry him; and he wouldn't, he wouldn't. Not until she had given him some sign.

And he wished to God he'd never met her; and he wished to God that he could be cured of this "set off" as he had of all the others.

And he shaved himself carefully, carefully; and cleaned his nails, and brushed his hair and donned his best clothes, self-immolate, votary of the unknown goddess.

He remembered the pork; which assured Mrs. Fuller and, ten minutes later, Mrs. Greenway, that all was well. He drove Damask to Muchanger; he kissed her, she turned into stone. She let him call for her; she chatted away, as friendly as could be, and then as soon as he touched her, she turned into stone. . . .

That night, rattling home over the Stone Bridge, he saw Sally Ashpole standing back in one of the recesses to let the cart pass. There'd been a time when he had been set on Sally Ashpole, black-haired, easygoing, good-natured trollop that she was, and she was not one of the girls who turned nasty when he ceased paying her attentions; they were still on terms of friendly banter. Sally had been anything but cold and hard and demanding, he remembered. With a feeling that he was making a gesture of defiance—though against whom or what he could not have said—he stopped the cart and called, "Hi, Sally . . ."

That was towards the end of March, and once March was over the year moved rapidly into spring. Mrs. Greenway persuaded herself that the warmer weather eased her stiff bones and stitched away diligently, entertaining herself with secret thoughts about three of everything, about a golden-brown lindsey dress, about Damask's attaining the security and comfort that she herself had missed. Mrs. Fuller, with her pullets beginning to lay, her broody hens beginning to set, and all the bother of the calf-rearing season approaching, stitched away with equal diligence at the quilt and entertained herself with thoughts of grandchildren.

And a tall sailing ship with her hull packed with tea, with bales of silk and muslin from India, to which had been added a consignment of pepper, nutmeg, and mace, taken on from the Dutch East India post at the Cape of Good Hope, came buffeting up through the Bay of Biscay on the last lap of her long journey. The pheasants in their wicker cage were quite tame now and would take food from Linda's hand.

The third Saturday of May in the year 1796 was one of those perfect late spring days which come all too rarely. In the pastures the hay, white with marguerite daisies, misted red with sorrel, stood knee high; the ditches frothed with meadowsweet, and all the air was sweet with the last rich fragrance of the lilacs and gillyflowers. While Damask made the beef pudding, Julie rather timidly displayed the result of her month's stitching, timidly because it included some feather stitching and a little drawn thread work here and there. And to her great relief Damask only said, "How pretty. You must have worked very hard!" Not a word about vanity.

Then Danny had called, on foot and early, bringing with him fresh evidence of his mother's approval in the shape of a plump roasting fowl, which Mrs. Fuller, forgetful of Steve's remark about Methodist ways, had thought would be nice for Sunday dinner. Julie was emboldened to open the little tin which served her as a tea caddy, and which had been opened only once—on Christmas Day—since Amos had issued his veto on tea in October. Amos and Abel Shipton had gone down to Bywater to inspect some old ships' timber in a breaker's yard there. The search for cheap timber had so far proved disappointing and disillusioning, and they were being driven to try makeshift methods.

The heat of the day and the exertions of her work had brought a flush to Damask's cheeks and loosened her hair a little; she looked quite pretty, her mother thought, still regretting the colour and fashion of the ugly dress which Damask had chosen made for herself. Danny described, with some homely wit, his mother's attempts to cook out of doors now that the weather was warm and the parlour, used as kitchen, unbearably stuffy; Mrs. Fuller had said that if gypsies could cook over an open outdoor fire, so could she; but she made the fire too near the house and the thatch had begun to smoulder. Altogether it was a very merry tea drinking.

"We'd better start," Danny said. "Father wouldn't let me bring the horse out, he's resting up for his hay-carting labours. My legs aren't so valuable in Father's eyes."

Damask said quickly, almost as though she had been awaiting the opportunity to say it:

"You needn't walk all that way with me, Danny. It's still light; I can quite well go by myself."

They both looked at her curiously, Danny in simple puzzlement, Julie with a flash of unusual cynicism. Was the girl really very clever, and deep and cunning? Was the secret of her success where so many had failed the simple expedient of pretending not to care whether Danny came or went?

"But of course I shall go with you. What d'you think I'm here for?" Danny said.

Julie looked at him; the handsome merry face, the thickly growing vigorous hair, the size and power of him; something long buried stirred in her defeated heart and withered frame. She remembered her own youth, the good-looking boisterous young cobbler whom nobody had thought a good match for a farmer's daughter who'd finished her apprenticeship and was clever with her fingers and lively and smart. But she'd known where her joy was to be found; and though it had lasted so short a time it had been sweet. . . . She hoped that Damask would find that same joy and that it would last longer.

"I thought we'd cut alongside the Waste and go through Layer. The bluebells should be out, it'd be pretty," Danny said. "And it isn't much further, we don't have to go all the way along the ride. I know a short cut."

"All right," Damask said with no pleasure in her voice.

To cover the lack Julie said, "It should be a lovely walk. When I could get about I used to go to Layer every year just to see the bluebells. . . ."

Even Mother—closer as they seemed these days to one another—had no notion, Damask thought. No notion how, all day, from the moment when she had risen in the dew-soaked, bird-loud dawn, she had been doing battle with herself; how every call of the cuckoo, every petal and leaf, every ray of sunshine had been lining up on the Devil's side, putting such thoughts into her head as nobody would believe.

They set off through the soft lingering light. One cuckoo in the depths of Layer Wood and one in the dense shrubbery of the Dower House were keeping up their eternal question and answer, and in the comparative coolness which had come with the evening all the scents of the approaching summer had magnified.

She was not self-analytical enough to realise that in truth her nature was sensuous and amorous, that even her "conversion" was all confused with the scent of hay and honeysuckle and the way the light had fallen on a man's hair; but she knew that the season's beauty, the world's loveliness this evening, would just make it more difficult to behave as she should.

They spoke little and the few words they used had a brittle, unreal sound.

The bluebells were out, misting with blue the distances between the trees and contributing their open peculiar scent of honey to the evening's incense. They wandered along, idly gathering the flowers until their hands were full.

"You take these," Danny said, pushing his bunch into her hands. "I'll pick another bunch for Mother. She often talks of gathering them when she first came to Clevely to live."

Suddenly Damask found herself staring down at the flowers through a dazzle of tears. The words sounded so innocent and so disarming—and she remembered that she hadn't wanted to come through the beautiful wood at all; and there was no danger, nothing wrong except the wickedness of her own heart. She looked at Danny's big, brown, work-scarred hands gently gathering the flowers and her love for him was a physical pain. Oh, how she loved him; how she wished that he would ask her to marry him!

Twilight seemed to rise from the ground, blotting out the distances and blurring the trunks of the trees while the upper branches were washed with light. The cuckoos ceased their calling, and immediately a wood dove resumed its long lament. Quite suddenly, without a word spoken, they both stopped, dropped their flowers, and turned to one another with a gesture older than time.

Their identities dropped with the flowers; no more Damask Greenway, no more Danny Fuller. Just a man and a maid in a summer wood.

All the old pagan gods came rustling up through the flower-filled thickets; they understood human nature, indulged it, exploited it, were tolerant of it because they could mould it so easily, and held it in contempt. Just one more couple with the summer in their blood.

But one of this couple had, for almost five years now, been in the service of another God who also understood human nature; had small indulgence for it and no contempt for because of it He had fashioned saints and martyrs and other curious creatures, such as girls with natural appetites leashed to touchy consciences. Just at—from the moralist's point of view—the right moment Damask's conscience jerked the leash. She cried breathlessly, "No. No. It'd be wicked!" She unclasped her arms and, putting both hands against his chest, began to push herself free. He tried to pull her close again and said in a thick strangled voice, "I'll marry you, Damask. We'll get married as soon as we can fix it. Aw . . . Damask . . ."

He had now spoken the words she had been longing to hear, but the time was not right; she knew her Devil and recognised his trickery. It was just like when he tempted Jesus in the wilderness, saying, "If thou therefore wilt worship me, all shall be thine." She struggled more violently and freed herself, sobbing with effort, and with the shock of having found herself so nearly in the pit of sin.

Her bodice was undone; she fastened it with unsteady fingers, brushed the bits of crushed leaf and petal from her skirts, pulled a twig from her hair. And all the time Danny did not move or speak. As she pulled away from him, he had rolled over and put his face on his folded arms. She imagined that he also was ashamed. Presently she said, very gently:

"It's all right, Danny. I'm not angry."

He did not answer immediately; then he said:

"I'm sorry, Damask. I should have known better." A more perceptive ear than hers might have heard less of apology than ironic comment in the words.

She retrieved the flowers, noticing that they were wilting already, and laying the stems into two neat bunches.

And still Danny did not move. He lay there quite overcome by the strangeness, the utter uniqueness of the thing which had happened to him in the last few minutes. He was cured! When she said, "I'm not angry," only politeness had held back his true rejoinder, "I don't give a damn whether you're angry or not." He now lay, savouring his relief, his joy at being his own man again. But he was still puzzled; this affair had begun in a curious way, it had followed an unusual course, and it had ended in a fashion which, only half an hour ago, he would have said was impossible. Such a rebuff at such a moment should, by all the rules, have quickened his desire; but it hadn't, it had killed it stone-dead. It was as though he had been bargaining for something and the seller kept putting the price up until in the end he'd no longer wanted it. When he had wrenched out the words about marriage he'd ached for her; when she pushed him away again it was suddenly all over. He'd been mad; he'd gone stark-mad in October and now he was sane again. He lay face downwards and looked forward to a future when he hadn't to go to chapel and could go into the Black Horse.

"It's getting dark, Danny."

He jumped up at once and said with an impersonal kindness which many a girl in the six parishes would have recognised as ominous:

"So it is and we have to get you home. I'll carry the flowers."

So it ended, as oddly as it had begun. And perhaps the strangest thing about it was the memory which it left. It was natural that Damask should remember. But Danny? Danny who grew into such a stout, red-faced, top-booted, sporting farmer of the period as was to be immortalised as "John Bull," why should he remember and feel something stirring, deep in his bulk, when such a day visited the earth, and sometimes shove aside, with an impatient gesture, the jar of bluebells which one of his daughters had set on the dinner table, and distort the simple facts of what he remembered until it seemed as though he had been cheated? Why should he? Only the gods, the ones in the thicket and the One who tweaked the leash of a conscience, could answer *that*.

Danny was not at chapel; he did not come to take Damask home on her June Saturday, but that was understandable. The hay harvest was in full swing and from the moment when the morning dew had dried off until darkness fell, men were busy. On that June Saturday, Damask made the beef pudding and a quantity of gooseberry jam; and Mrs. Greenway, encouraged by the reception of the featherstitching, embarked upon some real embroidery, true-lovers' knots and little posies. She also asked whether Damask had thought any more about the golden-brown lindsey, and Damask said she had had her quarter's money and had asked Miss Lee, the governess at Muchanger, to buy the stuff for her when she took Miss Amelia to the dentist in Colchester.

Damask was radiant that day; radiant with virtue, radiant with hope, for Danny *had* asked her to marry him. Once more she had proved the truth of the Bible. "But rather seek ye the kingdom of God; and all these things shall be added unto you."

CHAPTER 5

RICHARD SHELMADINE HAD COLLECTED THE QUARTER'S SAL-
ary due to him when he returned to Fort St. George; and as a
ship was ready to sail within two days, and there was nothing
upon which to waste money during the voyage, he arrived in
England with money in his pocket. Not being the man to take
thought for the morrow, he picked out the most comfortable-
looking hackney carriage, had his baggage loaded, helped in
Linda, who was wan and frail from the last bout of seasickness,
and said to the driver:

"Mrs. Everton's; Soho Square."

Linda so far forgot her policy of noninterference as to say:

"We owed Angelina money when we left. She won't have
forgotten."

"Nor have I, my pretty one. It is not customary amongst
gentlemen to regard a debt as a reason for patronising a rival
establishment."

The smooth snub was his instant retaliation for the criticism
implied by her reminder, but it went almost unnoticed. The
day was long past when reference to her middle-class origin
could plant a barb. "I thought Angelina *had* no rivals."

"A true word," Richard said.

Angelina Everton, born plain Aggie Stubbs, had spent the

first thirty years of her life pitting her moderate good looks, her lively wits, her indomitable spirit against the world, which had received her unwillingly and promised her nothing but poverty, degradation, and disease. She had served ale in a pothouse, exposed her limbs and sung vulgar songs on the stage, been one of the gossamer-veiled "virgins" in Mr. Scudamore's short-lived, infamous Temple of Diana—all before she was seventeen years of age. She left the Temple to become mistress to a foolish, wealthy young man who kept her just long enough to set her foot on the bottom of the ladder which led to the bedchamber of the Duke of Brittlesford, who, like the psalmist David, had "waxed cold" with age and asked little but kindliness and comfort from his bedfellow. He had always promised Angelina that he would provide for her; she need never wrestle with the world again, but he failed in his promise and when he died he left Angelina, then forty-two, nothing that he knew of; she had helped herself to the deeds of the house in Soho Square and coarsely invited the outraged family to take what action they liked to recover them. She had saved and swindled small amounts over the twelve years and had two thousand pounds laid by; she had jewellery worth perhaps a thousand more. She could have lived in modest comfort for the rest of her days, but modest comfort was not what she desired. Her tastes were extravagant; she craved excitement.

So she turned the house in Soho Square into . . . what, exactly? It depended upon what you were looking for. There was a great drawing room whose four tall windows looked out upon an "Italian" garden of reassuring primness and formality, and there, under the glittering chandeliers, ladies and gentlemen of the most unimpeachable character could gather to hear the best musicians and singers in London. Mrs. Everton's fortnightly musical gatherings were something not to be missed by anyone who wished to be regarded as the possessor of taste. At other times the chandeliers scattered their prismatic lights upon livelier, but still formal, assemblies where the conversation and the presence of the literary celebrities, and even more the literary-minded great, were the attraction. But Mrs. Everton also catered for the lighter tastes, still well on the respectable side; she sponsored a number of fortunetellers, giving preference to those of foreign origin; lectures on every subject of fashionable interest had been given from the little platform of her "Forest Room"—so called from the two or three dozen exotic plants, survivors of several thousands, which grew and hung and trailed against its panelled walls.

It was a large house, however; and the wide hall where the primmest matron in London might be seen drinking coffee or chocolate or sipping a glass of Madeira, the great drawing room and the Forest Room—only entered by invitation or ticket— were far from comprising the whole house. A few people, all men of liberal mind and Catholic taste, knew as much of it as was open to the public; but on the whole those who visited Angelina's ground-floor rooms were strangers to those above-stairs while those who visited the upper floor were seldom to be seen at the concerts and lectures below. On the first floor there were three public rooms, two devoted to gaming and one where food was served, excellent food, served grudgingly, purely for the convenience of patrons who could spare only a little time between games. Nobody ever went to Angelina's in order simply to eat. "I do not run a chophouse," she said. And although behind the three public rooms there were a number of very comfortably appointed sleeping chambers, nobody could go there and hire a room; they were for the convenience of gentlemen who, playing deep, and drinking deep as they played, were too late, or too early, to go home to their own beds.

But there was another staircase, another floor; a honeycomb of small, luxurious cells, each, one might say, occupied by a queen bee, about whom the male drones clustered. And now and then, as from humbler hives, one of the queen bees took wing, flew some distance, and settled, the acknowledged ruler of some great house as Angelina had been in her day; and now and then, as in humbler hives, a male drone died untimely. The clusterings, the flights, and the deaths were all hushed away; everything concerning that topmost floor was hushed, discreet, secret. Just occasionally scandal broke loose, but Angelina had many friends; quite a number of her queen bees had outflown her and attained what she had missed, married status; they, and those who had been content with less, were always ready to weigh in with the favourable word. After all, but for Angelina, where would they have been?

Mr. and Mrs. Shelmadine were on their way to Angelina's; they would arrive, their luggage would be taken to some hidden place; Linda would go and sit in what Angelina called her "Pretty Parlour" and Richard would climb the stairs towards the gaming rooms. Habitués would say, "Ha, Shelmadine, we've missed you," and would hardly know whether he had been away five days or five months or five years; and he would settle down and lose everything he had, and that would entitle him to one of the bedrooms at the back of the house, the charge for which, unless enough loose change remained in his pocket when he left the tables, would be docketed against him. She, in the Pretty Parlour, would be served with tea; would look through the current periodicals on the gate-legged table and wait . . . and wait. And there would be—one must admit and be philosophical about it—one night in a comfortable bed. It was folly to look beyond that.

"Mr. Shelmadine, sir! Welcome back, sir. Madam, your servant!" The big Negro doorman, one of the features of Angelina's, whose greeting was—once you understood things—an exact barometer of your standing and credit in the house, was, considering the unpaid debt, now five years old, surprisingly warm in his welcome.

"Miz' Everton, sir, sez whenever you come back, do it be in the middle of the night, she is to be told, sir. And you is to wait in the Pretty Parlour."

It sounded as though Angelina did not intend to allow Richard on to the gaming floor until that debt was paid.

One migdet page—deliberately gin-dwarfed—led the way to the parlour; another vanished through the door which led to Angelina's own sacrosanct part of the house. It was the dead hour of the day, three o'clock in the afternoon, and the hall and parlour were alike empty. Linda sat down thankfully in the comfortable chair and began to glance through the new papers; Richard walked about, cracking his fingers and cursing in a mumbling undertone. They were not alone long; the door was flung upon and there was Angelina with her inscrutable thickly painted mask of a face, the piled-up mass of dead-white hair, the eyes as cold and black as flint. She never smiled, never frowned—perhaps on account of the false china surface of her face; even when she spoke she moved her lips as little as possible; yet it was her mouth which indicated her mood. When she was angry her lips, scarlet paint and all, disappeared; when she was pleased they swelled, two sated leeches, the lower one more prominent than the other. She was pleased now. She stood in the doorway and dropped a mocking little curtsey towards Richard and at the same time shot a flinty glance at Linda.

"Welcome home, Sir Richard," she said.

* * *

It was July. The hay from the common pasture had been cut and scrupulously divided amongst those who had rights to it, and the cows and the calves born to them this season were turned out to graze upon the tussocks which the scythes had left and the young grass springing up anew. In the Layer Field a glint of gold was spreading through the green of the corn; in Old Tom an embroidery of poppies and scabious and knapweed and thistles gave evidence that though he had lain fallow he had not been idle this season. The new Squire was up at the Manor and had already made two rounds of his estate, accompanied not by Lawyer Turnbull or Sir Edward Follesmark, who had attended to things during the interval, but by Mr. Montague of Greston.

That was significant; to Steve Fuller, Bert Crabtree, and one or two others who had for years hankered after enclosure, it was the star rising in the East, promising the imminence of the millennium. To a number of others, especially the freeholders on the Waste, it was a very ominous sign. Greston had boasted the biggest commonland in the East of England, its cottagers had been the envy of every village in Suffolk and Essex. Then Greston had been enclosed and all the Greston common had come under the plough—Mr. Montague's plough. And, as Sir Charles had so often said, forty decent families, hitherto self-supporting after their fashion, had been thrown upon the parish. If the new Squire meditated enclosing and took Mr. Montague and Greston as his pattern it was an ill lookout for those who lived in the cottages on the Waste. Matt Juby's old cow might cough day and night, but she kept the family in milk. Shad Jarvey's donkey might be of an incredible age but, given time and enough stick, he could perform a number of profitable errands in the course of a year. If this new Squire, with his yellow-bilious face, went hobnobbing with Mr. Montague, things would go ill for people like Amos Greenway, Shad Jarvey, Matt Juby, and Matt Ashpole.

Matt Ashpole owned a gun; it was old and demanded skill of its user; it threw high and slightly to the left. Moreover, Matt was not legally entitled to own it at all. He did not hold a freehold of a hundred pounds a year, a leasehold of a hundred and fifty, he was not the son of heir apparent of an esquire or person of greater degree; and every time he fired—aiming low and slightly to the right—he was committing a felony. Still, he had kept his gun, and more than once when the larder was empty he had used it both in Layer Wood and in the coppice which lay between Bridge Farm and Wood Farm.

One evening towards the end of July he took out his gun, cleaned it carefully and loaded it, carried it to the place where the Waste ended with the Dyke and hid it there, under the gorse bushes, with a bit of sailcloth to protect it from any rain or dew which might fall. He'd had, in the past week, a little talk with his daughter Sally; and he had seen the new Squire out with Mr. Montague. And he had made his plan. Every evening, regular as sunset, Danny Fuller went down to the pasture just to make sure that whatever might have happened to other beasts, those belonging to the Fullers were on their feet and feeding well. Matt stood on the wooden bridge this evening, and when Danny came and jumped the little ditch between the pasture and the Lower Road, he turned and hailed him cheerily.

"I got something up at my place that you'd like to see, and I'd like you to hev a look at it," he said. "Got a minnit to spare?"

"What is it, Matt?"

"Something I picked up real cheap and want to get off me place. No room for it," Matt said mysteriously. "All right then, if you must know, thass a horse; lovely blood mare. But she was lame, see, hoppy-go-bob, off to the knacker's. I doctored her up and she's a clinker. Fred Clopton, he want her, but you know me, Danny, I don't favour Fred Clopton, all airs and graces these days. I'd ruther you had her."

"I doubt if I could afford it, Matt."

"Dirt-cheap. Five pound."

"Well . . ." That might be managed. He knew now that he would never marry. He just wasn't made to stick to one girl long enough. And that reminded him. "I don't much fancy coming up to your place, Matt. You know how it is."

"I do," said Matt heartily. "But this what I hev to show you is only just past the Dyke."

He dived into the sagging pocket of his dirty, ragged old coat, and produced, most surprisingly, one of the flat, capped hunting flasks which gentlemen carried. "Here," he said, "hev a pull at this. Right good stuff that is, French brandy."

"And a nice flask, too."

"Put in with a job lot, over at Summerfield, when they sold old Major Telford's stuff; can't think what they were about; four cracked jugs and a brass fender, a pair of bellows and this boy, bought the lot for a shilling. But the stuff in it I got from

... well, that'd be telling. You taste it and tell me if you ever had the like. You got quite a bit of drinking to catch up on like, ain't that so?" He watched Danny's face and went on, kindly, "There's no pleasing 'em, is there? So drink up and thank God for good liquor!"

They drank, turn and turn about until the flask was empty, and then walked in warm, brandy-flavoured friendliness towards the Dyke and reached the place where Matt had hidden his gun.

"Half a minnit," he said, stopping to retrieve it. Having done so, instead of putting it under his arm and walking on, he stood still, holding the gun as though he hoped to see something at which to take a pot shot. The brandy—which was like nothing he'd ever drunk before—was by this time moving swiftly in Danny's blood, breeding dreams in his brain. He saw himself, the bachelor, the misogynist, riding about the six parishes, to and from market, on the blood mare that Fred Clopton envied.

"Come on, Matt," he said impatiently.

"We ain't in no hurry." Matt's voice, though still amiable, had suffered a slight change. "I s'pose you ain't minded to marry my gal Sally?"

"Good God, no!"

"Then you'd better be! Don't move, Danny; this here owd gun is likely to go off and blow you to Glory. 'Naccident that'd be; but they'd only hev to look at it to see how unaccountable she is on the trigger." His voice was laconic, but his stare was flinty and Danny knew that he was not joking. Nevertheless, he said:

"Don't be daft, Matt. And don't point the old blunderbuss at me, even in joke."

"I ain't joking. Nor I ain't preaching. We're all young once. But there's my gal in the family way and she hold you to blame, so..."

"But I... I haven't had anything to do with Sally since last Midsummer Fair."

"You think again. 'Bout March, I seem to recollect..."

"Yes. That's true. But we only went for a bit of a ride. Nothing *happened*."

"Ah, thass what you think! Fact is we're most of us better bulls than we reckon—or wanta be at times. We 'on't argyfy about *that*. There's Sally, four months gone, you can see by the hang of her apron, and you was out with her in March; and if you ain't ready to stand up like a man and do the right thing by her, I swear to God you 'on't stand up never no more, Danny Fuller."

"I don't want to marry Sally, nor anybody."

"'Tain't what you want, 'swhat I want; and I'm the one with the gun! I warned you; stand still, don't this touchy trigger might cut short your meditations! I'm fair; giving you a chance to think, I am. But think quick. And don't go off with some half-cocked idea about saying yes now and no tomorrow. That hare 'on't run. If you diddle me I shall wait for you and get you for certain. Anyway I'm sick of this argyfying. Yes or no? I'm gonna count three now; then this gun is gonna go off. One . . ."

It was all very well to think, This is ludicrous, this can't be happening to me. It was happening. Matt's eyes were the eyes of a man with a purpose. The worn, touchy trigger was there, his finger was ready.

"Two," Matt said in a voice of doom.

And there was nobody about; here on the edge of the Waste it was as though they two were alone in the world.

"All right then. If I must, I must."

"Thass the spirit. Now I should be obliged if you'd just stroll along to Parson's and fix for the banns, starting Sunday. I shall be right behind you, but I'll be careful. And as soon's thass done we'll go along to the owd Horse and wet the bargain. You could hev done worse, you know, Danny. Sal's a bit wild but a clout or two'll settle her; and she do make as good a dumpling when she's in the mind as ever I set my teeth into."

The banns had been read twice and were due to be read for the third time on the morrow, when Damask's August Saturday came round. How soon after the first reading the news had reached Amos' ears no one could know. He did not report it and Julie learned it by overhearing a chance conversation started by somebody bringing a pair of shoes to be cobbled. Never before had she realised the full bitterness and exasperation of having a husband whose mind was set "on higher things." Amos refused to share her feelings, refused to speculate upon the truth or falsity of the rumour, refused to be concerned.

"Somebody must go and break the news to Damask, *gently*," Julie said.

"Well I ain't got time to go chasing over to Muchanger to

carry a bit of gossip. We're still digging out the foundations and the timber is due to arrive any day now."

"Then will you ask Shad if I could hev the donkey rig?"

"I shall hev enough favours to ask of Shad time we start carting the timber, Julie. Besides, if you go to Muchanger in the donkey rig, Damask'd think there'd been a death, to say the least."

"It's as bad as."

"Don't talk so wild, woman. Danny Fuller he backslid, there's the long and the short of it. He fell into sin and got a girl into trouble and is making the only amends he can. We should be glad he's going to make an honest woman of the poor girl. Why Damask should mind and say it's as bad as a death I fail to see."

"But she thought he was going to marry her. You must have seen that!"

"And I thought he'd turned over a new leaf. And maybe he did. Maybe if it wasn't for his mended ways he'd hev left the girl in the lurch. Ah, there is that to think of."

"It's Damask he's left in the lurch!" Julie said, beginning to cry.

"Now thass a shocking thing to say, and I'm surprised at you, her own mother. Damask is a good girl, she'd never do, with Danny Fuller nor no other man, anything so he could leave her in the lurch. You know that. Why you should be so upset and seem to reckon she'll be, I can't understand."

"But she loved him. I'm sure of that, though she never said it in so many words."

"Come, come, Mother! How could you know? And even so, well, we all hev our troubles and trials; the Lord knows what is best for us; the Lord knows what is best for Damask! You just take comfort in that thought! Remember the psalmist, 'The Lord is my shepherd.'"

It was quite useless. All she could hope was that Damask could not hear the dreadful news from somebody casual or cruel. Then, as the day for the visit drew near and she realised that if Damask arrived in ignorance she would have the task of telling her, she almost wished that someone might have forestalled her.

The day came and Damask came running in, carrying the parcel of beef pieces and another, larger parcel. It was a hot sultry day and a faint odour of meat already on the turn was perceptible immediately.

"I must get this on quicker than usual, it's half cooked already," Damask said as soon as she had greeted her mother.

The kitchen table was bare; not one of the "three of everything" was to be seen. She laid the large parcel aside carefully and began to gather together the things she needed for the pudding making. Then she realised that her mother was looking at her queerly, and that she seemed to have shrivelled and shrunk.

"Are you all right, Mother?" she asked, dipping a cup into the flour sack.

"*I'm* all right," Julie said in a tone which implied that her health was the one lonely thing that was right in the world. She looked at the larger parcel. "Thass your stuff? Oh, my dear, my dear!" She burst into tears.

(Miss Lee, kindly and obliging, had tried to buy a golden-brown lindsey away back in the spring, had put it on order, and here it was and Mother crying over it.)

"Mother, what is the matter?" Damask stood still, holding a cup of flour and the bowl into which she had meant to pour it. "Is it Father? What then? Has anything happened?"

"Lots has happened," sobbed Julie. "Ain't *you* heard anything? Ain't you got even a glimmer of suspicion?" It sounded as though she pleaded with Damask to know, to suspect, to spare her the task of telling.

"Danny?"

Julie nodded.

"Ill? Not dead? What is it then? Tell me. Tell me."

"He's going to marry Sally Ashpole. He got her in the family way, my dear, so he . . ." She broke off, shocked by pallor, "the very look of death," as she said later, which had come into her daughter's face.

"It isn't true," the white lips said.

"My poor dear, it is. Spitty Last brought his shoes, but you know how he mumble, I couldn't hear all, and you know your dad, what ain't said about chapel might as well not be said, for all he know. So I went across to the Ashpoles' and asked straight out. And there the hussy was, four months gone if a day and as proud as Punch and Mrs. Ashpole the same, telling me the banns had been asked . . ."

She saw the girl sway and hobbled forward, hoping to catch her, but she was too late. There Damask lay, rigid and white on the floor, surrounded by the spilt flour and the bits of broken crockery.

In the airless room where Julie had stitched away her girl-hood fainting fits had been a commonplace; she knew all the simple ready-to-hand remedies and she applied them, convinced though she was from the first that this was no mere faint. Nor was it a convulsive fit, so horrible to see with its writhings and frothings. The girl lay there as rigid and cold and still as a twelve-hour corpse and only a noisy, battling breath drawn at long intervals showed that she still lived.

When Julie had tried all she knew and the hot little kitchen reeked of burnt feathers, of hartshorn, of sliced onion, of vinegar and pepper recklessly scattered in the hope of provoking a sneeze, Julie thought of the one thing she had not yet tried—brandy. There was, naturally, none in the house, but more likely than not Matt Ashpole would have some. She shrank from the idea of going to their house again—they would guess at and triumph over the cause of Damask's fit—but she couldn't let Damask die for such a nicety. Hobbling as fast as she could, she went across to the Ashpoles' and was fortunate enough to find Matt alone in the yard, halfheartedly at work gathering his plums.

"Aye," he said, when she had gasped out her request and the reason for it, "hot enough to fell a bullock, ain't it? Less see now, I might hev, and again I might not." He came down from the ladder, picked up his old jacket, took the hunting flask from the pocket, and gave it a shake.

"Ah," he said in a satisfied voice, "here's a drop o' the best. That'll do the trick." He handed over the flask and then said, "Want me to come and give you a hand?"

"Oh no, thank you," Julie said hurriedly. "Thank you very much, I'll bring this back soon."

"No hurry," Matt said. He looked at the laden plum tree with ungrateful distaste, and diving into his pocket again, produced his clay pipe and a screw of tobacco. He'd known all along that it was too hot for working.

Julie hurried back and arrived panting. Damask, still as white as death, was on her feet, once more assembling the pudding materials, her movements so abrupt and jerky that Julie was reminded of an unskilfully handled puppet.

"Are you all right?" she gasped out.

"Quite all right. I'm sorry about the bowl. It was the heat, and I'd hurried."

"You set down, my dear, and I'll make a cup of tea. Never

mind about the pudding today. We'll hang the meat down the
well and I'll deal with it on Monday."

"I'm dealing with it now. What's that you have in your
hand?"

"A little drop of brandy I borrowed." She felt the need to
excuse such an action. "I couldn't bring you round, you see.
I got frightened. I don't really see the harm . . . not in illness."

"I'm all right. I'd like a cup of tea though."

"You still look queer," Julie said, pulling the kettle from
the hob to the centre of the fire. Damask went on with the
pudding, the jerky puppet movements oddly efficient, her face
completely composed. Save for the jerkiness and the ghastly
pallor there was nothing to show that she had been shocked
into an unconsciousness which must have lasted a full hour;
certainly there was no real reason why Julie should feel as
though her daughter had died there on the floor and that this
was a stranger, someone queer and rather frightening, just pretending to be Damask Greenway making the usual pudding.
But that was how she did feel.

Julie lifted off the kettle and made the tea, and Damask
slipped the pudding saucepan into the kettle's place.

"Now you set down and hev a nice cup of tea," Julie said.
She felt that over the tea they might talk, and Damask might
cry and she could comfort her and this feeling of strangeness
would pass. Tears, anger, protests, anything would seem more
natural.

Damask drank half a cup of tea, then she reached out and
picked up Matt's flask from the corner of the table where Julie
had laid it. She unscrewed the cap, poured brandy into Julie's
cup, and then into her own.

"Try that," she said. "It's good." Julie just stared, unbe-
lieving. "The cook at Muchanger always laces her tea if Mr.
Hook, the butler, has managed to refill their bottle."

"And hev *you* ever . . . ?"

"No." A slight smile, not in the least like any smile Julie
had ever seen on her daughter's face before, flitted across
Damask's lips. Unaccountably frightened again, she said stur-
dily:

"Well, it'll do you good. It'll do us both good. I had a fright,
too."

She could feel it doing her good. Every rare cup of tea she
ever tasted did her good, made her feel more cheerful, and
loosened something tight and knotted which crippled her spirit

as the rheumatism crippled her limbs, and now the tea laced
with brandy did her twice the good, acted twice as fast. She'd
hardly swallowed three mouthfuls before she found the courage
and spirit to say, "You know, my dear, there's as good fish in
the sea as ever came out."

The stranger across the table jerked her arm up and drank
and set the cup down and said, "If you don't mind, we won't
talk about it."

"Oh, of course not," Julie agreed hurriedly. "I shan't say a
word. We must put a good face on it. Even that time when I
told you I went across to ask, I did it casual-like, and I said,
'I congratulate you, I'm sure' as natural as natural, though I
did feel as though I'd been . . ."

"Didn't I say not to talk about it?"

"But, my dear, that ain't natural! Believe me, I know. Living
with your father all these years, having to keep everything
bottled up. Things turn sour in you. I know. I often think loose
tongues and easy tears was what God gave women to help them
to bear their burdens . . ."

"I'd like another cup of tea," Damask said. When she had
drunk it she went, despite all Julie's protests, and tidied the
workroom.

The rest of the afternoon and evening—except for the fact
that Julie did no sewing—passed as usual. At dusk, and now
in August's third week, the days were beginning to draw in,
Amos came home from his foundation digging, and resumed
his monologue about the chapel-building. The pudding was
dished up and eaten. It was just like an ordinary day, yet Julie's
anxiety and feeling of disaster persisted. When it was time for
Damask to go, she went with her to the door, and, holding her
by the arm, said timidly:

"You will be all right, won't you?"

"I am all right," Damask said.

"You're a right brave girl and I'm sure it'll all turn out for
the best." She gave Damask one of her rare kisses.

Back in the kitchen, knowing well what reception the remark
would receive, she could not refrain from saying:

"She bore up well, but it was a cruel shock to her."

"What was?" She told him.

"Oh, that. I told you it was nowt to her. All that fuss!"

"Well, I don't know." Some control, long strained, gave
way; Julie's voice became sharp and shrill. "I don't like it,"
she said. "I didn't like the way she went into a faint that lasted

an hour and then got up looking and acting like somebody that
had been dead a hundred years nor I didn't like the way she
looked when you said you'd see her Sunday week in chapel.
You may think it's nowt; I think her heart's broke."

PART III

HIGH NOON OF
A CHANGELING

CHAPTER 6

OUTSIDE THE HOUSE, IN THE DARK JUST BEFORE MOONRISE,
she stood still and listened to all the voices that were making
confusion in her mind. Julie's voice saying with the steady
monotony of a pulse, "He's going to marry Sally Ashpole,
Ashpole, Ashpole; he's going to marry . . ."; Amos' voice, so
certain, so unaware, so righteous, "See you in chapel Sunday
week; see you in chapel, chapel," and that other voice, ef-
fortlessly bearing down the others, saying, "There you are,
that's the reward of virtue! You've got the reward of virtue,
Damask Greenway. Sally Ashpole has the wages of sin." There
the voice went off into peals of satirical laughter, in which, at
last, now that she was alone in the dark, she could join. She
stood by the bed where the marigolds were dying and let the
laughter shake her like the wind, and all the time the tears
poured from her eyes unnoticed. When the hysteria had exhausted itself she could think again, and the thought was like
yet another voice within her head. "I've really known all along,"
it said with great calm. "Look at Jesus, He never did a sin at
all, and how was He treated? God deserted Him at the end
too."

She had always had a peculiar awareness of the bitterness
of that last cry from the Cross. Her ardent imagination, with

little to nourish it save what fragments of folklore were allowed to cross Amos' guarded threshold, had seized avidly upon all the Bible stories; Jericho, with Rahab the harlot's marked house, was quite as real to her as Baildon, a few miles away, but never visited; and Jerusalem, and Bethlehem and Nazareth and Bethsaida, where the waters were troubled and miraculous cures affected, were all far more part of her mental landscape than the six parishes familiar to her ear and eye. She knew Golgotha, the Place of the Skull; in Nettleton Chapel she had sat and watched the drama there, seen the nails and the blood and the darkening sky, the torn veil of the temple, and heard that last despairing cry. And always she had been sorry for Jesus . . .

And she had been right. Blind and ignorant, but right. God always failed you. . . .

Without surprise as without intention, she found herself walking not in the direction of Muchanger, but towards the Stone Bridge. Some time had passed, the moon was now rising, a wide bronze disc in the blue-black sky. Time no longer mattered. She was not going back to Muchanger; never again was she going to be industrious, punctual, patient, virtuous. What she would be instead and where she would be it she had, as yet, no notion. She walked towards the Stone Bridge like a sleepwalker and presently stood in one of its embrasures, staring down at the water upon whose late-summer, smoothly running surface the moon presently cast a lacquering of gold. At some such immense distance that it only just made contact with her consciousness was the certainty that presently something would happen. But even that seemed unimportant. Nothing mattered any more, nothing would ever matter again.

She was not startled when a voice from behind her, a voice unmistakably human and real, said, "Poor child, are you from the Poor Farm?"

She turned slowly, almost unwillingly, and faced the questioner. A strange figure in the moonlight, an old woman, very tall, of skeletal thinness, with a wild mass of white hair framing a face like a death's head, a bone-white jutting nose, eyes that seemed only dark hollows, and a mouth which was a changing shape of blackness as it asked again, "Are you from the Poor Farm?"

"No," Damask said.

"If you are," the woman said quite briskly, "there's no need to be ashamed. Not with me. A good strong girl who had run away from the Poor Farm would be more welcome to my sight

than Solomon in all his glory. That is a Poor Farm dress, surely.
And the way they do their hair. It always made me so sorry.
Charity suffereth long and *is kind*, according to the Bible, so
why the girls should always be made to look so very ugly . . .
Oh no, no, you're not ugly, I don't mean that, just the dress . . ."
She advanced another soundless step and laid a hand on Da-
mask's sleeve.

"Umm . . ." she made a little satisfied sound. "You *are* from
the Poor Farm. Just what I wanted. For months and months
I've said to myself . . . I mean anyone who could come to full
growth in such circumstances would be strong and resilient and
used to standing up for herself, and that is just what I need. I
do need help so very badly because you see . . ." She broke
off, edged into the embrasure beside Damask, and said, "Shush,"
in a whisper. Damask listened, sorting out the sounds which
made up the silence of the late-summer night, the small muted
sound of the water under the bridge, a bird's cry, a dog barking
at the other end of the village, and nearer at hand the sound
of a creaking gate.

"I've run away myself, you see," the old woman whispered.
"I will *not* be treated as though I were mad. I am not mad.
Occasionally—very occasionally—I forget things. Sometimes
I even forget what I have come out for, but tonight I remember
quite clearly. I came out to find somebody to help me. And I
have found *you*. You will come home with me and help me to
turn those people out, won't you?"

"What people?"

"Saunders and his wife. All the rest have gone. Mr. Turnbull
insists that I should count myself fortunate to have *them*. He
little knows; on several occasions the woman has *struck* me.
Imagine that; but if you will come home with me and support
me, everything will be all right. The thing to be careful about
is not to take her shilling; that commits you quite as deeply as
taking the King's shilling. Time and again somebody has come
back with me and she says, "Thank you very much," and gives
them a shilling and then I am all undone again. You don't need
her shilling; if you stay with me I will give you all you wish.
I'm no longer well-to-do but I'm not so poor as they would
have me believe. I know where my money goes. Mr. Turnbull,
of course, is scrupulously honest himself but, as I tell him, to
connive at other people's dishonesty is to assume a share of
their guilt."

She had forgotten whatever it was that had made her whisper, and her voice had regained its brisk and vibrant tone. Damask listened to the flood of garrulity and gave it some part of her attention while another part of her mind considered her earlier feelings that she had come to this place for some purpose which was now becoming plain.

". . . so you will come back with me, won't you? And refuse her shilling and stay by me. I swear you shall never regret it."

"I'll come with you," Damask said, thinking of Muchanger and the dinner party for twelve that was planned for the next day and the extra work which her absence would throw on the cook, who had so often sneered at her for being "Methody."

"Where do you live?" There was a sudden, ominous silence. Perhaps the old woman *was* mad after all and the whole story a fandango of nonsense.

Then, on a note of profound triumph, came the answer:

"I live at the Dower House. There! You see. Just for a moment I thought I had forgotten again. But you see, you waited; you had patience and didn't begin to shout at me, and so I remembered. I'm quite sure that if you would only stay with me and be my friend and get rid of those awful people everything would be all right. Of course it was very ill-advised of me to tell you that she had struck me—I did tell you that, didn't I? Does that intimidate you? I hoped that being from the Poor Farm . . ."

"I am not from the Poor Farm and I am not scared by anything you have said. Shall we go to your house?"

"I can't walk very quickly I'm afraid. You see I have to watch my opportunity and came out wearing my slippers, which are inclined to fall off." She laid her thin hand on Damask's arm. "Oh, horrible material," she said as they began to walk. "You shall have such pretty dresses, my dear. I have dozens of such pretty dresses which would fit you with a little alteration. She's so stout, you see; cloaks and muffs and tippets she has made very free with but the dresses were useless to her. You shall have them all. . . ."

The gate creaked as they pushed it open; this was the gate whose creaking had made the old woman say "Shush" and drop her voice to a whisper; the drive between the overgown trees and shrubs was a dark tunnel, and the moss underfoot deadened the sound of their feet; at the end of the tunnel the big, unlighted house stood in the moonlight, immensely sinister. Only yesterday, Damask thought, this would all have seemed frightening. . . .

The front door opened upon a high wide hall lighted by a solitary candle upon a side table and what light emerged from a half-open doorway at the back, beyond the curving stairs. As soon as they entered a voice called, "Is that you, Jem? Did you find the old . . . ?" and the figure of a stout, square-shouldered female was outlined against the oblong of light.

"Now don't be frightened; you stick by me and I'll stick by you," said Miss Parsons as she released her hold on Damask's arm, but in the second before her hand fell away Damask felt the tremor which ran through it.

The woman advanced, saying in a changed voice, "Oh, ma'am, you had us that worried; going off like that in your slippers and all. There's Saunders out hunting for you and me nigh distracted. And you fell in with somebody goodhearted again, thank God." As she reached the table where the candle stood she paused and fumbled, and within a few seconds three or four other candles were alight. Now she could see who had brought home the wanderer: a female, young, harmless. Her manner changed again, became affable and condescending.

"I'm very much obliged to you, young woman. Poor lady, she isn't quite . . . you understand; and now and again she get a wandering fit and we're so afraid that something might . . . Still, there we are all safe and sound. I hope bringing her back hasn't taken you far out of your way, my dear. Thank you again." She put her hand into the pocket which hung from her waist and brought out a shilling. "Please accept this for your pains."

Making no move to take the coin, Damask glanced at Miss Parsons, who had drawn a little apart and now stood watching with the interested yet impersonal expression of someone watching an incident in the street.

"It's all right," the woman said soothingly, "she'd wish you to have it, I'm sure. When she realise she'll be as grateful to you as I am. I'll get her to bed now, after all this excitement. You take this and be getting along." She thrust out the shilling again. Deliberately Damask waited in silence until the posture of offering an unaccepted tip had made its small contribution towards the woman's discomfiture; then she spoke.

"I've come to stay," she said.

Mrs. Saunders recovered herself quickly and laughed a little.

"Oh, dear me, has she been at that game again? That's part of her trouble, poor lady. She used to keep six or seven servants, you see, and now she can't really afford any if the truth was told. But over and over again she'll go out and come back with some poor innocent girl like you . . . I'm sorry, my dear, there's no job here. It's a shame she should have raised your hopes but there, you can't really blame her, can you? You take your shilling and get along. You're a nice tidy girl, you'll soon find a place."

"Miss Parsons asked me to come and stay here with her and that I am going to do."

"Now that is daft talk. I've told you how it is. She ain't responsible. You get along now and don't stand there wasting my time." Damask stood still and silent; Miss Parsons watched. When the woman spoke again her voice was shriller. "What are you waiting for? Ain't a shilling enough? You insolent little baggage. Be off, I tell you. If you got enough sense to understand her telling you there is a job here you got enough sense to understand me telling you there ain't. Get along with you. Or do you want me to put you out?"

"Do you want to try?"

The woman made a sound of complete exasperation and came forward, two hasty steps and one hesitant. The belligerent expression in her eyes gave way under Damask's calm stare. Suddenly she looked baffled.

"My husband'll be back in a minute. He'll deal with you," she muttered.

Miss Parsons broke into a delighted cackle of laughter.

"Now let us go upstairs and get rid of that very unbecoming dress," she said. She snatched up a candlestick and, holding it so that drops of grease fell upon each step, she led the way upstairs. Damask followed. Mrs. Saunders stood watching, incredulous. It could not be true . . . just a little scrap of a thing like that; why hadn't she taken her by the scruff of the neck and thrown her out?

Twenty minutes later when Saunders had returned, heard the news, and gone storming upstairs and came down again looking stupid and scared, she asked him the same question.

"I meant to," he said. "I went up to her and said, 'Come on, out of this!' and made to get hold of her. Then I just couldn't. You know how I am about cats, that same sort of feeling came over me."

"But I don't mind cats, and that same feeling came over me too," Mrs. Saunders said. They stared at one another in silent dismay for a moment, then she said, "But we must do *something*. What are we going to do?"

"We'll leave it till morning," Saunders said. He had a distinct feeling that daylight would bring courage.

CHAPTER 7

EVEN THOSE NEIGHBOURS WHO HAD BEEN AFFECTIONATELY disposed towards the old Squire and were thus inclined to lay the blame for the breach on his son, admitted at last that possibly there had been fault on both sides; or else the years and the long exile had improved Richard. Some of them remembered that the last quarrel had taken place at the time of Richard's marriage, and these had been prepared to find the new Lady Shelmadine a quite impossible person; pretty perhaps—or why should he have married her?—but pretty in a blousy way, vulgar, ignorant, and now that she was newly rich, extravagant and ostentatious. To them Linda was a pleasant surprise. The ladies especially were strong in their approval. The gentlemen remained a little puzzled; she seemed the last kind of female for a man of Richard's reputation to have married. Was it perhaps possible that his wildness had been exaggerated? After all, even those who were fond of Sir Charles were bound to admit that some of his views had been very hidebound.

All through the late summer and autumn of that year there was much coming and going between Clevely and the big houses in the neighbourhood, Ockley and Mortiboys and Merravay, Greston Park and Muchanger and Nettleton New House.

Richard took pains to be charming, and in the privacy of the connubial bedchamber made no secret of his purpose.

"My father had a great reputation for honesty and since he always represented me as a devil, I can see them all waiting for the cloven hoof to peep out. As no doubt it will, but not before I have cast some doubt upon his honesty or his judgement—I don't care which."

To behave in accordance of the unexacting standard demanded by a group of Suffolk squires was not difficult and it was made easier for him by the fact that he was, at the moment, delighted with his heritage and had not had time to be bored. He rode round the estate being extremely affable to everyone; he instituted no unpopular changes and missed no opportunity of showing generosity. This year, in addition to the Harvest Horkey, the villagers of Clevely enjoyed a Cricket Supper.

It was taken for granted that he would enclose, and the matter came under discussion at the first dinner party which the Shelmadines attended at Ockley. Sir Evelyn Fennel then said:

"When you do, let Monty here be your model. My father enclosed in '74; when he began he owned fifteen hundred acres and when he'd finished he had fourteen hundred and ten. Monty, when he tacked up his notice, had two thousand three hundred, and when he put up his last fence, had four thousand of them."

"And that, Sir Richard, is not the pawadox that it sounds. The first figure, of course, was just the awable and the pasture; the second included my share of the common Waste."

Richard, who upon being introduced to Mr. Montague Ryde Montague, had dismissed him as a lisping young fool, now turned to him with attention.

"Greston? Where forty decent poor men . . . eh?" He spoke the last words in a tolerable imitation of his father's voice. Everybody laughed.

"All the same," Sir Evelyn said, "they *do* fall on the rates, damn them; never having worked in their lives, they expect to be kept in idleness. The thing to *do*, I understand, is to demolish the damned hovels. Once they're homeless they move off and find work."

"But that is stwickly illegal."

"So are lots of other things." Sir Evelyn's voice was dry.

"Well, it's pwobably sentimental of me, but I would dwaw the line at destwoying their homes."

"Having enclosed to such advantage, you can afford to pay your rates."

"That is twue. The thing is, Shelmadine, if you wish to get your enclosure bill thwough *this* year you must look sharp. The last act demands that you tack up your notice for thwee Sundays in August or September."

"So there's a close season for enclosing, is there?" Richard said. "I didn't know. There are a good many points on which I am ignorant. I should be very grateful for your advice."

"I adore giving advice," said Mr. Montague.

Two days later he rode over to Clevely and he and Richard shut themselves in the library with a map of the village and all the papers relevant to tenancies and sales and purchases of land which Richard had managed to sort out from the fantastic jumble in which his father had kept such things.

Lisping, elegant, effete-looking as he was, Mr. Montague showed himself a good man of business, shrewd and orderly of mind.

"I cannot, of course, guawantee that you will do as well out of your enclosure as I did at Gweston," he warned. "I was deucedly lucky in my commissioners and in the number of fellows who either had no claim to show or couldn't pay their share of the expenses. Now *there* is a hint! Don't twy to keep down expenses. As the largest pwopwietor you will naturally have to bear the greater share of them, but if, in the end you have only two small pwopwietors who can't meet their costs, then their land falls into the common pool, of which you get the gweatest share, and in the long run you are better off. I twust I make myself clear."

He brooded over the map and the papers, the fine lace of shirt cuff casting a little shimmering pattern as he traced the boundaries of this man's holding and that, his eye all the while as keen and calculating as a butcher's studying a carcass.

"I think you may do vewy well, Wichard. Even if half your Waste fellows have a legal claim—and that would be most extwaordinawy bad luck—you'd still do well because there are so few landowners for it to be divided amongst. Miss Parsons, Fred Clopton, Abel Shipton—they're the ones worth considewing—the west own so little that when the Waste is shared out pwoportionately they'll only get an acre or two extwa, and that pwobably wubbish if you dwaw weasonable commissioners and make yourself civil to them. There's another hint—the commissioners allot the land, and some is good and some is bad ... Enough said?"

"I will take pains with the commissioners," Richard said.

"But tactfully, my fwiend, tactfully," said Mr. Montague, lifting an elegant finger. "Once evewy hundwed years an absolutely incowuptible fellow gets an appointment and will scweam 'Bwibery' at the top of his voice at the first opportunity. So tact is needed there." He looked down at the table again. "This Cawoline Amelia Parsons, *not* old Captain Parsons' daughter? She must be a hundwed!"

"She's eighty. The Rector says she is dotty."

"Ah ... there now. There might be something for you *there*, Wichard. She might be just sane enough to sign in favour of enclosure but not sane enough to look out for her wights. Enclosure is like wevolution, you know, full of opportunities for the wide-awake. Well, that completes our pweliminawy weconnaissance, I think. Now you must dwaw up your notice and get the signatures of all the other people who *own* land. I pwesume that everybody is agweed."

"How could anyone not? Fellows like Clopton and Shipton who are enclosed already stand to get a bit of the Waste; old what's-his-name, Bowyer, and Wellman and Crabtree surely will see that to have their land altogether, plus their small share of the Waste is better than going on in this old-fashioned way."

"You can never be too sure," said Mr. Montague sagely. "At Gweston I had just one old man who owned twelve acres, six in one field, six in the other, and make his mark he would not. I twied every persuasion, even offered him twice the market pwice for his land, to buy him out, you know. He wouldn't budge."

"So what did you do?"

"Just went ahead without his signature. It was a wisk! He could have gone popping off to the authorities and made a fuss, but he didn't. They don't know their own power. I should say the only one who could make difficulty for you if she wished is the old dame ... but then, if she's dotty ... Now, shall we begin to make a list of those whose signatures you wequire?"

"I think not," Richard said. The first signs of boredom were making themselves felt within him. The idea of becoming richer, of extending his land and increasing its value, was attractive and had borne him along so far, but to ask him to sit down and copy out a list of names was too much.

"I have a new bailiff fellow arriving tomorrow," he said,

"he can do all that. Do him good to get familiar with their names and acreages and so on."

"Then let us take a wide awound and look at the land itself. I was never welcome here in your father's time," said Mr. Montague.

So they set off on the ride which warned Clevely of the Squire's intentions and made Matt Ashpole get out his gun. Matt knew that he had no claim, save right of usage, to his cottage, his garden, his pasture on the Waste, and he was foresighted enough to visualise a time when his old horse would be homeless; but the Fullers, he reasoned, would always have a farm and Danny could never refuse house room to his father-in-law's old horse.

By the first week in September, Hadstock, the new bailiff, had written out in clear firm hand the notice which was to be fixed to the church door; and he had also made a list of all the landowners in Clevely, large and small, who would sign the paper.

The notice read, "We the undersigned, being the Lord on the Manor, the titheholder, proprietors, and freeholders of the Manor and Parish of Clevely in the County of Suffolk, do hereby give notice to whomsoever it may concern that we propose to approach His Majesty's House of Commons through the good offices of Sir Thomas Blyborough M.P. for an order for the enclosing of the arable land, pasture and wasteland of the aforesaid parish."

Richard, with the deadly depression of boredom rising in him, set out to collect the necessary signatures. He would gladly have deputed this task to Hadstock, but Mr. Montague—and one must always remember that *his* enclosure had been superbly successful—had said, "It is infinitely better, Wichard, to pweserve the personal touch in such affairs. Fellows who might easily be disposed to say 'no' to a mere bailiff will sign at a nod fwom you. We're losing gwound every day, as evewybody knows, but it still takes a bwave man to defy us to our faces."

Richard started his round with a call at Flocky Hall, where Fred Clopton, though not defiant, showed himself to be dubious and reluctant. "I've no wish to stand in your way, sir," he said, "but I've got to think of myself."

Restraining his impatience and forcing himself to speak amiably, Richard said, "In what way, Clopton?"

"I'm benefiting now by being enclosed," Clopton said slowly.

"Sounds selfish maybe, but we're all selfish when you get to the root of us. I can grow turnips, I can grow clover, I can winter-feed my beasts just because I *am* enclosed and free to do as I like. When everybody is the same I shan't get the price I do now for the things I have to sell and everybody don't."

"With more land, which would cost you nothing except the fencing, and with your experience in the new methods you'd still be well ahead of the others," Richard said.

"More land?"

"As a landowner you would get a share of the Waste; it might be quite considerable."

"Are you sure of that? I don't mean," he said quickly in answer to Richard's swift scowl, "I don't mean to doubt what you say, but it sounds peculiar. You see, my freehold never carried any rights to the Waste—not that I minded, I wouldn't want my beasts to run with all those poor ill-conditioned creatures."

"Naturally not. But if you sign this petition, as a landowner you will get a proportional share, enclosed, and not necessarily of the Waste, if you can understand that. An increase of your acreage, in proportion. It would be for the commissioners to decide where it was."

"Well, in that case of course, I'll sign gladly, sir."

The next three farmers on the list were all small proprietors, owning strips in the open fields. Bert Crabtree signed with alacrity. "I allust wanted it, but I never reckoned it'd come in my lifetime," he said. "If you'll be so kind as to write my name, sir, I'll put my mark to it. I bain't no scholar." Clem Bowyer listened to Richard's explanation and then said, "I'd be for it, sir, tooth and nail, if I was just twenty year younger; but I be old and I don't fancy no changes and upheavals at my time of life." The third man, Ricky Wellman, was more forthright; he was, in fact, Mr. Montague's "bwave man." "I'm agin it, same as the old Squire allust was, and when I'm agin a thing I'm agin it," he said.

They both looked, to Richard's casual eye, stupid, bovine creatures, only very slightly the intellectual superiors of the beasts they reared; remembering Monty's story of his obstinate old man, he decided that their opposition was not worth bothering about, so he wasted no eloquence on them but rode on to Bridge Farm to interview Abel Shipton.

"But that don't—er concern me—er, sir," Shipton said. "I

am—er enclosed. This farm—er was fenced—er around—er at the same time as Flocky."

"I know, I know. The point is . . ." And he repeated, in a voice of poisonous patience, the argument he had laid before Fred Clopton. Shipton listened, looking more and more uncomfortable and glancing now and then in the direction of the kitchen door. Finally he said:

"Only owners sign—er? Then it wouldn't be right—er for me to. To tell you the truth—er I ain't owned this land—er this last four years—er."

"Oh. Who does then?"

Shipton shot another uneasy glance at the kitchen door and then told his tale. He'd been in what he called a muddle and at his wits' end for ready money four years previously, and he couldn't sell the farm because Mrs. Shipton had put the whole of her dowry into it when they married; he hadn't even dared to tell her what a muddle he was in. Then one day "somebody" had offered to buy his farm and let him stay on at a ridiculously small rent on condition that the change of ownership remained a secret. "And that—er," Shipton ended, "seemed like a miracle to me—er; an answer to prayer if ever there was one—er."

"Certainly very fortunate for you. But a curious arrangement. Who is this somebody?"

Shipton looked at Richard with harassed eyes and a nerve began to twitch in his cheek.

"'Twas part—er of the bargain, sir. Heving took—er advantage of it like—er, 'twouldn't be right—er for me to tell—er."

His disability increased with his nervousness and was in itself enough to annoy his listener past bearing.

"Such a sale could be easily traced, you foolish fellow," Richard said. "You can save me time and considerable displeasure by telling me."

Shipton looked down at his feet and cracked his knuckles.

"Oh well, possibly Mrs. Shipton could hazard a guess!"

"You wouldn't tell—er her, sir?"

"Would I not?" Richard's smile sent something cold through Shipton's blood.

"If I tell—er . . . ?"

"Then I need make no inquiries."

"'Twas Miss Parsons, up—er at Dower House—er."

"Oh." Richard sat for a moment, mentally adding the acreage

of Bridge Farm to the amount of land which Miss Parsons owned openly and speculating upon the form of madness which would lead a woman to buy land on such a strange condition. Then he rode away. And soon he found that another man, ostensibly the owner of several strips in Old Tom and in Layer, had in fact sold his land to "somebody" who wished the deal to remain secret.

"Not so much of a secret," Richard ventured. "Miss Parsons' kindness is better known than she realises."

"She saved me from beggary," the man said simply. "I'd had a run of bad luck and to top all broke my leg. Old Scrat alone know where I'd have been but for being able to sell out yet stay on for such a small rent."

"Most fortunate for you," said Richard absently. And perhaps, he thought, fortunate for me, too. He remembered Monty's remark about the old woman being perhaps sane enough to make her mark and not quite sane enough to watch her rights. Certainly she now ranked second to himself as a landowner and her claims to the Waste when it was divided would be considerable. He set out to visit the Dower House.

Miss Parsons was feeling very well. It was a long time since she had felt so well in body and so clear in mind. Damask, dear child, had now been with her a fortnight, and in that brief time had worked wonders. Saunders and his dreadful wife had gone. How that miracle had been brought about Miss Parsons did not fully understand; Damask had told her to stay out of the way while she dismissed them, but she had been worried and had gone down and stood outside the kitchen door, ready to go in and support the child if necessary. No sounds of strife reached her, however, only the sound of voices, Damask speaking quietly, the man and the woman muttering at first, and then becoming quiet. Later in the day they had left the house and Miss Parsons had been hysterical with relief. When she was calm again she said, "And you promise to stay with me, *promise*."

"Of course I shall stay," Damask said.

"Then would it not be wise of me to write to the Poor Farm?"

"I am *not* from the Poor Farm. It might be as well to write to Mrs. Cobbold, at Muchanger. That was where I was working and my quarter isn't up until Michaelmas. She might make a fuss if she knew I was here."

"Oh no, not if I write and say how much I depend on you. I'll do it at once."

She showed Damask the letter when it was written. It began well, the courteous, formally phrased letter of one lady to another, asking as a favour that she should allow a maidservant to break her time and enter new employment. Then it deteriorated suddenly because Miss Parsons' mind had slipped a cog and it was fifty years earlier and she was writing to thank another Mrs. Cobbold for a very pleasant dinner party on the previous evening and asking whether anyone had picked up a silver button which had dropped from the Captain's waistcoat— of no value, no value at all and if it had not been found no one was to bother to search for it . . .

"That will do very well," Damask said, rightly concluding that this unmistakable evidence of the state of Miss Parsons' mind would strengthen the force of the appeal in the opening sentences. Mrs. Cobbold, when the letter reached her, said to her husband, "Oh well, this explains. Now which do I answer, the first half or the second? Poor old thing, she must be quite demented! Still, she chose well, that solemn little creature will not take advantage. And Cook always resented her going out on a Sunday. . . ."

So that was settled. Miss Parsons' next concern was the finding of substitutes for the Saunderses. "I'm not going to have you ruining your pretty hands and working yourself to death, dear child. If you did you might just as well have stayed at the Poor Farm. Could you go and find some servants in the village?"

"I could," Damask said. "But some from away would be better if you want me to keep them in order."

"Of course, of course. Oh, how clever you are! And how stupid of me. I know what I shall do. I shall write to Mr. Turnbull."

She did so. That letter, too, was most oddly compounded of reason and dementia; but it roused the old lawyer's sense of responsibility towards his client and resulted in the arrival, ten days later, of an elderly married couple, the woman stone-deaf, the man, an old sailor, lacking some fingers on his right hand. Conscious of their handicaps, they were delighted to find employment, touchingly anxious to give satisfaction, and when Richard Shelmadine came to pay his visit to Miss Parsons, the house was cleaner than it had been for years and a considerable stretch of the lawn in front of the house had been roughly scythed.

Nevertheless, as he approached the house, he wondered

again why anyone living in such obviously straitened circumstances should have bought land and then accepted such nonsensical rents.

Miss Parsons, on this bright September morning, was alone in the library at the back of the house, busily and happily mixing the ingredients of potpourri in a large Chinese bowl. It was years since she had made potpourri. Damask had suggested it, had dried the rose leaves for her and emptied and washed the small bowls which now stood ready to receive the mixture when it was blended. The room was clean and in perfect order, the sun shone in at the wide window and gleamed on the polished floor and the surface of the furniture. Miss Parsons was calm and lucid of mind; it was all like old times.

Into the calm came Bennett, the old sailor, saying:

"Sir Richard Shelmadine to see you, ma'am."

Miss Parsons took her fingers out of the potpourri and held them to her nose. Scents, more than anything else, are evocative of memory; everything slipped backward in time.

"Show him in. And bring Madeira and biscuits," she said. Charles always enjoyed a midmorning glass of Madeira. Charles? Oh, how foolish . . . Oh dear! Richard, of course, the man had said. Richard. And now here he was, smiling and bowing over her hand and saying that he hoped she remembered him.

"Oh, very well, very well indeed," she assured him. It was not true; entering the room unannounced, he would have seemed a stranger. He bore no resemblance either to his father or to the young man of nineteen or twenty whom she did remember.

As soon as he was seated Richard began to apologise for not having called upon her earlier, pleading press of business; there had, he said, been so many things to see to.

"Oh, I do not expect to be visited nowadays," she said abruptly. "I expect you want something now. What is it?"

He exerted his charm. "Of course I wanted something—to renew our acquaintance. In the old days I always greatly enjoyed coming here; you have so many curious and interesting things; and the fact that you used to offer me a sip of wine and a biscuit as though I were grown-up much endeared you to me."

"In those days the fact that you were your father's son endeared you to me," she retorted crisply. "Later on I deplored the way you behaved to him; the fact that the poor man is dead makes no difference to that. I'm still alive and able to speak my mind."

He had guessed that it would not be an easy interview; he had expected to find her senile and vague, probably cantankerous, but not inimical to him personally. Nobody else had held his behavior to his father against him; why should she?

The entry of the servant, rather flustered, explaining that he could find no Madeira, was a welcome interruption, giving him time to consider his next words. It would be unwise to make any further reference to the past, he decided.

"No, I know. That horrid man drank it. But it doesn't matter. It doesn't matter at all," Miss Parsons said, justifying the old sailor's opinion of her as an employer, "easygoing but very changeable in her mind."

Richard took out the paper which bore the notice, and said in a more businesslike manner, "The second reason for my visit is this. It speaks for itself, I think, but if there is anything you wish to ask about it I will explain to the best of my ability."

She took the paper and, holding it at arms' length because age had made her very long-sighted, studied it for a moment and then laid it down beside the Chinese bowl.

"Your father," she said, with apparent irrelevance, "was a very foolish young man and he grew into a very foolish old man. Always talking about what he would do *one* day, as happily careless as a schoolboy talking about what he will do in his holiday. I knew it would come to this, and I took my precautions. That is why there is no Madeira. It really was comical, he looked so *disgusted* the day I offered him an inferior wine. And it was all his fault." A smile of wry amusement began to reassemble the wrinkles around her mouth and eyes; then it faded; her whole expression clouded as she realised that she had lost track of what she was saying. And there was no help, no guidance to be had from this stranger who was watching her so closely, yet so coldly. She said, with some defiance, "It's all right. I know, I know. I must just . . ." She turned away and plunged both hands into the potpourri, willing herself to remember. She *must* remember. Here was the potpourri; she had been making it when this stranger arrived—that was obvious; and they must have spoken to one another. But about what, and who he was, she could not recall. The very effort to do so led to greater confusion, and after what seemed to her a long, an impolitely long time, she lifted her hands and said piteously:

"I'm sorry, I have forgotten what we were talking about. I do forget. That is my trouble."

He said gently, "Please don't worry. We all have these little lapses. Why, once in London, I hired a hackney carriage and gave the man the address of a house where I hadn't lived for four years! Actually we were talking about this"—he reached out and touched the paper—"and you were just going to sign your name, here." He indicated the space where he wished her to place her signature.

Still confused, and wishing to conceal her confusion, she said in a more animated voice, "Was I really? Well, that seems very simple, doesn't it?" The quill stand and the inkpot, used for the letters to Mrs. Cobbold and Mr. Turnbull, stood on the far end of the table. Miss Parsons looked at them, and then at Richard again. Something, not what she was reaching for, but something, fell into place in her mind. Signing things had some connexion with Mr. Turnbull. . . .

"Why didn't Mr. Turnbull come himself?" she inquired.

"It was hardly of sufficient importance," Richard said after only the briefest hesitation. "A mere formality." She selected and dipped a quill, took up the paper and held it at arms' length again. The word "enclosing" leapt out at her. Her mind cleared and she knew what it was she had been saying before she digressed to mention the Madeira and lost her way.

"But that was what I was about to tell you. I knew he would procrastinate too long. So I took action." Her expression became cunning. "You can't enclose unless I sign, can you? And I shall never sign. I own more land than you realize. I shall have quite a voice. That is why I have had to live in this meager fashion, to make my plans and keep my secret. But you can't enclose unless I consent, can you? So we might as well tear this up."

Taking the top edge of the paper between her two hands, she began to tear it, and had torn three inches before Richard lunged forward and seized her by the wrists. At his touch she reacted exactly as she had done to Mrs. Saunders' attempts at violence, resisting fiercely and screaming like a maniac. As she fought against him the tear in the paper continued to lengthen and Richard realised that he was helping her to destroy it; so he let go her wrists and put his hands on her shoulders and shook her, partly in the hope of making her drop the paper, partly in genuine rage. He thought later, when he had time to think, how easy and how delightful it would have been to shake her to death. The shrill screams were actually giving way to jerky, breathless little cries when the door opened and Damask rushed into the room. Shouting "Stop it," she launched herself at him and would have seized him by the elbows but for the fact that he immediately released his hold and stepped back, feeling immensely foolish. Miss Parsons fell limply into her chair and the paper fluttered to the ground.

"He tried to murder me," she said shakily.

"Ma'am, I assure you . . . I was merely trying to prevent her from tearing an important document," Richard said, feeling more foolish. He stooped to retrieve the paper and held it out to show the torn edge. "She had taken up the pen in order to sign, then suddenly she began to tear it instead."

The girl was not looking at him; she was stooping over the old woman and had placed her arm about her.

"There, there," she said, as though to a child. "It's all right now. I'm here. It's all right." She tucked back a whisp of the white hair and fastened one or two buttons which had opened in front of the old woman's bodice, and then she lifted her head and looked into Richard's face with a stare which was neither accusing, nor tinged with complicity, nor amused. It seemed indeed to have no connexion with the unusual scene just ended; it was a long, cool, measuring stare under which his lack of ease increased to the fidgeting stage. Touching his hair and then his cravat, he said again, "I assure you . . ."

"He tried to murder me," Miss Parsons repeated.

"No, no. Nobody would do that. It was just a misunderstanding. Look, you go on with the potpourri and I'll take him away."

Her attention thus distracted, Miss Parsons muttered something about not wanting any more interruptions and resumed her mixing in the bowl. Richard, almost reduced to similar childlike obedience—"I'll take him away," indeed!—stepped forward and opened the door and then followed Damask through it.

"I had no idea," he said as soon as they stood in the hall. "She seemed to be so rational, and then suddenly . . ."

"You must have done something to upset her," Damask said, stating the fact without blame, but equally without excuse.

Richard felt fury begin to move in him again; that detached cool manner of hers was extremely annoying, the more so because she was young and pretty and should, he felt, have been either apologetic and flustered by the whole incident, or inclined to giggle about it. He looked her over before he spoke again. There was nothing prim about the tight-waisted, full-skirted muslin dress, yellow in colour and tied with an amber velvet sash, nor in the clustering bright brown curls amongst which the amber ear-bobs swayed, nor in the necklet of heavy amber globes tied with a matching velvet on the nape of the smooth white neck. Everything about her looked as though it had been chosen and donned with an intent to charm—and she could have been charming, should have been charming, yet her glance and her manner towards him, acceptable perhaps from some sour elderly female, was, from her, subtly insulting. Yet, because she had handled the old woman so well that in the circumstances it might be wise to enlist, or attempt to enlist her aid, he spoke smoothly.

"Perhaps I did, but if so unintentionally. The unseemly scuffle which you interrupted—and I am grateful that you did—was, as I said, merely my attempt to prevent her tearing up a list of signatures which has taken me some time to collect and which I have no time to gather again. You, of course, handle her marvellously, if I may say so. You have had much practice?"

Who was she? He imagined a relative, a great-niece or some such to the old lunatic. There was, now he came to think of it, something rustic about her; it showed, not in her looks or deportment, but in her voice and ... yes, her hands! He had noticed them as she soothed the old woman, her hands and about half her forearms between wrist and elbow were not as white and smooth as one would have expected. Some poor relative, perhaps, chosen to act as companion and caretaker; and that queer manner might be the result of shyness.

Yet there was nothing shy about the girl's voice as she said—ignoring his question—"What was it you wanted her to sign? May I see?"

"Certainly. I don't suppose you will understand it, but I can assure you that to sign would be to your"—he waited just long enough for her to supply the missing word, but she did not—"to Miss Parsons' advantage. And, as I say, she was on the very point of signing when her mood changed and she began to tear it instead."

As they talked they had moved by a progress so gradual as to be almost imperceptible away from the library door and now stood almost opposite another. Damask, ignoring the paper which he held out towards her, leaned forward and turned the knob of the door and pushed it open upon the large square drawing room, whose furniture and two chandeliers were shrouded in ghostly linen and whose shutters were closed.

She went over to one of the long windows and flung back the shutters, so that the sunshine streamed in. Just for a moment she stood in its path, a golden gleam and shimmer; really, he thought, a most attractive little creature, but for that manner which reminded him of somebody about to pull one's teeth. Shyness? Ignorance? It occurred to him that no introductions had been made.

"Permit me," he said, "to introduce myself. Sir Richard Shelmadine, at your service, ma'am."

"My name is Damask Greenway. May I see the paper?"

"A very lovely and unusual name," he said. Damn it, he was doing his best! "And if I may be permitted to say so, extremely suitable." To that there was no response. He handed her the paper and, assuming ignorance on her part, began to explain. She cut him short.

"I understand about enclosure. I have lived in Clevely all my life and heard enough about it. And about Greston . . ."

"'Where forty decent poor families were thrown upon the parish,'" he said, just as he had said it at Sir Evelyn's table. She did not smile. She said:

"So this is how it all begins. And it ends by making all the farmers as prosperous as Fred Clopton."

He thought then that he understood. Not a relative; some farmer's daughter with just the necessary smatter of education . . . back home, helping in the dairy and with the hens and then gladly escaping, taking a post of amanuensis to a daft old woman . . . much as Linda had gone to her cousin Maud.

"Yes," he said, "it will be a great thing for the farmers. But, of course, if Miss Parsons remains obdurate, everything may be held up indefinitely. All the landowners are supposed to be unanimous—to give their consent. Two of the freeholders have refused to sign, but their opposition can, I think, safely be overlooked. This is different, Miss Parsons owns a good deal of land, and unless she changes her mind very quickly she will delay the whole scheme for another year at least."

She gave her attention to the paper, reading, he observed, in the slow, careful manner of the unpractised, and frowning as she read.

"I'm sorry to bother you about it," he said as pleasantly as possible. "It is not, I know, a matter about which a pretty young lady should be asked to concern herself."

"Oh, it concerns me," she said. "It concerns me very much."

Expectations from the old woman's will, no doubt.

"I can assure you the enclosure will be greatly to Miss Parson's advantage. For one thing enclosed land is always of greater value than land in open fields; farmers become more prosperous and rents go up: for another her share of the Waste would be considered, it will be divided proportionally, you see."

"My father is one of those who lives on the Waste."

"Your father?"

"Amos Greenway, the cobbler." As she spoke she raised her eyes, and for the first time he saw her gaze tinged with some expression, and it was one of mockery. It was as though she said, "Now change your manner to me, and see if I care!"

"I see," he said. "Well, of course he could be safeguarded. He may, of course, have a claim of some sort—the commissioners, that is the men who make the division, have grown more lenient of late. But suppose he can produce no shadow of claim, it would be very easy for me to make him some allotment. What would you suggest?"

"I can't tell you because I can't picture in my mind how big an acre is. He must have enough."

"That could be arranged. If you would bring a little persuasion . . ."

"That isn't all. There is a man called Fuller."

"Ah yes, I know. But he is a tenant. The enclosure would not affect him, except of course that his land would be all in one piece and fenced around."

"Yes. That is what he has always wanted."

"Well, then . . . ?"

"That is what I don't want him to have." She brought out the words with a deadly simplicity. "He shouldn't have it, either. The very last thing Sir Charles did was to give him notice. On the day he died. His lease ran out on Lady Day and he should have gone then; but nobody knew, and he hoped nobody *would* know. I'm not going to coax anybody to sign anything that will make the Fullers as rich as the Cloptons and set Sal—Mrs. Fuller up in a gig!"

The spite in the last sentence brought a smile to Richard's lips. Some girlish squabble which the other female, Sal—Mrs. Fuller, had probably forgotten, brooded over by this cold-eyed little cat and resulting in that venomous statement. How very odd and amusing.

But he remembered something which Miss Damask did not know—that Miss Parsons' refusal to sign was not, as he pretended, just an arbitrary mood. From the few things she had said he had pieced together another story; long ago, sanely and quite cunningly, the old woman had set herself to carry on his father's opposition to enclosure. He'd tried to trick her into signing, but she wasn't mad enough to be easily tricked. It seemed as though his one hope lay with this girl.

"Do you think you could persuade Miss Parsons to sign this?"

"I could try."

"On condition that your father is provided for and Fuller sacked?" She nodded. "Very well, that suits me. Fuller, I understand, is an excellent tenant, but that is no rarity. When do you think you can let me have the papers?"

"Tomorrow."

"That would be excellent. And I promise that if you manage to persuade Miss Parsons to sign I shall keep my side of the bargain."

She looked at him again with that calm, expressionless stare; and again he was disconcerted. Once outside, mounted and on his way home, he smiled derisively at the idea that this mere girl, a cobbler's daughter, could, without saying a word, have threatened him, Richard Shelmadine. Nevertheless, at that moment, as their eyes met, some definite communication was made to him, some warning given, as though something quite apart from the girl, and infinitely powerful, had said, "You would be wise to do so."

CHAPTER 8

DURING THAT LAST WEEK OF AUGUST WHICH FOLLOWED DA-
mask's free Saturday, Julie worried about her daughter a good
deal. During the next week she found herself looking forward
to the moment when Amos would return from chapel on the
Sunday evening and, if questioned closely enough, tell her
whether the girl was looking well or poorly. When that time
came, however, all that Amos had to report was that Damask
had not been to service at all and he entirely failed to share
Julie's concern over her absence.

"She've missed Sundays afore this. When I fixed for her to
hev a Sunday every month nobody said which one. She'll be
there next week."

"I'm worried," Julie said. "A shock like that don't show all
at once. I remember that time when a girl, Jennie Brook her
name was, set aside of me, sewing on the same skirt, and
dropped dead. I never shrieked nor anything, then two days
later I started to shake so I couldn't hold a needle. Had to go
home and take a fortnight off. S'pose it took Damask that way."

"You're too fanciful," Amos said.

"Fanciful or not," said Julie with unusual firmness, "one of
us has got to go to Muchanger and *ask*. Will it be you, or shall
I hev Shad's donkey rig?"

"You'll just make yourself look silly," Amos said.

Taking that as permission, Julie arranged to borrow the donkey next day in the afternoon.

When he helped her into the low flat cart, Shad handed her a stout stick and said, "Now thass no use just a-tapping him, missus. Nowt on earth'll make him run, as you well know, but a whack'll keep him moving. And I'm sure I hope you'll find the little maid all right."

"Thank you, Shad," Julie said. She took up the reins and made the sort of sound likely to encourage a donkey.

"Go on, fetch him a whack, don't he'll never start," Shad cried.

Julie used the stick, timidly at first and then firmly, and the donkey moved away. Even at his slow pace Julie felt the jolting of the cart in all her stiffened joints, and when he stopped, as he soon did, she waited for some moments before rousing him to action again. Between home and the crossroads, where the grave was, bright this afternoon with scabious and knapweed, he stopped twice more and Julie began to be conscious of time's passing.

"Oh, get along, get along," she cried. "I surely ain't so heavy as some loads you take!"

The slow, intermittent progress continued, and at last three quarters of their journey was done and Muchanger only another mile away. Then the donkey stopped once more, and Julie hit him as usual. This time, instead of moving along, he seemed to crumple, went down on his knees and then heeled over sideways, tilting the little cart. A shaft snapped, and the cart righted itself, so Julie escaped without even a bruise, but Shad's donkey, that legendary animal, the wonder of six parishes, had stopped for the last time.

This would happen to me, with Amos so against me borrowing him and all, she thought as she climbed awkwardly out of the car and looked down at the little grey heap. She was sorry about the donkey, too; for as long as she could remember he had been part of the landscape of the Waste. And she regretted that last blow.

"I'm sorry, Neddy, but I couldn't know, could I? And what am I going to do with you now? And how'm I going to get to Muchanger and back?"

She looked helplessly up and down the road. Nobody in sight. She was now miserably sure that bad news awaited her at Muchanger; this was an ill omen, surely. Tears filled her eyes.

Well, it was no use standing here crying. She must get to Muchanger somehow and know the worst. She set out to hobble the last slow mile.

The mere mention of Damask Greenway's name infuriated the Muchanger cook, always an irascible woman.

"She ain't here, thass all I know and all I can tell you. Went off a fortnight ago for her free day and never came back, and me with a dinner party on my hands on the Sunday. Thass your creeping Méthodist what had to hev a Sunday off every month so's she could go to *chapel*!"

"Didn't nobody get word?"

"Mrs. Cobbold got a letter and said to me that little Greenway ain't coming back. And I say good riddance."

"Is Mrs. Cobbold at home?" Julie asked humbly.

"No, she ain't; the master neither. They're in Norfolk."

"So nobody knows. Was it Damask wrote the letter? She can write."

"Oh, she can write." The woman's voice was sour. "Always above herself, she was. How should I know who wrote the letter, I worn't told a word but what I've told you and 'twasn't my place to ask. My job was to muddle along shorthanded till another girl was found, and not a Methody this time, thank God."

As Julie turned to hobble away, the cook fired her final shaft:

"Gone to the bad, like as not. Them quiet sort is always the worst."

Hearing it put like that, Julie knew that that was what she had, all along, feared without admitting it to herself. She had never been able to rid herself of the memory of the way in which Damask had poured the brandy into the tea; it had indicated a deliberate about-face. . . .

She had not gone a quarter of a mile before she realised that it had been the desire to get to Muchanger which had enabled her to walk there. Now, with no desire to go anywhere, least of all home, where she must break the news about the donkey to Shad and the news about Damask to Amos, every step became more painful. She began to cry again, and was shuffling along, now and again wiping her eyes with the edge of her shawl, when she heard the clop-clop of hoofs and the rattle of wheels behind her. On such a day it was almost too much to expect that she might fall in with somebody who would give her a lift to the crossroads, so it was with a hopeless kind of hope that she lifted her head when the vehicle drew level. And it was Matt Ashpole.

He reined in quickly, but he had gone a little past her already. Twisting round in his seat, he shouted in an astonished voice:

"Julie Greenway! Why, for God's sake, Julie, what're you doing here? How'd you get here? And what're you howling for? Here, come along now, give us your hand." He helped her into the cart and made room for her beside him. "There now, there now," he said in a soothing voice. "Tell us whass gone wrong."

"Oh, Matt," she sobbed, "I never was so glad to see anybody in the whole of my life. There's my Damask gone from Muchanger, nobody can tell where. And I've killed Shad's poor old donkey and I didn't think I'd ever get home."

"Giddap, Gyp!" Matt said, shaking the rein. "There now, you stop blaring, Julie. We'll see you safe home. You tell me all about it."

She did so, omitting only the reason for her concern over Damask's well-being, merely saying that she had missed her Sunday. By the time she had ended her tale they had reached the scene of the disaster. "And there he lay," she said, pointing.

Matt drove just past the wreck and drew to a halt.

"Well, now I've seen all," he said in an interested voice which somehow seemed to make the whole thing less tragic. "That ought to be put on show, that do! They say you never see a dead donkey and I never did afore, not in all my days. Well, well. Now we gotta get him home, I reckon; can't leave him here on the highway; besides, Shad'd never believe you; he'd think you'd swapped him for half a pound of tea!" He swung himself over the side of the cart. There was no one on earth, Julie thought, comforted, better able to deal with a dead donkey and a broken cart than Matt.

First he loosed the harness and turned the little cart and hitched it behind his own. Then with a grunt he lifted the little grey carcass into the cart which it had drawn so many miles. His movements were competent and sparing of effort and in no time at all he was climbing back into his own vehicle.

"Well, here we go, missus! Reg'lar Lord Mayor's show, ain't we? Giddap, Gyp!"

Shad's grief and rage knew no measure.

"You med him run, thass what you did," he shouted at Julie.

"Thass women all over, no sense, no patience. I let you hev him out of the goodness of my heart, and you kilt him. He'd hev lasted out my time but for you. You're a murderer, Julie Greenway, same as if you'd killed a pusson—and there's a heap of them could hev been better spared!"

The commotion brought everybody out of the cottages; even Amos looked out to see what was afoot. Seeing Julie wilting in the center of the group, he came and joined her, hammer in hand, half a dozen brads held in his teeth.

When Shad renewed his accusations, Amos was moved to loyalty; spitting the brads into his hand, he said:

"Come, come, man, thass no way to talk. Poor old Neddy been due to die this last five year. 'Twas just bad luck my missus happened to be out with him." He put his arm through Julie's and she leaned on it gratefully.

"How'm I gonna make a living without my old Neddy?" Shad demanded.

"We'll cap round for you," Matt said. "All of us here, eh?" There were murmurs of assent, varying in enthusiasm, but unanimous. "And I'll ask all the chaps down the old Horse and all about. I'll start you off with a shilling," Matt said, reckless with generosity, "and I'll keep my eyes open for a nice cheap donkey for you."

Amos drew Julie towards their cottage. There his manner changed.

"I told you," he said, "but you would go running off. Now there's a shilling gone outa what I was saving for the chapel! You being out with the creature we can't very well give less than Ashpole. And if you'd just stayed here you've hev seen Damask."

"Seen her? You mean to say she was here?"

"No more than ten minutes arter you'd gone galloping off. She've changed her job and gone just acrost the road to Miss Parsons. Said she'd hev come over afore to let us know but the house was in a terrible state and there worn't nobody to leave the old lady with till lately."

"Well, thank God for that," Julie said, almost crying again from relief.

"Thass right enough to thank God," said Amos in his pulpit manner, "but you should trust Him too. 'Rest in the Lord and wait patiently for Him,' as the Good Book says. If you'd hev done that, Julie, the chapel'd be the better off by a shilling!"

"I'll put my wits to work and try to think out some way to

make that shilling right with you, Amos," Julie said meekly. "Did Damask look well? Did she seem like herself?"

"Now I come to think of it, she didn't. Well enough. But her hair was all over the place and her dress worn't suitable. I remarked about it but she said it was Miss Parsons' wish she should wear it."

"Funny she should be *there*," said Julie meditatively. "Her time at Muchanger wasn't up till Michaelmas."

"Seems Miss Parsons wrote to Mrs. Cobbold and asked for her. There, I've told you all I know, and she said she'd be running over again very soon. Now I gotta get back to work, I've wasted enough time as it is."

The death of the donkey and the collection of contributions for a new one remained a focus of interest amongst the Waste dwellers for just a few days and then droped into limbo suddenly. For on the next Sunday morning there was the preliminary notice about the intention to enclose tacked on to the church door.

Those Waste dwellers who through piety or policy attended morning service brought back the shocking news.

"Well now," said Matt when he heard it, "I reckoned he'd do it but I never reckoned he'd move so fast. You'd think he'd wait till he'd settled his bum in the old chap's saddle afore turning everything topsy-turvy. Well, boys, this is serious. We gotta move fast, too; and we gotta move all together if what happened at Greston ain't to happen here."

Amos, who was preaching at Summerfield that Sunday morning and attending chapel at Nettleton in the evening, first heard the news on Monday at about six o'clock in the evening. He had been hard at work all day and he was just about to set off for Bridge Farm to squeeze in an hour's work on the new chapel before darkness fell. Never in his life before had he so deplored the shortening of the daylight hours which came with summer's end. Very soon, he decided, he would change the programme of his days. He would work on the chapel in the morning and do his ordinary work at home by candlelight; but that change must be postponed as long as possible because then he would work alone and his progress would be very slow. It took two to handle the timbers properly.

As he opened his door he was confronted with a group of his male neighbours, headed by Matt Ashpole.

"You off somewhere, Amos? We was just coming to see you. We want a bit of help."

That was an appeal which Amos could not ignore, pressed for time as he was, so with an inward sigh he asked what it was they wanted of him, and Matt, who had taken on the role of spokesman, explained that everybody on the Waste must join in the endeavor to resist the enclosure, and that his neighbours were counting on Amos for help, "You being handy with your pen, Amos, and glib with your tongue, as we all know."

More concerned with the waning of the light than with the future of the Waste, Amos said hurriedly that he'd think it over; it was a thing which needed thinking over anyway, and just now he had a job to do. They could come and talk to him about it again, towards the end of the week.

"But we've gotta look lively, Amos," Matt protested. "This is a serious business."

"So is my chapel." Already he thought of it as his. The idea to build had been his, he had persuaded Shipton to give the plot of land; he had thought up the way of getting round the timber problem by buying the old ship's timbers; and he had done by far the greater part of the work. His chapel seemed near and urgent, this enclosure business something distant and concerned with the future. So having said he would think it over, he pushed his way through the group and hurried away, but he did not go fast enough to be out of earshot when Matt said disgustedly, "Him and his blasted chapel! Can't the silly sod see this is his tater patch in danger as well as ours?"

That speech may have helped Amos, when he came to think the matter over, to decide to disassociate himself from the resistance effort. He certainly thought over the question of time; if he were to ply his trade diligently enough to feed himself and Julie and keep up his contributions to the building fund and also go on with the building he would have no time to run hither and thither trying to prevent something the Squire had set his mind on and which would thus happen in any case. So, when next approached about the matter, he said that he had thought it over and had come to the conclusion that this was one of those situations covered by the text, "Render therefore unto Caesar the things which are Caesar's; and unto God the things that are God's."

"Seizer," said Matt. "Who the devil . . . ? Oh, I see. Ha-ha. Thass a good 'un, Amos! Squire, he mean, boys. Ah, he's a seizer, all right. And naturally I'm all for letting Seizer hev what is Seizer's; what I ain't in favour of is letting him hev what is ours and was our fathers' afore us, even if we don't hev no bloody papers to prove it." There was a murmur of assent, then somebody said:

"Ah, boy, but how're you going to stop him?"

"Thass what we've got to think out. But I can remember back when they cut up Greston Common and so many folks was in misery, heving lost their all. Something was said then about they left it too late to put their case. One chap'd even got his paper, little old black scrap of stuff that was too, and nobody could read it, but he went and dug up the damn thing too late, fences was up then. I've hunted my place like a dog hunting fleas, I ain't found no paper, but I shan't let that daunt me."

Talk turned for several minutes upon papers; how diligently they had been hunted; the unlikely places that had been searched. Only Matt Juby had found anything that looked as though it might have value in this connexion.

"Well then, all the rest of our granddaddies were damned careless old fellows. And maybe as well they were, don't we shouldn't be here to tell the tale!" At this point Amos turned away and went on with the stitching upon which he had been engaged when they entered his workroom to ask whether he'd thought things over.

"So, we ain't got no papers," Matt went on, "but we still can *try*. And to start with we should tackle Squire and state our case. If Amos here 'on't go, I will." He ran his bright little eyes over the gathering and halted them on Widow Hayward's son, lately come back from his soldiering and lacking an arm. "You shall come with me, Ricky. You got a case. There you are, fought for your King and country, give your arm for England, where'll you be without that bit of Waste to grub in and grow taters and keep a pig? I don't say Seizer'll listen, I don't say he'll take no notice, what I do say we'll hev tried."

Richard received the deputation civilly enough, listened to what Matt had to say, promised to bear it all in mind, and sent them away to drink beer in the kitchen. Ricky Hayward was satisfied and reassured, but then he was a simple soldier and had not Matt's lifelong experience of horse dealers and other tricksters to draw upon.

"He was all right, very smooth-talking," Matt said. "But I noticed something I didn't like. He says, 'Hev any of you got anything to show in the way of papers?' and I says, 'Only Matt Juby,' and a sort of glitter showed in his eye, like it will in a chap's that hev just sold you a broken winded nag smartly doctored. Arter that I couldn't stomach his talk about not wanting to ruin anybody and most like we could all count on allotments. If he didn't want to ruin anybody why should he be glad we hadn't got no papers? Still, there we are, we ain't done yet. I'm going to talk to the next on the list and thass Miss Parsons."

"Fat lot of good that'll do. She's dotty."

"She ain't too dotty to write her name. She'd hev the next loudest voice to Squire's when the time come and maybe she's dotty enough to speak for us."

So it was from Matt Ashpole's tongue that Miss Parsons learned that her signature was on the paper after all.

The September evening had turned chilly and Miss Parsons and Damask were sitting by the fire in the library. Damask was shortening another dress to her own length—a velvet one this time—and Miss Parsons was reading aloud from *Robinson Crusoe* to entertain her as she sewed. Upon this quiet domestic scene Bennett came to say that two men were at the back door asking to speak to Miss Parsons, and that one gave his name as Matt Ashpole.

"Oh yes, I know him. He often does odd jobs for me. Let him come in."

Matt, to whom shyness was unknown, stepped in boldly, followed more diffidently by Ricky. Miss Parsons said, "Good evening, Ashpole," and Matt said, "Good evening, ma'am." And then he saw Damask and, as he later said, he could have been knocked down with a feather. He did almost for a moment lose sight of his errand. Mindful of his manners, he said, "Excuse me, ma'am," and then turned to Damask accusingly. "So thass where you got to! Whyn't you let your pore old mum know? There was she rushing over to Muchanger, killing Shad's old donkey and crying her pore eyes out; and you only just acrost the road all the time."

("And then," he said, reporting the incident later on, "she ups and give me a look and says, 'I went across and told my father where I was at the first opportunity.' Now them's ordinary words enough, ain't they, and she said them quite pleasant, but the look she give me went clean through me like a cold knife.")

Recovering himself, he turned back to Miss Parsons and said, "Excuse me, ma'am. It was just that seeing her here and thinking her mum didn't know yet put me off what we come about." Then since the old lady was looking at him with no sign of dottiness at all, he proceeded to tell her exactly what he had come about, with Ricky, as support, now and then saying, "Ah," or, "Thass so."

In the interval since Richard's visit Miss Parsons had made still further improvement. Now when her memory lapsed a little or she contradicted herself, there was nobody to shout at her or mock her or say she was mad. Little Damask had a wonderful way of saying very gently, "Now wait a minute . . ." and then telling her just what she had been saying when her memory failed, or what she had said yesterday which conflicted with what she was saying today. As a result, she was no longer frightened or worried; she was well fed, well served, and much happier than she had been at any time since her father's death. This evening she was quite capable of listening intelligently to what Matt had to say, and when he had done she said in a clear, firm voice:

"I quite agree with you. I'm very much against enclosure."

"Then if I may make so bold as to ask, ma'am, why did you sign the paper in favour of it?"

"But I did not. That is just what I would not do. Sir Richard came here and he . . ." Part of her affliction was not that she forgot but that she remembered too many things too vividly, so that the past, instead of being in perspective, decently remote, was always encroaching upon the present. Now in her memory she relived, without the buffering of the past tense, the moment when Richard had started to shake her. "He tried to murder me," she said.

Matt did not believe that, and fearing lest his disbelief and astonishment should show in his eyes, he removed his gaze from her, looking at Damask, who bent her head over the needlework, and then at Ricky, who—parade-ground trained—could express a great deal without moving any feature much. His face now said, "There y'are, I told you the old gal was dotty."

For a moment Matt was at a loss, then once again experience came to his aid; he remembered his grandmother who had lived with the family when he was small; she too was a bit dotty and inclined to accuse people of acts of unbelievable malevolence. The thing to do was to take no notice. So now he ignored the accusation against Sir Richard and said bluntly:

"Well, ma'am, if you didn't sign, how do you reckon your name got on to that there paper?"

"It cannot be on it," Miss Parsons said. But her voice was losing its assurance; something in her head, just behind her eyes, was beginning to pull tight and knot itself. Her expression clouded.

"But, ma'am, there it *is*, writ plain for all to see. On the church door," Matt insisted.

"But I . . . There was . . . The church door, you say? The church door . . ." She had a sudden, immensely clear, mental vision of the church door. On the Sunday morning when Charles had brought his wife out of the church on his arm for the first time. Out of the shadow, into the sunshine; so fair, so radiant, so very beautiful.

"I don't think I can bear it," said Miss Parsons, speaking aloud, after all these years, the words she had so resolutely repressed then. To stand there, surrounded by the gaping, admiring villagers, and to look down the long dark tunnel of the years, alone, alone. "I don't think I can bear it," she said again, and pressing her hands to her face, she began to cry desolately.

Damask rose, without haste, to her feet and went over to where Miss Parsons sat and touched her on the shoulder.

"Now there's no need to upset yourself, no need at all," she said. "I'm here and everything is all right. I'll send them away. Don't cry. Everything is all right." Miss Parsons ceased crying and Damask, turning her head, signed to Matt and Ricky to go away. Ricky actually set himself in motion, but Matt stood his ground.

"To my manner of thinking thass just what it ain't. All right, I mean," he said, allowing a trace of truculence to creep into his voice now that he was talking to Damask. "That look to me like there's been some jiggery-pokery somewhere. The lady say she never signed, yet there it is, her name, writ plain. You stand aside, Damask, my girl, and let us get this kinda straight!"

"I am not going to allow you to upset Miss Parsons with any more of your nonsense," Damask said. She straightened herself and turned towards him, looking him full in the face.

"Go home, Matt Ashpole," she said.

"I don't take orders from . . ." He blinked and swallowed and started again. "I come here to talk to Miss Parsons . . ." His voice trailed off inconclusively on the last word and his mouth stayed a little open. Then, abruptly, he turned and followed Ricky, who was already on his way out of the room.

Damask picked up the book and the magnifying glass which

helped Miss Parsons to read and placed them in the old lady's hands.

"Oh yes," Miss Parsons said, an expression of simple pleasure lighting her face, "we were reading, were we not? And just coming to the exciting part, dear child!"

Holding the book well away from her and manipulating the glass with skill, she read on and reached the moment when Crusoe found the footprint in the sand.

Damask had taken up her work and resumed her stitching, her head bent. She was conscious of Miss Parsons' voice and polite enough to make, now and then, a small appreciative sound, but her mind was far away, in the strange place into which she had fallen when the news of Danny's betrothal had felled her to the floor, the place of the Voice and the Promise, the things for which there were no human words. From that place she had emerged with a power of whose nature and magnitude she had no conception; she had handled it tentatively at first, as a man might try an unfamiliar tool. Now confidence was growing, and skill, and ambition. . . .

"There!" said Miss Parsons with satisfaction, "was not that exciting?"

"Immensely exciting," Damask said.

Outside the Dower House, Ricky Wellman straightened his shoulders and drew a deep breath.

"Pore owd gal, mad as a March hare!" he said. Matt made no answer and Ricky imagined that he was depressed by the failure of the interview.

"I tell you what, Matt, I don't reckon they'll none of them take no notice of our plight. Not so as to be a help. I reckon thass every man for himself now."

Matt grunted. They reached the gate and Ricky made as though to turn to the right, cross the Stone Bridge, and go to the village, but Matt turned left, towards home.

"Hi, come on," Ricky said, "less go down to the old Horse and wet our whistles. I can do with a drink after all that shindy."

"I'm going home," Matt said. "I don't feel like seeing the chaps tonight," he added, explaining to himself, as much as to Ricky, the reason for his unusual choice. There was certainly no connexion, in his mind, between Damask's words, "Go home, Matt Ashpole," and his sudden feeling that home was the one place where he wished to be, and if anyone had pointed it out he would have called him mad.

"They'll know you done your best, Matt," Ricky said.

"There's nowt you *can* do when you're up agin them in power. Cheer up and come along. I'll treat you."

"Thass kind of you, boy, but not tonight. I feel like getting home and getting my boots off." That was it; he wanted to take his boots off.

He turned towards the Waste, and Ricky, after a moment's wavering, turned that way too and fell into step beside him. They walked in silence for a while and then, just as they reached the edge of the Waste, Matt said:

"Rum how the old gal shut off the blaring, worn't it. Once I seen something like that afore. A gyppo it was that had a way with horses. Nappiest horse there ever was he'd go up to it, be it kicking and carrying on ever so, and just lay a hand on it and speak a word and there it'd stand, quiet as a lamb."

"She hev a rare masterful way of giving orders," Ricky said. "Make a good sergeant, she would. And I call to mind the time when she was mim as a mouse. Got right nice-looking too, ain't she?"

Matt ignored that and there was silence again until they reached Widow Hayward's door. There Matt paused.

"I dunno," he said. "That kinda stick in my mind—the old gal being so sure she never signed that paper. I reckon that could bear looking into, Ricky."

"You can't pay any heed to what she say. She's off her head. Said Squire tried to murder her."

"Well s'pose he wanted her to and she wouldn't and started to blare and carry on; maybe he did. 'Snuff to make any man feel like murder, talking sense one minnit and rubbish the next. Just like my old granny—and many a clout she had from my dad, *and* my mum, come to that! I fare to recollect that Mr. Turnbull look after Miss Parsons' affairs; I reckon 'twould do no harm to hev a word with him, if I can get near him."

"I done running up and down on this job, Matt. They got all the guns and all the powder, you might as well face it. If they mean to grab the Waste they'll grab it. All we can do is retreat in good order."

"But we got nowhere to retreat to, you fool," said Matt angrily. "I know what a loony say ain't much to go on, but thass something, and maybe we could make more of it. Damn it all, boy, I kept alive and brung up a family just by making a little something into a bit more."

* * *

Next morning Miss Parsons woke and found herself very clear in her mind. She lay and watched the strengthening light and thought over Matt Ashpole's visit and everything he had said; she remembered it all. When, at eight o'clock, Damask appeared, as was her habit, with the breakfast tray, Miss Parsons said:

"My dear, I have been thinking. I must go along to the church and see for myself whether he told me the truth. You were there when Sir Richard tried to force me to sign, weren't you? And you *know* I didn't, don't you? So what the man was talking about I really do not know, but I must find out."

"There isn't the slightest need for you to bother yourself about anything he said." As she spoke Damask leaned forward; with rather less than the width of the tray between them their eyes met. "I won't have you exciting yourself about every bit of nonsense stupid people come and tell you. Forget it. Just remember that everything is all right."

And of course it was. So long as Damask was there, everything must be all right. The old lady ate her breakfast placidly and with enjoyment. Damask removed the tray and went out into the garden to cut, from the weed-smothered beds and borders, enough of the hardy survivors of the flowers as would decorate the house. She left Miss Parsons to dress herself as usual.

Halfway through her dressing Miss Parsons went to the window and looked out into the garden. A brisk breeze was stirring and the first leaves were loosening their hold. Far away, across the stretches of roughly scythed lawn, Damask was moving about, a wide basket on her arm.

I shall need some outdoor clothes, Miss Parsons said to herself, and went to the cupboard. There she asked herself why? And gave herself the answer. Because she was going to the church to see if what that man had said was true. And she must slip away without Damask's knowing, because the dear child didn't want her to be worried.

It was all perfectly plain. She was not even deterred to find that the outdoor clothes which she thought were hanging in the cupboard were no longer there. That was nothing to get excited about; she knew where they had gone. Mrs. Saunders had taken them. And that she remembered proved, did it not, how very clear she was in her mind; Damask, dear child, of course didn't realise how much better she was; she had first encountered her when, what with one thing and another, she had been in a very bad state, so naturally she now tried to protect her, to shield her from all worry. But really there was no need....

She found an old black cloak which Mrs. Saunders had despised and a tricorne hat with a broken feather. Having put them on, she took another crafty peep through the window and saw Damask busy gathering sprays of rose trees which had almost reverted to the wild stage and were, at this season, laden with bright red berries, similar to those found in the hedges, but plumper and more rounded.

Miss Parsons went downstairs and let herself out of the house.

She encountered nobody and nothing happened to distract her during her walk and she arrived at the church gate with her purpose intact; and although on the previous evening a memory, with the church as background, had caused a disturbance in her mind, this morning she faced the church itself without a tremor. Her swift gliding steps carried her along the path where the shadows of the ancient yews lay blackly, and up to the porch.

And there it was, indisputable. Amelia Caroline Parsons, just in the space where Richard Shelmadine had asked her to write it, and in her own fine Italianate hand—the only decently written signature on the paper.

She stood motionless and stared at it for a long time. Then, as the deadly significance of it was bore in upon her shrinking mind, she began to cry, not the loud protesting sobs which were her usual form of expressing distress, but a low, desperate moaning, broken now and then by muttered words.

"I am mad. I must be mad. I *am* mad."

Hitherto, however glaring her lapses of memory, she had always held firmly to her belief in her sanity; even when she had run away from the Saunderses and then, in emotional stress, forgotten her very name or where she lived, as soon as she was capable of thought again her first thought had been that she was *not* mad, she merely forgot things. But now she knew. Never, save it a fit of stark, staring madness, would she have written her name on that paper and thus given her consent to the very thing she had planned for years to prevent.

She sank down, trembling, on the church steps and put her head in her hands and went on moaning and muttering. There, very shortly—since it was easy to guess her whereabouts—Damask found her. Distraught as she was, she recognised "the dear child" and, taking her hands from her head, laid hold of

Damask's, clinging to them with the frenzied clutch of the drowning, admitting over and over again that she *was* mad, begging Damask to stay with her and look after her and not let her be locked up.

When she had abased herself sufficiently, Damask spoke. She said, "Of course I shall look after you. That is what I am here for. Listen . . . everything is all right. I am here and everything is all right. Look at me . . . There's nothing at all for you to worry about. Come home now and be happy. . . ." And happiness and comfort and assurance and a sense of well-being flowed in from the touch of her hand, the sound of her voice, the steady, calm gaze of her eyes.

Quite happily Miss Parsons allowed herself to be led home.

That Mr. Turnbull, Mr. Lawyer Turnbull as many people called him, was a kindly man was evident in the way in which he received his roughly dressed, roughly spoken visitor, and allowed him to sit down and tell his story without interruption. But when Matt had finished, the lawyer allowed his amusement to show plainly.

"Really," he said, "one of the most ingenious ideas I have ever encountered." He leaned back in his chair and gave Matt an appreciative look. "Whose idea was it?"

Matt was not quite sure of the meaning of "ingenious" nor of "encountered," so he hesitated for a moment before committing himself and then said cautiously:

"It was me that had the idea something might be a bit odd-like, sir."

"And I suspect that you hoped that if the signature were questioned at this last moment, everything might be held up for another year."

"Well, if it did that it'd be all to the good. Arter all, a year's a year when you look like losing everything."

"Indeed yes. Leaving the matter of Miss Parsons' signature aside for a moment, tell me—how many of the Clevely Wasteholders have anything to show in the way of a claim?"

The Squire had asked the very same question. Watching the lawyer very closely, Matt said:

"Matt Juby dug up a paper and Amos Greenway—though he ain't with us in this thing—did come down to tacks and spell it out for him and that told how 'way back his careful old great-great-granddad did get leave from the Squire to build a cottage and graze his beasts. And only yesterday Bert Sadler's wife hunted out one that looked just the same to my eye, but we ain't had time to get Amos' word for it yet. Thass about all, I reckon."

No glint of pleasure shone in Mr. Turnbull's eye; he looked serious and concerned and Matt was encouraged to say:

"Maybe we all had papers in the past, but you know how it is, sir, folks that can't read or write don't set such store by papers as them that can. And there ain't much space for hoarding such things . . ."

"No, unfortunately. Well, I'm afraid that in that case the most rest of you can hope for will be a charitable allotment. And that rather depends . . ."

He broke off, thinking how much better the small people of Clevely would have fared if the old Squire could have been persuaded to enclose, or by some means forced to enclose. Sir Charles' very horror of the results of enclosure would have led him to mitigate its evils as far as possible. Mr. Turnbull's dealings with Richard had led him to conclude that the new Squire was pleasant, but not at all inclined to be sentimental.

"That depend," Matt said, "on what the owners say, you mean? And that was what I had in mind when I went to see Squire. Then I reckoned I'd put it to Miss Parsons, too, and as I just told you, she said she was against the whole thing and never had signed no paper. Yet there her name is, plain as print. So I thought I'd ask you what you made out of it."

"I think that it was genuine forgetfulness on her part. She is very forgetful. Or it might be that your request embarrassed her and she didn't want to promise you anything and at the same time didn't like to refuse point-blank, and so took refuge in . . . well, an untruth. I've known women tell far worse lies than that merely to avoid a moment's unpleasantness, haven't you?"

"There is such a thing as forgery, as you should know, sir," Matt persisted.

"Indeed there is. But to forge a signature and then expose it in a public place under the very nose of the person whose signature it was supposed to be would be unusual, to say the least. And to whose profit would it be to commit forgery in this case? Nobody would gain anything . . ."

"Except somebody as wanted to enclose and knew the old lady was dead against it," Matt said shrewdly.

"Now, now," said the lawyer warningly, "you mustn't start making such suggestions."

"And mark you," Matt pressed on, "anybody that thought of it could count on the old g—lady never seeing it. She don't go about. The chance is she never would of known the paper was there, not less I went and told her. And I don't reckon there's many folks in Clevely know how Miss Parsons write. But that you *do*, sir, and so I reckoned I'd come to you."

"Well, if it would ease your mind at all, I'm willing to look at it; but I'm sure my opinion will only confirm it. I visit Miss Parsons once a quarter. I'll come next week, on Tuesday."

"Thass very good of you, sir, and I'm sorry to hev took up your time."

But the getting together, the waiting to see whether Amos would speak for them, the visit to the Squire, the visit to Miss Parsons, the framing of the intention to visit the lawyer and fitting in that visit, had all taken time; Matt, like everybody else, had to devote some attention to make a living. So there was a Sunday between Matt's visit to Mr. Turnbull and Mr. Turnbull's visit to Clevely and that Sunday was the third of the three demanded by the act for the public display of the notice. There it had hung for the required time, no formal objection had been brought forward by anyone important enough to be considered, and by the day of the lawyer's visit the notice, with certain other relevant papers, were well on their way to London, where, upon receipt of them, Sir Thomas Blyborough M.P. was ready to set the machine in motion.

CHAPTER 9

AS SOON AS HE HAD DONE HIS PART TOWARDS PROMOTING THE enclosure of Clevely, Richard was free to turn his attention to the next item of his programme of reversing his father's policy—the alteration of the Manor House itself.

Had she had the power to oppose him, Linda would have done so; as it was, at the first mention of his schemes she allowed herself to say, most indiscreetly, "Oh, but it is so lovely as it is." He made the predictable retort:

"Doubtless to *you*, my dear, but then your experience has been unfortunate." He then spent a happy ten minutes pointing out the practical inconveniences and the aesthetic faults of the building she thought "so lovely."

Compared with Flocky Hall, Bridge Farm, the house where the Fullers lived, and many other buildings in the parish, the greater portion of the Manor was in its infancy. Richard's grandfather had been in the middle of a building spree when the financial disaster of 1720 overtook him. He had added a Queen Anne façade, done away with many leaded casement windows, removed or concealed many heavy Tudor beams. Sir Charles, with his love of all antique things, had often said, with truth, that he preferred Flocky Hall and had had a perennial joke with Mrs. Abram Clopton, one day, when they both had time for such an upheaval, they would change houses.

Richard only compared his home with Greston Park, which Mr. Montague, vastly enriched by his enclosure, had been able to demolish and rebuild in the Palladian style; he craved the wreaths and swags and medallions of the new plasterwork made fashionable by the brothers Adam, the closed-in hearths with basket grates, the pillard entrance.

His own mother, during her brief reign, had succeeded in persuading her husband to have the dark panelling painted, the drawing room white and gold, the dining room a pale blue green, and Linda, arriving forty years later, thought both rooms very beautiful, even though the unrenewed surface of the paint had faded and developed myriad cracks, fine as a cobweb. Richard said that the panelling must go; and both rooms be lengthened by fifteen feet. Fluted and carved marble fireplaces were ordered.

The prospect of steady work all through the winter for local labourers did a good deal to compensate the loss of popularity amongst the poorer people which the move to enclose had cost the new Squire. It became evident, for instance, that Mrs. Sam Jarvey at the inn no longer welcomed the discussions and grumbles about the proposed enclosure in which Matt Ashpole and the other Waste dwellers spent their time. The work at the Manor brought a good deal of custom to her house, carpenters and bricklayers and plasterers earned good money and spent it recklessly. One day she spoke out, as she had told Sam she would if Matt and his lot kept on bellyaching about the Squire; she leaned over the bar and said clearly, "Now that'll do, Matt Ashpole. This is a decent house, I would hev you know, and I don't like your language."

"I ain't using no language, Mrs. Sam, that I ain't used these thutty years gone by. Hev you gone Methody or something?"

"No. I ain't. But I don't like to hear Sir Richard miscalled. He may not suit you, but he suit some all right."

"Meaning he suit you! Well, you don't want to be short-sighted, missus! All that new trade'll go back where it come from. Us from the Waste'll still be here, and if we don't hev a spare ha'penny for ale you'll feel the draught the same as us and you'll only hev the bloody Squire, what suit you so well, to thank." Having made this reasonable statement, and seen it received without sympathy, with in fact a sour disapproval,

Matt went on, "What is more, if my language don't please your fancy, I'll find a place where thass welcome, along with my custom. Come on, chaps! My old hoss and cart is still good for a jog into Nettleton."

Once he had given his orders and made sure that the builder, a man called Farrow, understood them and was capable of carrying them out, Richard suffered an attack of boredom. Having deliberately sought and gained the goodwill of his neighbours, he now found their company tedious in the extreme; the hunting and shooting with which they whiled away their country winters demanded an energy and fortitude towards cold weather which he did not possess and the prospect of returning to his old haunts in London, this time with money in his pocket, was irresistible.

He asked Linda whether she wished to accompany him. The question sent the clever little tightropewalker in her mind out on another tricky little trip. There had been a time when it had been possible for her to get what she wanted by the simple expedient of expressing a wish for the opposite; but Richard had seen through that device and was apt now to say, "Very well, so it shall be." She knew what she wanted in this instance; all summer she had known that she could be very happy—by her modest standards—in Clevely if she could be free of Richard's company. She liked the house, and the village; she liked most of her neighbours. She had, after all, been born and reared in the country and had now, after long exile, come home. But to say outright that she wished to remain here would be to invite frustration. So she said dully:

"For me it is a choice between two boredoms. In London you will, I imagine, spend most of your time in Soho Square, so I should be alone with nothing to do, and here I shall be alone with nothing to do."

"That," he said, "is where you make your mistake, my pretty one. You will be here, alone except when Mrs. Cobbold and Lady Fennel and others of the sisterhood come to cheer your solitude by drinking tea with you, but you will have plenty to do. For one thing you will see that the workmen carry out their orders. And if it is not asking too much, I wish you to keep an eye on Master Hadstock."

"But I don't know anything about farming," she said quickly.

"No. For a country girl you are singularly ignorant of the practical side. But then if you were as capable as Lady Fennel

I should hardly have been obliged to engage a bailiff. I know nothing about farming either, but I know that Hadstock is as self-opinionated as he is competent; that is why I shall arrange for you to overlook him. It'll do him good to be obliged to consult with and report to you."

Really, she thought, his ability to contrive discomfort for others had a smack of genius. In the three or four months since Hadstock had been engaged to supervise the agricultural side of the estate, he and Richard had had several violent differences of opinion; Hadstock was always right, Richard wrong, and Richard knew it but he derived great pleasure from provoking the man just up to the verge of saying, "Run your farms yourself then!" At that point Richard, knowing Hadstock's worth, would withdraw and, without actually making an apology, smooth over the differences with a false and mannered courtesy which again seemed to put Hadstock in the wrong. To arrange that this man, so knowledgeable and experienced, should consult with and report to a completely ignorant woman was the kind of plan which it delighted Richard to devise. It was on a level with the manner in which he had amused himself by causing domestic friction ever since their return. He had managed to combine a perpetual complaint and carping about the food and service with a campaign of charm directed at the servants, so that every complaint appeared to originate from Linda. He had thus, in a subtle manner, made use of the natural suspicion and reserve with which all the old retainers greeted the new regime. Naturally the new Squire could not be a patch on the old, now sanctified by death and a model of all virtues; so somebody had to be disliked, and since the Squire was so smiling and charming, his lady constantly making suggestions for improving this and that, in no time at all the dislike was concentrated upon her. Linda bore it with the wry resignation with which she had borne so many other things. And now Richard was off to London and she would be left alone in peace at Clevely; she could rehabilitate herself.

On the day of this departure Richard made an early start, for the autumn days were short. It was a mild November morning with a slight bluish fog shredding away as the sun rose. Linda stood by the side door, which, during the alteration to the front of the house, was used as a main exit and entrance and watched the carriage disappear along the avenue. Her relief was so profound that she was almost ashamed of it. Deliberately she looked back, remembering the time when she had looked forward, with such eagerness, to his coming; had thought him so wonderful and looked upon his attentions to herself as nothing short of miraculous. Charmed, and dazzled and flattered, completely under the spell she had been, and oh, so humble! Now she was glad to see him go.

She walked round to the front of the house, where the work was in progress, and knew a shame even deeper. Not only was she glad to see Richard go; for one shocking moment she had entertained a wish that he had gone for ever. Looking upon that scene of activity, now in its most destructive stage, she had thought for a moment how wonderful it would be if Richard were never coming back; then she could stop it all; tell them to close in the two pleasant rooms, now so indecently exposed, replace the old panelling, put back the heavy old door with its fanlight and portico, restore as far as possible the portion of garden now trampled and dug up and ruined, and go away. No, not quite so abruptly. Before they went she would give them a job that would be a genuine improvement—they could put windows into some of the servants' bedrooms, those dim little warrens high under the roof at the back, some of which were lighted by two panes of glass in the ceiling and provided with air by a grating high in the door. In the summer when, soon after her arrival, she had made a careful inspection of every corner of the house she had been aghast at the atmosphere in some of those apartments. Richard had pooh-poohed the suggestion that while the builders were on the premises some windows which would open could be made. "Walk round the village some warm evening and see how many windows that will open *are* open," he said. "Cottage people dislike fresh air."

Still, to think about what she would do if she had control was surely the most fruitless way of spending time and energy; she set about making the most of her unusual freedom.

In the afternoon she went for a walk through Layer Wood and was pleased to catch a glimpse of her two golden pheasants. They had been so tame by the time they arrived at Clevely that it had seemed safe to turn them loose in the grounds; there for some weeks they had remained, stalking on their delicate feet through the flower beds and over the lawns, and coming up with friendly condescension to take food from Linda's hand, as they had learned to do on the ship. Then, at the beginning of October, they had disappeared. There had been one or two light frosts, so it was not unreasonable, perhaps, for Richard to say lightly, "I expect they died. After all, they're tropical birds, they could hardly be expected to weather an English winter." He went on to say that he was himself feeling the cold severely and to ask whether this poor apology for a fire was really the best the house could provide.

Linda mourned the pheasants until someone from the village told Jim Jarvey, the lodgekeeper, who carried the news to the house, that "a masterous gaudy old bird" had been seen in Layer Wood.

"They won't be there long," said Richard. "Yes, of course we could warn everybody not to shoot them, but what about poachers? *My* preserves are pretty sharply looked to, but Layer isn't all mine, and everybody isn't so strict. I'm afraid you've seen the last of them."

However, they were there this afternoon and Linda called to them and flattered herself that they did hesitate for a moment before taking wing. Perhaps it was as well, she thought, that, since they had gone back to the wild, they should have abandoned their former tameness completely. Safer so.

It was dusk when she reached home and full dark by the time she had taken off her outdoor clothes and settled down by the fire in the small sitting room, with a tea tray on a table beside her. The whole long peaceful evening stretched before her; she was luxuriating in the thought when a servant came and asked when would it please her to see the bailiff, now or later on.

"I'll see him now," Linda said, and laid aside her book.

When the man entered she greeted him with a tentative smile, and saw with dismay that she had been right in thinking that he would resent these interviews. He returned her greeting civilly enough, bringing one big brown hand up to the lock of straw-coloured hair which fell over his brow, but his expression, which was surly, did not lighten.

"Sir Richard said, my lady, that you wished me to come and report to you every day."

That was, of course, exactly how Richard would put it, making it seem as though the idea were hers. And she could not—in the circumstances—contradict. Also, she thought, with just a flash of spirit, suppose she *had* said so; would it have been so extraordinary? While Richard was away she *was* in charge and had a perfect right to demand that the bailiff report twice a day if she wished. But this bout of self-assertion lasted only a second; the rightness of her position was undermined by her knowledge that Richard had arranged these interviews as a form of penance for them both. Richard's malice poisoned everything.

"Well, you see," she said placatingly, "I shall be sending letters to my husband regularly, and what you tell me will give me something to write about. Please sit down."

He was not placated; and too late she realised that to mention the matter of letter-writing was a tactless mistake; it sounded like a spy reporting.

"Thank you, no, my lady. I'm in my working clothes. That was one thing I wanted to ask you. Do you wish me to come when we knock off work, or later on, when I'm cleaned? I've taken the worst off my boots, but I'm still a bit doubtful whether they're fit to be in the same room with a lady."

"That depends entirely upon which you prefer. To come back would mean more walking, wouldn't it?" She seemed to remember hearing Richard say that Hadstock, offered the choice between lodging at the smithy and a cottage in Berry Lane, had chosen the latter.

"I always make a round after supper," Hadstock said.

"In that case then, if you prefer it, look in later on. But now, please sit down. Do you drink tea? I know many men despise it."

"I like it, but I won't have any now, thank you all the same. I shall be making my own later on."

"Do you live alone?"

"I live alone."

"In Berry Lane, isn't it?"

"Yes, my lady."

The brief, unyielding replies might, she thought, be put down to awe of her—but she had heard from Richard some verbatim accounts of things Hadstock had said to *him* during their differences; and his manner might also be the result of shyness in the presence of a female; yet nothing in his posture or expression indicated shyness; he sat at ease, not fidgeting, and looked straight at her with a cool, unabashed look. His eyes were greyish blue, light against the weather-beaten skin, and numerous little lines radiated from their outer corners. He was defying her to put the interview on an easier footing, and with a sigh, Linda abandoned the attempt and asked the question which she had been deferring. What was there to tell about the day's work?

As though he had memorised a distasteful lesson, he reeled

off the day's doings. Because of her ignorance hardly any of the things he mentioned evoked any mental image in her mind, and when he had finished all she could think of to say was:

"You seem to have been very busy."

"I am glad that you are satisfied, my lady," he said, and rose to his feet. "Have you any orders to give me about tomorrow?"

"Orders?"

"Sir Richard said I was to report to you each evening and take my orders from you, my lady."

"I think he meant only in the event of his having sent some special orders from London, Hadstock. He knows that I know nothing about farming. And I am sure that he knows also that *you* know exactly what to do."

"Then I'll wish you good night, my lady."

"Good night, Hadstock."

Except that the succeeding interviews took place in the evening, that Linda never repeated her gesture of offering refreshment, and that Hadstock had changed out of his working clothes, that first meeting between them set the pattern.

Then, when Richard had been gone a little more than a fortnight, something happened.

At midmorning on a bleak, windy day, Farrow, the builder in charge, was shown into Linda's room. He seemed to be in a state of excitement.

"We've come on something we hadn't reckoned for, my lady," he said. "There's a hole and something beyond it just where the new foundations are being dug. Job Ramsden stood there digging and then he disappeared. He ain't hurt. But to find a hole just where the foundations was to go'll put out all our plans. I thought you should know."

"I'll come and look at it," Linda said.

"Wrap up warm, my lady. It's raw out."

The trench which was being dug for the new front wall of the house ran across the space where, forty years earlier, Richard's mother had planned her "purple" garden, the fashionable craze of the year after her marriage. Linda picked her way through the uprooted and dying lilacs and wisteria and perennials which had gone on yielding their purple blooms unheeded year after year. At a point where the new trench was nearing its limit, its neat, narrow line gave way to a rounded depression with a hole in its centre. Close to it a dazed-looking man was wiping soil from his eyes and ears and spitting.

"It's probably an old well," Linda said to Farrow as they neared the spot.

"Begging your pardon, no, my lady. There's stairs, and Job said something about an arch. More like a cellar."

They stood by the hole. The reason for the collapse was plain to see in the ragged edges of ancient rotted timbers which projected from the soil. Down into the hole ran the flight of shallow stairs, smothered with earth and stones and fragments of spongelike wood.

"'Tain't no cellar, ma'am, m'lady, I mean," said the man who had fallen. "So far as I could see in the gloom, it looked more like a church arch, all carved-like."

"Ah," said Farrow, "some of them old monks' doings. They was all about here, back in the old times when they started the sheep up at Flocky."

Linda stooped and took up a branch of one of the murdered lilac trees—and buds which should have been next year's leaves and flowers were already there, with their promise—and with it scratched away the soil and stones from the uppermost stair. White and smooth the marble which the roman galleys had brought to this barbarian, marbleless colony gleamed up at her. Of the Romans, of the galleys she knew nothing; but she recognised marble. No cellar entry, this.

"Get a lantern," she said. Then, turning to Job, she asked, "Are you really unhurt?"

"A bit shook up, m'lady. Thought I was a gonna for a minute, I did, earth opening under me feet that way. Then I hit the stairs and went down on me—like youngsters go downstairs, m'lady. And then what with the arch and a great space beyond, all dark. Aye, that shook me up."

"And yelled he did as though Old Scrat had got hold of him!" Farrow said. But he spoke absently. Job's accident and the hole and the stairs and the arch and whatever lay beyond were of no moment to him; he was working out what the find meant in terms of constructional difficulty.

The man who had gone for a lantern arrived panting.

Farrow took it.

"Best let me go first, my lady. Something else might give way."

He descended the stairs, his boots crunching on the soil and stones and fragments of wood. He disappeared under the flat canopy where the unbroken timbers still supported the three-foot depth of root-threaded soil, and those above waited and listened. After an interval they heard his feet on the hidden lower stairs, and then he came into view again. He looked awed and did not speak until Linda asked impatiently, "Well, what is it?"

"A church, I reckon, but such a one as I never see . . . all pillars, my lady, and statchers, and the floor all coloured." He blinked and seemed to shake himself. "Thass safe enough. I know what happened; they shored over the entrance, whoever they was, and they knew their job, I'll say that for them. But where the timbers ended they sopped up the damp like, and when Job stood just on their ends they give way. Further in them pillars take the weight anyway. Thass safe enough, but I ain't sure . . ." He looked at Linda dubiously. Cursory as his inspection had been, in the dim lantern light, some of the "statchers" had shocked him. But of course the "gentry" had different notions; his sister, who before her marriage had been parlourmaid at Nettleton New House, had told him about some of the things they regarded as ornamental: Negresses without a stitch to their name, holding candles; little china boys, naked as frogs, supporting fruit dishes.

"What aren't you sure about, Farrow?" Linda asked.

"How this is going to work out with the building," Farrow said, almost truthfully, for part of his mind was grappling with that problem.

"Oh yes, of course. And I shall have to write to Sir Richard . . . but now I must see it."

That evening she was in the middle of writing to Richard when Hadstock arrived to act his part in the daily ritual. Laying down her pen, she said, "Oh, Hadstock, have you heard the news?"

"About the church found underground; yes, my lady. I had heard."

"I am just writing to Sir Richard about it; and I find that I have forgotten—or rather that I did not notice—many details. I wonder, Hadstock, would you, instead of saying all those same things over again, come with me while I take another look?"

"But of course. Certainly, my lady." And behind those simple words were a statement and a question. You give orders, I take them. Why ask me?

"I went down this morning with Farrow," Linda said, answering the question. "He hurried me round. There are some statues which, I am sure, he found embarrassing. But I have lived in India . . . and I assure you that these are, by comparison, most respectable."

She checked herself. What on earth had provoked her to speak so confidentially to Hadstock, who might, for all she knew, share Farrow's views and prejudices? She started again:

"I could have asked Walters, or one of the Jarveys or Daniel to come with me . . . but to tell you the truth, all the servants seem a little . . . scared of it. They seem to think that anything so old and underground must be . . . sinister."

And why should Hadstock think otherwise? He was a servant too.

With the first real feeling he had ever allowed any word of his to reveal, Hadstock said:

"I should regard it as a favour to be allowed to look round, my lady. As a matter of fact, I intended to ask your permission to do so before I went home tonight. I have my lantern."

"We'll go then," she said.

As they walked towards the place, with the lantern light casting a yellow circle about their feet, she said with cautious primness:

"You mentioned an underground church. It isn't *quite* that. The statues are more of a . . . classical nature."

"Or possibly pre-Reformation English," Hadstock said, as though speaking to himself.

"Would they use marble so much then?" Linda asked. "This place is all marble—or at least I think so."

"Indeed, my lady?" Holding the lantern in one hand, Hadstock with the other rolled back the piece of sailcloth with which Farrow had covered the hole. Then he descended five or six stairs and turned, offering Linda his hand.

"With only one lantern," he said, as though to excuse this familiarity, "one of us must walk in the dark, so I'll light my own steps and guide you down."

"I meant to count this morning. I will now," Linda said.

There were twenty-four stairs. Between them and the arched entrance was a square space of tessellated pavement, thinly covered with soil and debris brought down by Job when he fell. Then there was the arch, and within the pillared space, three times as long as it was wide, and lined with the figures which Linda had modestly described as "classical."

Hadstock seemed not to share Farrow's embarrassment; holding the lantern high, he studied each one and moved on.

Neither he nor Linda spoke. In fact, within a few moments of entering the place she would have found speech difficult for she was forced to press her teeth together to prevent them chattering. There was a deathly chill in the place; a chill of which she had not been aware on her earlier visit, when, in contrast with the atmosphere aboveground, the subterranean space had seemed warm.

There was also—and she became increasingly aware of it as their progress brought them to the farther end—a sense of somebody watching. She attributed this to the statuary. All the figures, even those in the most unusual postures, were extremely lifelike, and as Hadstock caused the light to fall upon one it was rather like being introduced to a person; then the light moved on, darkness engulfed the figure, but it was still there, and watchful. Before their slow progress brought them back to the arched entrance, Linda had decided that, as in so many other things, the simple untutored instinct of the servants had been right; there was something frightening about the place, and perhaps Mrs. Hart, who when invited to go down and view the wonders, had said, "No, thank *you*! To my mind anything that's once bin buried is best left buried," had spoken more truly than she knew.

Outside on the square of pavement Hadstock stopped after Linda had stepped on to the stairs.

"Just a minute, my lady, if you don't mind," he said, and with his foot cleared a space and looked down, moving the lantern backwards and forward.

"What is it?" Linda asked, her teeth chattering.

"Look," he said.

Pale stone-coloured squares and brown ones and some of bright greenish blue, and some of pink and black and terra cotta colour were arranged to make a picture, a huge black bull being slaughtered by a slim pale youth wearing a blue loincloth.

"You're cold," Hadstock said, and held the lantern to light the stairs ahead.

In the open the November night seemed warm as June, and the starlight more than ordinarily friendly. Linda drew a deep steadying breath and said:

"Well, what did you think of it? It isn't a church, is it?"

"Not as we understand it. A place of worship, yes."

"Heathen?"

"Pre-Christian." He looked down at the stairway thoughtfully. "You should warn Farrow, I think, my lady, that he may stumble across another entrance."

"Oh, what makes you think so?"

"Bulls were sacrificed there," Hadstock said, "and you'd never get a bull dead or alive down by those stairs, they're not wide enough."

Linda allowed herself the shudder she had suppressed.

"I felt something horrid about it. At least tonight I did. I didn't notice it this morning; nor the cold."

"No. He was a sun god."

"Who was?"

"Mithras," Hadstock said.

Strangely enough, it was not until she had returned to her letter to Richard that it struck Linda as being remarkable that the bailiff should seem so well informed. She had actually written the words, "Hadstock thinks that the place is . . ." when she realised that Richard would neither welcome nor believe Hadstock's theories and would, at the same time, be surprised to learn that he had any and that she gave them any credence. At that point she was surprised herself and, looking back, realised another thing—Hadstock, giving his views and theories about the mysterious underground place, had spoken with more assurance, more ease of manner than usual.

She scored out the last words she had written and, taking a fresh sheet of paper, wrote a hasty note to Mr. Avery, the Rector, telling him of the find and inviting him to inspect it and give his opinion. Mr. Avery, whose antiquarian interests were genuine, though curbed by his slothfulness, was eager to visit any remains already excavated which appeared to bear out his theories about the Roman occupation of Clevely. He was at the Manor soon after breakfast; and Linda, finishing her letter to Richard at midday, was able to say, "Mr. Avery has seen the place and thinks that it was, long ago in Roman times, a temple of Mithras."

She conveyed to Farrow Hadstock's warning about another entrance, and after that digging was done in a gingerly manner since Job Ramsden's experience might at any moment be repeated. Farrow went down and gave the place a more thorough inspection and did find, at the end farthest from the stairway, a great stone slab. "But do that mark t'other doorway," he said, "thass nowt to do with us, that lay right under the house. I only wish this un did too." The delay—for nothing could be done until Squire had had his letter and replied to it—irked Farrow sadly; the days were so short, and getting shorter.

Amos also was worrying about the shortening of the daylight hours. Every day now he set off for Bridge Farm in the morning twilight and laboured away till dinnertime; but the work was slow and growing slower because each successive layer of timber had to be lifted higher and was more difficult to hold in place singlehanded while the nails were driven in. He had ingeniously dug a ladder into the ground at one corner, so that its staves held the far end of the planks steady while he nailed his end, and that helped; but the staves and the planks were not of equal measure, and sometimes the planks slipped and sometimes the ladder shifted. Several times Amos had been obliged to call upon Shipton to come to his aid and that had resulted in a really nasty scene with Mrs. Shipton.

Mrs. Shipton, who never had any time or desire to gossip with anybody and who went to chapel, not to church, had remained ignorant of the notice on the church door until long after it had been taken down. However, at the back of the house at Bridge Farm there stood three fine walnut trees, and in years when the crop was heavy there were more nuts than Shipton could spare time to collect and market. Shipton, for some reason which no one could name, was always muddled and behind with his ordinary farm work. But collecting walnuts—helped by a few of the youngsters from the Waste—and marketing them in the small quantities which made most profit was just Matt Ashpole's job. So when the nuts were ripe he went along, paid so much a tree into Mrs. Shipton's hand, and while his small minions toiled, had time to talk about enclosure. And there came that awful moment when Mrs. Shipton said:

"Abel, something's going on that ain't right. Why worn't your name on that there paper? You're an owner; why should you be overlooked? Matt Ashpole say you 'on't get your rights when the Waste's cut up!"

She had the whole story out of him in no time and she was just as furious as he feared she would be.

Next time Amos loped along to the kitchen door and asked could she tell him where Abel was because he wanted him just to come and lend a hand, Mrs. Shipton made short work of him.

"Chapel I am, allust hev been and allust shall be," she said fiercely, "but there's chapel and chapel, I'd hev you to know.

Thass one thing to live righteous and another to live daft! You're daft, Amos Greenway, and you've made Abel daft. That there little bit of meadow was where I allust had my duck pen; that you must hev. Now you must have Shipton wasting his time. The chapel at Nettleton allust hev been good enough—them that grudge walking a few miles to their worship ain't worth anything to the Lord, nor to me, nor to you. You get along with your rubbish and leave Abel be. If I catch him wasting another minute on that wooden hutch of yours I'll burn it down. I mean that, Amos Greenway."

Amos believed her. He'd suspected all along that every evidence of Shipton's "lukewarmness" could be traced to his wife. Nevertheless, he started to read her a sermon about putting God and God's business first.

Mrs. Shipton cut that short.

"We ain't in chapel now," she said truthfully, and went in and slammed the kitchen door.

So Amos toiled on alone, except on Saturdays, when a few earnest souls came along to help him; and as the walls of the little chapel grew, so did the labour of adding to them.

CHAPTER 10

LINDA'S LETTER ARRIVED AT RICHARD'S LONDON APARTMENTS less than an hour after he had left for Angelina's on what his servant guessed would be an all-night session, so he dutifully ran along to Soho Square with it and it was handed to Richard at the card table. He glanced at it, recognised Linda's hand, and laid it aside. Some hours later, when play ended and he was about to rise from the table, in a bad mood for he had lost heavily, he would have left it lying on the console table on to which he had tossed it but for the intervention of a man against whom he had been playing.

"Sir, you are forgetting your letter."

Richard glared at him. He was the man whose luck had been as consistently good as his own had been bad. He was also—which obscurely added to his crime—a stranger to Angelina's. Now that he came to think of it, Richard remembered that as they sat down one of the other players had made an introduction, but lack of interest had prevented him from noticing the name sufficiently to retain it. A dim-looking fellow with something vaguely clerical about him, either in his face or his clothing; and the face looked as though it had been carved from suet, with two bits of coal stuck in for eyes . . . but his luck had been quite phenomenal!

Richard reached for the letter, remarking as he did so:

"You had devilish good luck this evening."

"I am usually lucky at cards," the man admitted. "That is why I play so seldom. One becomes unpopular; also—and this may surprise you—consistently good luck eventually becomes as tedious as the other kind. But I am preventing you from reading your letter."

He turned away from Richard and stood sipping the brandy which he had ordered when play ended.

Richard—though he was careful not to become too much intoxicated when at the tables—was no longer clearheaded enough to absorb much of the meaning of Linda's letter. What it conveyed to him was succinctly expressed when a man on his way out paused and said casually, "You'll be here tomorrow, Shelmadine?"

"No. I shall have to go to Suffolk. It's an infernal nuisance. I've some work being done and they've blundered on to something that puts out the plans."

The other man said, with interest, "A priest hole? We came across one when we made our alterations. Cunningly hidden too . . ."

"Underground, my wife says. Something to do with Mithras, whoever he may be."

"Never head of him. Well, get back as soon as you can. Suffolk in November! Ugh!"

"Ugh, indeed," Richard said. He folded the letter and looked round for the waiter. The stranger had swung round and now said:

"Did I hear you make mention of Mithras?"

"Possibly," said Richard, watching the waiter's passage across the room.

"If you don't mind my asking—in what connexion?"

"Perhaps you would like to read this letter!"

Impervious to sarcasm, the man said eagerly:

"Indeed I should. Thank you."

Richard tossed it to him and then turned his back and strolled over to another table where play had ceased and last drinks were being ordered. Dropping into a chair, he said to his neighbour.

"Do you know that fellow?" He indicated the man who stood reading the letter.

"Good God, yes! That's Mundford." He reached out and

touched another man on the elbow. "I say, Errington, Mundford's turned up again. Over there, look!"

"So it is. Funny I hadn't noticed him."

"He was probably invisible last time you looked!" There
was a spurt of laughter, hearty enough, but with just a hint of
uneasiness in it, like the laughter with which schoolboys greet
a joke from a master by whom they are intimidated.

"Don't draw his attention," Mr. Errington said. "I owe the
brute seventy pounds!"

"His luck tonight was unbelievable," Richard said.

"Oh. Have you been playing with him? Stripped you, eh?
He invariably wins. They say the Devil engaged to stand by
his elbow and see that the cards fell right for him."

"Not to mention endowing him with perpetual youth!"

There was another spurt of the same laughter.

"Well, he *was* one of Francis Dashwood's merry Medmenham boys," said Errington. "And the Hell Fire Club closed
down in . . . let me think . . . '61 or '62; and he wasn't young
then."

"He certainly wasn't," said a youngish man on the other
side of the table. "I know," he explained, "because my uncle
Borthwick fagged for him at Eton and Uncle B is seventy-five.
Had his birthday last week and, like the damned ass I am, I
forgot to offer my felicitations."

"Alas for your expectations," Errington said. "You can't
expectate if you don't felicitate. But to return to Mundford,
the sight of whom makes me expectorate, he must be hard on
eighty; and he doesn't look it, does he?"

"So perhaps the rumours are right. He always wins; he does
not grow old. . . ."

"He is looking this way. In that embalmed brain the memory
of seventy pounds is stirring! I'll wish you good night, gentlemen, fellow gamblers, and scoundrels all!"

But it was at Richard that the coal-chip eyes were looking,
and as the group around the table hastily broke up, Mundford
approached and held out the letter.

"Thank you for allowing me to read it, sir. Most interesting.
You do realise, don't you, that if what your local cleric suspects
is true, you have there a property of incalculable value."

Value . . . a hole in the ground? Ah, but there was something
else . . .

"Oh, all those marble figures, eh?" asked Richard, remembering.

"They doubtless would have some value, antique relics, works of art," said Mundford smoothly. "It was of the site itself I was thinking. If it is indeed a Mithraic temple—and it certainly sounds . . . I myself would give you two thousand pounds for the use of it . . . for one evening."

Momentarily speechless, Richard gaped at him.

"For the use of it, a little secrecy, and possibly some small collaboration on your part. And believe me, Sir Richard, the sum mentioned was not just an attempt to strike a bargain; it was a surety of my sincere interest."

"Well, if you're interested to that extent, you'd better come with me tomorrow and take a look at it."

"How very kind of you. I am most infinitely obliged to you. There is nothing in the world that I would rather do."

His voice was calm, but something so avid shone on his face that Richard gave voice to words of unusual sincerity.

"I wish to God," he said, "that there was anything in the world that I *really* wanted to do."

As he spoke, the limitless boredom moved in him like a sickness; the boredom that had driven him from one excess to another, which had set in early and grown great as his interests narrowed and his emotions cooled and one diversion after another failed him.

Mundford said, almost as though speaking to himself:

"There are always new worlds to explore," and passed on to ask about their place of meeting, their mode of travel on the morrow.

CHAPTER 11

LINDA WAS SURPRISED AT THE INTEREST WHICH RICHARD evinced in the underground place; he had shown none at all in the ruins of a temple reputed to be two thousand years old, nor in a deserted city said to be even older than that, nor in an aqueduct which had last served its purpose in Akbar's time, all of which had been the object of visits from other white people in India. She, of course, had joined the expeditions and stood and stared and exercised her sense of wonder to the full.

His attitude towards *this* antiquity she attributed to Mr. Mundford and reflected that there was novelty also in Richard's relationship with this man. Never before had she known him to be on such terms with anyone. Acquaintances he had in plenty, but no friends, and she had often hated herself for taking advantage of her knowledge that one way to amuse Richard was to decry or make mock of his acquaintances. This Mr. Mundford was different, no word of criticism must be used concerning him, as she quickly learned. Towards him Richard had something of the reverence which a young schoolboy has for one older, stronger, and more popular.

It was all very strange and perhaps a little comic, but although she disliked Mr. Mundford and found him physically repellent, she could not regret Richard's friendship with him.

It seemed to have eased something which had always been provoking Richard to be unpleasant, to take pleasure in being unpleasant. One might think it strange that friendship with such an ugly, dim-looking little man should oil the rasping wheels of their marriage, but it seemed to do so; Richard was much kinder to her than he had been for longer than she could remember and actually said that she had behaved sensibly over the find. "Many women would have thought only of getting the house refronted and would have had the hole filled in at once."

And that made her think of Hadstock, who, on the evening after their visit to the place, had abandoned reserve and formality long enough to say that if he had his way he would have the opening closed over at once. And she had said, "I feel the same." Their relationship, at that moment, advanced a step.

For two days after their arrival Richard and Mr. Mundford went up and down the marble stairs and into and out of the house. They said little about the find in Linda's presence, but sat up late, talking. On the third day, much to Farrow's relief and joy, Richard gave orders that the hole was to be closed. At that point the foundations were to be deepened and strengthened for safety's sake; then the building would go on as usual and no one would ever guess what lay just by the long sash window, one of three, in the new dining room.

No one questioned Richard's action. "A queer old place, full of statchers, all of 'em naked and some of 'em nasty," as Farrow described it, had been found on a gentleman's private property; the gentleman had come from London to look at the find and had sensibly decided not to let it interfere with his building plans. The days of publicity lay far ahead in the future and every one of the few people most nearly concerned would have laughed to be told that if, one hundred and fifty years later, one fragment of one of the statues should come to light it would receive nationwide attention. Mr. Avery, the Rector, was heard mildly to lament that a friend of his at Cambridge had not been able to view the find; but even he realised that nothing must stand in the way of Sir Richard's new dining room. To the workmen Job's sudden disappearance into the earth and his lucky escape were far more matter for wonder and talk than the discovery to which the fall had led.

Richard and his new friend went back to London and in a few days it was all forgotten.

*   *   *

Hadstock resumed his evening visits. During the first of these Linda asked the question which had lain in her mind since their inspection of the temple.

"You were the first person to identify that place," she said suddenly. "How did you know?"

"I guessed."

"Anyone could have guessed. I could have guessed—but I shouldn't have been right. You were. You must have had something to go upon."

"I read a little, my lady."

Although in its wording the sentence might have been an opening towards conversation, its tone had a finality, and Linda asked no more questions. She began, however, to entertain a curiosity about Hadstock, who lived alone, who held himself apart from everyone, and who "read a little" and was informed upon matters about which one would have expected a farm bailiff to be ignorant.

Once, on a short November afternoon, the last of the month, she walked along Berry Lane and stood and stared at the cottage as though it could afford some clue. It shared its occupant's secretiveness; its two small windows, one up, one down, were curtained with some ugly drab material; the tiny garden was untilled, thickly buried under the leaf fall of a solitary, age-twisted apple tree. When she had passed and could see, looking back, the space behind the cottage, she had a view of a linen line slung between two posts. Limp in the windless air hung two of Hadstock's shirts, his working blue, the white one into which he changed in the evening, three handkerchiefs, and two pairs of socks. Did he do everything for himself, she wondered, or did a village woman work for him? The idea of Hadstock washing, perhaps even ironing, his clothes was amusing, and yet pathetic.

She might never have known any more about the man than she did on that November afternoon had it not been for the accident which took place during the second week in December.

During his brief visit Richard had ordered, or had told Hadstock to order, a new bull. The two men who had delivered it, each holding a pole hooked into the ring through its nose, had warned Hadstock of its savage disposition. A stout leather collar had been slipped over its head and attached by a chain to one of the solid posts by the side of the manger, but even thus shackled it had, in the few days, managed to intimidate anyone who had attempted to feed it. Hadstock had undertaken the job himself, ". . . until the creature has settled." The stockman, in his first entrances, had always gone armed with a pitchfork; Hadstock, believing this to be provocative, had relied upon the bull pole, slipping the hook through the ring as the great head turned upon his entry and, by pressing on the pole, warding the creature off while he emptied the food into the manger within its reach.

The days were now so short that the evening feeding had to be done by lantern light; and on the second Thursday in December, Hadstock entered the bull stall, a skep of food embraced by his left arm, the lantern and the bull pole held in his right hand. He set the lantern down and in the murky light advanced, slipped the hook, as he thought, into the ring, pressed, felt some resistance, and edged himself towards the manger. But the hook had missed the ring and was pressing against the bull's nose. It moved its head slightly, the hook fell away, and there was Hadstock, close to the manger. He realised instantly what had happened and without releasing his hold on the skep— a stout wicker basket capable of holding a bushel—leapt away. The skep saved his life, deflecting the full force of the impact of the animal's attack. One horn struck the upper part of his arm, tearing it to the bone, and as he fell backward he hit his head on the edge of the manger. But the fall carried him out of reach of further attack and the bull's supper fell back too and was scattered on the floor. So there was Hadstock lying senseless and the bull, held by the chain, prevented from doing murder and also from enjoying his supper. Very soon the bull began to lament in a loud voice the folly of his recent action; he could smell his food, but he could not reach it.

"Din't Mr. 'Adstock feed that there owd devil?" Tim Palmer asked Boy Jarvey, as, having finished their own rounds, they were on their way home.

"I see him go off with the skep. Ain't sin him since."

"'E don't generally make that row time 'e's eating," Tim said, leaving it to Boy's wit to know that he was referring to the bull, not the bailiff. "'Old your lantern out the way a minnit, Boy. Ah, I thought so, there's a light in the beast's stall."

"He's a talking to him," said Boy with that deep irony of which only the very simple are capable. "Soothing, like he towd me time he see me fending him off with a pitchfork. Come on, Tim, thass gonna freeze cruel. Less get along."

"I don't like the sound of yon," said Tim, who was not

without experience. "You don't reckon the owd devil got Mr. 'Adstock down, do you?"

"Serve him right if he did," Boy said, but the callousness was superficial for he added immediately, "Mebbe we'd best take a look." There was, also at a superficial level, curiosity, the chance of drama, and below that, deeply rooted, the old loyalty, man against beast.

They entered the bull pen cautiously and pulled Hadstock out by the legs, Tim Palmer, even at that moment, sparing attention and breath to address the bull sardonically:

"Thass right, you go on a-blaring, you owd——. Reckon anybody'll feed you arter this?" Then he said, "'E's 'urt bad, Boy. Run along to the 'ouse and tell them."

"But of course he must be brought in here," Linda said. "And somebody must go for the doctor." So Hadstock was carried into the room where Mr. Mundford had slept during his brief visit and somebody rode, helter-skelter, for the doctor who lived in Baildon and came somewhat unwillingly, since he, like Boy Jarvey, expected frost and had, by careful questioning, made quite sure that neither Sir Richard nor his lady was in need of his attentions. And when, much later, he arrived, there was nothing that he could do, because Lady Shelmadine had already bandaged the gash in the man's arm, and when he suggested bleeding the patient in the hope of restoring him to consciousness she said, "Oh, but he has bled a great deal already . . ."

The doctor was comforted, however, by presently being set down to an excellent game pie and as much port and brandy as he could take, and a little later he had the satisfaction of watching the victim of the accident return to his senses—or at least show signs of life.

They stood, the doctor flushed and expansive, Linda pale and tense, by the foot of the bed when Hadstock's eyelids flickered, and he said, in a voice which surprised the doctor, who had, after all, only the working clothes and some gasped-out words about a bailiff whom a bull had gored, to go upon:

"So there you are! I knew that somewhere in the Elysian fields . . . it could *not* be otherwise, or how could Heaven be?" The blurred gaze focussed, sharpened, came to rest on the doctor's flushed face; and then, very slowly but surely, the curtain of reserve dropped again. "I was wrong," Hadstock said, "I should have taken a pitchfork."

* * *
Next day, though ghastly pale and obviously in pain, Hadstock suggested going home to his cottage.

"But you can't. You couldn't look after yourself, one-handed."

"Then I'll hire an old crone."

"But *why* do you want to go home? Aren't you comfortable? Is there anything I can do? Books? I have several, some quite new; let me fetch . . ."

"I wish to go home," Hadstock said in a manner only just short of being rude and ungrateful.

"I forbid it. You must stay at least until the doctor has been again and we are sure that the wound is not inflamed. Then, if you must, and if I am sure some able-bodied woman is there to look after you, I will allow you to go."

It was obvious from the way he set his mouth that it was with an effort of will that he prevented himself from speaking words of anger. They looked sternly at one another. Then Linda said, with dignity:

"There are plenty of servants; you give no trouble. And if you wish to be alone you can have solitude here quite as well as in Berry Lane. Alfred will look after you; and if you wish for anything, just tell him."

"Now you're angry," Hadstock said, surprising her. "Don't be angry. I'm not ungrateful, I assure you. I know you mean kindly, but you don't . . . It's just that, for a sick man, home is the only place."

"Then just for a day or two you must regard this as your home."

She walked to the fireplace and laid on two logs and then went out of the room. She did not enter it again that day, nor the next, but contented herself by ordering light, nourishing invalidish meals, telling Alfred to tell Hadstock that she had made kind inquiries about his health and sending him two of her newest and most entertaining books.

On Sunday morning her caution was justified. Alfred reported that Mr. Hadstock was out of his mind, mumbling and muttering and carrying on very strange. Later in the day the doctor, fetched from Baildon in a hurry, had his moment of sweet self-justification. He was able to say, "I expected this," and to do his bleeding, after all, audibly hoping that it was not too late.

The bleeding, and certain nostrums which he administered,

silenced Hadstock temporarily; but presently he resumed his muttering and mumbling and carrying on, and Linda, having listened to him for a while, took the sensible precaution of sending Alfred away for a well-earned rest. It would never do to have Alfred exercising his simple mind on the subject of what Hadstock was talking about. A good deal of it was well out of his range—Shakespeare's sonnets, so much quoted, for example, "Shall I compare thee to a summer's day? Thou art more lovely . . ." "Being your slave, what should I do but tend Upon the hours and times of your desire?" That was all innocuous enough; but Hadstock, wildly quoting, wildly commentated too. "The hours and times," he said, "shall it be the time when I'm all in a muck, and sweaty and stinking, or later on when I am, if nothing else, clean? Just as you wish, Hadstock, of course it is nothing to me. Clean or dirty, all one! She'll offer you tea, however much you stink. Oh, most gracious. 'I know many men despise it,' just for a minute setting you alongside the rest of them, a man, like the others. I will not take the Borgia draught. Lower the fence and let the tiger in! Halt by the shop window and stare, wet-lipped with longing! Not I!"

It went on and on.

There was fear in the house. Everybody knew someone, or someone's close relative, who had been gored by a bull and died. Even though he had had the benefit of a doctor's attentions the bailiff would go the way of all the rest. There was a special venom about a bull's horns, as about a toad's tongue, a serpent's tooth, and a cat's claw. Accidents went in threes, and death was catching. As the year moved towards its darker nadir everyone was content, indeed, deeply glad to leave it to Linda to sit in the sickroom, to thrust spoonfuls of black syrup into the sunken mouth, to lay wet cloths on the burning brow and listen to the interminable ravings.

Hadstock was sane again and on the mend when Richard arrived, unannounced, bringing Mr. Mundford to keep Christmas with him. Of the accident he said only that it was entirely Hadstock's fault, he had been careless and oversure of himself. And he expressed surprise that the bailiff had been accommodated in the guest room.

"With three good rooms out of use on account of the alterations, and Christmas upon us, I should have thought even you would have had better sense."

"For a time he was very ill, and I was helping to look after him; it was convenient for me to have him in this part of the house."

"I wonder you did not think of my room; that is nearer, and has a communicating door!"

There was nothing, Linda knew, behind that remark save a jeering sarcasm; their own disastrous physical relationship, for which he held her entirely to blame, had convinced him that she was cold and without sexual attraction; he was incapable of jealousy where she was concerned. Nevertheless, she was obliged to turn away quickly to hide the dark wave of colour which ran upwards from her throat to her hair.

"I'll see that the room is cleared and cleaned immediately. It shall be ready for Mr. Mundford in less than an hour," she said.

Hadstock was already up and dressed; the coat sleeve taut over the bandaged arm. She had seen very little of him since he returned to his senses with the fever's abatement, confining her visits to brief inquiries made at the open door and leaving the care of him to Alfred. Now, in order to regain a footing in safe everyday terrain once more, she said briskly:

"I'm afraid it won't be a very cheerful Christmas for you, Hadstock. You must allow me to send you up some festive fare."

"I've already arranged with old Widow Hayward of the Waste to come and do things for me, my lady. And now, before I go, I must thank you for all the care, and the attention, and the kindness. Very few ladies would have . . ."

"Oh, I did very little," Linda said hurriedly. "Alfred bore the brunt of it."

Hadstock looked into her face as he said, "Alfred has been most conscientious." Then, shifting his gaze, he went on, "But I did ask him whether I talked much nonsense and he said he hardly knew as you sat with me, my lady, most of that time. A man at such a moment has no guard on his tongue . . . and if I used rough language or . . . or said anything to offend you I do most humbly beg your pardon and ask your forgiveness."

"You cannot claim credit or take blame for the bulk of what you said, Hadstock," Linda said lightly. "You quoted from Shakespeare most of the time; so fluently and extensively that I began to wonder whether at some time you had been on the stage."

The years of enforced falsity with Richard had not been wasted, she reflected. The words had exactly the right ring and the hint of curiosity gave the final touch of authenticity.

"Why, no," Hadstock said, relief plain on his face. "I've not done *that*. But I did once have a schoolmaster who would assign long passages of Shakespeare to be learned by heart as punishment. It seemed barbarous at the time, and later on, blasphemous—but if it gives a man something to babble about when he's in delirium it has served its turn."

The Christmas season passed more pleasantly than she had anticipated. Richard donned his affable face again. Invitations which she had not known whether to accept or refuse, not knowing whether Richard would be at home or not, were hastily accepted; other invitations as hastily issued. There was the usual Christmas feast for the villagers and the distribution of the "Christmas dole." She was saved, by the activities and by Mr. Mundford's soothing presence, from the trivial persecutions which Richard's company ordinarily involved. The two men were now on Christian-name terms and seemed to have endless things to talk about; often they sat up far into the night. Frequently they were joined by Mr. Montague, who had been introduced at one of the gatherings and who seemed to be as unaccountably charmed by him as Richard was.

The subject of enclosure seemed to have receded to the background of Richard's mind and was mentioned only once when someone asked how things were going. Richard replied carelessly that everything had gone without a hitch and that the commissioners were expected to begin their work of assigning claims early in the new year.

For Damask, too, this was a pleasant Christmas. Last year she had been a humble receiver of "doles," this year she was a giver. It was very pleasant, when the carol singers with their lanterns came and hoarsely chanted the traditional songs at the door of the Dower House, to open the door and see their faces as she revealed herself in her velvet dress and the little fur wrap which she had put round her shoulders before opening the door on the cold night. Most of them were Waste dwellers; she knew their names, they knew her although Amos' prejudices and then her own Methodist ways had precluded any real familiarity. There had always been a slight gulf and often, in her childhood, she had seemed to be on the wrong side. Now, thanks to the miracle, the gulf was a great chasm, and she was very much on the right side of it. She distributed pennies and

oranges and mince pies with a regal air. The youngest of
Matt Ashpole's brood, a boy of twelve who had inherited his
father's shrewd little eyes as well as a full measure of his
cheekiness, had fully made up his mind that, when his turn
came, he was going to say, "Thank you, *your ladyship*," just
to show her. But when his pennies and orange and mince pie
were handed to him, his courage deserted him and he said,
"Thank you, miss," as meekly as the others.

On Christmas Eve, Damask, carrying a large basket, walked
across to the cottage on the edge of the Waste. She had made
regular visits ever since the one when she had found Amos
alone and he had "remarked upon" her changed appearance.
Since then she had, so far as possible, timed her visits to fit
in with his absences. He was still working on the chapel each
morning—or at least each morning until so much neglected
work had accumulated that he was obliged to stay at home and
deal with it. Twice during that late autumn and winter he had
been at home when she paid her visit and she had discovered
that he was one person who could not be overawed, or intimidated, or stared down. He scolded her about her appearance,
rebuked her soundly for ever taking a job where she could not
get leave to attend chapel at least once a month, and inquired
sharply about the gifts of tea and sugar and cheese and bacon
which she brought to Julie. Did Miss Parsons know the stuff
had been brought out of the house? Were the goods regarded
as part of her wages, or what? She directed upon Amos the
stare which had disconcerted Sir Richard Shelmadine, quelled
the Saunderses, silenced Matt Ashpole; and Amos stared back,
grave, concerned, reproachful. On another visit, reaching the
cottage door and hearing within the sound of Amos' hammer,
she had turned back giving herself as her reason, though honest
enough to know that is was, in reality, not the reason, the
excuse that with Amos there, Julie's pleasure in the visit was
marred. When she found her mother alone, the visits were
delightful. Julie gloated over the dresses, admired the hairdress,
was delighted that Damask's hands had grown smooth and
white. She accepted the gifts with a pathetic humility and never
questioned Damask's right to bestow them. They would brew
tea and drink it together and everything was cosy and pleasant.

Early in December, when Bennett slipped on an ice-lacquered
path and hurt his knee and had to have the doctor's attentions,
Damask spoke to the doctor about Julie's rheumatism, and next
time he passed—on his way to visit the bailiff at the Manor—

he left at the Dower House two large bottles of mixture which, he assured Damask, had been most efficacious in the relief of cases similar to the one about which she had consulted him. One was a medicine; one a general tonic. The medicine was a sweet syrup, heavily loaded with opium, and Julie did not exaggerate when she said that it relieved her aches and pains; the tonic, which smelt strongly of cloves, had a base of cheap brandy, and she was speaking the truth when she said it made her feel a great deal better. Every time she took a dose of either mixture, brewed a cup of tea, fried a slice of bacon, or nibbled a piece of cheese Julie was happily amazed at the way things had turned out. Damask was a good girl, and she had been rewarded; far better off, she was, than that slatternly Sally Ashpole, with a baby on her hands, a husband back in his old wild drinking ways, and the whole family with notice to quit at Lady Day next March and at their wits' end where to go. It was, Julie reflected with fustian philosophy, very queer how things that looked bad had turned out for the best after all, and the other way about, come to that!

So on Christmas Eve she welcomed Damask with joy and accepted all the gifts in the basket with expressions of pleasure, and Damask, walking back to the Dover House, was well pleased with herself.

Just before he left for London again Richard said, "Oh, by the way, a box will arrive. Have it put just as it is into Alec's room—they're some things he wants us to store for him."

The box arrived a few days later; a heavy, black, iron-banded trunk, furnished with solid locks. It was carried up to the room as Richard had ordered and she thought no more about it.

She had a new interest in life.

Three or four days after Richard's departure, when Hadstock, still holding one arm in stiff immobility, came for his evening interview, he said:

"Do you like dogs, my lady?"

"Oh yes, very much."

"But not in the house, perhaps?"

She was embarrassed, hesitated, and then decided to be frank; after all, there was nothing unnatural about disliking dogs and she need not go into any detail.

"I do," she said, "but Sir Richard objects to them in the house."

She remembered, with distaste, that time when, the enchantment over, she had tried to free herself of slavery; Richard was set to subject her then *against* her will and had found, in her pet spaniel, a tool ready to hand. Twice she had given the dog away, twice it had found its way home, once from a considerable distance. She had then paid somebody to shoot it, and had never since had any pet, unless the golden pheasants could be so regarded.

"I rather thought," Hadstock said, "that a dog'd be company for you on your walks and evenings when you're alone here. And I had the chance of getting hold of something rather unusual...but of course if Sir Richard..."

"What is it? What kind?"

"Would you care to look at it, my lady?" He went to the door, opened it and spoke, and in walked, with immense dignity, a dog that seemed, to Linda's astonished eyes, as large as a donkey; it was pure white all over and had a thick, glossy pelt.

"How perfectly beautiful," Linda said as the animal paused just inside the room and took stock of its new surroundings. At the sound of her voice it looked at her and then moved over to Hadstock and laid its head for a moment against his hand.

"He's used to me now. I've had him since Christmas Eve. I had thought...for Christmas, my lady; but perhaps in the circumstances it was just as well."

"Oh, but I should love to have him. He's so beautiful and would be such company. But it is... I mean dogs get fond of you and then it is rather difficult to find them a place where they can be happy when someone who doesn't care for them ...Oh, you know what I mean, Hadstock."

A glimmer of understanding more profound than was justified by anything she had said showed for a moment on Hadstock's face, and then, impassive again, he said:

"Well, he knows me now and I'll see him every evening. I could always take him home with me if that seemed desirable."

"Oh, on those terms I could have him. That would be such pleasure. Thank you, Hadstock, thank you. Now do please sit down and tell me all about him, his name and everything."

Of the dog's breed Hadstock spoke freely. His grandparents were foreign dogs, of a kind originally bred in the Pyrenees to protect sheep from wolves; their courage had been proved time and time again. The name of this one was Simon; he was eight months old and wouldn't grow any larger, though he would thicken out somewhat. How and where he had come by him

Hadstock seemed to slur over—someone he knew, he said, had imported two of the dogs and hoped to make the breed popular in England...

"But in that case... I mean anything new is always so very expensive," Linda said.

"He didn't cost me anything, my lady. And even if he had I should still be very deeply in your debt."

"Oh, nonsense," Linda said. "I am now very deeply in yours—for the kind thoughts as well as the dog. Will he come to me, do you think? Simon. Simon."

"Go to her," Hadstock said, speaking to the dog as though it were a person. "You belong there now."

A faint, far echo of something that same voice had said about belonging, something that the man did not know he had ever said, stirred in Linda's mind. She felt the colour in her face again and was glad that at that moment the dog left Hadstock and walked towards her. She bent over him until she was composed enough to go through the silly evening ritual.

After that the dog went with her everywhere and slept on a rug beside her bed. His allegiance was soon entirely transferred to her and though he greeted Hadstock in a friendly fashion he would not leave Linda's side even when Hadstock entered.

He was by her side one morning as she came out of her own room and saw that the door of Mr. Mundford's, ordinarily closed, was open and that a maid was within it, giving it the "turn-out" to which even empty guest rooms are subjected in well-regulated households. Linda remembered that she had something to say to the maid, so she went into the room and began, "Oh, Annie, I wanted to tell you..." She broke off and sniffed. "What a peculiar smell! Is it the polish you are using?"

The girl, who had been polishing the floor, had risen to her feet, still holding the cloth.

"No, my lady. It's wearing off now, the smell, I mean. It was something the gentleman used. It used to be awful in the mornings when he was here."

"Open the window." The girl turned to do so and let out a startled exclamation. Linda turned to her and, following the direction of her gaze, saw that Simon was advancing towards the trunk. His attitude was strange, he crouched down so that his belly fur almost brushed the carpet as he advanced; his ears were flat to his head, his tail low. Within a foot of the trunk he paused and began to growl, far back in his throat; then, as Linda and the maid watched, he made a different sound, a shrill kind of yelp, twirled about, and dashed from the room.

Seeing the girl's pallor, Linda said as steadily as she could, "I suppose he has never seen a trunk before. Let me see, we were going to open the window, weren't we?" The girl fumbled and Linda went to help her, noticing with shame that her own hands were not quite steady. "There," she said, "that will freshen the air."

Simon was in the corridor waiting for her, lifting his paws, thrashing his tail, and trying to lick her hand as though he had committed an offence and were making an apology. It was merely fanciful, Linda told herself as they went side by side down the wide shallow stairway, to think that he had sensed something sinister about Mr. Mundford's trunk and had committed what must in his sheep-dog eyes be the worst crime— desertion in the face of danger. Merely fanciful. (But on her way to bed that night she paused by the door of the guest room, opened it, reached inside for the key, and locked the door on the outside.)

The maid, the moment Linda had gone down the corridor in one direction, emerged from the room and bolted into the other, towards the back stairs. And next time that room was dusted and polished, two maids, both eyeing the trunk and competing with one another in suggesting what gruesome objects were contained therein, did the least possible amount of work there in the least possible time.

The year turned and began the slow climb upwards to summer. A few snowdrops, strangely immaculate, pushed their way through the black soil at the edges of the shrubberies; a few yellow aconites stood stiffly in their little frilled ruffs at midday; most noticeable of all was the change in the quality of the afternoon light. Sometimes, even when snow lay on the ground, the sky, just before sunset, would take on a luminous look, palely green and full of promise. It was winter still but spring was on the way.

On one such January afternoon, a Saturday, a thin young man rode into Clevely, hitched his horse outside the church gate, vanished into the shade of the yew trees; and after a few minutes emerged again and rode away. The body of the old Squire lay in quiet corruption under the great stone tombstone, and his ghost did nothing to forestall or hinder the young man in his action, which was strange. For it had happened; enclosure had come. The new notice stated that the necessary act for the enclosure of the parish had been passed and that all those who had claim to the Waste and had not already done so should furnish a clear and correct statement of those rights within one week, either to Sir Richard Shelmadine's bailiff or to the office of Mr. Turnbull, attorney, in Baildon. It looked official, but harmless enough, and even Matt Ashpole, when it had been read slowly and distinctly twice over to him, said:

"Well, that ain't so bad as I feared. That don't say nowt about mucky little owd bits of paper. That say a correct and clear claim. Well, all of us hev claims that are correct and Amos shall see that they're set down clear. Of course we'll take Matt Juby's owd paper and Bert Sadler's, just to show the sort of thing we all had no doubt, till some silly young bitch used 'em as hair curlers; and for the rest Amos shall write out clear and correct statements. I'll give him the gist of it and he'll put it proper-like."

Amos, duly approached, said, "Well, it's like this here, Matt. You don't go to chapel and I don't care about the Waste; so if I bother with your business, you'll hev to bother with mine. I got the chapel walls so high now that I can't manage any longer singlehanded and with the days so short and the roads so bad I can't get anybody to labour with me regular. S'pose I say I'll draw up your papers, will you come and help me with the last three layers of timber? I don't aim to go much higher than that and anyway I ain't got much wood left. Next thing I'll hev to reckon with is the roof. . . ."

"Now you come right down off that there roof of yours," Matt said. "I do wish you'd get it into your skull, Amos, that you ain't doing us no mortal favour. *You* live on the Waste, same as us; so do Shad's new donkey that I got for him, best bargain I ever struck. Now when you want leather fetched from Baildon, who cart it? Shad do. You picture for yourself when there ain't no Waste, nor no donkey. Nor my owd hoss. I did reckon I'd got him provided for, come what might, but I was wrong!" Matt's voice turned sour. The ejectment of the Fullers had been a heavy blow to him. "None the less, Amos, if you'll scribe out a decent paper for us, all right, I'll come and give you a hand with your tabernacle, though I'm church myself," said Matt, who never went near the church, but did occasionally send his children so that they might qualify for the Parson's dole.

After much argument and much crossing out and insertion of phrases, a fair copy of the statement was produced; a strange combination of pomposity and naïvety.

To Sir Richard Shelmadine, Bart: His Majesty's House of Commons; the Commissioners for the enclosing of Clevely parish and all else whom it may concern— We the undersigned be the dwellers on the Waste in the said parish and this be our case. From time immemorial we have lived on the Waste and made our living thereby; saving Matt Juby and Bert Sadler, we don't have papers to show; theirs are enclosed herewith as a sample of the lot. We beg leave of your honours to say that in the eyes of God and by right of custom we have claim for some provision to be made for us when the Waste shall be divided. We think your honours would not wish to have on your conscience the misery and hardship that would come upon us if we be driven off the land where we support ourselves as our fathers and forefathers did in years gone by. Trusting your honours to consider our rights and throwing ourselves upon your justice and mercy, we be, sirs, your humble and obedient servants—

"Ah," Matt said judicially when Amos read out the final draft, "that read very well." He savoured the businesslike sound of "sample of the lot," his own contribution. "Now you sign, proper fashion, Amos, and if you'll be so kind as to write my name for me, I'll make shift to copy it somehow; then Ricky Hayward can put his, he can write a bit. Amos, maybe we should of made special mention of Ricky, him losing his arm and all. . . ."

"It would be hard to work it in now," Amos said. He was tired of the whole business.

"It could go in after 'divided.' It could read on, 'specially in the case of Ricky Hayward, what give his arm for King and Country'; that'd read very well, Amos."

"I don't think it'd be wise to make any special cases. Once you start, where would you stop? You could go on and mention Shad with his donkey to provide for and old Mrs. Hayward who must hev somewhere to hang out her wash. Best leave it as 'tis, to my mind." ·

There was still quite a lot to do. Amos had to write out Matt's name to be copied; and for the others, less ambitious, he must write the name on the paper itself, Kate Hayward, her mark; Matt Juby, his mark, quite a number of names; then the marks must be made.

It was Wednesday by the time the paper was ready, the two legal claims folded within, the whole enclosed in a clean sheet, sealed with a blob of cobbler's wax, and addressed to Mr. Turnbull.

"I'll journey into Baildon tomorrow to deliver it all safe and sound," Matt said. It was he who had insisted that the paper should go to Mr. Turnbull, not to Mr. Hadstock. Mr. Hadstock was Squire's man, the lawyer, he thought, was impartial.

"And then on Friday," Amos said, "you'll come and give me a hand with the chapel."

"Oh b—— the chapel," Matt said. "I ain't earned nowt this week yet, Amos, galloping to and fro on this job. Gimme Friday to knock up a crust, don't I'll be too weak and feeble to heave for you. Thass all right for you—I see that there mawther of yours carting a bloody great basket of goodies for you every week—not that I blame or grudge, mark you. I only wish one of mine had done as well for herself. Look, I'll give you a hand Satterday."

A few minutes later Amos said to Julie, "Next time Damask brings anything across the road, whether I'm here or not, you tell her to take it straight back. I never did feel easy about it and I ain't heving Matt Ashpole saying we take charity. I always hev earned what we need and so long as God give me health and strength so I will. We don't need no luxuries!"

One could only hope, Julie thought, behind the meek mask which she presented to Amos, that Damask would choose her time for visiting carefully. It was such an easement to have a cup of tea whenever one felt like it.

Mr. Turnbull admitted that he had a sentimental side; so he permitted himself to sigh a little as he opened the package and spread out the paper which bore the mark of several different dirty thumbs and fingers, and which seemed to have been in close contact with onions, leather, human sweat, and horse manure. It had, the old lawyer thought, another odour, too; the sad smell of simple man's invincible trust and hope for justice and mercy: in this case all misplaced and doomed to disappointment, Mr. Turnbull thought as he laid aside the modern document and turned to the enclosed, aged ones. They, at least, did constitute valid claims; Matt Juby and Bert Sadler would probably receive an acre or two apiece to compensate them for their lost rights. As for the rest . . .

And really this was no way for a man of law to be thinking, he reflected briskly; rights were rights, legal documents must be preserved and ready to produce when called for, or where would lawyers be in the scheme of things?

Nevertheless, the phrase, "in the eyes of God and by right of custom," had an oddly haunting quality.

The three commissioners—the same ones who had surveyed and redistributed the parish of Greston—set up their headquarters at Baildon, at the Hawk in Hand, an ancient little hostelry within reasonable reach of the acres which were to be rattled into fragments and then painstakingly reassembled after the manner of a jigsaw puzzle. Unfortunately the eldest member of the group, a Mr. Sawston, was assigned the largest and best-furnished bedchamber, which faced East, and on the first night of his stay the wind blew, unhindered, straight across from Russia, across the flat plains of northern Europe, across the ruffled North Sea, in at the estuary where Bywater stood, and on until it came to the old, ill-fitting casement window of the Hawk in Hand at Baildon. Mr. Sawston arose next morning with a very stiff neck, which made him irritable and impatient. He and his colleagues were receiving two guineas a day apiece, which was a considerable remuneration in a period when a farm labourer earned seven shillings for a week's hard toil and a country clergyman was "passing rich" with fifty pounds a year. But Mr. Sawston, moving about, with his head a little on one side in an aura of pungent embrocation, was in no state to linger over the job, fond as he was of money and useful as he found it. His one idea was to get back to his comfortable chambers in Chancery Lane. Under his guidance the commission carved up Clevely with the despatch of a butcher, with a shop full of customers, jointing a new carcass.

There came a day—it was in late February, a day of alternating sunshine and brief bitter squalls of snow—when a list of lands assigned, claims admitted, and expenses to be met was exposed on the church door, accompanied by a rough map drawn up by the surveyor who had worked with the commissioners.

On that day, late in the afternoon, Steve Fuller walked into the kitchen which had once been a parlour and dropped from his shoulders the bit of damp-spattered sacking which had been his protection against the snow. He sat down by the table, rested his elbows on it, and dropped his haggard face into his hands, which seemed so disproportionately large for his body.

"If only I'd waited," he groaned. "If only I'd had the sense to wait. There it is, all in the one piece. 'Tenancy at present known as "Fuller's," property of Sir Richard Shelmadine, Bart.' All in one piece, just what I allust longed for and now to let! 'Tain't to be borne."

Mrs. Fuller crossed the room and laid her red puffy hand on his bowed shoulder. She was no longer quite the cheerful buxom creature from whom Sir Charles had accepted the offering of cake and home-brewed wine. There were more lines in her face and more grey hairs amongst the curls. But her spirit was unimpaired.

"Don't you fret, Steve. Don't you fret, my dear, my dear. We'll manage. I give Annie Jackson good warning and she've been on the lookout for a little shop for me; and she've found one, in Friargate. You give me just a year or two there and we'll live close, and we'll hev the money to buy us an acre or two. Danny'll get a job. There's a room right up in the roof, we'll hev a lodger, Sally can help there, and with the cooking. We ain't beat yet, Steve, not by a long chalk. Come on, don't you fret. I got a nice dumpling just ready."

"I couldn't eat a crumb," Fuller said. "I doubt if I'll ever eat anything again. To hev it happen, just like I allust wanted it and me under notice to quit; and all on account of my damn hastiness. I could cut off my hand what hammered the nails in that there rack and that there manger, so I could."

Sally, who had been nursing her baby, now laid him in the old black hand-carved cradle which had rocked seven generations of Fullers.

"Once," she said, fastening her bodice, "I had a job at the Hawk in Hand. I dessay I could get it back if it come to a pinch."

Fuller took no notice and Mrs. Fuller hesitated before she spoke. Danny's marriage had been a dreadful shock and disappointment to her; and to her simple nature things would have seemed easier if she could wholeheartedly have disliked the girl. If she had done so Mrs. Fuller could have given her what she obscurely called "bell tinker." When Danny had come home back last summer and sheepishly announced that he was going to marry Sally Ashpole and that she was going to have a baby in the autumn and that was why, Mrs. Fuller had said, "Sally Ashpole, dirty little slut and careless too. I'll give her bell tinker." But there was something rather disarming about the girl's good nature; and she had a sense of humour; and the baby was a boy—though nothing like Danny to look at. Mrs. Fuller disapproved of her daughter-in-law, but she could not wholly dislike her. Disapproval, however, came uppermost now as she said:

"I've no doubt you mean well enough, but that wouldn't *do*! We've allust been a respectable family, and don't you forget it."

"And a hell of a lot of good we've done ourselves," Fuller said bitterly. "Even that damned surveyor fellow, when he went round, said my land was the best cultivated of the lot. So because I worked my guts out manuring and coddling that mucky old top end of Old Tom, some other chap is going to hire the neat little holding I should hev had. 'Senough to break your mind just to think on."

"We'll manage," Mrs. Fuller said again.

"We'll manage," Sally echoed.

After a moment Fuller stood up, rising slowly and heavily like an old man.

"Damn beasts gotta be fed, come what may," he said, and went out into the yard.

"Well, that's the worst yet," Mrs. Fuller said, lifting the saucepan lid and peeping at the dumpling. "Things'll mend now. You and me'll drive into Baildon as soon as there come a decent day, Sally, and take a look at this place my cousin found me. This dumpling's ready to dish. He'll fare better when he's got a good bite inside him."

In the byre that had once been the kitchen, Fuller stood still, staring with sick eyes at the rack which worked his ruin. Slowly, with the movements of a sleepwalker, he reached out and took up a halter and set about the only thing that was left for him to do in this world. . . .

Mrs. Fuller's spirit was equal to this last challenge. If it could be managed, Steve was going to have proper burial, in consecrated soil, and with all the rites. She managed very well. As soon as the limp body had been neatly laid in its bed, Sally was sent through the snow, which had settled in for the night, to tell the Rector that Fuller had taken a chill and that Mrs. Fuller didn't much like the way he was wheezing and that Fuller himself was nervous and thought he was going to die.

They'd all be much obliged if the Rector would call and talk to him, not tonight, tomorrow. This message, carried from the back door to the cosy study where the Rector was brooding over the commissioners' decisions and drinking port wine, distressed him very much. He disliked all thought of illness and of death. He seized upon the one cheerful note in the appeal, "not tonight, tomorrow," and sent back a reply that he would make a visit tomorrow, if necessary, but that he sincerely hoped—and that was true—that Fuller would be much better by morning. Morning, with snow still falling, brought another message to say that Fuller was dead.

Mrs. Fuller dug into the "egg and butter" money which she had been saving towards setting up her little shop and gave Steve a funeral which set a standard for all time in the six parishes and became a byword; seventy, eighty years later people in an attempt to convey a description of splendour would say, "Grand as Fuller's funeral."

Having managed that, Mrs. Fuller retired from management. She talked no more of the little shop and made no alternative plans.

"You'll hev to fend for you and yours now, Danny," she said. "If you want me I'll come with you, if not I can allust go and live with Annie Jackson."

The responsibility thus thrust upon him, combined with the shock of coming home to find his father dead, and the remorse of having been absent—drinking at the village inn—at a moment when his presence might have prevented a tragedy, sobered Danny entirely. He'd thought that the worst thing of all had happened to him when he found himself married to a girl whose brief attention for him had waned; he was morally certain that the baby who bore his name was not of his getting; he'd tried for half a year to escape the reality of his life, leaving everything but his share of the manual work to his father and mother. Now decision and management must be shouldered.

"Father—and he was the best farmer in six parishes—couldn't find land to hire," he said, "so I doubt if it's much use my trying; but maybe I could get a job like Mr. Hadstock up at the Manor, if I tried. And of course you'll come with us, Mother. You can mind the baby and Sally can get a job too. We'll manage."

Nobody noticed that he had used the words so often on Mrs. Fuller's lips; but in the speaking of them Danny entered into his manhood.

* * *

Fuller was not the only casualty of the enclosure bill. Old Clem Bowyer, he who had refused to sign, saying that he was too old for changes, received by word of mouth the news of the assignment to him of a neat packet of land, and of the share which he must pay towards the expenses of the commissioners, and the fencing. He had the details repeated to him three times, so that they were fixed in his mind, and then went home and said to his daughter, who kept house for him:

"I fare sorta tired, Martha. Reckon I'll go to bed early."

She was a good daughter; she took him a brick, hot from the oven, wrapped in flannel to warm his feet and a great pewter mug full of hot black currant tea to warm his innards, and Clem turned his face to the wall and slept very well. But he did not attempt to rise in the morning. As soon as he woke he thought about all the changes and the expenses and he knew he could not face them.

"I fare sorta tired, Martha," he said when his daughter came to see why he was not stirring. "Reckon I'll bide where I be today."

He never left his bed again, and in ten days was dead.

Ricky Wellman, who had also refused to sign, saying that when he was against a thing he was against it, changed his views completely when he discovered that despite his refusal to demand enclosure, enclosure had been thrust upon him and that his thirty acres—now all in one piece—included two upon which Fuller had toiled so earnestly. "I were a rare silly owd fool," he confessed, "trying to stand in me own light, like I did." He then took a stout knife and pried up one of the bricks near the hearth in the kitchen floor and lifted from its hiding place the leather bag which held his life savings. One or two of the coins were already rarities, guineas first minted in the reign of Charles II, hoarded away by Grandfather Wellman. Ricky counted them, the coins clumsily lifted and set out by his great gnarled fingers; there was enough to pay his share of expenses, do the fencing, and leave plenty over; he could go in for newfangled things like turnips and clover and winter-feeding if he had a mind. Twenty years dropped away with his prejudices.

At the Bridge Farm the enclosure had a result which was logical, but quite shocking, as logical things often are in this illogical world.

In a manner ominously calm Mrs. Shipton said, "Well, there

you are, Abel Shipton. If you'd given your mind to your business and not messed away your farm and my money you'd now hev a bit of the Waste to add to it. Now Miss Parsons being the owner get the share of the Waste what go with this farm, and she's old and she'll die and we'll end with notice to quit same as the Fullers. Thass what chapel done for you, my man, and thass what you've done for me, and there's no getting away from it."

There was no argument either, and Shipton attempted none. He remembered the text, "Blessed are ye, when men shall revile you . . . for my sake," and in silence obeyed the Biblical precept of turning the other cheek.

Next morning, all in the snow, Mrs. Shipton, having fed her fowls, tramped on to where the new chapel stood, the walls reared to about the height of ten feet, as Amos and Matt had left them when the timber gave out. She looked at it a long time, remembering the duck pen which had stood on the site; remembering the hours which Abel had wasted helping Amos Greenway to dig the foundations and begin the walls; remembering the hours—and the devoted attention—which Abel had given to the other chapel, at Nettleton.

Mrs. Shipton was at a dangerous age for women; the hot flush which, despite the cold, scalded her neck and face, the feeling of dizziness and nausea were no new things to her; ordinarily she drank a cup of cold water straight from the well and sat down for a few minutes. Today she did not attempt any palliative; she stood there, nursing her grudge and growing more flushed and more dizzy and more nauseated as she stared at the little chapel. Eventually she turned away and walked unsteadily into the house; and there in the kitchen Shipton presently found her. Not meeting her eye, he said sheepishly:

"I'm taking—er them pigs—er into market. Is there anything you wish—er I should—er fetch home?"

"No, thank you. Unless you know someplace where they sell gumption!" said Mrs. Shipton curtly.

Still turning the other cheek, still thinking "Blessed are the meek," Shipton turned away and went off to market. And as soon as he was safely away Mrs. Shipton took a really nice dry faggot and the tar bucket and the bellows from the hook where they hung by the kitchen stove; she carried them away and then she came back and shovelled out of the stove a dustpan full of glowing red embers.

Mrs. Shipton had more affinity with the Old Testament than with the New.

While all these events were taking place in various parts of Clevely, consternation and dismay reigned in the Waste. Of its dozen or so families only three were provided for, or even recognised as having existence. Matt Juby and Bert Sadler were granted half an acre apiece. "To be enclosed and fenced about from that portion of the said Waste immediately contiguous to the dwellings of the said copyholders, Matt Juby and Bert Sadler," whatever that might mean; and Amos Greenway, cobbler, was awarded twenty acres—no reason given. The others, like the forty poor decent families at Greston, faced real destitution.

Human nature, consciously or unconsciously, demands a scapegoat who can bear the blame for its woes; and the scapegoat must be handy, within reach and sight. Sir Richard Shelmadine and the Parliament men were in London; the commissioners dispersed, Mr. Turnbull in Baildon. The obvious scapegoat was Amos Greenway, who had written out the paper and now had twenty acres awarded him. What had he added to, or subtracted from, that writing? Who could know?

Ill feeling, though running high, took no outward form for two days, partly because a kind of paralysis had overtaken the Waste, but chiefly because the selection and persecution of the scapegoat demands the services of a high priest, and Matt Ashpole, obviously the choice for that role, was not sober enough to stand up at any moment during those forty-eight hours. So Amos went, unmolested, down to Bridge Farm and viewed the smouldering remains of his chapel, and came home and knelt down by his workbench and addressed his God in words which, if the Deity had any moment at all, must have reminded him sharply of another faithful servant named Job.

While Amos wrestled with his God, and Matt Ashpole lolled in drunken stupor, too far gone to notice that his lurcher bitch was whelping again, and the other Waste dwellers gathered in little groups and bewailed their fate, nobody noticed that Ricky Hayward, the one-armed ex-soldier, had disappeared; and when, more than a week later, news drifted in from Nettleton, which was on the coach road, that the coach from London had been held up and robbed on the other side of Colchester, nobody connected that with Ricky Hayward, or spared any sympathy for the passengers, who had—so said the rumor—been robbed of watches, jewellery, and cash worth ninety pounds. Everybody was interested, and envious, when, a few days after that, Ricky reappeared, stolid-looking as usual, and said that he got himself a job as footman with one of the officers of his old regiment who had now retired and was off to settle in America. His old mother was going with him; and that news did make a stir. In future the Waste dwellers, when they starved to death would have no one to lay them out, nor, if miraculously they should survive and go on breeding, would they have the services of a midwife. But they thought Ricky lucky and told him so and he gave no sign of what he knew—that he had not been lucky, merely enterprising and desperate.

At the end of the second day after the posting of the enclosure results, Matt Ashpole was sober for the simple reason that his supply of liquor was exhausted and he had no money to replenish it. He noticed the puppies for the first time and said, "Pore owd Ripper, had to manage all on your own; done well too, though how we're gonna feed the little buggers this time beats me." He then took his old gun, and said in quite another voice, "Now I'm gonna talk to Amos."

By the time he arrived at the cobbler's door almost every male dweller on the Waste was behind him, even Matt Juby and Bert Sadler thought it wise to join the group. On the fringe a number of little boys hovered, and two girls. There were no women in the crowd; Mrs. Ashpole had spoken for the whole of her logical sex when she said, "S'pose you do for Amos; what'll that get you? You'll swing and his twenty acres'll drop back into Squire's hand as like as not." Naturally Matt took no notice at *that*.

They came to the cobbler's door. Amos was not working; he had done no work since the previous day, when he had seen the ruins of his chapel; he was reading his Bible, searching for comfort and understanding, and since he read in the kitchen, it had been impossible for Julie to make herself a cup of tea all that day. When the knocking came on the door, some slight hope stirred in her; the knocker, whoever it was, might hold Amos engaged just long enough for her to make a brew . . . the kettle was boiling.

Amos went to the door.

"So there you are, you Methody twister," Matt said at once. "We're come to hear how you account for writing yourself into twenty acres while the rest of us get nowt."

"Ah," and, "Thass right," said the crowd.

"I can't account for it," Amos said, bringing his mind back to mundane matters. "No, there's no accounting for that, so far as I can see." No accounting for anything in a world where it could happen that a man received, one day, enough land to ensure that the chapel would be roofed, and on the next news that the chapel was burned down. "I can't account for it at all," Amos said again.

No impartial observer could have failed to see that, so far from being elated by his unaccountable award, Amos looked ill and sick at heart; all the harsh lines in his face were graved deeper, a patchy pallor lay around his mouth and eyes, and his lids were red with sleeplessness; but there was no impartial observer in that crowd and all anyone saw was the man who had, not very willingly, drawn up the paper from which they had gained nothing and he twenty acres, for which he now said he could not account.

"You was the one said let Seizer hev what was Seizer's, ain't you?" Matt said accusingly. "And beyond doubt thass what you *wrote*, you——! And got all us bloody iggerunt lot to sign it. They give you twenty acres for your services, you crooked sod, you! I see it all as clear as——day!" He believed that he did. He'd taken no solid food during his two-day drinking bout and now, half lightheaded with fasting, was in a state to believe anything.

When he had left his hovel, carrying the gun, he'd had no intention of using it; he meant to frighten Amos, to scare him thoroughly, and force some kind of explanation from him. Now he had found his own explanation, and there stood the rogue, entirely unrepentant, not attempting any explanation, and not looking in the least scared. "If you reckon you're gonna gloat over your ill-got gains, Amos Greenway, while the rest of us starve on the parish, you're mistook. I'm gonna shoot you for the damned rotten treacherous swine you are!"

Even then he might not have done it had not Amos stood there so exasperatingly calm. As it was, he swung the old gun into position and pulled the trigger. There was a flash, a muffled kind of explosion, a strong smell of gunpowder, and a cloud of blue smoke which hovered for a moment between the two men and then drifted outwards over the heads of the crowd and inwards across the workroom to the kitchen door, from which Julie, her tea forgotten, was fearfully peeping. As the smoke cleared, Amos could see Matt again, standing there holding out his scorched and bleeding hands, and the twisted broken thing which had been his gun lying at his feet.

"You'd best come inside," Amos said, reaching out an arm. "You, Bert, take his other side; the rest of you go home."

They helped Matt on to the bench by the worktable and Amos called to Julie to bring water and something for a bandage. Matt then showed his mettle. White-lipped, he said:

"We don't want no water, Amos; gunpowder's the best cleaner. I've put a pinch and sparked it off on many a wound afore now. Jest you tie me up. And you, Bert, get out and find me a drink of *some* sort, somewhere, for the love of God."

"Julie'll make you a cup of tea," Amos said.

Julie did; she also, remembering Matt's several kindnesses to her in the past, produced the big black bottle of the medicine which was so effective for easing her pains, and gave him, since he was a man, a double dose, which soon did its merciful work. Then the four drank tea together, even Amos drinking the strong, heavily sugared beverage gladly; and presently Bert took Matt home. It was generally agreed that nothing but a miracle had saved Amos and Matt and those nearest to them from death, mutilation, or blindness, and the jubilation was in no way mitigated by thoughts about quick death being preferable to slow death by starvation, which seemed to be the fate in store for many Waste dwellers just then.

CHAPTER 12

AS SOON AS HIS HANDS WERE PARTIALLY HEALED AND HE FELT
capable of carrying on the campaign Matt attempted to talk to
the Squire again; but Richard, wary perhaps of such attempts,
stayed in London the whole of that spring; so Matt drove into
Baildon again and was again kindly received and listened to
by Mr. Turnbull, who said, yes, he had received the papers
and, yes, he had noted what they said, and then mentioned that
he had taken on himself to advise Sir Richard and the commissioners to make some allotment, however small, to the
Waste dwellers.

"I could only *advise*, you know, because all that side of the
business was nothing at all to do with me; and because, except
for the two who had papers, none of you had even the shadow
of a legal claim. But I think I explained that before."

"Seem to me they took your advice, sir, and made some
allotment, twenty acres; but all to one man, Amos Greenway,
the cobbler. Now why should that be? Twenty acres divided
out among us all would hev done us well and satisfied everybody. Why all to one and nowt for the rest of us?"

"That is a question quite beyond my power to answer. Greenway has no claim that I know of, and the land granted him
came from Sir Richard's personal allotment of the Waste. Sir

Richard may have had some private reason—I understand that Greenway is a very industrious workman."

"So are we all in our way; and we are dependent on the Waste, which Amos ain't. He could cobble shoes anywhere."

"Yes, I admit that it seems very hard. But I have to tell you frankly that you have no redress, no hope of redress. The distribution was done legally and justly and you would be best advised to accept it and to look about for some means of making a livelihood when the Waste is fenced, as it will be very soon."

A more discouraging interview could hardly be imagined, and Matt had to stiffen his courage to attempt the next one. He braced himself and early one evening walked up to the Manor again and asked, this time, to speak to Lady Shelmadine. He'd seen her about and rather admired her looks, her hair was pretty; and it was well known that she had been more than ordinary kind to the bailiff when he had his accident. A pretty woman, thought Matt—knowing nothing of the circumstances—might well have some influence on her husband, and a kind woman might be disposed to use that influence in the cause of right and justice. He was astonished at himself for not having thought of it before.

Linda received him kindly and listened to his story, which was more succinct and less full of rancour than she had expected when he began and she realised the reason for his visit. When he had finished she said gently, "I will, of course, *speak* to Sir Richard about you and the rest of them; I promise you that; and if I thought any persuasions of mine could have any effect..." She broke off, imagining exactly what the result of such pleadings would be. "It's Sir Richard's land," she said, "and if he has decided not to make any allotments, as it seems he has, I'm afraid that nothing I could say would change his mind."

"But you will *try*, my lady? Afore thass too late, if you don't mind my saying so."

"I'll write to him tomorrow. I'll put the case just as you have put it to me. But... I do beg of you, don't pin your faith on my efforts."

Seen close to, she was even prettier than he had thought, because her eyes were so soft and gentle-looking, in fact not unlike old Ripper's; and when she smiled, as she did when bidding him good night, she was very sweet-looking indeed. It was funny—Matt thought—that she should have so little faith in her powers of persuasion; he knew several lumpish women with faces like the hindquarters of a cart horse who got their own way with their menfolk every time. And it wasn't because "the gentry" were different; everybody knew that Lady Fennel ruled Ockley, and not by sweet smiles and saying "please." Them that smiled and said please—like poor old Julie Greenway—most often didn't get much, Matt reflected; and that brought him back to the hopeful hopelessness which had led him to go to the Manor. If this failed what else could they do? What'd become of them when their front doors opened on the highroad and their back doors on the fenced in Waste? What'd become of Shad's new donkey and his own old horse? You could pay for animals to be pastured, of course, but then to turn that necessary extra penny you'd have to work the poor beasts to death—and yourself too. My God, Matt thought, we are all in a mucky mess and that's the truth.

That evening, when Hadstock paid his routine visit and had said his piece, Linda mentioned Matt Ashpole's visit and its reason. "It really is dreadfully hard for them, and I do feel sorry; but of course there is nothing I can do. I can write, of course, but I can't alter something that has been done legally."

"No. All progress has to be made over somebody's dead body," Hadstock said.

"They won't *all die*, surely?"

"No, no, of course not. Don't look so horrified," said Hadstock, adding, just too late, "my lady." "I only meant," he went on, "that all change hurts somebody."

"You do think that enclosure *is* progress?"

"Beyond all doubt. The open field system was the right, the only one when men, even while they worked, had to be ready to beat off their enemies, human or . . . well, wolves, for example. Once those times were past it became a clog, preventing improvement, chaining the best man to the pace of the slowest. Enclosure was bound to come and it was bound to hurt somebody; but they'll adjust themselves, the Waste dwellers, I mean, and in the end, not yet, but eventually, more produce per acre will make food more plentiful, and cheaper, and the poor will benefit by that."

"And that will be a good thing. I speak feelingly," she explained, "because I know what it is to be poor. Enclosure was partly to blame for *that*. My father was a clergyman, quite unbelievably unworldly, so he took no care of his rights, and when Didsborough was enclosed he lost almost all his tithe and received nothing in exchange. So we were poor, but we were a very happy family." Her voice, though she did not know it, took on a wistful, nostalgic note.

"I'm glad of that. I mean, my lady, that a happy childhood is a wonderful, enviable thing, something that—if you don't have it—nothing that comes later can make up for. I missed it . . ."

"Were you poor?"

He laughed, briefly, harshly. "No, quite the reverse in fact." He looked her in the face and seemed to take a sudden decision. "Not to put too fine a point upon it, my lady, my father, like many others of his kind, was scrupulously careful to provide for his illegitimate children, of whom he had a great many."

"Oh, Hadstock," she said, using the surname in such a warm intimate way that it might well have been a term of affection, "I am sorry I asked. At least, I mean only that I am sorry if it made you tell me something you would rather not. Though, really, if you look at it sensibly, it doesn't . . . doesn't make any difference; not really, does it?"

"It depends who does the looking," he said bitterly. "They don't *think*, these fine gentlemen in search of an hour's diversion; or *if* they think, they believe their poisonous money can make amends for everything; bring the brat up in luxury, send it to school, make it an allowance, what more can be expected? All perfectly honourable; the stigma falls on the poor wretch who didn't ask to be born, should never have been born, or being born, should be drowned at birth."

"Oh, Hadstock, no. Don't say that. Surely life . . . to be alive . . ." Embarrassment at the situation which her simple question had brought about, and a desire to comfort the man, banished all discretion. "If you weren't alive," she said, "I should miss you very much. You've no idea how much I rely . . . and that reminds me of something I've wanted to ask you for a long time. You're so knowledgeable; can *you* tell me what there could possibly be in a locked trunk that could frighten a dog?"

The sudden change of subject seemed to leave Hadstock at a loss for a moment. Then he said, "Do you mean Simon, my lady?"

"I mean Simon, and the trunk belongs to Mr. Mundford; it contains things he wanted to store here." She told him about the morning when Simon had entered the spare room and how he had behaved. "That night," she said, "I locked the door.

But now every night when we go past—he sleeps in my room, you know—he behaves strangely. Sometimes he scratches at the door and sometimes he slinks past it as if he were frightened. And I . . . well, I know it sounds silly, just a locked trunk, but at night, alone in this part of the house . . . it gives me a creepy feeling. There's a strange smell too, even though we opened the window; it doesn't go away; I think it comes from the trunk."

"You're not suggesting . . ."

"Dead bodies?" She laughed rather uncertainly. "Oh no; I believe Annie and Polly did start up some tale—Annie was there that morning when Simon . . . No, this is a strange smell, but not altogether unpleasant."

"Do you mind if I go into the room and see and smell? I'll take the dog. Here, Simon, come along."

The dog raised his head and pricked his ears at the sound of his name but did not move from Linda's side.

"I will come too," she said, adding as they went from the room, "This is going to present a problem, I'm afraid, when the time comes for him to go home with you. But perhaps that won't be necessary, after all." Richard's moods were less virulent nowadays, she thought, and also there was a difference between this large, strong, potentially fierce dog and a small fawning spaniel; even Richard would see that. That Simon was capable of ferocity she had proved several times, and that made his behaviour with regard to the trunk the more remarkable and disconcerting.

As often before Simon ran down the corridor and scratched at the door, growling in his throat as though some enemy were within the room; but when Linda turned the key and opened the door he did not attempt to enter with them, but hung back, ceased growling, and took on a cowed air again.

Hadstock sniffed. Then he said in a relieved voice:

"Why, it's incense; that's all."

"Then how silly of me not to recognise it. Some churches . . ."

"This, I should say, is particularly strong and pure—the best, and very expensive. And if I may hazard a guess I should say that Mr. Mundford has impregnated some clothes with it, as a deterrent to moths."

"And why should Simon . . . ?"

Hadstock hesitated for a moment.

"It sounds a long guess, but it is feasible. Race memory. Where his parents come from all churches smell of incense;

and dogs are not allowed in church, are, in fact, kept out with shouts and blows. So a devoted dog, once a week, sees his master disappear into a place where he is not allowed, consequently he hates the place and the very smell of it. After many generations such a prejudice may be inborn and qualify to be called instinct."

"I suppose it could. That is the *only* explanation, isn't it. Oh, thank you, Hadstock, you have relieved my mind."

"What were you imagining?" Hadstock asked curiously.

"I don't know," she said slowly. "Something . . . well, evil, in some obscure way. Actually, to be honest, I never feel very comfortable in Mr. Mundford's presence."

"That may be a prejudice, too. All those old stories are bound to create an impression."

"What old stories? I never heard any in connexion with Mr. Mundford. Did you?"

"Oh, nothing specific. Just a generally bad reputation."

"In what way?"

"The usual way," Hadstock said. "Shall we lock this door again—for Simon's peace of mind?"

"If your theory is correct, the locked door and the scent within will only increase his prejudice."

"Clever as he is, will he know that the door is locked?"

"For *my* peace of mind, then, yes, please lock it."

When they reached the spot where Simon was lurking, Hadstock put out a hand and gave him a friendly clout.

"I'm ashamed of you," he said, "and so are all your ancestors."

"But they," Linda said, "are to blame for his behaviour again if your theory is correct."

Hadstock laughed. But as he followed her and the dog downstairs he said, serious again:

"If you feel nervous at night why don't you have some servants in this part of the house?"

"It would be so silly," she said. "Servants are so very nervous themselves, it would never do to allow them to suspect that I was nervous too. Besides, at the moment, on account of the alterations, there are only three rooms, Mr. Mundford's, Sir Richard's, and mine in use in this part of the house."

"I see."

They came to a standstill at the foot of the stairs. Then Hadstock said, staring about as though taking his bearings:

"If your room is beyond the one we've just inspected it shouldn't be too far from the stable yard."

"It isn't. One of my windows looks on to the yard."

"Then, if you like, while you are alone here, I'll come and camp over the stable. There is a room, unused. Then, if at any time your imagination produced any fears, you could shout, or blow a whistle, and summon *my* imagination to produce the explanation. I assure you the arrangement would not inconvenience me at all."

"It is extremely kind of you to suggest it," she said. "I do thank you, very much. But of *course* I'm not really frightened, and I have the dog and the servants are not far away. I wouldn't dream of putting you to such inconvenience, for it would be that, whatever you may say."

"Very well; as you wish, my lady. There are times when it is a convenience for me to be on the spot and I had marked that room for my purpose. So if you ever look out and see a light rather late, you'll know."

After that the times when it was convenient for Hadstock to sleep over the stables appeared to recur very frequently. Seldom, for the rest of that winter, during Richard's absences did she look out and fail to find the faithful little light.

CHAPTER 13

DURING MARCH OF THAT YEAR LINDA RECEIVED THREE LET-
ters from Richard, all urging her to urge on the workmen as
he expected to find the alterations completed in April when he
returned. The letters also contained detailed instructions for the
placing of various articles of furniture, new carpets, mirrors,
and ornaments which began to arrive at Clevely in almost daily
consignments. The enclosure had gone as Richard had desired
and his income would be larger in the coming year; also, as
he wrote, in a moment of unusual expansion, his luck at cards
since Christmas had been phenomenal. (He did not mention
that shortly after his return to London he had again mentioned
to Alec Mundford the matter of luck, and that Alec had said,
"Well, as I said, I'm bored with it. I'll lend it to you and see
how you like it." He had bunched the tips of his tallowy fingers
and thumb together and lightly touched the back of Richard's
left hand, using his left, too. And that evening Richard's luck
had changed and had continued good.)

On the second day of April, Linda received another letter.
Richard wrote that his plans had changed; he and Alec were
going for a short visit to France, to a place called Loudun.
They would return in May and come direct to Clevely, bringing
company with them; two gentlemen and five ladies. "Now that

the house is habitable—or shortly to become so or there will
be something to be said—we can begin to entertain a little, at
least enough to leaven the lump of local company. These are
a lively crowd; you, my dear, will probably think them too
lively; but, as you are well aware by this time, I do not insist
upon your sharing my interests any more than I inquire too
closely into yours! So long as you have an eye to the material
comforts and needs of our guests you may abstain from their
company if you so desire and gather your primroses and catkins
in peace! I will advise you of the date of our arrival nearer the
time. . . ."

Linda read this letter with an emotion which it was not
written to evoke—a deep relief. Save for the finishing touches
the house *was* ready, that was a comforting thought; and so
was the plain implication that when the "lively company" arrived she would not be expected to participate in its activities.

Inevitably, as April passed, alternating days of warm sweet
promise with others of biting wind, and Richard's final letter
arrived, and then May came and at last the day of the arrival
dawned, Linda's relief gave way to a mounting anxiety. It was
the first time in all her life when she had been responsible for
a houseful of guests; she feared Richard's censure if anything
was unsatisfactory; she became timid of the guests, especially
the female ones. She knew Richard's taste in female company;
the pattern had been set long before her time by that Mrs.
Davison who had been the cause of one of the first quarrels
between old Sir Charles and his son. Richard favoured married
women, smart, sophisticated women who for some reason or
another had fallen from, or abandoned, the strictest standards
of "ladyhood." They were invariably past their first youth, not
too financially secure, widows, or married to men who were
merely shadowy figures in the background; but they were,
invariably, what was called "well bred"; and that meant that
they would know and notice if in any detail the housekeeping
and service at Clevely Manor should fall short of standard.
Quite humbly Linda admitted to herself that life at the Didsborough Rectory, in Cousin Maud's comfortable middle-class
establishment, and in the places where she had lived with Richard during their married life, had not equipped her to make a
good showing as the hostess of a country house.

So on first sight she was relieved, and at the same time,
being human, slightly annoyed, to find that all five ladies were
extremely young and what the French called "women of the

people." All were very pretty; well dressed, exquisite and even elegant in their equipment, but they were all of humble origin, and each pair of pretty, high-heeled feet was set on the bottom rung of the ladder which Angelina had scaled so successfully. On the first evening, looking at all the lustrous young eyes, the slim young waists, the rounded young bosoms, the full, painted young lips, and listening to the voices, frankly rustic or painfully genteel, Linda thought to herself, with the inward honesty which was at once her curse and her salvation, Here we have the makings of a very superior brothel and any minute now one of them is going to call me "Madam," which will put me in my place!

That notion, followed to its conclusion, brought dismay. Was it right to be so compliant? Suppose Sir Evelyn Fennel turned up at Ockley with five such guests; what would Lady Fennel say, do? What ought Lady Shelmadine to do?

Lady Shelmadine sat there, weakly, feebly glad that her guests were not more intimidating. They seemed, indeed, to be in awe of her; and this attitude was encouraged—almost deliberately, it seemed—by the behaviour of the male guests towards their hostess. They treated her with the most elaborate civility, as Alec Mundford had always done, and as Richard was doing. Both the men were "gentlemen"; one old and rather shabby, with a cynical face and—it was revealed—a cruel, witty tongue; the other was young, and foppish, not unlike Mr. Montague, who was, Linda was not surprised to learn, invited to make the tenth member of the party.

On the first evening, tired by travelling, everyone went to bed early. On the second, at about nine o'clock, Richard said, "We are going to play cards and shall be late. If you prefer to retire, my dear, we will excuse you."

"If you propose to be late you will need some refreshments. Shall I order them?"

"That would be as well. Have them brought here and tell the servants they can go to bed. We can wait upon ourselves."

The extension of the front of the house had resulted in more bedrooms, but still, in order to accommodate properly the ladies whom she had imagined would be critical, Linda had remained in the room which she had used during the alterations; and to it, having ordered cold food and wine and brandy, she retired. Hadstock's faithful little light still burned in the window above the stable. She had not seen him since Richard's return and probably would not see him as long as the visit lasted; looking at the light, she now wondered what explanation Hadstock had given for his change of sleeping place, or whether he had indeed given any; and also why he had not taken the opportunity to return to his cottage, the house now being full enough of company to reassure the most insanely nervous person.

And yet, to her, dismissed to bed like a child—for the outwardly considerate words which Richard had spoken were nothing less than dismissal from her own drawing room—the little light was obscurely a comfort; a recognition of her identity; proof that she mattered to *someone*. Upon that thought she slept.

She was awakened by Simon, who was moving about and growling that same low, stifled growl which he had emitted so often outside the door of Mr. Mundford's room. She roused herself and listened. Quiet movements in the next room, muffled by the thickness of the old walls, reassured her. She did not trouble to make a light, but spoke softly to the dog.

"Don't be silly, Simon. Come here and lie down. It is only Mr. Mundford going to bed."

Simon remained restless for a while, then at last flung himself down with a sigh. Linda returned to sleep.

The house guests slept late next morning. Linda breakfasted alone, interviewed Mrs. Hart, who, surly before the guests' arrival, had now cheered up under Richard's lavish praise of *her* arrangements, and then went into the garden, where the first irises of the year were showing colour. She stood admiring them, Simon by her side, when one of his sudden, defensive movements warned her that someone was approaching her from behind. She turned and saw one of "the girls" coming across the lawn from the house, walking rapidly. As the girl drew near, Linda made an effort to fix a name to this young body, this pretty face, and succeeded: this was Miss Smith, the one they called Rose, the one who, by just a trifle, was the youngest and prettiest of the lot. This morning her face was puffy— with sleep, Linda thought at first; then she noticed that in her clenched hand Rose held a sodden handkerchief.

She said, "Good morning, Miss Smith. Isn't it a beautiful morning."

"Lady Shelmadine, can I speak to you for a minute?"

"But of course."

"Privately," the girl said, looking back at the house.

"We'll go through here," Linda said, and walked towards

an opening in the thick yew hedge which backed the border where the irises grew. Another yew hedge grew on the opposite side of a wide grass path, and at the end of the path a third hedge made an enclosure in which stood a sundial and a stone bench. At this time of day, at this season, the sun fell on the bench and the yew hedges shielded it from the wind; it had seemed the perfect place to sit, Linda had thought. But it was, she discovered, melancholy. The dark hedges were gloomy even in sunshine, and the sundial, with its trite little motto, "It is later than you think," was not cheerful company.

They sat down together on the sun-warmed stone, and after a moment's silence Linda said:

"Now, what did you want to ask me?"

"It's a favour. I want you to lend me—the coach fare back to London. I know it's a lot to ask—in the circumstances I mean—but I gotta go and I can't very well pad the hoof like this . . ." She indicated her flimsy, high-heeled shoes, her long, wide silken skirts.

"Of course not," Linda agreed, "why should you? I'm sure my husband will . . ."

"Oh!" said Rose, her hand flying to her mouth. "I got off on the wrong foot, as usual, but I did say *privately*, didn't I? I meant just between you and me, my lady, nobody else to know till I was safely away. Lend it to me, will you? I swear I'll pay you back."

"That isn't what bothers me. I'd give it to you . . . but to tell you the truth, I haven't more than a few shillings."

She attempted to explain this statement, which was true. Richard allowed her money for current expenses, enough and no more. The allowance for April was spent, and now it was May and he was home and she would have no more money until he went away and left her in charge again. She had not, had never had, the price of the coach fare to London for her own; Richard housed and clothed and fed her, what more did she need?

The attempt to explain was drowned by Rose's bursting into sobs, noisy, uncontrolled as a child's with a broken knee. She appeared to be in such distress that Linda's mind flitted from the financial to the emotional problem; placing her hand on the girl's smooth, silken knees, she said:

"What is the matter? Is someone ill? I'll think of some way . . . if only you'll hush and let me think. Why can't you tell my husband and ask him for the money?"

Rose hushed, drew a quavering breath, let it out in a final sob, and began to talk.

"I'm daft," she said, "that's what's a matter with me. It all sounded lovely, a 'oliday in the country and nothing to it but the usual. I ain't all that particular don't I shouldn't be. . . . You must of seen through us, my lady; you know what we are, shut your eyes as you may. Even so, even if it was what it looked like, it was a rotten crying shame. I knew that the first night, but me . . . All right, I'm daft . . . and I'm scared. I'm too scared to go on with it, promise what they may. I know the difference between right and wrong; I *do* wrong . . . I know that, but a natural sort of wrong, if you can understand that, my lady. This is different . . . nothing else ever scared me. Now I'm scared and I've gotta get away without their knowing. They'd be that angry! And I wouldn't put it past that Mundford to be sitting there in his bedroom and hearing every word I'm saying now. . . ."

And deep down, far under the foundations of reason and experience, something in Linda's mind popped up its head and said distinctly, "Neither would I!" And that was, of course, absolutely sheer nonsense.

"That is nonsense," she said aloud. "No one could possibly hear from such a distance; and no one could approach us and listen. My dog would give warning. What is it that has frightened you?"

The girl lifted her head and looked at Linda; her eyes were very beautiful, a clear hazel in colour, with a tinge of blue in their whites, and with thick, rather short black lashes.

"No use asking me that. I took me oath not to say. I dussent say, and if I did you wouldn't believe me. I don't want to talk about it, I just want to get out. If you can't lend me the money I'll chance me luck and just go. I've gotta foot it into this place—Baildon, ain't it?—to get the coach anyway."

"On some days the coach runs through Nettleton, which is much nearer."

"Less hope this is one of them days. I can get into the park without goin' back to the 'ouse, can't I? Then I'm off. Goodbye, your ladyship."

She jumped to her feet, gathered up a handful of her skirts in either hand, displaying slim ankles and the promise of well-turned calves, and set off along the path, running lightly, with something of a swallow's swoop in her gait. Linda looked after her for a moment and then dropped her head into her hands.

It was possible to ignore or discount everything the girl had said except one thing. "You must of seen through us . . . you know what we are." She had seen, on the first evening; she had known all along. And she had done nothing, said nothing, had accepted the situation with a meekness which she now saw was shameful, despicable. "You must of seen through us . . ." That had been said to her by a pretty little London prostitute— and four others were there, under what was technically *her* roof, and they were doubtless thinking the same thing . . . and so were Mundford and Montague and old Dunhill and young Saxstead. She saw suddenly the depths of the abyss into which Richard had thrust her, one small push following another all through these years. . . .

Suddenly she stood up and began to walk towards the house.

Richard and Alec Mundford were in the breakfast room. The older man had before him a plate well filled with bacon and grilled kidneys and was making a hearty breakfast, though his pallor was almost phosphorescent; Richard was sipping coffee. His hands were unsteady and so was his head, she had seen that convulsive, only just perceptible tremor shake it on many mornings, in many places.

She greeted neither of them, from the doorway she said:

"Richard, I want to speak to you—alone."

"Oh, do you? Well, I don't want to be spoken to in that tone of voice," Richard said, instantly turning nasty. "If you can be civil, you may say anything you wish to say in Alec's presence."

"Come, come," said Mr. Mundford, balancing food on his fork and speaking good-humouredly, "why involve me? If every other room in the house is occupied, I shall be finished in about five minutes and will go into the garden."

What was the power behind those words, strong enough to make Richard, furious as he was, set down his coffee cup and get up and open the door that led into the little sitting room which she used when she was alone, saying as he did so:

"No, no, finish your breakfast in comfort."

Inside the room he faced her. "Well, what is it?" And she found that the words which had been ready in her mouth only two minutes ago were now not easily spoken; she could have said them when she walked into the breakfast room, now they sounded melodramatic. But that was the kind of hampering, undermining thought which had allowed her to be brought to this pass. This time she would speak, no matter how the words sounded, no matter how much Richard was enraged.

"It's this. Either those women must leave this house, or I do!"

Richard began to laugh, and even at that moment she observed that there was nothing false or forced about his mirth; he laughed as heartily, as almost painfully, as a normal man would laugh at some remark of exquisite humour. He sat down, laughing, in a chair and, laughing, put up a hand to steady his tremulous head. . . . It was quite a moment before he could speak.

"What an alternative," he said. "Then they must go, must they not? They can go back to Angelina's, but you, where would you go?" When she did not immediately answer, he went on, "It is difficult to choose, is it not? You have so many friends! And of course there is always the Rectory at Didsborough—what difference would one more mouth make amongst so many? I'm sure your holy brother would welcome you heartily, if only to help wipe the nine little noses; it is nine, or have I lost count?"

"Where I go," she said, with some wonder that her voice should sound so clear and steady, "is not important. What I am telling you is that it is impossible for me to remain here with those young women. Their presence puts me in a hideous, false position; if you have a glimmer of reason left you must see that."

"Could it be that at this late hour you are becoming jealous, Lady Shelmadine?"

"I have no reason, you should know that! Where you are concerned, Richard, nobody could take anything from me because I have nothing. But that only you and I know. In the eyes of the world, in the eyes of the young women themselves I look like a compliant, conniving wife, nothing more nor less than a procuress. And that I cannot, will not bear."

"It *is* a pity that there are no footlights," Richard said. "Mistress Shelmadine in her celebrated part, *The Wronged Wife*! I have invited, into my own house, four gentlemen of my acquaintance and a few young women to keep them company. I have not, you may have noticed, attempted to thrust them into the society of the fat Suffolk squires and their wives, whom you regard so highly, nor have I demanded that you should show them more than the merest civility. So what all the to-do is about I completely fail to see."

And so, by that time, alas, did a considerable part of Linda's own mind. The impulse which had brought her in from the garden, which had seemed so strong and right and valid, had dwindled now, seemed, in the light of Richard's words, quite ridiculous. Mentally she fingered Rose's words again, "You must of seen through us, you know what we are," but they had lost their accusation; all she could think was that she had not Rose's courage. Rose had run off, penniless . . . but then, she had her looks, and her lack of standards, and a destination.

"In any case, it is only until Monday," Richard said, with a return to his smooth, affable manner. "After that the sanctity of the rooftree will be restored . . . though we shall be back," he added.

Better perhaps to wait. In the interval lay by some money; find a post . . . housekeeper, governess. "Your name? You have references?" Dear God, where could one turn?

"And now, if that little bout of hysteria has cleared the air," said Richard, rising, "I should be very glad if you would ask Mrs. Hart to tell the cook that the kidneys she serves are fit only for cannibals. How Alec could stomach them I *do* not know, it made me feel sick to watch. In fact"—his voice took on a note of mock approval—"on the whole, my dear, your interruption was not untimely." He strolled back to the breakfast room, leaving her to the bitterness of one more defeat. Afterwards, in the calm of emotional exhaustion, there was plenty of time to remember the other things which Rose had said, and to wonder.

On the morning after the party had left—even the liveliest of the young women now quiet and jaded—Linda saw that the door of Mr. Mundford's room had been left open. The black trunk had gone from the place where it had stood so long. Yet it had not been amongst the luggage which the travellers had taken with them, she was sure of that. She added this new mystery to the things which she wished to talk over with Hadstock. He did not come to the house on the day of the departure, presumably Richard had given enough instructions to last out that day; but on the evening of Tuesday he presented himself as usual, and as usual began his mechanical report.

"Oh, leave that," Linda said, "we both know that it means nothing. There are so many things I want to consult you about. I know you'll think I'm silly again—like with the incense— but they are things that worry me, and I have no one else to

tell. So please sit down and listen, and then tell me I'm silly—
even that will be some relief."

Hadstock sat down and regarded her gravely.

"I don't think your fears—they are fears, aren't they?—are
silly at all, my lady."

"Fears? That sounds so very definite. Yet one of those girls
ran away. She said she was scared. And Simon was scared—
the trunk has gone, by the way. And where? Not to London.
I know, because there was such confusion, so many people
shouting and giving contradictory orders and the young women
seemed half asleep, so I went and overlooked the loading."

"Oh yes," Hadstock said. His voice was carefully noncom-
mittal but her conscience—sensitive at this point—thought that
it detected astonishment and disapproval. No doubt Hadstock
had "seen through" the female guests and wondered that she
should tolerate them. And beyond Hadstock there was the village, and beyond that the dinner tables of the neighbours: gossip, speculation; condemnation. She looked down at her hands
for a moment while the hot blush rose and subsided, then she
raised her eyes and looked at Hadstock almost defiantly.

"It's a mystery, isn't it—the disappearance of the trunk, I
mean."

He looked at her steadily, assessingly before he spoke.

"If I told you what I think, what I suspect, you would hardly
believe me. And I might frighten you, which I wouldn't do for
anything in the world. Yet if I leave it unsaid and this goes
on—and on—I leave you in an intolerable situation. I'm in
an intolerable situation myself. . . ."

"I think I should believe almost anything you said, Hadstock
. . . and just to show that somebody else suspected . . . well,
incredible things, would be a comfort in a way. There was that
girl who ran away. She asked me to lend her the coach fare; I
had no money at the time, so she just went off, on foot. . . .
Nobody mentioned her, asked about her, commented on her
absence. That sounds unbelievable, does it not? You see . . ."
She hesitated; in all these years she had never confided in
anyone, never voiced a complaint about Richard, and on the
surface of her mind floated the thought that it was strange to
begin now, to Richard's own bailiff. But below the surface
there were depths. She knew that Hadstock was knowledgeable,
trustworthy, and on her side. And below that again, other depths;
the little lighted window over the stable . . . his own remark,
still audible, that he would not frighten her for anything in the

world. "You see, I did make a protest, and he said that he had simply invited his friends to stay and had provided the young women for company. It sounded... well, somehow, so plausible when he said it, and yet when Rose—that was her name— just disappeared, nobody took any notice. And for me, that put another face on the matter... that and the trunk's disappearance. If I told you what was in *my* mind, Hadstock, you'd hardly believe *me*!"

"And what have you in mind?"

"I think," she said slowly, "that in some peculiar way it is all—Mr. Mundford, the girls, the trunk, and everything— somehow connected with that place—the temple of Mithras. I think Mr. Mundford, absurd as it sounds, here in the eighteenth century, worships Mithras and I think the girls were brought here to act as... priestesses or something. The one who ran away said to me, 'I *do* wrong, I know that, but a natural sort of wrong; this is different.' Those were her very words. I've thought and thought about them, and a few other things, and that is the only conclusion I can come to."

She ended on an apologetic note, half expecting Hadstock to laugh, half hoping that he would produce some rational explanation of it all, as he had done when consulted about Simon's behaviour over the trunk. When at last he spoke his words fell heavily upon her hopes of comfort.

"I think you're still a bit short of the mark," he said. "My lady, does the name Medmenham mean anything to you?"

"Medmenham? I don't think... no, nothing. Why?"

"It is a place in Buckinghamshire," Hadstock said. "And there, only forty years ago, in this enlightened eighteenth century, a little group of gentlemen used to worship the Devil. That is known fact. The moving spirit of the group was a Sir Francis Dashwood, and they used to call themselves the Franciscans and dress up as monks of that order, the more perversely to indulge in every kind of vice and debauch. It sounds like nonsense, doesn't it, childish, nasty nonsense... but there was more in it. After all, a belief in God presupposes a belief in the Devil, doesn't it? There is Biblical evidence; if you believe that Christ said, "Love your enemies," you should also believe that He said, "Get thee hence, Satan." Anyway, one of these Franciscans—they also called themselves the Hell Fire Club— a man named Baker, went mad and died, raving, in the same lodginghouse where a man who had some talent at versemaking lived. Baker's ravings, just as they emerged, but shaped into rhyme, went into a broadsheet which had a tremendous sale in London in 1760. There was a great scandal and the Hell Fire Club broke up the next year. Most of the members died violently, or untimely. But Alec Mundford lived on . . . just as Baker said was promised him. I should remind you, my lady," said Hadstock with a slight smile, "that the broadsheet was sheer doggerel. In its own words, the promise to Mr. Mundford was:

Thou shalt live on and wondrous luck shall know,
Until of life and luck thou hast enow!
When thou art weary, thou shalt make thy plea
In the right hour and I will come for thee!

And I know it sounds crazy and farfetched to the point of fantasy; but, like you, I've thought and thought about it and I have come to believe . . ."

"What, Hadstock?"

"That Mr. Mundford is attempting to re-form, here, the Hell Fire Club. I think that trunk contained clothes—vestments— probably those same monks' costumes from Medmenham, and the set of church plates. And I think you were right about the place. They must have stumbled upon the other entrance."

"From the cellars," Linda said. "You remember Farrow said it would be somewhere under the house! Oh, and I remember now . . . Woods, do you remember the butler named Woods? On Mr. Mundford's very first visit, in the middle of the night, Woods roused the house saying there was someone in the cellar. He'd been out very late and came in and heard voices or saw a light or something. They—Mr. Mundford and my husband— couldn't be found for a moment, then they appeared, and my husband was very angry. He said he had taken Mr. Mundford down to choose a bottle of wine and that Woods was drunk to be making such a fuss. Woods left soon after. It's funny, isn't it, how everything seems to fit in, and yet all adds up to something so ridiculous!"

"There's a side to it that is not ridiculous, my lady," Hadstock said. "It's a free country . . . nobody *minds* what they do except in so far as it involves . . . It's you I mind for, my lady."

"Well, of course," she said, making an effort to be reasonable, "I am not much involved. Richard would never . . ." She broke off as she realised that she had referred in this informal way to Richard. "And we have no proof, have we?" she went on hastily.

"And if we had, there's very little we could do." Hadstock's voice was suddenly heavy. "At least, you, my lady. . . . Would it not be possible for you to make a prolonged visit somewhere until this has blown over, whatever it is?"

He looked so troubled that she said, more brightly:

"Why, yes, of course, I could always do that. But I think I have been making a fuss about nothing. It's strange how bothersome, puzzling things grow less when one talks them over, isn't it? I *am* so glad I can talk to you."

"Well, I'm there to be talked to, or called upon, if ever there is anything I can *do*. In fact, I'm entirely at your service, my lady." He brought out the last sentence with a mocking imitation of a fine gentleman's formal utterance of the phrase.

"I know. And I'm very grateful," Linda said.

PART IV

NIGHT OF A NECROMANCER

CHAPTER 14

ONCE AGAIN MATT ASHPOLE HAD BEEN FORESIGHTED. SO FAR all his plans and schemes had gone wrong but it was difficult to see what could go wrong with this one. He'd obtained several old pine trees and a two-handled saw and, having worked at it with his wife and those of his children still at home just long enough to demonstrate the management of the tool, had set them to saw five-foot lengths and then split them into fencing stakes. There'd been a slight difficulty with Mrs. Ashpole, who protested that it was not woman's work.

"Don't be a dunderhead," Matt said, "stand to reason, don't it, I can't stand here a-sawing—that is unless you'd care to take owd Gyp and knock up a living for us. We gotta eat till them stakes are ready and sold." Mrs. Ashpole, who was as fond of her food as any woman, saw the force of that argument and later used it herself. As soon as Matt had gone off in the cart, she abandoned her end of the saw, saying, "Now you boys get on; stand to reason I can't stand here a-sawing—that is unless one of you'd care to make a stew. We gotta eat!" She did more cooking in the next few weeks than she had done in the previous two years. She also kept the boys at work by the simple expedient of setting so much work to be done before food was served. The pile of stakes grew steadily.

There would soon be a brisk demand for them.

The commissioners had borne in mind the European situation; England and France were at war, the island kingdom must feed itself or go hungry; not even the enclosure of Clevely must be allowed to reduce, by one grain, the year's harvest. A greater yield next year must be arranged for in every possible way. So they had ruled that the Waste should be fenced by the end of May—which would give its new owners a chance to plough it if they intended to try cultivation, or to gather a hay crop; and Old Tom and Layer were to be fenced by the end of November. Any land remaining unfenced by that date was forfeited. As Mr. Sawston truly said, "Any man who can't afford to fence after harvest must be a very inefficient farmer and should not have land at all."

By the end of May the fences were up, and on some claims the ploughs were out. The desperate situation which Matt had foreseen, when the Waste cottages lay landless between the fence and the highroad, had come about. There were other Waste dwellers, more blindly optimistic, or too stupidly incredulous, who seemed to be taken by surprise.

Mrs. Palfrey was one of these. Spitty, her husband, was no good, he was frail in body and feeble in mind, the last to get a job when seasonal labour was in demand, the first to lose it. Mrs. Palfrey had kept food in the many mouths of her large family by growing potatoes, rearing a pig on the potato peelings, and keeping a few geese and hens. Nine pregnancies and several miscarriages had not interfered with her simple yearly routine. She had always begun to plant her potatoes on Good Friday; and on that date, in 1797, she planted them as usual, despite the warnings of more farsighted persons who told her she would never gather the crop. All through her married life she had done her best, and that included planting potatoes; her dim mind could not visualise a future which did not include a potato crop.

Three weeks later she stood by the brand-new fence which stood within arm's length of her hovel door and watched the ploughshare turn out the potatoes, "All sprouted beautiful," as she said. She shed no tears, she had learned the futility of them in the first four years of her life; she stood and watched with an expression of dumb animal hopelessness on her face and then went in and shut the door. She had four geese and six hens in the precarious shelter of Matt Juby's half acre; she had enough potatoes to last until late July. "There'll be no taters this year; we can't live athout taters," she said to herself over and over again. Two more of the children must get work; Emmeline, aged nine, who, like Spitty, was not quite bright; and Tommy, seven. And she herself must leave the younger ones to Spitty's care and go out to work. In June she made hay at Wood Farm and earned eight shillings; in July she picked stones from a section of the newly ploughed Waste; twopence a bushel they paid her and she earned fifteen shillings. The one hundred and seventy bushels of stones did, as she said, "drag you down a bit"; but by August she knew that the down dragging was not all due to the stones. She was pregnant again. Soon she would be unemployable since lithe, active women were ten a penny. In the old days she could go out and dig a few potatoes, and catch her breath and lean on the spade, her own woman, on her own plot; now there'd be nothing for it but to starve or go on the parish! Nobody looking at her, gaunt, despairing, ragged, dirty creature as she was, would have credited her with any pride; yet she had been proud, proud of the fact that though they had been hungry, and cold, and barefooted, they'd never yet been on the parish. . . .

Matt Juby had enclosed his half acre as soon as he had paid the one shilling and sixpence which was his share of the commissioners' expenses. He hacked into the thinnest possible slivers a wooden bedstead, the back door of his hovel, a ladder whose staves had rotted, and the body of an old wheel-less wagon which Matt Ashpole bought for a shilling, dragged home, and sold for half a crown. Each stake was linked to its neighbour by a piece of string, a length of knotted rag, or some twisted reeds and rushes. "That don't look a mucher, but there 'tis, thass fenced, and nobody can say it ain't," Matt Juby said. Few were in a position to criticise the fencing, for most people were begging Juby to house some bit of livestock or other, "just till we know where we are." Bert Sadler, the other fortunate legal possessor of a half acre, had put it all down to potatoes immediately, foreseeing a time when potatoes would be in demand amongst his neighbours. Matt Juby "took lodgers." The rickety fence established his claim and satisfied—apparently—the letter of the law, but it did not act as a retaining wall, so anybody who struck a bargain with Juby and gained a lodging for his beast or bird must do a bit of fencing on his own account. Mrs. Palfrey's four geese and six hens penned in a corner surrounded by a fence made of the stouter sticks of a faggot gathered by Emmeline and Tommy from the edge of Layer Wood; the thinner sticks were woven in and out and formed a kind of basketwork. But geese eat a great deal of grass and very soon the patch was bare and then, in the struggle for the possession of the boiled potato peelings and "gleanings" which Mrs. Palfrey brought for the hens, the geese always won; so the hens starved and laid no eggs and it was only reasonable to kill them off one by one while there was flesh on their bones. Matt Juby had bargained for one goose as rent for the corner, so the Palfreys ate three geese and six scrawny hens in nine weeks and then settled down to an unvaried diet of potatoes again.

For a while Shad's donkey also lodged with Matt Juby, not fenced in, but attached to a stake which allowed him only a limited amount of grazing, for which Shad paid sixpence a week. The donkey did not realise how privileged he was; he could only remember that when he was free on the Waste he stayed as near as possible to a certain black door which would often open and a woman would come out and give him a crust, or an apple core. Five times in four weeks he managed to grub up his stake, trot to the flimsy fence, lean against it, and get back to the door where three times he received a titbit and twice—complaints having been made—a clout on the rump. At the end of the month Juby said to Shad, "Sixpence a week or no sixpence a week, I can't afford to house that donkey. He might hev my fence down one time when they come to inspect and then where would I be?"

So then Shad's donkey went to join Matt Ashpole's horse, which was staked out on the narrow grass verge of the road which ran through Nettleton to Baildon. Juby—on the whole ungratefully considering that Matt had got him the wagon cheap—had refused to house the horse, so Matt had taken to the roadside, where the animal, eating steadily, was moving every day farther and farther from his owner's house. "He'll end in Baildon, so any time I want to drive in there I'll hetta walk there first to fetch him," Matt said.

Amos had also been faced with the fencing problem. His twenty acres, that unaccountable gift from Heaven, did not lie near his house at all. About five acres of it consisted of the tip of the common pasture, where it ran up to the Stone Bridge, the other fifteen acres were on the Waste just across the river.

It was all moist, soggy ground, the grass freely interspersed with clumps of reeds, and though it afforded pasture of a kind it was useless for cultivation. As an allotment made to someone who was not a proprietor and had no rights, it did not carry with it the demand for a share of the expenses, but it must be fenced by the end of May and Amos had no money.

"S'pose I fence her for you, Amos," Matt Ashpole said, grasping out to catch another slippery opportunity. "S'pose I fence her, real good and proper, and for payment take pasture for my owd hoss for—well, less say five year. End of that time do I still *hev* a hoss I'll start to pay you sixpence a week—regular. Thass a fair offer, Amos."

"A fair offer," Amos repeated. "But I dunno . . . that stick in my mind that God didn't bring all this about jest to give your old horse a home. There's purpose behind all this and I've gotta puzzle it out."

"What d'you mean, a purpose?"

"A purpose. The will of God. There I am, my chapel burnt down and twenty acres of land I can't afford to fence. That don't make sense to me, but there must be some purpose there, part of the eternal plan. Seems to me, if I could sell the land, then I could build a chapel . . ."

"And who the hell'd buy that mucky marshy bit?" Matt demanded. "There's Martha Bowyer, she can't afford to fence what her owd man left, either he didn't hev no cash money or he hid it where she can't find it; hers is good land and that ain't snapped up yet. Fact is, Amos, all about here, just this time, them thass got cash got land as well and folks like me that is land-hungry is money-hungry too. Nobody'd bid for your bit; you'd do best to let me fence it like I said."

"Well, I 'on't refuse right away, Matt, but I gotta give God a chance. Heving all eternity, He move a bit slow, but I reckon everything'll work out afore the end of May . . ."

Apart from mentioning here and there that he had a bit of land for sale, Amos did not exert himself. He was busy; with hay time and harvest approaching there was a good deal of harness to repair; and the light evenings brought a spate of outdoor meetings in villages which had no chapels. Amos attended as many of these as he could, and preached at several, and when he thought about the land which must be fenced or forfeited before the end of May he reminded himself that the Lord would provide.

He was coming home from an outdoor meeting, a very well-attended and successful one, on a Saturday evening when May had only ten more days to run, when he overtook Danny Fuller, walking rather wearily towards Clevely.

The Fullers had left the village in March, that much Amos knew, so he was surprised to see Danny, so late, in the dusk, going that way.

"Hullo, Danny," he said as he drew level.

"Oh, hullo, Amos," Danny said. There was a slight constraint. It was, Danny remembered, a year ago this very day since he'd set off with Damask to take the way through Layer Wood to Muchanger—it seemed hundreds of years; so much had happened—and he'd never really come face to face with Amos since. And Amos was remembering that Danny was a backslider, which was, in a way, worse than being a heathen. Heathen didn't know what they missed, backsliders did and scorned it. Still . . . raking in his mind, Amos turned out the fact that Danny had done the right thing by Sally Ashpole . . . and then Julie had said . . . and there was Damask . . . His mind shot away from the thought of Damask, all wrong, all wrong somehow; he'd argued and rebuked every time he saw her. It was no use dwelling on your failures. . . .

"How're you faring, Danny? I misremember for the moment where you went and set up."

"We went to Baildon, in the Friargate. Handy for me. I got a job with Mr. Thurlow Lamb, the auctioneer."

"Did you so? And your mother? Well, I hope?"

"She's all right, in health, I mean. Still pining. Houses seem to mean a lot to women. She never got over being uprooted."

That was the explanation that he and Sally gave one another for Mrs. Fuller's decline in energy and efficiency. Danny could remember the time when, at every turn, his mother would mention, either as a threat or a promise, what she could do with a little shop in Baildon. Now she had the little shop and took no interest in it. Her cooking had deteriorated and every time the bell rang she'd say, "Oh, bother that bell," or, "You go, Sally." And she was always harking back. "Just about now that apple tree is in full blow . . . I reckon them lilacs smell sweet this morning."

Danny thrust the uncomfortable thought away and said more briskly:

"You live on the Waste, Amos, you can tell me. Did Fred Clopton plough his piece or leave it for grass?"

"I never noticed."

"Oh well, I can but ask. I never did like Fred and I used to show it, like a fool, and I daresay there'll be a bit of humble pie to swallow; but I reckoned he might hire me ten or twelve acres. I don't know who else to ask."

"What do you want it for?"

"I held on to my best beasts when we quitted, but it's been the devil's own job finding them pasture, everybody ploughing up on account of the corn prices. Four moves they've had in the last seven weeks. Maybe I was daft to try to keep them— but I had in mind that I might one day hire some land again, or find a bit cheap . . ." He laughed derisively.

"I got twenty acres—I mean nineteen—Danny, that I aim to sell. 'Tain't fenced, and 'tain't very good. Maybe you know it." He described its position. "I'd take a pound an acre for it."

Danny stood still in the road.

"I could manage that! My God, Amos, that's wonderful!"

"Now there's no need to be taking the Lord's name in vain, Danny. You'd hev to fence it, and be quick. But Matt Ashpole'd do it for you, and cheap, too, if you'd let his old horse run along with your beasts."

"That'd be wonderful," Danny said.

"What is more," said Amos, with growing eagerness, "if you keep your beasts there all winter you'll want a shed. I'll help with your building if you'll help with mine."

"Why, what are you building, Amos?"

"A chapel of course! Thass worked out wonderful. Them that trust in the Lord shall never be confounded; no truer word was ever writ."

Nineteen pounds to spend on timer, and a far better site than the old one, stuck away there behind Shipton's barn. The new chapel would be very conspicuous; he'd have some big notices outside it, so that those who could read could read out for those who could not such edifying remarks as, THE WAGES OF SIN IS DEATH; and on Sunday evenings when the men and boys gathered to lounge on the Stone Bridge and gossip and spit into the water, the sound of the good hymns and prayers would rise up and reach them.

Danny was dreaming too. He'd heard about the wonderful things that were being done with drains up in the fens near Ely; maybe he could drain his piece, grow better pasture, rear more beasts, somehow or other get into farming again.

They walked along for quite a distance without speaking

again. Once Amos did open his mouth to say, "All things work together for good for them that love God," and that he did not say the words aloud was in no sense due to doubt of their truth, it was because he remembered that this scheme was going to benefit Matt Ashpole, and his horse, Danny Fuller and his bullocks. . . .

Danny's nineteen-acre plot, now known by the name which it was to bear for many years—Cobbler's Corner—was fenced by the end of May and his bullocks and Matt's horse installed. Matt, owning only limited human sight, had no idea that his original scheme for ensuring his horse a home had seemed to fail, had gone underground, and then burrowed its way to open triumph again, so he regarded the whole transaction of the fencing and Danny's return as a piece of lucky business. He was quite willing, therefore, to hang about Baildon Market each Wednesday and Saturday and wait until the auctioneer's office closed and then give Danny a lift to Clevely and on Saturday nights he also provided what he called a "shake-down," so that Danny would stay over and spend Sunday with the bullocks. By late June the shed which was to shelter the beasts through the winter was under construction, and so was Amos' chapel; the two men helped one another with the planting of their corner posts, and Matt helped with the hauling of the timber. There was marked amity.

On Wednesdays, Danny had to walk back to Baildon after his evening's labour and the exertion, stripping the flesh from his bones, brought out the marked resemblance to his father, causing Mrs. Fuller to fret a little. Lethargic as she had become in other ways, she always stayed up on Wednesdays to serve him a late hot meal. One Wednesday, seeing him off to the market, she said, "You'll be going to Clevely, I s'pose?" and then added one of her wistful remarks, "I reckon that pink rose by the parlour window'll be all in bloom now. I planted that the year afore you was born."

That evening Danny left off work while there was still light in the sky, crossed the highroad, and entered Berry Lane. He intended to ask the new tenant of the house to allow him, as a favour, to gather half a dozen of the pink roses. To his surprise the house still stood empty, the garden thick with a summer's unchecked weeds, the nettles beginning to invade the little yard. The door of the byre that had been the kitchen was open and Danny could see the ill-fated manger and rack.

He pushed his way to the front of the house and gathered

a big bunch of the sweet pink roses and then walked rapidly through the dusk towards Baildon. But on the Waste he stopped and had a word with Matt Ashpole, who would know, if anyone did, why the house was standing empty. Matt knew. The tenant who had hired the holding was building a new house.

"The land, you see, Danny, when they shuffled it about, was all in a piece down by the Lower Road, so he reckoned it best to live there. He's a warmish chap, Grigg his name is, son to old Grigg, the biggest butcher in Bywater, so he could afford to build like. Come in, boy. Hev a bit of a set down and a sup of my brew. I've took to making me own in these hard times, ain't got it right yet, but it's a drink."

"No, thanks," Danny said. "I reckon ... No, too late to-night. Mother will sit up and she'd fret. On the other hand, if I wait till Saturday, somebody might go and snap it up."

"Whass bothering you, boy?"

"That house. I'd like to see Mr. Hadstock."

"About hiring it again, you mean? Well, I wouldn't go rapping him up about that this time of night, might make him oiled. Tell you what, Danny, if you like I'll hev a word with him tomorrer morning. I got a errand up at the Manor as 'smatter of fact. He ain't a bad chap in hisself, apart from owd Seizer, I mean. I'll put in a word for you, and let you know Satterday."

Hadstock, who had always considered the Fuller family ill-done by, promised Matt that he would do what he could to arrange the tenancy; and that evening spoke to Linda about the matter. Matt had told a glib story, there was Mrs. Fuller, he said, "peaking and pining away, fretting for her owd home," and there was Danny, "killing hisself running backwards and forrards." Linda said it would be very nice for Mrs. Fuller to come back to Clevely. "I never did understand that business," she said. "In all other matters my husband went dead against old Sir Charles' arrangements, but he confirmed the Fullers' notice to quit. I thought it strange at the time. And of course he may object to their return."

"I wonder," Hadstock said. "Five pounds' rent is better than having the place empty until it rots. There've been no other applicants. And I hear that old Wellman is now intending to build a new house in the middle of his holding, others will too, as they can afford it. There won't be much demand for houses without land. I wonder ..."

"I think we're both thinking of the same thing," Linda said, smiling. "Just to write and say a *suitable tenant* has offered to rent the house. . . ."

"That *was* in my mind," said Hadstock, returning the smile.

"Let's try it," Linda said. There are relationships in which such a humble, harmless piece of connivance is more significant than a passionate embrace; theirs was one such.

Richard did not even trouble to reply to the letter which informed him that a tenant for a five-pound-a-year property had been found. Why should he? Why should he keep a bailiff if not to attend to just such trivialities? Besides, he had other things to think about. He was discovering how right Alec had been when he said that consistent good luck could be embarrassing and in the end tedious. He ignored the unpopularity which resulted, his touchy temper and perverse behaviour had rendered him unpopular before his luck changed; the trouble now was to find a game. At Angelina's the tables were either filled against him, or the players, after a game or two, made excuses and drifted away. He had to seek new places, find strangers to play with; and although he gloated over his winnings he found gambling boring nowadays, the very spirit of the game wilted when you knew, before you turned it over, that the card you had drawn would be the very one you wanted.

In Baildon, Mrs. Fuller returned to life as soon as a return to Clevely came under discussion. She took out the quilt with the true-lovers' knot pattern which she had made for Damask and never been able to bring herself to give to Sally and draped it over a screen at the back of the little shop. Every customer who entered for a twopenny pie or a pennyworth of gingerbread admired it; many asked if it was for sale. "I dunno," said Mrs. Fuller. "I made it special; thass not a pattern you see every day. I hung it there to brighten the place like." Soon people were asking, "S'pose it was for sale, what would you be asking for it?"

"Oh, I'd want five pounds for that one," said Mrs. Fuller.

Five pounds for a quilt! Over the teacups women asked one another, had such a price ever been heard of? But of course it was a very unusual pattern, and all silk, not a bit of cotton stuff in it. Finally Mrs. Thurlow Lamb, assiduously visiting a sick friend of slightly superior social status, saw one of Mrs. Fuller's quilts, ten years old, but as good as new, on the sickbed;

and the next day she went to the shop in the Friargate and bought the true-lovers' knots.

"So there you are, you can get a horse, Danny; stabling 'on't cost nothing back home, and you can ride in and out so long as you hev to and that'll o'ny be till we get on our feet again. Give me back my diary and my fowls," said Mrs. Fuller, "and we'll be on the mend again in no time. We'll live close for a bit and sell the best." She made that concession to fate, thinking of Steve's mother as she did so. "But not for long," she added stoutly. "I'll manage."

Just before the move Danny took two days' holiday and went to Clevely, where, aided by Matt Ashpole, Spitty Palfrey, Shad Jarvey, and one of the Gardiner boys, he whitewashed the house inside and out, and moved the rack and the manger into the now almost completed bullock shed on Cobbler's Corner. He noticed how easy it was to get people to work nowadays—the mere smell of a job brought all the Waste dwellers running. Oh, if only he could lay hands on some more land, arable land, any land...

By evening of the moving day Fuller's was, in all but one respect, itself again. The black dresser was back in its rightful place in the kitchen and the firelight was red on the sides of the pewter mugs which Mrs. Fuller had set Sally to polish. Mrs. Fuller was frying a pan of eggs and bacon, standing to do so within inches of the spot where Steve's body had swung from the turnip rack. That fact, as fact, she did not bear in mind, but other memories of Steve were there, newly poignant on account of the surroundings, so that her pleasure was dimmed and soured. Deliberately she turned away from them, scowling at the bought eggs as she turned them in the pan. The bacon she had cured herself, last autumn, taken into Baildon, and brought back again; *that* was all right, but *bought* eggs at Fuller's! She thought of fowls clucking around the back door, of brown eggs warm from the nest; she thought of bright yellow butter and pale yellow cheese. And she thought again of Steve, poor man, poor man; still she'd done her best for him, dead and alive, and fretting did nobody any good, it'd just weaken her for the long pull and the strong pull which lay ahead if they were to make a success of this new venture. Deliberately she left Steve to his rest and faced her labour. She'd manage....

In June, Mr. Turnbull came to bring Miss Parsons her quarterly allowance, as usual. It was his fourth visit since Miss

Greenway had been installed as companion and he had ceased to wonder at the improved appearance of the place and its owner. Miss Parsons indeed was coming quite plump and placid. Today she was making what looked like a bead purse—the girl was skilful in contriving little peaceful occupations for her; she seemed always to be busy with something nowadays.

As usual, he chatted a little; handed over the money and watched Miss Greenway put it in a drawer and fetch the ink and the quill stand. Miss Parsons signed the receipt with her usual flourish, though she muttered something about signing things being dangerous. She then resumed the beadwork.

"Oh dear," Damask said, "I'm afraid she has forgotten again. For the last three weeks she has been worrying about something and wanting me to send for you, but I knew you would be coming. May I offer you a glass of wine?"

"That would be very kind." A decanter and three fluted glasses stood on a table behind the chair in which Miss Parsons sat, and as she went towards it Damask paused and said, as though to an earnest child, "You are making it pretty!" The old lady looked up and smiled in a pleased way and the girl just touched her shoulder, an affectionate, approving pat. It was a pleasing little scene and the old lawyer smiled and then sighed. He could remember a very self-assured, domineering Amelia Caroline Parsons, and he thought it was sad the way age altered people, even their personalities. His own seventieth birthday was in sight! Still, of course, a man, a trained mind, disciplined to a profession...

He let the thought fall as Damask handed him, very prettily, one of the fluted glasses and at the same moment, as though to underline his mental comment about Miss Parsons' earlier self, the old lady said with much of her former vigour and decisiveness:

"I wish to make my will!"

Carrying the wineglass, he moved to a chair and sat down near her.

"You made a will, you know. Five years ago ... yes, just five years."

"Then I wish to make another."

That put Mr. Turnbull in a quandary. He could hardly look an old, respected client in the face and say what was in his mind: "Madam, you made a will when you were competent to do so; you are not now so competent." Instead he sipped his wine and murmured, "A most excellent Madeira," and in the moment so gained framed the next sentence.

"Five years is not long. With so recent a will I would hardly advise any changes."

The girl handed Miss Parsons her glass of wine and said soothingly, "There, you see, you *had* made one. So there's nothing to worry about."

Her glance met Mr. Turnbull's and he noticed, as Richard Shelmadine had done, the lack of the expected expression. The glance did not say, "Poor old thing!" or, "I manage her well, don't I?" Nothing. Yet the glance itself started a train of thought in the lawyer's mind. Of course, Miss Parsons wished to leave the girl a legacy, and that was reasonable enough. She deserved something. And even if, by the strictest legal standards, Miss Parsons was not in her right mind, she was, on the other hand, certainly not a lunatic and there was nothing in the least out of the way in her wishing to reward the devoted attention of one who had come into her life since the other will was made.

"I wish to make my will," Miss Parsons said.

"There is no need to make a new will, you know..." And, dear me, he thought, it would be easier if the young woman were not present.

"Everything to Damask," said Miss Parsons. "This is Damask. Damask Greenway, my only friend."

The girl set down her glass and said, "Dear, I asked you not to bother. Please don't bother." To the lawyer she said, "This is all very embarrassing for me. You talk to her." She walked away through the open french window into the garden.

Mr. Turnbull breathed more freely and began to make legal phrases in his mind. "... if still in my employ." That was it. How much? Well, feeble-minded people often lived to a great age and became very cantankerous. The girl might have an ordeal ahead of her... say five hundred pounds.

"I wish to make my will. Everything to Damask. To Damask Greenway, everything."

"Yes, yes, I heard you. I think that you would be hasty and unwise. After all, she might leave you, get married, or... or leave for some other reason..."

"She would *not*. She promised. She promised and I promised..." She jumped to her feet, spilling the beads, which fell in a little tinkling shower. "Plenty of lawyers," she cried in a rising voice, "about, I mean, plenty of lawyers about. My money, all my money and my will. I wish to make my will. Everything to Damask, Damask Greenway. ..."

"Now, please, please, my dear madam, don't upset yourself ... I am not trying to cross you. I only say that such a matter ... You see, in your case everything is a considerable bequest, very considerable. I think it should be discussed calmly."

"Calmly. Calmly." Miss Parsons repeated the word as though she had never heard it before. Then her face took on an expression of immense cunning. "She didn't say that. *I* only say what *she* says. That is the safest way. You see, I'm very forgetful, very forgetful indeed." She looked about vaguely and presently saw all the tiny beads, pink and blue and green and silver, scattered on the floor. "Now you've made me drop my beads," she said, her face crumpling like a child's. "Oh dear, oh dear." She began to cry, loudly and complainingly, like a child.

"Now, please, please," said Mr. Turnbull. "Look, I'll collect..." He dropped, with a cracking sound as though twigs were breaking, to his knees and began to gather up the little beads with fingers which were suddenly ten times their usual size. Miss Parsons, crying more and more loudly, stood stock-still, so that he was groveling almost under her skirts and he had a sudden memory of the first time he had ever been in this house ... fifty years or so ago, with his father, just after the Captain's death and she'd been ... and he'd been ... dear, dear, the damage the years did. ...

He was conscious of nothing but relief when the girl came hurrying through the french window again.

She took the old lady by the arm and said, "I *told* you not to upset yourself. Just over some spilled beads. Please, Mr. Turnbull ... I can pick them all up in a moment. There now, everything is all right. There, there."

She had Miss Parsons in her chair again. Mr. Turnbull got stiffly to his feet. Their eyes met.

"I wish to make my will," Miss Parsons said with all the vigour and freshness of someone making a statement for the first time.

Mr. Turnbull remembered that the one thing he dreaded was an apoplectic fit, and never, so far, had he been so dangerously near it.

"Darling, you don't need to make a will," the girl said. "You *have* one nice will already."

Mr. Turnbull made his escape with those ridiculous words ringing in his ears. Nothing, no protests, no attestations on oath could have so firmly established in his mind the conviction of the young woman's complete integrity. "You have one nice will already!" And she'd been there when he mentioned that that will was five years old . . . she was no fool, she must know what that meant. And her one thought had been to comfort the poor demented old woman. It seemed unbelievable, but there it was, he had seen with his own eyes, heard with his own ears. Completely disinterested. And why, in the name of God, should the Guildhall Feoffees, who had never done anything for, never even heard of Miss Parsons, benefit from her estate instead of that truly remarkable, selfless creature, Damask Greenway? And after all, with every bit of mind and will left to her, his client had expressed *her* feelings. Should they not be respected?

Before he retired on that lovely June evening, Mr. Turnbull made a short simple draft of a new will, by which Amelia Caroline Parsons bequeathed her whole estate to Damask Greenway.

He then went to bed and slept well and waked to the burst of song with which the birds were greeting the dawn. He felt restored and refreshed by the sound sleep he had enjoyed and remembered, with amusement, his feeling of threatening stroke on the previous afternoon. Absolute nonsense; it just showed what tricks one's mind could play one. And then, suddenly quite irrelevantly, when he was thinking so rationally about Miss Parsons and her will, he remembered a performing dog which he had seen at Baildon Fair, long ago when he was young enough to take interest in that event. The sole point of the performance was that the dog did exactly the opposite of what its master commanded. Extremely easy to train a dog that way, dogs not being aware of the difference between "stand" and "sit," "come" and "go"; but it would surely not be easy, would in fact be impossible, fantastically impossible to train an old lady, however feeble of mind, to the point when you said, "Don't bother," she began to bother madly, and when you said, "You are making it pretty," she took that as cue to say, "I wish to make my will." Really, thought Mr. Turnbull, that I should dream of that comparison shows that my mind is not what it was . . . or that I am still half asleep. He plumped up his pillow, and then, the birds having exhausted their first exuberance, went back to sleep again. But in the morning he handed the rough draft of the new will to his clerk, who would make a fair copy.

CHAPTER 15

THE HARVEST RIPENED AND WAS GATHERED. FOR ALL WITH corn to reap that was a fortunate year. Labour was very cheap. Out from the Waste cottages, now besieged between the new fences and the sterile highroad, came every being who could totter on its young legs or stagger on its old ones; so the price of labour went down and down. But the price of the garnered corn stayed, on account of the war, at its peak.

That year even Captain Rout, that inefficient farmer, had his rent money ready for Michaelmas, and was also able to increase his order for smuggled brandy brought in by the gang who operated from Bywater. He was, moreover, able to buy his wife a fine new dress, the first she had had for years. That meant that when, just before All Hallows' E'en, Mrs. Fred Clopton of Flocky Hall invited them both to a party—as she had done in previous years—Mrs. Rout was able to accept. Similar invitations she had refused scornfully, concealing her true reason, which was that it was unbecoming for the wife of a gentleman who had, when all was said and done, borne the King's commission to appear at any gathering where she could not outshine a farmer's wife, however up-and-coming that farmer might be. Mrs. Clopton had attributed the refusals to sheer snobbishness, for which she had at once admired and hated

238

Mrs. Rout, and had persisted with her invitations. When the final acceptance arrived, she said to Fred, "Ah, I knew the time would come when she was sick of her own company! And I'm glad it's this year, when Mrs. Thurlow Lamb is coming, with her airs and graces. It'll show *her*!" An obscure statement, but perfectly lucid to Fred, who understood his wife's social aspirations and indeed shared them so far as his daughters were concerned. He agreed that there was no point in sending the girls to the Female Academy at Baildon, and having them taught French and the pianoforte, and drilled on the blackboard, if they were then to come home and revert to mere farmer's daughters, as their mother assured him they would, unless *some* exertion was made. Money, which he was making "hand over fist," wasn't enough, social advancement was needed as well.

The Harvest Horkey that year was a particularly lavish affair, as well it might be, the Squire having done so well out of the enclosure. Going home, replete and exhausted, the villagers remarked less upon what there was to eat and drink and upon the wonderful fiddling of the little hunchback who had come to supplement Jim Lantern's playing than upon the peculiar game which the Squire's friend, Mr. Mundford, had played with some of the girls. There was no point in it, no prize, no result. He just went round offering one girl after another a bit of pale pinkish stone, like a pebble. "Will you be good enough to hold this in your hand while I count ten? Thank you, that will do." Daft-like, wasn't it?

Even Richard, when they were drinking together late in the library, mustered curiosity enough to ask, "What were you up to all evening, Alec?"

"Reconnoitering," said Mr. Mundford simply. "You may be grieved, if not surprised, to learn that of your villagers between the ages of sixteen and twenty not one is a virgin." He took the stone from his pocket and fingered it.

"That tallies with the Rector's theory that no man will ask for banns to be put up until he's well and truly caught," Richard said. Then he added curiously, "But how can you tell . . . ? There wasn't time . . ."

"I passed this about. It's a very special piece of stone. I bought it from a slaver in Zanzibar—you will appreciate its value to *him* when I tell you that in the hand of a virgin it changes colour and turns blue. Which is also interesting; you can trace there the derivative trend of Christianity, Mary's colour is blue, is it not? I gave two hundred guineas for this and it is worth every penny. Tonight, for example . . . it turned colour once, a little creature with flaxen hair and a pink dress. Before I could reach you and ask you her name she'd vanished and presently she slipped back into the dance, looking rather sheepish. I invited her to hold it again . . . and alas . . ." He ended with a laugh. Then, abruptly serious, he said, "After all, it is a thing we must face. We need one by the end of October and *some* preparation will be necessary. They're so damned coy. I know, I've been through this before. It is very difficult to make them believe that it's a purely passive part. To have one handy, one capable of being worked upon, would be very convenient. The best subject I ever found was at Medmenham, quite simple-minded, with a passion for port wine. Believe it or not, it had no effect upon her, she drank it as a kitten drinks milk, liking the taste and wanting more and more. I only wish I had her now," said Mr. Mundford wistfully. "She was just right, but then Medmenham, as I've told you before, was *wrong*. I said so at the time. If you credit one side with power, then you must credit the other, and that *was* an abbey, consecrated soil, and there was the stumbling block. Dashwood didn't really believe either way . . . what I attained I attained despite him and the other fools." As always on the rare occasions when he spoke frankly of his intentions and aims, a startling change came over him; into his suetty face and tallowy fingers the blood seemed to flow, carrying warmth and colour and vitality; his ordinarily cold eyes grew luminous. When he spoke of the power he sought, it seemed to be already his, when he spoke of the Power he worshipped it seemed to be there, in the room, oppressively overwhelming, even to Richard Shelmadine; he could make the incredible seem credible, the fantastic merely a matter of common sense.

Damask first learned of the Fullers' return from exile when she met Danny face to face halfway along the drive just before dusk on a Saturday evening late in September—the evening of the Harvest Horkey. She usually chose Saturday evenings for her visits to her mother since Amos was almost certain to be out of the house then, either working on his new chapel or attending a week-night meeting in one already established. She had, with some reluctance, abandoned the attempt to give Julie bacon and cheese and butter and plum cake and other solid comestibles which seemed of such small value in the Dower House and of such enormous worth on the Waste. Julie dared only accept a little tea and sugar and, at intervals, fresh bottles of the medicines, and these she hid away furtively.

Julie, of course, knew that Danny had come back and that Amos had sold him the land, and once or twice the mention of the facts had been "on the tip of her tongue," as she put it to herself, but she shrank from saying anything which might cast the slightest gloom over these brief bright visits. Damask had survived, had enjoyed, indeed, a stroke of wonderful good fortune; still, you never knew how deep such a wound might have gone or how it might ache, all hidden away. Once, during the summer, Julie herself had suffered a pang when she saw Sally Ashpole—Mrs. Danny Fuller—visiting her mother and carrying a really bonny bouncing baby in her arms. Nice dresses and pretty ornaments and what Julie called "plenty to do with" were all very well, but did they entirely make up? Her grandmotherly instincts cried out that they did not. On that day she had felt with renewed force that Amos, in selling Danny the land, had been disloyal to his daughter.

Damask closed the door of the Dower House behind her that Saturday evening, settled the basket with the tea and sugar and medicines more comfortably on her arm, and began to trip along the drive. It curved slightly around a clump of laurels, now neatly clipped back, and as she rounded the curve there was Danny. They came face to face and it was a perceptible while before he recognised her. Matt Ashpole had said in his gossipy way that she was at the Dower House and the old lady thought the world of her, but that had not prepared him for this elegant vision; he had indeed been wondering whether she would answer the door to him, and what their attitude towards one another would be. Now, recognising her, he gave a sheepish grin and said, "Why, hullo, Damask."

"Good evening," she said coldly. "What are you doing here, Danny Fuller?" As she spoke she lifted one slim, white, be-ringed hand and settled the gauzy scarf which lay, light as mist, over her curls and then encircled her neck; she had felt the pulse in her throat leap to life and pulled the scarf closer to hide it.

"I wanted to have a word with Miss Parsons. Is she at home?"

"She's always at home. But you can't see her now. She never sees anyone unless I am there and I am just going out. What did you want with her?"

"Just a bit of business." Be damned if he'd tell her, acting so highhanded. "I'll come another time."

"You might just as well tell me now and save yourself a long walk. I handle all her business now."

"I don't mean housekeeping. I mean *business*. And it isn't a long walk—we're back in the old house, didn't you know?"

"No! I . . . why I . . ." She collected herself quickly. "I'm out of touch with village gossip nowadays. No, I hadn't heard. Did you get the land back, too?"

"Why, no! Just the house. I've got some land, nineteen acres your own father sold me. Didn't you even know that? Nineteen acres, but that's not enough. That was why I was calling on Miss Parsons. She got her share of the Waste and I wondered whether she'd rent me a bit. You see, I . . ."

"I can answer that now. None of Miss Parsons' land is for hire."

"Now you can't answer for *that*, Damask. Not without even asking. I'd pay a good rent and get the land in good heart . . ."

"Not Miss Parsons' land you won't."

"I don't see how you can be so sure . . ." By this time she was completely mistress of herself again and able to meet his eyes. She looked at him and strangely, since nothing in the situation had altered, he was certain that Miss Parsons had no land for hire. "Well, if you're so sure," he said, all the spirit and hope and fight seeping out of him.

"I'm sure. And now if you'll excuse me." She began to walk along the drive again. He turned and began to walk in the same direction, not quite with her, about half a pace behind, as a dog might.

"You're angry with me, aren't you? Rightly so, I reckon. It was just—aw, something I couldn't talk about, Damask. But I . . . well, I'm sorry if I . . . if I made you angry." It was the best he could do on the spur of the moment, taken aback as he'd been by the way she looked and then shattered by that cold, strange stare. And so much had happened during the last eighteen months, and he himself had changed so much, was now so worn down by work and worry that he could hardly remember exactly what had been between them . . . at least, that was not quite true; he could remember her saying, "I don't want to be one of your jilts"—that was at the beginning; and he could remember the scene in the wood—that was at the end; but there were blanks.

She gave a little light laugh, a lady's laugh, and said:

"Why should I be angry with you? You did me no wrong. And the girl you *did* wrong you married, didn't you? Why should anybody be angry?"

She was still slightly ahead of him, walking so quickly, so lightly, and not turning her head, that he forgot that look she had given him and remembered only his land hunger.

"No," he said in eager agreement, "I never did you much wrong, Damask. And if you feel that way and aren't angry with me, you might put in a word with Miss Parsons. Her bit of the Waste now, it's fenced, but not ploughed..."

"It is being ploughed on Monday," Damask said. They had reached the gate, and she halted and waited as a lady should so that he could open it for her. She passed through, and while he was engaged in closing the gate she said, "Good night," and was gone, walking swiftly, lightly in the direction of the Waste cottages.

On the next evening, which was Sunday, she went to the Manor House. All her fury and discomfiture had now focused itself and the voice in which she spoke to the footman who opened the door and the glance she gave him cancelled out the small consideration that ladies of importance did not arrive alone, on foot, after dark. He sped to announce her.

Richard, Mr. Mundford, and Mr. Montague were playing cards and interest had been lent to the game by Mr. Mundford's having "taken back" his luck. Just before Mr. Montague had arrived, Richard had said, "You were right, as usual. It *is* tedious to play and know that you will win."

"Tedious in the end, not at the beginning, you will agree? Well, it was only a loan, give it back!" Alec said lightly. He cupped his hand, seemed to pluck something from the back of Richard's left, and then paused, holding his hand as though something indescribably fragile and precious were balanced in his palm. "And if I lend it to dear Monty, then we shall know how every game will go! Never mind, I'll think of something."

A little later, as Linda moved to take her place at the end of the dinner table, Mr. Mundford reached out and touched the lace of her sleeve with fingers which looked, she thought, in some way afflicted.

"Beautiful," he said, "beautiful. Venetian, is it not?"

"I don't know," she said. "I'm afraid I don't know much about lace."

"Nor about luck," said Richard, with what seemed like complete irrelevance, had dropped into his own chair laughing.

Mr. Mundford, for some reason, seemed displeased and shot him a quelling glance.

The "devil's own luck" was thus safely away, gone with Linda, who had said good night and left the three men to their play, and Richard was enjoying the game more than any he had played for a long time when the doorbell sounded an urgent peal and presently a footman came and said, rather breathlessly, that Miss Greenway wished to see Sir Richard.

"Greenway . . . Greenway," said Richard, looking up from his cards. "Oh yes, I remember." She'd done him a favour, persuaded the old lunatic to sign, and he'd kept his bargain, given her father twenty acres—not the best—and sacked somebody she had a grudge against. What did she want now?

They were playing in the library; Linda, unless she had gone to bed unusually early, would be in the small sitting room.

"Ask her to wait in there," he said, indicating the door of the breakfast room, which lay between the library and the room which Linda used most. He laid his cards on the table and said, "Excuse me. I shan't be a minute."

Damask stood, very straight and still, with her back to the branching candlestick on the side table, so that her face was in shadow.

Richard said with his easy, spurious pleasantness:

"Good evening, Miss Greenway."

She waited just long enough so that he began to wonder whether she had heard him, and then said:

"I do not wish you good evening or anything good, Sir Richard. You cheated me."

"Cheated!" He savoured the word, disliked it, and said with some vehemence, "That is no word to use. If I remember rightly I promised to see that your father received an allotment of land and that the . . ."

"Fullers."

". . . the Fullers should receive notice. Both those conditions I performed to the letter. What do you mean," he demanded, his anger rising, "by coming here and abusing me? You are a very insolent young woman."

"I'm very angry," she said coolly. "The Fullers are back in Clevely."

"God in Heaven!" he said. "Who cares whether you're angry or not. Who cares where the Fullers are? You coaxed your lunatic mistress to sign her name and I rewarded you, and that is the end of that! Lunacy must be contagious." He moved to the hearth and pulled the bell rope. "The servant will show you out," he said, and went towards the door of the library. As he put his hand on the knob, Damask turned and lifted the candlestick and said:

"Sir Richard."

He was aware of the shifting light and turned and, seeing the candlestick in her hand, imagined that the half-jibing remark about the contagion of lunacy was sober truth and that she planned to set fire to something.

"Put that down!" he exclaimed. "What in hell do you think you're doing?"

She set the candlestick on the table so that it flowered with its seven golden blooms between them. He saw her face clearly for the first time that evening and noticed, half idly, that her eyes, instead of reflecting the light as one would have expected, seemed to glow, yellow and transparent, as though the light were behind them. A most curious effect, he thought, even while his mind was busy framing a sentence that would really hurt her. The desire to hurt her had, he suddenly realised, lurked in him ever since that first interview.

"You should, you know, ask Miss Parsons to add to her other favours by teaching you some rudimentary manners," he said silkily, and watched to see the barb strike.

Her face remained impassive; she hardly heard him. Her mind reached backwards—the Saunderses, scoundrels with a bad conscience between them; poor old Miss Parsons, unsound of mind; Mr. Turnbull—but there possibly Miss Parsons' authority had borne some weight; Matt Ashpole, just an ignorant lout. *This* was the real test; and the power welled up to meet the challenge.

"Sit down," she said gently. "Sit down, Richard Shelmadine."

He fought it for a moment; delayed so long despite the weakening of his knees that in the end he had only just time to drag a chair under him and prevent himself from sitting on the floor.

"Insolent," she said musingly. "Wouldn't you be?"

He went red, and then white with rage, gripped the edge of the table, and tried to heave himself up, then put his hands on the edge of the chair and tried to lever himself to his feet. It was useless, he might have had no legs at all. Damask watched his struggles with an expressionless detachment that was more wounding than mockery. At last he slumped in the chair and muttered:

"All right. What do you want?"

"An apology—for breaking your word."

"I swear until you told me I didn't know the Fullers were back. Where are they? You see, I don't even know that."

"They're back in the same house. They've some land already and are looking for more."

"It was without my knowledge." Surreptitiously he pressed his hands against the sides of the chair again and tried to lever himself up. Sweat sprang in little shining drops on his brow. "Without my knowledge," he repeated. "I remember now, Hadstock, my bailiff, wrote that he had found a tenant for the empty house; he gave no name. How should I know?"

"Oh well," she said, accepting the explanation, "it would have been better if you had told me that in the first place instead of calling me insolent."

Deliberately she removed her gaze and stared about the room with a naïve and puppyish interest. Apparently the spell held even when she was not staring at her victim.

Presently she ventured a move and went over to the sideboard to inspect something which had roused her curiosity; a silver dish with a silver grid over it and three short stout candles under the grid. What was its purpose? Oh, of course, to keep dishes warm while they waited. What an excellent idea! What extreme luxury! Not even at Muchanger had she seen such a contrivance. They must have one at the Dower House.

The sweat had gathered now and was running down the harsh lines of the Squire's yellow face. His spruce white neckcloth was greying with damp and collapsing upon itself. She looked at him without amusement, but with immense satisfaction.

"The word," he said, as though he were being throttled, "was ill chosen. I retract it. I apologise."

Delicately she smoothed her gloves and adjusted the filmy scarf which covered her hair.

"You can't," he gasped out, "just go away . . . and leave me here. I'll put the Fullers out again. I'll do . . . I'll . . . What do you want of me?"

"Nothing. Nothing at all but just to sit there until I let you up."

* * *

"He's a damned long time," Mr. Montague said, glancing at the door which led into the breakfast room.

"Wench trouble, I suspect," said Mr. Mundford. "*Miss* Greenway, I noticed, and Richard looked blank for a moment and then remembered something and went with some alacrity."

"And they're suspiciously *quiet*," said Mr. Montague, who was not without experience. "Some women shout and throw things and then you get angwy yourself and you're saved. But when they cwy, quietly, that is dangewous, you begin to pwomise them things. Do you think that perhaps Wichard would welcome an intewuption?"

"I should welcome a glimpse of the lady," said Mr. Mundford.

"To the wescue then!" cried Mr. Montague. He got up and opened the door into the breakfast room, tentatively and politely, saying:

"Wichard, we are waiting for you." Then he saw the way the girl was standing, plainly triumphantly, and the way Richard was sagging, sweating profusely in his chair. Too late, he thought, he's promised her two hundred a year!

Mr. Mundford had taken a look, too, and interpreted the scene otherwise. As Mr. Montague stepped back from the doorway, he moved forward.

"We," said Damask, turning the stare upon him, "are having a private conversation."

"Which one member of the party seems not to be enjoying very much," said Mr. Mundford smoothly. "Sometimes, you know, an impartial third person..." He moved towards the chair and said in a bantering voice, "Manners, man, manners, get up and introduce me." Richard looked at him with agonised eyes and scrabbled with his fingers on the table's edge, and sweated more profusely.

Mr. Mundford looked at Damask, who looked back at him. Blundering fool... just when she was proving...

"We have no wish to be interrupted," she said brusquely. They fought one another over the candles for a moment.

"And I have no wish to be intrusive," said Mr. Mundford blandly. "Helpful, yes."

"Then for God's sake help me, if you can," said Richard thickly.

"Is it not remarkable," said Mr. Mundford, with his eyes on Damask, "how, in an extremity, people not ordinarily attentive to the Deity appeal to other people in his name?" He smiled as he spoke and, reaching out one leg, kicked the leg of the chair in which Richard sat. "Get up," he said. And Richard was in possession of his legs again.

"Monty is alone, and you need a drink," said Mr. Mundford, ushering Richard out of his own breakfast room.

"Try on me," said Mr. Mundford, before Damask could speak. As proof of his willingness to be "tried on" he moved to stand conveniently for dropping into the chair.

"It would be no use," she said rather sullenly.

"Never mind. Try. My name is Alec Mundford."

All right, she thought, she'd show him! Coming in like that and spoiling everything. An upsurge of anger, which in the circumstances was understandably mistaken for an uprush of power, swept over her.

"Sit down, Alec Mundford," she said, desperately willing it to happen. But he remained standing.

"No," he said, "I am stronger than you—as yet. But you are young. And I confess that I felt a weakening of the knees. . . . Tell me, how long have you practised this art, and to what purpose?"

"It came, a year ago in August. Quite suddenly. A woman was going to throw me out of somewhere where I wanted to stay . . . and she couldn't; nor could her husband. Then I knew."

"And what happened in August a year ago?"

Sullen again, she said, "Nothing."

"Come, come," said Mr. Mundford, "*you* remember! You and I must be frank with one another if we are to work together."

"Work together?"

"Why not? It would never do for us to oppose one another, would it? But we'll speak of that later. Tell me what happened in August last year."

"I had . . . a shock. And it was a hot day. I fainted; my mother thought I was dead."

"And where were you during that time?"

"How did you know?" she asked sharply. He did not bother to answer, he just looked at her and waited.

"In a place," she said at last. He nodded. "And there were voices . . . and light was something you could touch and handle, and colour . . . colour was something you could taste . . . and time was . . . you could see it. It sounds all confused, but that was how it was, and I understood it . . . then."

"And you returned with this power?"

"That was how it seemed. Nobody had ever done what I wanted them to do until then."

He nodded again. "Now do something for me," he said. He took from his pocket the lump of pale pink stone. "Hold this in your hand, will you?"

She hesitated. "What is it? I don't want anything else to happen to me. You leave me alone and I'll leave you alone—and Sir Richard if he's your friend, though he did cheat me."

"I'm not going to take anything away from you. I told you, we must work together. Just hold this in your hand."

Reluctantly she took the stone and held it.

"Now give it back." He snatched it quickly and looked at it eagerly. "'And colour,'" he quoted delightedly, "'was something you could taste.'" He slipped the stone back into his pocket. "Working together," he said, "there would be no limit to what we could do." He brooded for a moment. Then he said:

"Tell me, what do you want most in this world?"

The pulse began to beat in her throat again.

"Something I can never have now."

"Why not?"

"It is too late."

"Ah, but you forget. 'Time was . . . you could see it,' remember? By that measure it can never be too late. What is it that you want? I swear to you—by the things we both know—that if you will work with me, you shall have it."

"But he's married now."

"How young you are," Mr. Mundford said, almost dotingly. "How young, and how innocent. . . ."

CHAPTER 16

Once the harvest was over the year seemed to go down-hill rapidly; the evenings drew in; the usual early October gales stripped the trees and howled around the ill-fitting doors of the Waste cottages, presaging worse weather to come. Those who had potatoes to dig dug them thankfully, watched by envious eyes.

Matt Ashpole, in that October, received what he called "a smack on the snout," one against which even his remarkable foresight had not warned him. He *had* foreseen and had spoken to Mrs. Sam Jarvey about the "draught" which would blow, cold and bitter, when destitution overtook the Waste dwellers. He had himself lately felt its breath; quite a third of his carrier's business had been concerned with taking little bits and pieces of produce to market and buying other little bits and pieces for his neighbours. That trade was now virtually dead. But he had sold all his fencing stakes and he was counting on Shipton's walnuts. So one blustery October morning he drove along to Bridge Farm to come to terms with Mrs. Shipton as he had done in previous years.

She was not in the kitchen; he banged on the door and shouted and, receiving no answer, took Gyp by the bridle and led him to the rickety fence which separated the yard from the stackyard and left him so close to one of Shipton's haystacks that no sensible horse could have failed to take advantage of the position. He then went, on foot, to take a look at the walnut crop. And there, to his surprise and horror, he found Shipton and his missus—her head tied up in a duster—armed with linen props, beating down the nuts with their own hands.

"Hullo, hullo!" he said. "Ain't late this year, am I?"

Shipton gave him a sour, sheepish look and went on with his beating, but Mrs. Shipton lowered her prop and stood with it like a standard-bearer while she said briskly:

"This year we're gathering 'em, sacking 'em, and selling 'em, and taking what profit there is to be had, Matt Ashpole. Letting you do it was all part of the loplolly state of affairs what brought us to ruin!"

"Ruin, missus?" said Matt, remembering all the fat pigs in the straw, all the stacks in the stackyard. "Come now, you ain't the one to talk about ruin, surely!"

"I ain't *talking* about it; I'm dealing with it," retorted Mrs. Shipton.

The old bitch must be mad, Matt thought; and there was nothing to be gained by arguing with a mad woman armed with a linen prop. He shot Shipton a glance, a nice blend of sympathy and derision, which Abel affected not to see, and walked slowly back to where he had left his old horse, which, being a prudent animal, had made the most of its chance.

"Come on, Gyp," he said, climbing into the cart, "we've gotta find some other way of turning a honest penny. I don't know what things are coming to, that I don't."

Even his sturdy spirit was cast down for a while as he remembered better days, when sometimes—not often, but sometimes—a job would go begging, when Matt Juby maybe would rap on his door and say, "Matt, do us a favour. Dead rat under the floor at Flocky and I promised to go and hunt it this morning and now my cow is dropping her calf." Nowadays the smell of a dead rat to be hunted and disposed of, a dead sheep to be buried, an overflowing privy to be emptied brought half a dozen men running, all ready to accept a cutthroat price for the job. Terrible times we live in, Matt thought. But the rhythm of the old horse's plodding hoofs soothed him, and the sight of the animal itself, narrow-hocked, bony-ribbed, sway-backed, ewe-necked as it was, was a cheering sight. He was better off than most; he still had his old horse and sooner or later he'd find something to buy and sell again. His leathery lips curved in a smile as he remembered Shipton's face, the rasp in Mrs. Shipton's voice. Poor old devil, for all his acres!

The increased poverty amongst his neighbours would, in the end, affect Amos unfavourably too, since in past years the sale of the pig or the geese or the half-grown calf had generally led to an order for shoes for some member of the family. This year nobody would order new shoes, but a good many people were willing to come and lend him a hand with the chapel-building in return for a patch on an upper or a clump on the sole. The new chapel grew much faster than its ruined predecessor, and after labouring on it all through the evenings, Amos worked for hours by candlelight fulfilling his obligations to his helpers. Every evening after he had left the house, Julie made a pot of tea and drank it slowly, savouring every drop.

The second week in October, just when he had decided that it was time to change his routine and build in the mornings again, the weather turned wet. For days on end it rained relentlessly, heavy driving rain against which even a sack offered little protection, so Amos stayed at home and made up great arrears of work and Julie had no tea. Then a fine morning dawned, and as soon as he had noticed the weather, Amos, with a piece of bread, meagrely spread with lard, in his hand, set off for Cobbler's Corner. Thank God for that, Julie thought piously, and put the kettle on, reached down her little brown teapot and the blue jug of skim milk. Ordinarily they washed down the larded bread with a cup of the milk and hot water, unsweetened; this morning Amos hadn't even waited for that.

With the hot sweet tea even the stale bread and thinly spread lard made a feast and Julie lingered over it, thinking kindly of Damask. She had just poured fresh water into the pot to liven up the brew when the door of the workroom opened and closed, heavy stumbling steps approached the kitchen door, it opened, and there was Amos, looking so pale and stricken that she cried, "Oh! Are you ill?" getting clumsily to her feet as she spoke.

"Gone all lopsided," he said in a terrible voice, and sat down and put his head in his hands.

"What hev?"

"My chapel," he groaned.

"Oh dear me," she said, concealing her inward relief.

"Thass a sad job." She looked at his bowed head with a glance void of sympathy but rich in pity. She knew the toil and

the self-denial that had gone into that building, not to mention
the nineteen pounds! A secret feeling of guilt stirred in her;
she had so much resented the immediate sinking of that capital,
which had seemed like a gift from Heaven, in the chapel,
inevitable as she knew it to be. She had *almost* wished ill on
the place at times.

"What happened?" she asked tenderly, as though interest at
this point could retract the grudging of earlier thoughts.

Amos did not answer immediately; he was probably praying.
After a few minutes he raised his head.

"I must bear in mind, 'whom the Lord loveth He chasteneth.'
But the shock of the sight of it made me lose heart for a minute."

"What happened?" Julie asked again.

"Thass sunk, four—five inches all along one side—Danny
Fuller's side. I reckon thass all on account of the draining he
been doing. Stand to reason, don't it? The ground down there
was all plumped out like a fresh apple, he drain, and that shrivel
like an old apple thass lost its juice. The ground shrivelled,
and pulled the timber away. One place at the corner it gaped
so I could put my hand through."

Far, far back in Julie's mind framed the sentence: "That's
what come of selling land to a chap who jilted your own daughter." The sentence could never be spoken, of course. Instead
she said:

"Maybe you should of drained your bit when he did his."

"Maybe I should. I didn't reckon on his being so hasty.
Mention draining he did, the first night, afore he'd even bought
the land. And that do seem a queer thing, Julie; there he is
working away for the glory of Danny Fuller and me for the
glory of God and his drains work, all the reeds and rushes hev
died down and he've got good pasture for the price of rubbish
and I hev one chapel burnt and the other gone lopsided. That
do seem hard."

As soon as she knew that he was not stricken with mortal
illness she had remembered the tea and moved so that she stood
between him and the table. Now pity overcame her caution
and she went back to her chair, saying:

"You mustn't take it to heart, Amos. Hev a cup of tea. It'll
pull you together."

He stared at the teapot, the jug, and the cup and the saucer,
and was tempted. Julie meant it kindly; and there'd be relief
in sitting here, drinking tea and talking over the mystery of

God's ways, accepting the comfort of a sympathetic human being.

It was a temptation; he recognised it as such and thrust it away. A whole jumble of admonitory texts took possession of his mind: A house divided against itself could not stand; the beam must be taken from your own eye before you could take the mote from your neighbours; except the Lord build the house their labour is but vain. . . . He saw exactly where he had been at fault and why he had failed.

"Julie," he said, "that tea come from Damask, didn't it? I towd you months ago to send her back with what she brought. And I towd you two years ago, no more tea in this house till the chapel is built. Both ways you disobeyed me and one way you deceived me. I've wrestled with Damask; every time I see her I've towd her about the way she look and act and never come to chapel, but she don't heed me. She've backslidden, too. And there's you taking what she smuggle out of the house and don't even try to account for. The Lord, no doubt, think I turn a blind eye on these things. Here . . ." he said, and reached out and took up the little brown teapot and dashed it into the hearth; it cracked with a small sound which seemed to be echoed by Julie. "Oh," she said, as though something in her had broken too. Yet when he turned he saw on her face no hurt, no pleading look, only a red, almost jubilant anger which held him motionless and speechless with astonishment.

"Thass the end," Julie said. "I've borne with you and borne you all these years and on'y a minnit ago I was downright sorry for you and offered you a cup of tea for your comfort. Now you've chucked away the one thing thass been my comfort all these weary years. I never asked much," she said, her voice rising. "I've scrimped and screwed and gone shabby when there was no need to, and lived as hard as if I'd married a poor tool like Spitty Palfrey, not a man with a trade to his name, and I've come to the point where all I ask is a cup of tea what didn't cost you anything, nor took anything away from your chapel, a cup of tea my own daughter give me. What if she do curl her hair a bit and wear a pretty dress?" Julie's voice rose again as the old barrier fell and the ancient grievance poured out. "So did I till you went Methodist, and was I any the worse? My people was all good people, a good farmer my father was and good to them that worked for him and a kinder woman than my mother you'd be hard put to it to find, but they didn't think a curl or a frill or a cup of tea or a glass of ale, come to that, was a deadly sin. Nor wouldn't God, thass just you, with your ideas as lopsided as your chapel!"

Amos was as much astonished as that Biblical character, Baalam, whose ass turned and spoke to him. He just stared.

"I can make tea in a jug," said Julie, "till Damask bring me a pot, which she will do when she hear what you did to my little brown 'un, what was a wedding present to me."

She got up, reached down another larger jug and the little tea tin, and pushed the kettle back to the fire.

"I'm gonna make a jug of tea now, Amos; and do you interfere with me I shall pour the water on you, so you'll be the sacrific. I don't aim to be your sacrifice no longer."

This was worse than finding the chapel lopsided; more shocking; more bewildering. Without a word Amos turned and went into the workroom and fell on his knees by the bench. "Take it to the Lord in prayer," the hymn said, and he did that; all the troubles and the puzzles and the hurts. Damask, he felt instinctively, was at the root of the trouble; he prayed for her, and he prayed for strength and guidance to help him to deal with her. . . .

His chance came on the following Saturday. He had felt for a long time that her visits were deliberately timed to avoid him and he saw no harm in a little subterfuge. He went out, as usual, in case his movements were watched, and then came back again.

The tea was made by that time and Julie and Damask were sitting over it, their elbows on the table, their heads together. Damask had asked at once what had happened to the little brown teapot and had been told.

"We ain't spoke a word to one another since," Julie said rather piteously. Her rage had flared and then died down like a fire of dry sticks with no log to kindle and she would have been glad to make peace if Amos had given a sign. If he had just admitted that he was hasty over the teapot she would have broken down and cried and apologised for the way she had spoken; but Amos remained silent, prayed more than ever, and regarded her coldly.

"That seem so queer," Julie said, "to live aside anybody as close as we do and not talk. Not that he ever minded what I said, or answered much . . . But if I give in now he'd think he was right and I know he ain't. I know there ain't no harm in a cup of tea, for instance; nor in you letting your hair curl, natural."

"I'll bring you a new teapot. There are several never used. Which would you like, a china one, painted with flowers, or a pewter, or a silver one?"

Some slight uneasiness flared in Julie.

"I thought, maybe, just an old one, past use. I mean . . . well, I couldn't go taking a *silver* teapot."

"Why not? Everything in the house is for me to do as I like with. Now that you've once stood up for yourself and don't have to hide things away any more I'll bring you lots of things. Anything you like, blankets, a down quilt, cushions for your chair. Why not? There's room after room in that house fully furnished and never entered except now and then for dusting."

"But . . . still, all Miss Parsons'," said Julie timidly, anxious not to offend.

"We share it. I look after her and she provides me with what I need; and if I need things for you, then I can have them."

Before Julie could express any of the wondering gratitude which she felt, the sound of the outer door opening reached their ears.

Her recent declaration of defiance had not rendered Julie immune from a feeling of guilt; she started and said, "Oh! There's your father!"

"Never mind. Just go on drinking your tea and take no notice of what he says." She put her hand briefly upon Julie's misshapen one and Julie smiled and was calm, much as Miss Parsons was when similarly handled; she was obedient too, and lifted her cup just as Amos opened the inner door.

He said, "Hullo, Damask," just as he always had done upon finding her at home. Then he added, "I'm glad you came tonight. I've got things to say to you."

She said, "Hullo, Father," and her red lips shaped a smile; above them the golden eyes were cold and deadly.

"One thing," Amos said, "is this here tea. Your mother says there's no harm in tea and I ain't saying there is, apart from it being a luxury and an indulgence of the flesh; but there's harm in bringing things out of your employer's house—and you never have yet looked me in the face and said that Miss Parsons give you leave to bring it. And there's harm in breaking your word, which is what you and your mother atwixt you hev made *me* do. No more tea in this house, I said, till the chapel is finished. The Lord expect a man to keep his own house in order and wouldn't take into account that you both went behind my back. That's one thing," said Amos, checking off a point made, much as he did when he was in the pulpit. "Then there is this business of you neglecting your worship. Great pains I took, time you first went out to work, to fix for you to come to chapel regular. Without a word to me you went and changed your job and never been inside the chapel since. That ain't right, and you know it. I don't know what manner of servant you call yourself nowadays, but you seem to hev a lot of freedom, and do Miss Parsons value you as highly as you make out, she'd give you time off to get to chapel once a month. And if you don't care to ask her, I will. I been sadly lax, letting all this time pass without doing nothing, but now I seen the error of my ways. That's the second thing. And now we come to the matter of your appearance. 'Tisn't seemly that you, my daughter, a well-brought-up, godly girl, should go about decked out like the whore of Babylon—that dress you're wearing this minute ain't decent, Damask, cut so low I can see where your breasts begin. Every time I see you, you look more of a scarlet woman—I ain't saying you *are*, but you look like it. And if, as you said to me the first time I spoke, 'tis Miss Parsons' wish you should look like a trollop, then there's only one thing to do and that is give in your notice."

At that point even his longwindedness, practised in exhortations, gave out.

Julie sat sipping her tea, and sipping her tea as though her very life depended on it. Save for the slight noise as she swallowed, the room was very still when Amos' voice ceased.

Damask put her elbows on the table again, shaking out the lace of her sleeves as though deliberately flaunting it; she linked her fingers and set her chin on them and eyed Amos steadily for a moment. Then she asked, with exaggerated sweetness:

"Have you quite finished? Then I have two things to say to you. The first is about Danny Fuller."

Despite the admonition to be calm, Julie gave another slight start at the sound of that name; and she'd have put her cup down but seemed unable to. Another sip would steady her, she thought, and drank again. "I didn't mind what Danny Fuller did," Damask said, "it was a good thing for me, in every way. But he could have made me look silly, walking me home from chapel and fetching me from here on my free days and then marrying Sally Ashpole. It just happened that I was saved from looking silly; but any decent father, with natural feelings for his daughter, would have thought twice before selling Danny Fuller the land he wanted. That's one thing," she said, with a sudden brutal mimicry of Amos' pulpit manner. "It isn't the important one though. That's the way you treat my mother. Years and years she's had no comforts, not because you couldn't earn money, but because you was"—oh dear, what a slip! How *did* that happen?—"were too good and holy to tend to your trade. Nobody minded that. But now that things have changed and she could have a few little pleasures and an easier time, you just grudge it. Your chapel didn't go lopsided because Mother had a cup of tea, and if you were honest with yourself you'd know it. And you didn't break her nice little brown teapot because you thought teamaking was wrong. You broke it because you had to take your temper out on *something*. You were angry with God, really; so you smashed a teapot!"

She thought that would make him flinch, or at least shake his calm.

"You're wrong there, my girl. 'Tain't for me nor any man to be angry with the Almighty. God was displeased with me, and rightly, as I've been pointing out to you."

He looked straight into her eyes. Something like fury moved in her; she remembered the Squire; even Mr. Mundford had said that he had felt his knees weakening. She gathered herself for the test.

"You'll apologise to Mother for breaking her teapot," she said. "Go on, apologise, Amos Greenway."

"Now that," said Amos, "is no way to speak to your father. That look to me as though you're forgetting the Fourth Commandment as well as a whole heap of other things. 'Honour thy father and thy mother,' I must remind you. Honouring ain't calling your father by his first name, nor honouring your mother ain't smuggling things out of one door into another just to pander to her. What else is in that basket?"

"No concern of yours. Put that basket down; put it down."

"Bottles," said Amos. "Now what do *they* contain?"

"Medicine. Stuff she should have had to ease her years ago if you'd been half a man." She was breathless with anger. Twice he'd defied her.

"Who paid for it?"

Insultingly she told him the truth, heedless of the result for Julie.

"It went on the bill with the doctor's fees for tending Bennett and the stuff Miss Parsons had for her cough. Pay for it yourself if you feel badly about taking it!"

"You know I can't do that. Doctors' medicine ain't for poor people. But you earn money seemingly, you pay for what you bring your mother—tea and sugar and all; and until I know you do, don't you let me see anything else brung into this house."

Once more she mustered all her forces and tried to beat down his eyes, but he outfaced her and she knew that this battle must be fought out of the level with ordinary human weapons. She had one ready, bright and sharp.

"You weren't so particular, were you, about taking twenty acres of land you'd no claim to. Everybody was asking how you came by that, but I didn't notice you concerning yourself. You can grab as greedily as anybody else when it's something *you* want. Maybe that's why the chapel went lopsided, built on ill-come-by ground!"

Now he was shaken; his face went grey and seemed to shrivel in on itself. He reached out his big work-scarred hands and set them on the back of a chair as though for support. Julie knew another pang of that same pity and let out a sound, half moan, half protest. Damask watched him with an almost visible amusement, gloatingly; he had defied her, let him suffer.

He spoke at last. "I never thought of it," he said. "Matt Ashpole and the rest come here asking me to account for it and I said I couldn't. Thass true I never asked a question, never made a move to find out. Maybe I stand condemned for that. Maybe in your rage agin me, Damask, you said a true word." He swallowed audibly. "There it was, it seemed all legal and aboveboard, and I took it and reckoned it a gift from God."

He had never, in any pulpit, spoken more movingly or with more dignity.

"I'll go straight to Mr. Hadstock tomorrow . . . and ask," he said, his voice faltering as he realised that the land was sold, the money spent. If something had been wrong about his allotment it was late now to set it right. He couldn't, but God could . . .

"This," he said more firmly, "is a matter for the Lord. And I ask you, my family, to come with me now to the mercy seat and ask forgiveness for past sins and errors and guidance in the future."

He looked from one face to another as he spoke; and then, as though to set an example, went down on his knees.

"I must go now," Damask said. She laid her hand on Julie's shoulder and whispered, "I'll come soon and bring you a teapot." Then she went hurriedly.

Almost as soon as she had gone, Julie moved stiffly from her chair and stiffly went down on her knees beside Amos, close enough to let him know that he was not alone in his misery and bewilderment and his search.

CHAPTER 17

ALL HALLOWS' E'EN DAWNED MURKILY. MRS. FRED CLOPTON, leaving the bed of unrest upon which she had worried the night away, peeped out at first light and burst into angry, nervous tears. It was going to be foggy and the party—the most ambitious one she had ever planned—would be ruined. Maternal love had made her bold and this year she had cast her net wide, except for Mr. Avery and the Routs from Wood Farm, all her choicest guests had some distance to travel, and if it stayed foggy... She wept hysterically as she thought of the waste: the floor polished to glassy perfection for the dancing, Miss Trent, the music teacher from Baildon, already in the house; old Lantern and the boy whom he had taught and of whom he spoke so highly, Jacky Fenn, bespoken to bring their fiddles; the elegant cold buffet supper to be served in the dining room; new dresses for herself and the girls. All to be wasted because the November weather had arrived a little too soon. Crazily she accepted it as a sign; her plans would fail, Ella and Phyllis would never have another chance; they would marry local yokels, comfortably off, perhaps, but unrefined. It would all be wasted.

"Cheer up, lass," Fred said, "'fog afore seven, clear afore eleven.'"

"Before," said Mrs. Clopton with a gulp and sob. "How can we ever hope to get on with you talking like a workman and then this fog?"

Mr. Mundford, looking out only a moment or two later, regarded the change in the weather with pleasure. He gave no outward sign, he did not smile, or rub his hands or make a sound of satisfaction, but something stirred, deep and cold and certain within him. With the discovery of Damask Greenway he had known that all his material needs were met, and his next act had been to work out, by a study of the moon's phases and certain astrological charts, the best possible date for what he still spoke of—modestly—as "the experiment." When, after the first casting, that date appeared to fall on All Hallows' E'en it had so astounded and amazed him that he had worked out all his calculations again, without changing the result. He knew then that success was certain. He had the right place; a place of worship, mellow with the memory of many men's yearning towards the unknown, the superhuman, yet free of the taint of the Nazarene. In that place, so long sealed away, the dark symbolic blood had drenched the altar in a ceremony that reached backward to the beginning of time. Mithras, old god as he was, was, in Mr. Mundford's sight, a newcomer, but his rites were the old ones; the legendary Abel, second generation of mankind, had sacrificed his animals, and so the blood sacrifice was a close link with that lost time when Lucifer was recognised for what he was, a rebellious angel, strong enough to do battle with those on the other side, Michael and his angels. Mr. Mundford, set upon disinterring the thing which had been overlaid and lost so long ago, lost, one might almost say, in the very Garden of Eden, was able to put the right value upon this tenuous link with that lost time. Yes, the place was perfect.

And he had—again by what seemed an accident—instead of an ignorant stupid female child, half unwilling, half frightened, bullied or bribed into collaboration, Damask Greenway. A mere novice, of course, but the sign was on her, some sort of vision had been vouchsafed her—oh the naïvety of her attempted description! "In a place . . . and light was something you could touch and handle, and colour . . . colour was something you could taste and time was . . . you could see it." She'd had one glimpse, that was all, but she had come back with something, the power to impose her will and the daring to use that power, even on Richard Shelmadine.

And he had instead of a batch of rowdy, reckless fellows who approached the whole thing as a game, much as they would have done a cockfight or a horse race, Richard Shelmadine, that gnawed out shell of a man, so emotionally void that he was neither credulous nor sceptical. He was curious, but his curiosity was merely the result of boredom; he'd tried everything and been eventually bored by everything; and he was greedy . . . he hoped to gain something. That his greed and his boredom actually cancelled one another out Mr. Mundford had proved by lending him his luck. Greed had been satisfied, dwindled and died, killed by boredom; yes, they cancelled one another out and left nothing. Richard Shelmadine was nothing, just the two necessary hands. . . .

And then, as a kind of decoration, the final finishing touch, there was the fact that by the moon and stars, this particular day, commonly known as All Hallows' E'en, was the chosen date.

Mr. Mundford saw the significance of that. Like Christmas and Easter and Lammastide and Whitsun and various other days, All Hallows' had roots in the past; the crafty organisers of the new Christian faith had seized on all the old landmarks of the year, given them new names, new reasons for being, and incorporated them into the Christian calendar. The horned masks and the licence of Saturnalia lurked behind the Christmas festival, the old rebirth of the year, symbolised by the egg ceremonies, behind the Easter celebrations, and behind the lesser, only just recognised anniversary known as All Hallows' E'en there was the dark and sinister history of the November eve covens. No date in the year would have so much suited his purpose; no kind of weather been so promising.

At eleven o'clock, fulfilling Fred Clopton's promise, the fog lifted and the sun gleamed out for a couple of hours. Every last clinging leaf and all the bare twigs shone damply in the sudden brief light. Then the air thickened, by three o'clock it was dusk and soon after four quite dark.

Mrs. Palfrey, walking heavily, came away from Flocky, where she had been helping with the last preparations for the party. She had earned a precious shilling and had also gained an unexpected prize. The whole skin, the "swathe," of a ham, with a good lining of fat, just as Mrs. Clopton had peeled it from the joint before applying the browned bread crumbs. The

Palfrey family had not tasted any form of animal food for at least six weeks. At the end of harvest Spitty had applied for parish relief. In the course of the investigations following this application, it had transpired that the Palfrey family was not the responsibility of Clevely; Spitty had been born in Baildon; his relief must be claimed there. He was, by law, entitled to the price of a one gallon loaf of bread per week, his wife and each dependent child to the price of a half gallon loaf. In that month the gallon loaf was worth one shilling and eightpence, so the allowance granted to the Palfrey family was five shillings, or sixty pence. And lest this grant should lead to idleness and pauperism, the careful guardians arranged that the week's dole should be divided into six equal parts, and Spitty was allowed to collect tenpence each day for six days a week. This made sure that he, at least, had never an idle moment. Lithe, able-bodied Danny Fuller with his heart light with hope had found the walk from Clevely to Baildon twice a week quite a strain; for poor, shambling Spitty, product of a lifetime's malnutrition, the walk twice a day was a task only just within his power. He had to set off early in the morning and returned late in the evening, utterly exhausted, yet despite the exhaustion so hungry that he would have found no difficulty in devouring the tenpenny loaf without help from his family. The spiteful and petty-minded arrangement worked the family woe in another way too, making it difficult for Mrs. Palfrey to take any small job which did happen to come her way, since it was impossible to leave three children, all under five years of age, alone in the house for long. In desperation she had done so on the day of Mrs. Clopton's party; she had tied the two youngest to the table legs, leaving four-and-a-half Betsy free and in charge. Mrs. Ashpole had promised to "look in" once or twice. So Mrs. Palfrey came home in triumph, sharpened the family knife, and chopped the ham skin into fine mincemeeat, the small yellowish-brown, semi-translucent fragments of boiled pigskin shining in the base of soft lardy fat. She would have fed the children and put them to bed before Spitty came home, but the last crumb of yesterday's bread had been eaten at midday. So they waited, the children wailing with hunger, until, very late on account of the fog, Spitty arrived, dewed all over with grey misty drops and almost dead with weariness. Seizing the stale tenpenny loaf, Mrs. Palfrey cut it into thick slices and spread them thinly with the minced "meat." She was ravenously hungry herself, but just as she spread the fifth slice the new child moved within her with a nauseating lurch. Tightening her mouth, she drew the knife twice across the slice, cutting it into four.

"I did my eating up at Flocky. So you all get a bit extra. Right a feast tonight, ain't it?" she said bravely.

Damask herself carried up Miss Parsons' tray. The old lady had developed a cold two days earlier and was keeping to her bed. Her appetite was good and she welcomed the tray with little eager sounds.

"Quite a feast tonight," Damask said, pausing to set one covered dish from the tray on the silver heater with the three thick candles under the grid and then carrying the tray itself to the bed. "Oxtail soup and a roast partridge, some grapes from the Ockley hothouses, and our own pears."

"Delicious!" said Miss Parsons. "Lying here, I have been thinking. One should cultivate gluttony, without practising it too much, in one's youth, so that one may have one dependable pleasure left in old age."

Thinking of Julie and the tea—Julie had, most oddly, veered clean over to Amos's side and refused the tea and the teapot and even the medicines which Damask had taken over on the day following the row—Damask said, "If one can afford it." She lifted the cover from the bowl of soup.

"And we can, can't we, dear child? There was a time when, when we, when I . . . nothing but cold mutton, the nastiest kind, all fat and little bones. That was before you came. Now you're here and everything is all right. You'll never go away, will you? Promise me."

"I have promised you. I shall never go away. I am going out for a little while this evening, though. Mrs. Bennett will come and make you comfortable for the night and I shall be here when you wake up in the morning."

"Oh dear, I shall be alone." Miss Parsons' wrinkled old lips, glistening with the rich soup, assumed a childish pout.

"I must go and see my mother. She isn't very well, you know." She had told Mr. Mundford to stop the carriage in which he was fetching her at the gate of the Dower House.

"I hope you find her better," Miss Parsons said untruthfully. With the passing of time she had grown more possessive about her "dear child," and jealous of Julie. It was, of course, natural and proper and admirable that the child should care for and visit her parents, but Miss Parsons grudged every one of the brief, infrequent visits. She rather hoped that Julie would die soon; then she would have Damask's undivided attention.

"I have a mother myself," she remarked as Damask removed the empty soup bowl and placed the partridge before her. "She doesn't care for me, though. Being a girl, you know—a great disappointment. My father says that in China—or is it India? No, China, I think, unwanted girl babies are put out to die of exposure. Did you know that?"

"No. What a horrible custom."

"Is he in the library?"

"Who?"

"Papa. If not, on the top shelf of the cupboard to the left of the window there is a big brown-covered book, a kind of journal which he kept when he was on his voyages. *Most* interesting. Not intended for female eyes, of course, but most enjoyable reading. We might peruse it together."

"Not this evening. I told you. I have to go out presently."

"You must wrap up well. I have a cold, you know."

"You have had. It is better now. I think you will be able to get up tomorrow."

"I sincerely hope so. It must be almost time for Charles to visit me, and it wouldn't do, would it, for me to receive him in my bedroom. His wife would object. She's very jealous, you know. And quite crazy, poor creature. I do sympathise with him, in a way. But they say, don't they, 'Fools and knaves are always paid out, but fools first.' He brought it on himself. Of course she is quite unbelievably beautiful and very well connected. I do realise that. Papa was quite disgusted and said, 'If that is gentlemanly behaviour, give me seafaring men every time.' This is a very young, tender partridge, or exceptionally well cooked."

"Eat it while it is hot."

"And afterwards we might play cards. We could play on the tray, or would you prefer it if I got up and sat by the fire?"

"We'll do that tomorrow. This evening I have to go out."

"Of course. I'm afraid I keep forgetting. I am *very* forgetful. But not mad, whatever that woman says."

The beauty of this kind of conversation was that one need not attend, need make no effort at all. One could go on, pursuing one's own thoughts, remembering all the things which Mr. Mundford had said, all the cajoleries and the promises and the mysterious, tantalising things which meant nothing, because one was young, and ignorant, "just a beginner," as Mr. Mundford pointed out. The promises she did understand; they shone, distant and golden, rather like a sunset, and outlined against them, stark and black, was the silhouette of Sally Fuller's figure, just as it had been when Damask, leaving the cobbler's cottage one evening, had seen it standing by the Ashpoles' door, full and ripe, bursting with promise, for Sally was big with her second child. At that sight the slight but vigorous vein of scepticism which in her Methodist days had often troubled her by producing doubts and questions about God began to work again, questioning this other Power. These questions were more quickly silenced; she had only to look around her, or down at her own hands, to find proof of *this* Power's favour towards her, its omniscience and potency. And there was Mr. Mundford, with his signs and wonders, always ready to encourage her.

Damask removed the tray, soothed Miss Parsons into a passive drowsiness and went to get ready to play her part in the great "experiment."

The fog, which from within the lighted room seemed so thick and baffling, was far less impenetrable when one was out of doors. That at least was something to be thankful for, Linda thought, as she stole, furtive as a thief, out by the side door and into the stable yard. She knew roughly where Simon was, for he had howled dolorously for an hour after being dragged away; but he was silent now, and with hands which no effort of will could make steady, she opened door after door before she found the right one and braced herself to meet the dog's overwhelming welcome. After that she wasted no time; she had made her plan. Between the Manor and Berry Lane, if you went directly, there were only a stretch of park and the Parson's glebe. Hadstock said that the walk took him barely ten minutes. With the dog close to her side, she left the yard and hurried into the park, where the long, tussocky grass, grey with the fog dampness, slowed her progress, until, after a few minutes, she struck the narrow track worn by Hadstock's feet. That was something else to be thankful for—and it was more; it was a sign. Out of all the horror and tumult and confusion and desperation, here she was, on the little path which led direct to Hadstock. His feet in their daily journeys had made the way smooth for hers.

The track led, ruler-straight, to the sunken ditch which divided the park from the glebe. Water, leaden-coloured against the greyed grass, ran in the ditch's bottom, but two great stones broke the surface, bridging it in two lengthy strides. She misjudged the first step and slipped, soaking one shoe and stocking and one side of her skirt, but she regained a precarious balance and reached the glebe, and Simon crossed in one lithe leap.

The uncurtained kitchen window of Hadstock's cottage showed as a yellow smudge on the prevailing grey before she reached the gate in the fence which separated his back yard from the glebe, and that again was a symbol of hope. For her most immediately pressing problem Hadstock would have a solution; and in asking his help she would be bound to explain a little; that would be a relief. As she opened the gate and walked into the small yard she reminded herself that she must be careful, controlled; the relationship between them was tenable only on those conditions.

She had not spoken to Hadstock since Richard's return to Clevely just before the Harvest Horkey, and she had seen him, in that time, only once, at the Horkey itself. Hadstock had remained aloof then, and left early. After the supper was ended and the trestle tables were cleared to leave room for the dancing, she had, as on the previous year, started the jig on the arm of Ricky Wellman, the oldest man present, while Richard hauled Mrs. Hart, all twelve stone of her, bulky in four petticoats, twice around the barn. A little later, when Richard said in his critical fashion, "You have not yet honoured the bailiff, my dear," she had said, "No, but I will," and turned very quickly lest something in her expression should betray her. The idea of dancing with Hadstock as part of the routine, a sharing out of favours, was repulsive to her; it would have been a secret betrayal of their unacknowledged intimacy. And it would have been something more—a test of fortitude. But Hadstock had gone, his early retirement eloquent and significant.

The lighted window was close now. As she moved towards it she saw the light obscured by Hadstock's bulk; he carried a kettle in his hand.

She knocked on the door and it opened. There was Hadstock in his shirt sleeves. He stared at her with unconcealed astonishment.

"You!" he said. Her face in the shadow of the cloak's hood had a luminous pallor, her eyes, with pupils dilated by the walk through the darkness, were black and huge, and she was trembling so much that the little globules of moisture along the edge of the hood and the wisps of hair which showed under it shimmered and gleamed.

"Is anything wrong? Come in," he said. As she entered the kitchen, he slammed the door to, as though to exclude some possible pursuer.

"Nothing very much. At least . . . Oh, Hadstock, I'm sorry to arrive like this and disturb you. But you did say that if ever . . . Do you think you could keep Simon for me?"

"Of course I can. Here, sit down." He pulled forward a high-backed chair, black with age, uncushioned. "Let me have your cloak, it's quite damp."

"I mustn't stay. It doesn't matter." But he took the cloak, shook it, and hung it on the peg on the door where his own jacket hung. The big white dog, close by Linda's chair, watched him. Another disappointing walk! Simon hated Linda to visit cottages; he liked to walk all the time, and have her full attention. But he knew how to behave; he stood by her side until the cottage's occupant had admired him, and the children, if any, had mauled him a little; then he lay down with his nose on his paws. This cottage belonged to someone he knew, and there were, apparently, no children, so he could lie down now. He did so, with a patient sigh, and stayed immobile, only cocking an eye when he heard his own name.

Hadstock turned back and looked at Linda. Some sort of shock, he thought; and nasty, despite the way in which she had said, "Nothing very much."

He moved to the hearth, and taking up a handful of the dried twigs which lay there, broke them small and fed them to the flames, which lapped about the kettle.

"I was just about to make some tea," he said untruthfully. He had fallen into the habit of shaving overnight; it saved time in the mornings and during Richard's absence enabled him to present himself to Linda freshly shaven. The kettle had been put on to heat the shaving water. "It'll be ready in a minute. Will you drink a cup while you tell me what has happened?"

She was already calmer. To a degree she had succeeded in her plan. Simon, at least, was safe. Pointing to the dog, she said:

"He bit Mr. Mundford this afternoon."

"Splendid dog!" said Hadstock, so impulsively that Linda began to laugh; and then checked herself, knowing where laughter would lead.

"It wasn't funny," she said.

"I know," Hadstock agreed instantly. "Like many most reasonable actions, it led to deplorable results. Sentence of death?"

"Yes." He was making it easy for her. Busying himself taking the teamaking things from a little cupboard beside the fireplace, not looking at her, and making the horrible things sound almost ordinary.

The kettle boiled with a spurt and a hiss. Hadstock put tea in the pot, his big hands moving with a care and delicacy that held a hint of pathos.

"He'll be quite safe with me," he said as he passed her a cup of tea. He pulled a stool out from under the table and sat down on it. He had seen how unsteady her hand was; his longing to comfort her was like a physical pain. "Now, tell me all about it. When, and where, and how, and how much bitten is Mr. Mundford?"

"When was just after we had returned from our walk this afternoon; and where was in my little sitting room. I've kept him—Simon—out of the way as much as possible, you know, kept him to my bedroom and that one room downstairs. We were there and Mr. Mundford came in, and that smell, the incense, came with him; he *reeked* of it. Simon bristled and flattened himself on the floor and went behind my chair. Mr. Mundford said something about thinking Richard might be with me and he also said something about . . . what happened earlier in the afternoon. Then he came close to me and mentioned this lace on my sleeve. A little while ago he remarked the lace on another dress; asked me was it Venetian, and just touched it. I happen to remember that because when he did so his fingers were all bunched together as though he had rheumatism. He said that the lace on this dress wasn't nearly so beautiful, and he just touched it, too; not with his fingers all together this time, more as though he were plucking something that hung from my wrist. Perhaps Simon thought he was taking something from me. He sprang at him, straight out from behind my chair, without warning. Fortunately Mr. Mundford wears a very voluminous cravat, stiffly starched, otherwise his throat would have been bitten. As it is, only his cheek is lacerated. Here." She put her hand to the place on her own clear jaw line. "I must say, in his favour, that he was very magnanimous about it. He said dogs always disliked him. But Richard was very angry and said Simon was vicious and must be destroyed. I just couldn't bear that."

"You don't have to," Hadstock said. "I'll take him out for

a bit each morning and evening, as I did when he lived with me before, and leave him locked up. I'll put the key in the hole in the thatch just over that window, so you can come and see him any time you want to."

"Thank you. It may not be for long. Richard generally takes notice of what Mr. Mundford says and he spoke in the dog's favour. Also—they've already stayed here five weeks."

"I know," said Hadstock with some feeling. The time had seemed interminable to him, missing his evening visits to Linda, brief and formal as they often were, and subjected daily to Richard's nagging, veiled insults, and interference. He shifted a little on his stool, linking his long brown fingers and letting his hands dangle between his knees. "And that is all that happened this afternoon?"

She looked at him, surprised. Did he know about the other happening? It was possible, the order might have been relayed through him.

"Not quite all. But I didn't mean to bother you with that. Did you have anything to do with the pheasants? Did you know?"

"What pheasants?"

"The two Chinese pheasants that lived in Layer Wood. They were . . . they belonged to me; I brought them back from India, where they were given to me in circumstances that made me value them very much. At first they stayed in the garden, then they moved into Layer, but I used to catch glimpses of them now and then. I hoped they'd breed this year, but I don't think they did. This afternoon Simon and I were just leaving the house by the side door—it isn't much used now that the front is completed, but we use it so as to go in and out unnoticed; today Mr. Mundford and Richard were there and so were my pheasants, in a crate! Mr. Mundford was saying something about everything falling into place. They both looked startled, rather confused when they saw me, and more so when I asked what the pheasants were doing there. Richard said that he intended to give them away. I asked to whom and he asked was that any of my business and I . . . I answered him sharply and said yes, it was, because they were my pheasants. . . ."

"A not unnatural remark," Hadstock said drily. "And then?"

"That is all. He was very angry, of course; and I feel that that is partly why he was so obdurate about poor Simon."

"What happened to the pheasants?"

"I don't know. They had gone when I returned. I admit I

was curious; I asked one or two of the servants—quite casually; they none of them knew anything about them. Mr. Mundford knows; I think he has had a hand in it, somehow. Ordinarily he is so very ready to put in a tactful word, but all the time we were talking about them he stood and stared at the birds and never even looked round. And then ... then later on when he came to my room he asked might he replace them by a more domesticated pet, and asked if I would like a parrot, or a monkey. I was aware then that I had behaved childishly; but those pheasants, though I saw them so little, were dear to me in a way." Hadstock was surprised to find himself instantly jealous of the donor of the pheasants, jealous in a different, deeper way than he was of Richard Shelmadine.

"Sentimental associations?"

"Yes ... and no. They were given to me by an old man, a cripple, who gave them to me for a keepsake, because they were all he had to give."

"Ah," said Hadstock. He visualised a beggar, making a precarious living perhaps by showing off the birds.

"He was so immensely rich, you see, he wouldn't have missed anything else; the pheasants were valuable to him because he had only had them two days."

She remembered how that truth had had to be concealed from Richard. And now here she was, offering it so simply to Hadstock, knowing that he would understand. Suddenly, in the light of that comparison, she saw the whole tragedy of her marriage; it wasn't only that by marrying the wrong man you brought misery to yourself and to him; you lost all chance of the happiness that you and some other man might have known.

"I think I should go now," she said. "If I am missed, there may be another fuss and I don't think I could bear any more today. Thank you for taking the dog and for listening to all my troubles."

Hot, hasty words beat their way to the surface of his mind. Don't go back; stay here with me; I love you ... But with the taste of them on his tongue he knew that he could never speak them. He was too old, too much experienced. He knew what it meant to be poor, having been rich, and what a descent in the social scale meant; he could visualise the search for work, the search for a home, the scandal, the friendlessness, the placelessness. He would, at that moment, gladly have lain down and died if his death could have benefited her, even a little, but such drama, he thought satirically, was denied him, like so many other things. So he rose and took her cloak from the peg and laid it on her shoulders, and said in an ordinary voice, "You will allow me to walk back with you. I have my rounds to make. Have you thought of how you will explain the dog's disappearance?"

"Not yet. My one concern was to get him away."

"We'll think of something as we walk," Hadstock said. He shrugged himself into his coat and reached down his lantern and carried it over to the fire, where he lighted it with a twig. The dog had gone with Linda towards the door and she had first bent over him and then gone down on her knees, hugging his white head to her breast.

"No. No. You must stay here, Simon. Just for a little while. Sit! Sit! Simon, stay here." By the light of the lantern Hadstock could see the tears in her eyes. He opened the door a little way and said brusquely, "You slip through. I'll keep him back." She did so, and as the dog lunged to follow her Hadstock caught him by the collar and heaved him into the middle of the kitchen. "For God's sake," he said, addressing the dog as though it were human, "don't make it harder for her.

"He'll be all right," he said, locking the door and putting the key in his pocket.

A loud, unearthly howl from the kitchen denied that Simon would be all right.

"It's quite plain to me," said Hadstock, "that his presence, like murder, cannot be hid. I shall say that *I* let him out of wherever he was confined and took him home with me. Sir Richard can make what he likes of that."

Linda's words of thanks were lost in the clatter of hoofs and rattle of wheels as Mr. Rout's gig and Mr. Thurlow Lamb's carriage followed one another along Berry Lane.

"Late traffic this evening," Hadstock commented, reaching forward to open the little gate.

"I expect the Cloptons have a party," Linda said. "It is All Hallows' E'en, you know."

"All Hallows'?" repeated Hadstock in a curious voice. "Why, so it is!"

Up on the Waste only two windows were lighted; people retired early, saving light and fuel. Candles had never been much used there; rushes, which cost nothing, dipped into animal fat, which was plentiful in due season, and allowed to harden had been the usual form of illumination. This year there had been a shortage of animal fat and a consequent dearth of rush-dips. Matt Ashpole was working by firelight; he missed his fuel rights from the Waste less than the others for, being able to get about in his cart, he was free of the countryside and always kept a sharp lookout for fallen branches or dead trees. Amos Greenway was burning a precious candle, which was justified, for he was finishing off a pair of top boots for Fred Clopton. They were exactly of the pattern and quality as those Sir Charles was wont to order—which just showed how Fred was prospering.

Matt was working on a still. He'd tried various kinds of brews in the last few months and been satisfied with none of them. Then he'd had the good fortune to fall in with an Irish cattleman at one of the markets and had listened attentively to an account of how what sounded like real good liquor was made in illicit stills in Ireland. By all accounts it wasn't only drinkable, it was saleable. Matt had straightway invested a few pence in a quantity of slightly damaged barley, which he said he needed for chicken food, and had made his "mash." If the strength of the resultant liquor should bear any relationship to the potency of the odour of the "mash" it would be liquor of no mean order. Tonight, with a large copper kettle, a bit of brass piping, some clay for sealing the joints, and a washtub for cooling, he was busy with his first experiment in distilling. The Irishman had warned him that homemade "potheen" should not be drunk straight from the still, but all Irishmen were notorious liars and Matt promised himself that if the still did not blow up in his face and if it produced anything resembling liquor, he would have a drink before he went to bed.

When Amos had put the last stitch into Fred Clopton's boots, there was still a good inch and a half of candle left. So he turned gladly to a task more to his taste. He had reluctantly postponed—not abandoned, but postponed—the chapel building. Until the spirit of the Lord moved more vigorously amongst the members of existent chapels at Nettleton, Baildon, and Summerfield, and more funds and more labour were forthcoming so that the site could be properly drained and the foundations properly laid, he knew himself defeated. But only temporarily. And the rickety, lurching building could be put to good use. Three of its walls were visible from various points in the road, and Amos was preparing three large boards.

He did not overestimate the literacy of the Clevely inhab-

itants, nor underestimate their curiosity. The boards would attract attention and those who could spell out a word or two
would be invited to read them out to the others. That was one
way of spreading the Word. The passer-by, halting with his
back to Berry Lane, would face the front of the chapel, where
the entrance should have been; and there he would see, in red
and black letters on a plain board, WHEN GOD SO WILLS
A CHAPEL SHALL STAND HERE. Coming up from the inn
or the smithy, anyone on the road could hardly avoid the sight
of the sagging south wall, where these words would meet his
eyes, THE WAGES OF SIN IS DEATH. Those two boards
were already completed, standing face to the wall behind the
workbench. Amos now set Clopton's boots aside, laid a plain
board on the bench, and thoughtfully stirred his paintbrush
around in the paint. This was the notice which would show
from Stone Bridge. It must be brief, because the paint was low
in the tin. With part of his mind selecting, testing, and dis-
carding various texts, Amos found himself entertaining an un-
dercurrent of thought. He remembered how, on the morning
after Damask's terrible attack on his integrity, he had gone to
call upon Mr. Hadstock to ask if the bailiff knew any reason
why he should have been given the grant of twenty acres.
Hadstock had been very reassuring. "I know of no reason, but
you may be sure there was one, and a good one, otherwise
you'd have been left like the rest."

"Well, I'd be grateful, sir, if you could find out for me."

Hadstock had asked Richard. "The man seemed genuinely
concerned . . ."

"Somewhat late in the day," Richard had said. "The allotment was made in February." He was half inclined to add, "Tell
him it was because he has a pretty daughter," but caution
prevailed.

"Oh, tell him anything. What has he done with the land?"

"Sold some and started to build a chapel on the rest, sir."

"Then tell him I made him that special allotment hoping he
would use it for that purpose. Don't look so sceptical, Hadstock. Do you doubt my altruism?"

So Amos, in taking the land as a gift from God, had been
right and Damask wrong. The chapel's collapse was not a
rebuke, it was just one more test of faith. And by using the
site as a place for displaying notices Amos was showing that
he was still full of faith and devotion and loyalty. What should
the third wall announce to the world? Suddenly he knew; the

message was brief, profoundly true, and voiced a fact of which many people in Clevely seemed to have lost sight and of which they might well be reminded.

THE EARTH IS THE LORD'S, Amos wrote.

(Soon after the three boards were in place some anonymous wit, profiting probably by the lessons he had received in Sunday school, scrawled along the lower edge of that one, "But Squire grabbed it.")

The carriage, its lights dimmed and yet magnified in size by the fog, was waiting at the gate of the Dower House. The driver, heavily muffled, sat aloft and neither stirred nor spoke as she approached. Mr. Mundford himself opened the door, alighted, and helped her in. Immediately the carriage set off. Inside the closed vehicle it was quite dark. Mr. Mundford had to fumble about in order to find her hand.

"You're cold," he said kindly. "Not nervous, are you? I assure you again that there is nothing to be nervous about, nothing in the least. But it has turned cold and we have quite a long drive. So . . ." His hand left hers, and she heard him moving about; then his hand found hers again and pressed a small flat bottle into her fingers.

"Take a good drink of that," he said, "it will warm you."

The liquid was itself cold, almost without flavour, and quite unrecognisable. Since the Saunderses' depredations had ceased and Miss Parsons' financial situation had improved, such luxuries as wine and brandy had returned to the Dower House; Mr. Mundford's draught was something quite unfamiliar, however, and rather disappointing, neither pleasing the palate nor warming the stomach. Soon, however, she felt its effect, a warm lassitude wove itself about her; it was as though she had crept into bed on a chilly night, felt the light weight of the blankets, the softness of the pillows, and begun to drift towards sleep. But she must not sleep now, that would never do. She had to help Mr. Mundford, and in return he would give her her heart's desire. She struggled against the torpor; and then, all at once, was free of it, free of everything, free of her body. The "I" which was Damask Greenway rose and floated, hovered somewhere in the space enclosed by the hood of the carriage, and looked down upon the body which it had inhabited. There it sat with its hair prettily curled, its yellow skirts demurely spread, its little white hands folded together . . . just like a doll waiting for somebody to pick it up and involve it in a game of make-believe. The real Damask, airy and free, watched with interested approval.

The carriage jolted and swayed, turned several corners; it was, as Mr. Mundford had said, quite a long drive, and slow, of course, because of the fog. But it stopped at last and Mr. Mundford alighted and held out his hand to the doll which rose with easy grace and stood beside him; the real Damask left the carriage at the same time and hovered, watchful, above the doll's head. The carriage drove away immediately. Mr. Mundford took the doll by the arm and led it through a doorway, along a passage, through another doorway, and down some stairs into what looked like a cellar, then through another doorway and down a long sloping passage where it was very cold. The doll shivered. They came to a place where a great stone slab had been removed from a wall, leaving a wide gap through which they all passed and entered a vast place lined with tall pillars and lighted by candles and decorated by large white figures which stood at intervals along the walls beyond the pillars. A strange place.

Almost immediately Sir Richard Shelmadine joined them. Mr. Mundford said in an ordinary voice, "All well?" and Sir Richard nodded and went close to the doll in the yellow dress, regarding it with interest, but no favour.

Mr. Mundford moved away a little and came back carrying two glasses and gave one each to the doll and Sir Richard; then he fetched a little plate upon which lay three tiny biscuits. They each took one. Mr. Mundford turned away again, and when he joined the group he held a glass and a little biscuit, too. The real Damask was rather afraid that the doll's porcelain fingers would break the biscuit, and that would be a bad thing because this was a ceremony. Before they ate or drank, Mr. Mundford said something which reminded Damask of Amos' "Grace before meat," but this was in a language she did not know. The doll managed beautifully, drank its wine, which was heavy and sweet, and ate the biscuit, which was so frail that it seemed to melt in the mouth. Then Mr. Mundford lighted some other candles, which immediately gave off a horrible, stifling odour; the real ones he extinguished, saying some more of the unknown words as each one went out. In the subdued light one noticed the fire for the first time; a red, glaring fire like a sunset on a stormy evening. In its glow the doll began to take off its clothes and there was no more embarrassment or any other feeling attached to that disrobing than there would have been to the undressing of a doll. After one glance the real Damask, hovering high under the groined roof, paid no more heed but turned her attention to what Mr. Mundford was doing to some birds which looked like pheasants, but more brightly feathered, more beautiful than any pheasants could ever be.

In the best bedroom at Fuller's, now the young couple's, the atmosphere grew stuffy and then foetid. Mrs. Fuller had started off with four good stout wax candles—quite enough to see the job through—but they had burned out and been replaced and then, anxious to do something to help, Danny had fetched up his lantern. The lights, the heat that came from the good roaring fire in the kitchen immediately below, and the heat of three sweating bodies combined to raise the temperature in the room to a point only just bearable.

Mrs. Fuller wiped the sweat from Sally's face and then from her own.

"I can't make it out," she gasped, too much distressed to remember any longer to be tactful in front of the sufferer. "Coming on like that so sudden and then taking this turn. Granted thass come feet first, but then many do, but they *move* nonetheless. Oh, what wouldn't I give to see old Widow Hayward walk in that door!"

Danny unclenched the teeth that gripped his lower lip.

"They say Mrs. Sam Jarvey is knowledgeable."

"So'm I. But fetch her, do."

Danny blundered away and Mrs. Fuller turned back to the bed.

"You gotta try to help yourself, Sally. This ain't your first; you know the worst wrench is the last. One good go and it'll be over. Come on now, take aholt of this and next time give a good heave."

But she knew that she was wasting her breath. Sally was past hearing or understanding; she just lay there, almost as though she were dead already, and the spasms had practically ceased.

The baby wasn't due for another month, that was the queer part, and babies that came early, though difficult to rear, usually came easily. Mrs. Fuller had said as much to Sally when the pains started suddenly midway through the afternoon. "Thass took us by surprise, like," she said, "and it may be a pingler, but you 'on't hev the trouble with it you had with *him*, bless his heart! Keep on the move, my dear, for a bit, and count on it being all over by suppertime."

But here it was long past supper, long past bedtime; the middle of the night had come and it looked as though Sally would die. In one blinding flash Mrs. Fuller realised how fond she really was of the girl, and how unfair she had been to her. She'd not made enough allowance for her faulty upbringing, not appreciated her good nature or her anxiety to please; she had even withheld the quilt with the true-lovers' knots. If Sally died . . .

Dashing away a fresh burst of sweat from her forehead, Mrs. Fuller racked her brain in an effort to remember any old wives' trick that she hadn't tried.

Danny, too, was suffering from remorse. This was a judgement on him. He'd been forced into marrying the girl and he had always held it against her. In retrospect it seemed easy to have defied Matt, he'd never have dared use that gun! Weak and flabby, that's what he'd been, and then spiteful, obstinately refusing to be pleased by anything Sal did or said. He'd been daft, too, hankering after that cold little bitch, Damask Greenway, who'd treated him like dirt all along. Fool, fool, fool.

When he reached the inn and learned from a shouted and not altogether amiable conversation with Sam, who leaned out of the window to conduct it, that Mrs. Sam was herself bedridden, a cask having slipped and crushed her foot that morning, Danny knew that there was no hope. Sal'd die, just as he was getting set on her, and it would serve him bloody well right!

When Linda and Hadstock left him, Simon howled for a while just as he had howled when Richard had had him dragged away and shut In the shed. Then he tired and lay down to wait patiently until his mistress should come and set him free again; he dozed and waked and dozed again in the timelessness that only animals knew. Then he woke again and leapt up, all his age-old instincts shrilling out their danger signals. Out there in the night the enemies were prowling; all was not well with the fold!

He rushed around the small kitchen, throwing his full weight against the door and uttering his deep, full-throated bark. Sometimes just that indication that a dog was awake and wary was enough. He was afraid of nothing now—the thing which had terrified him, which stank of evil and the dreaded unknown, had proved to be only flesh and blood after all. If only he could get out of this place! He jumped on to the table, scattering Hadstock's tea things, and there found himself level with the window. One bounding leap carried him through, the small panes and rotten woodwork giving way before him. Over the gate, across the glebe, over the ditch and into the park he went like a white streak; his nose dripped blood and the taste of it on his tongue raised his fierce spirit to frenzy. Thus and thus would the blood of the enemy taste.

He ran straight to the side door of the house and was there baulked again. Madness came upon him; he threw himself at the door, reckless of bruises, retreated, threw up his head and howled and barked, and renewed the assault. The servants heard him and cursed or shuddered according to their sex and disposition and buried their heads in the bedclothes. No one stirred. They all knew that the dog had been locked up for attacking Mr. Mundford. And a dog howling in the night boded no good, anyway.

Linda heard him. She had not gone to bed and was still huddled by the fire in her small sitting room, half paralytic with a fear she dared hardly examine or name to herself. Despite the fire which roared and crackled and blazed, the room grew colder and strange draughts troubled the candles. Closely woven into the fear was a sense of guilt; she'd known, really, and tried to take refuge in incredulity; had seen, and turned away, muffling her eyes with disbelief. But what could I have done? she asked herself again and again. What can I do now?

She knew what she *must* do when she heard the dog. Somehow or other Richard had found where he was and her imagination shuddered away from the thought of what was happening now. She got up on legs that felt stiff and hollow, as though they were made of bamboo, and took one of the flickering unreliable candles. She went out into the hall, where the stairs climbed up into the darkness and the cold came to meet her, walked resolutely across it, and opened the door on its farther side. It led to the gun room, disused since Sir Charles' death. Here the dog's noise, a rising crescendo of yelps and barking, reached her more clearly—she was on the right track—but then she'd known all along. As she crossed the room she looked at the neatly ranged guns and for the first time in her life wished that she had learned to use one and thought of Lady Fennel, by repute the best shot in Suffolk. If someone were torturing Lady Fennel's dog and there were guns within reach . . . But it was no good, she wasn't Lady Fennel, she knew nothing of guns, not even how to load one. . . .

On the far side of the gun room was the door to the little lobby which was just inside the side entrance. She opened that door and was making steadily along the passage towards the cellar door when Simon, who had momentarily ceased his noise, taken a run back, and turned for one more attempt to batter down the door, threw himself against it and snarled as it resisted him. So he wasn't down there in the cellar with *them*; he was outside. She turned and threw open the door, dreading what she might see. Simon, with his crazy eyes and his fur on end and his face and chest all spattered with blood, was a horrid sight, and he bounded in like a mad dog, pushing against her and sniffing (all right so far, all well with the flock), and then rushing off along the passage towards the cellar door. She cried out, put her hand on the door to steady herself from the impact of the dog's passing, and dropped her candlestick. At the same moment something else moved out there in the darkness, and something low down, near the ground, glimmered.

She would have screamed then, but she was voiceless, as one is in a nightmare, and no sound came.

"It's all right, my lady. I'm here," said Hadstock, and raised his lantern.

She could speak then and said, "Oh, Hadstock, oh, Hadstock!" over and over again, laughing and crying at the same time.

Miss Parsons woke suddenly, as the old do, and was immediately conscious of something wrong. No pain; and her breathing was certainly clearer; not too hot or too cold. What then? She raised her head and looked about her. The candle in its perforated china cover, specially designed to burn safely and slowly through the night, gave out its steady muted glow, but the fire was out. It must be very late. She reached for her watch and held it at arm's length near to one of the holes in the candle cover and squinted and scowled until she had it focussed and could see the time. Just after midnight. Then she must have been asleep. It was ten when she was settled for the night. Ah, yes, now she knew; she remembered. Mrs. Bennett had settled her for the night because Damask was out. And she'd meant to stay awake until the child came home, but she'd fallen asleep. That was what was wrong. Was it? Wasn't it rather the feeling that the next-door room was still unoccupied?

She could, of course, knock on the communicating wall, as she occasionally did, especially if she were unwell. But that seemed unkind. The child had been out with her sick mother and needed her sleep; but she herself would not sleep until she knew. She must know. She rose, put on her slippers and dressing gown, and took her candle.

The sight of the empty room threw her into a fluster. Up to that point her thinking had been logical and lucid and her anxiety natural enough. Now here she was, all alone, and she'd lost Damask. Her world began to break up. Secrecy, she thought wildly, that was the thing. Once the Saunderses knew that Damask had gone—oh dear, oh dear! They mustn't know. She trembled to think what would happen. They'd have it all their own way again. She must escape, get away and find somebody to help her. . . .

Furtive as a thief, she padded down the stairs and reached the front door. It was locked and the key had been removed; oh, how cunning they were. But not cunning enough, or else luck was with her, for the key lay there on the table in the hall. She inserted it, turned it, and opened the door, inch by inch, lest she should make a sound. There, she was out! And lucky again in that she had brought down the covered night candle— an ordinary one would have soon been quenched by the thick fog-laden air. She held the candle out well ahead of her and followed it, steering an erratic, zigzag course along the drive, sometimes plunging into the wet bushes of the shrubbery on one side, or blundering on to the wet grass of the lawn on the other and muttering to herself as she went. Eventually she reached the gate. This time it did not cry out its message of betrayal; somebody must have oiled it since her last attempt to escape for help. One of those kind people to whom Mrs. Saunders had given a shilling, perhaps.

Now, which way? The Stone Bridge was a good place; people often lingered there, people with nothing to do. On the other hand, that way led to the village where Charles and Felicity lived; she'd avoided the village since their marriage; she hadn't even attended church since that Sunday when Charles had come out of the porch with his bride on his arm. But in this fog it was safe enough. Even if they came by they wouldn't recognise her . . . wouldn't know that she was the one whom Charles had jilted in the very middle of a dance because over her shoulder he had seen the beautiful pink and white mask that hid the face of a mad devil. Funny the way men never

saw behind masks and women always did. She could have told
him. She could have said, "She'll want a purple garden, you
know, and a house in London and twenty-four pairs of high-
heeled shoes, and all that unnecessary expense will wreck your
plans for recuperating your finances." But of course to have
said that would have drawn attention to the fact that she was
herself an heiress; it would have been in bad taste. Besides,
she had never had a chance. Charles had avoided her for years.
Ashamed, no doubt. It was not until Felicity was dead and the
baby grown into quite a big boy that he had come visiting
again.

She had now reached the Stone Bridge, and having lost all
sense of time, was momentarily disappointed to find it deserted,
all its embrasures empty. But she was soon comforted, for she
recalled a dream. In the dream she had stood here, just like
this, waiting, and the girl in the ugly dress of the Poor Farm
had come along. So everything was all right, and she had only
to wait. In the dream it had been a warm night, with a great
copper-coloured moon; now there was no moon and the weather
was foggy and cold. Very cold, thought Miss Parsons, inef-
fectually huddling her dressing gown around her. The poor
child would feel the cold, too, in that thin print dress; she hoped
the waiting would not be too long. However, perhaps her name
would keep her warm; it was a warm, red name, Damask, like
the rose; the very word called up a picture of a dark, deephearted
rose, sweet-scented, basking in the sun against a dark red wall.
She said the word over and over again and the foggy darkness
took the sound, hushed it away into silence.

In the hidden place Mr. Mundford's "experiment" neared
its climax. And about time, too, Richard thought; the rites
seemed to have gone on for hours and were becoming tedious.
In the beginning he had watched Alec's actions with curiosity
and interest and been mildly surprised to discover that he was
himself still capable of physical revulsion. Blood he had been
prepared for. Alec had made no secret of his intentions to
sacrifice the pheasants, had indeed gloated over the beauty and
rarity which made them so suitable to his purpose; and to see
some of the blood drained off into a little brass bowl was
tolerable—after all, Richard had been cupped in his time!
Fastidiousness made its first protest when Alec dipped his tallowy fingers in the bowl, and using the blood as though it were
paint, began to draw strange patterns on the floor. Richard had

looked away, thinking that never again would he be able to watch those long pale fingers handling knives or forks at table or cards in a game without remembering how they looked at this minute.

The patterns were completed at last. The peculiarly vile-smelling candles shed little light on that part of the floor and all that Richard could see was a kind of cross with extra pieces added to each extremity and some interlinked triangles—or it could have been a star. Not that it mattered, he thought with growing scepticism as Alec took a measured pace backward and began to mutter a brief incantation.

Richard allowed his attention to drift towards the stone slab where Damask lay. Interest stirred again; the girl appeared to be dead! Not one of the sculptured figures was more white, more still, or—come to that—more shapely! He remembered, viciously, those moments when he had seemed nailed to his chair and how, soon after, Alec had announced in high glee that he had found the perfect instrument, and he had protested against any dealing with the insolent little baggage; Alec had said, "You may safely leave her to me!" Was this what he had then had in mind—human sacrifice?

The thought brought a sense of irony as he realised that the idea of Damask Greenway's losing her life in the cause of this fantastic nonsense moved him not at all, whereas what Alec was doing *now* . . . really, too utterly revolting. Even if one had retained one's childhood belief in the Devil, hoofs and horns and smell of brimstone and all, one could hardly credit that such a nasty, childishly nasty, performance could be pleasing to him.

Averting his eyes, Richard thought back over his association with Alec Mundford. There'd been the offer of the two thousand pounds, of course, and the indisputable matter of the luck with cards; but the rest was mainly talk; promises; hints. There'd been that time when they'd come down and brought Dunhill and Saxstead and the girls and there'd been what Alec called an attempt to establish the right atmosphere in the temple, and that, except for one detail, had seemed to Richard just another drunken orgy, carried to extremes but not, in essence, different from similar affairs in Angelina's house and other places. The only thing that made it memorable was the behaviour of the girl who ran away . . . Rose? Right at the height of the excitement she'd suddenly begun to scream and cry and pray and cross herself. There'd been also the visit they had made to

Loudun, where, years ago, there had, it was said, been an outbreak of demoniac possession. It was a small dismal place and there was nothing to see and Richard had been bored. Alec had said, "Mecca and Jerusalem aren't particularly pleasant places either but they have their pilgrims."

Now there was *this*, pompous, disgusting, going on and on and getting nowhere, just like everything else in life. Well, tomorrow he'd collect his two thousand pounds from Mundford and just drop him . . .

It was at that point that he realised that while he had been thinking Mr. Mundford had made a fire and thrown upon it something which gave off a powerful stench and a great deal of smoke; and now he was on his knees, praying, if you could call it that, praying aloud for something which appeared to put Richard's fee in jeopardy; for the burden of the eager, earnest prayer was that the Power which had granted him an increased span of years should now take away the gift and grant him instead instant and sudden death.

Richard listened and saw suddenly that the logical, reasonable, and inevitable conclusion of cynicism and boredom must be the desire for death, there was no other end; yet he himself did not wish to die. All he sought was release from boredom; and something vital still existed in him because he was still searching and, yes, hoping to find that relief. That was why he was here in this fantastic situation, taking part in this fraud. He was sure now that that was what it was . . .

And then, all at once, something of imminence and expectancy filled the temple, sweeping through it like the wind, with the rush and the sound and the overwhelming though invisible presence of the wind, and even Richard Shelmadine knew the almost forgotten, longed-for quickening of the blood.

Damask had gone. Her body lay there, slim, white, and virginal, but it was as inanimate as the other tools with which Mr. Mundford had busied himself. He had noticed the moment when the induced, drugged trance gave way to true coma and again congratulated himself upon his choice. The girl might even die.

She was back in the place which she had visited once before when she lay on the floor of her mother's kitchen and Julie had feared her dead. She recognised it with a sense of wonder that her memory of it should have been so blurred and imperfect and her one attempt to describe it to Mr. Mundford so halting and imprecise. Yet she understood—because here she understood everything—that this was because there were no words in which to convey a description of this place, this state. You could no more do it than you could describe colour to a man blind from birth.

She had remembered, and mentioned, voices . . . but voices were physical things utterly disconnected from the method of communication which one experienced here. . . .

In only one way did this place resemble the world, this state the state of being alive in a physical sense, and that was in the perpetual pull, the conflict between the good and the evil . . . names again, symbols . . . but how else could she explain to herself? For although she was here, knowing and understanding and experiencing, she was not part of it yet; she did not belong; the physical world, where "I" was a thing of hands and feet and eyes and ears and a mind which could only understand through a mesh of symbolism, was waiting to claim her again, soon, too soon, before she was ready, cleansed, and reinstated. For here, eyeless, handless, mindless, the naked spirit was still faced with the same choice as in the other place, the world . . . one side, or the other. She remembered the last time and how she had chosen and where in the end that choice had led. With the whole of her being she cried, "God forgive me and take me back!" knowing that the words "God" and "me" were also symbols, one standing for a great vibrating Power, the other for something no more than a dust mote, visible for one second in a ray of sunshine. But the dust mote was capable of choice; last time it had willed itself one way, now it willed itself the other and knew itself to be accepted. In its turn it accepted the fact that there would be pains to bear, difficult things to be done. "I'll do anything, anything. Only show me the way," she cried.

And it seemed that she was shown. Straight before her face was a great cloud of smoke, the heart of which slowly cleared into a tulip-shaped radiance. In the clear space she saw John Whitwell, exactly as he had looked when he stood in the barn in the evening light and called to her to come to Jesus, except that now the brightness about his head was spiked, clearly defined. Of course—the Crown of Thorns. And now behind his outstretched arms was a cross of rough wood; and there was Mr. Mundford, horned and hoofed, grinning maliciously, hammering home the nails.

She stared for a long while with a double awareness; the scene was as *real* as any she had ever looked at; yet at the same time she knew that John Whitwell and Mr. Mundford were only symbols, that understanding had to creep in this way just as the light of the sun must creep through the cracks of a shutter. But none of that was important; what mattered was what she must now *do*.

Mr. Mundford watched the core of brightness grow and knew that at last he had succeeded. Lucifer, Son of the Morning . . .

Richard Shelmadine watched too, his feeling of expectancy recoiling in the old familiar way. A complete hoax. Nothing but a nasty mess and a dead naked girl on a stone slab! He might have known, he thought.

Seeing nothing at all save a column of smoke, he was sufficiently in possession of his ordinary senses to be aware when the girl moved. Not dead then! It would be of some slight interest to observe her behaviour when she woke up and realised that she was stark-naked in the presence of two men, one of whom at least would stare at her with unfriendly eyes.

He saw her move, with the precise, weighted movements of a somnambulist, and reach out for the knife which Alec had used on the pheasants. He was a little slow in realising what she meant to do, and when he did he remembered that Alec now owed him two thousand pounds and that was not a debt which his heirs and executors were likely to honour. Alec, self-deluded fool, was now on his knees with his hands clasped over his eyes, gabbling away like a crazy man, praying for death, while death moved towards him.

Richard shouted, "Look out, man!" and moved between the two and reached out his hand to take the knife. Then the feeling of complete, incredulous wonder to which he had so long been a stranger was briefly his. The knife plunged home and with his lifeblood spurting out over his clenched hands he knew for a moment, too late, the value of life.

The spell was broken. Mr. Mundford felt his dark master's withdrawal and sagged forward with a cry of despair.

The spell was broken. Damask cried out too, for the re-welding of body and spirit was as painful as the birth wrench.

Up at Fuller's, inspiration came. "Danny," cried Mrs. Fuller, "I just thought of something. Fetch me the pepper, quick!" Danny blundered down the stairs and up again and thrust the wooden canister into her hand. Shaking a spoonful into her damp palm, she went to the bed and knew a decline of hope.

Sally's pudgy little nose had gone sharp, its pinched-in nostrils bluish-white, so dead-seeming that to hold out the pepper seemed almost like descecrating a corpse. Mrs. Fuller's hand trembled and some of the pepper spilled as she said, "S'too late, my pore dear, too late." But she was wrong, Sally drew a sniffling breath and the pepper stirred; then she gasped and gave a mighty sneeze, with, hard on its heels, a scream that rent the night. And there was the baby, as fine and lively as though he had arrived exactly at the right time and in the ordinary way. Mrs. Fuller didn't even have to slap him to make him draw his first breath, and that was just as well, for she was taken completely by surprise and was crying and saying, "Oh, thank God, thank God!" It was almost a minute before she could proceed with all she had to do.

It was perhaps only a minute that they had spent thus— standing just by the door with their arms around one another, Linda clinging to him as though he were the one solid thing in a disintegrating world, he holding her close and tight as though a flood or a whirlwind might tear her out of his arms— but it seemed a long time. Hadstock had time to remember her face of terror—but she had opened the door, so frightened and so brave. Oh, if only this comforting clasp in which he held her could be a symbol of real rescue, real support! If he could pick her up and carry her away and keep her safe so that nothing could ever frighten or trouble her again. Where to? asked the sardonic voice in his mind. The cottage in Berry Lane, which is part of your miserable remuneration and from which you will be ejected tomorrow morning? He imagined himself and Linda tramping the roads. Well, would it be worse than *this*? Had he been cowardly to hold back so long? Was it fair to decide for her, leave her to believe that she must go on . . . and on . . . alone? Above all, had he been coldhearted always to have rejected the alternative? Yes, he had; and though he would, even at this minute, with Linda in his arms, have preferred to cut off his hand than do it, he *would*. He'd go to the man who had begotten him and apologise, take back all those things he had said, humble himself, ask him for money. The sensual, genial old sinner would stamp and swear, but he'd be pleasant, triumphant, and he would make no effort to conceal his triumph. He'd take a fingerful of snuff and trumpet into his fine silk handkerchief and say, "What did I tell you? What's amiss with the wrong side of the blanket if that's where the money is? So now you've run off with another man's wife, have you? You'll have to amend your Puritan notions about bastards, my boy!"

No, no! Not that. He'd humble himself, he'd get the money, but nobody should ever know why. He'd take her away—if she wanted to go—and put her safely somewhere and love her for ever but never go near her. "And won't that be nice for you both?" asked the voice of the tormentor. Caught all ways, the worm on the pin.

Oh yes, there was plenty of time for Hadstock to do his thinking.

And for Linda, too. After all the pains she had taken to be careful. After all the self-derision: What need for all this care, you're not young, not pretty any more, you're imagining it all. Just because you're in love with him, were from the first moment when he was surly and defensive; just because he raved in delirium, muddling something you'd said to him with something Shakespeare had written . . .

But it is true, and it is wonderful. We'll go away and he can be somebody else's bailiff and we'll live in a little cottage and I'll wash his shirts and have supper ready when he comes home.

The inevitable sardonic voice in her mind reminded her that she had also been in love with Richard Shelmadine. And that there was no denying. Nor was the fact that for years, years and years, she had gone on, carrying that love, that dead thing, corrupt, past any breath of revival, any hope of warmth. Suddenly the burden of self-blame which she had shouldered rolled away. Never once in all their time together had Richard held her like this, with intent to comfort; never once in all those years had she felt that she could depend upon him. He'd flashed into her life like a meteor; she'd fallen into his orbit and hung there, attracted, dazzled, compelled . . . and now she had been thrown off.

She stirred in Hadstock's arms and he let her go immediately.

"I've always tried," she said shakily, "to behave properly . . . but this . . . well, I think you know. You do know, don't you?"

"I know. This is not the time, nor the place."

The whole thing could have hardly lasted a minute, for the blood from Simon's nose was still wet on her hand, sticky on the folds of her skirt.

"He was hurt," she said. "And now he is . . . We must get

him back. There's something horrible in this house tonight, and if he . . ."

She began to hurry along the passage. There, where it ended by the closed door of the cellar, Simon had found himself baffled for the third time. Silently he was flinging himself at the door. The battering-ram tactics had worked before, either the thing gave way or somebody came and opened to you. He was bracing himself for another assault when Hadstock, coming up behind him, whipped off his belt and slipped the end of it through his collar.

"There," said Hadstock, "he's safe." Linda gave a gasping breath of relief. The dog writhed and pulled against the constraint, snarled and pawed the door.

"Now," said Hadstock in a brisker voice, "may I see you to your room? Or would you"—he hesitated and then brought out the crucial words—"like to come back with me to the cottage? Unless, of course . . . Ockley? Muchanger?"

She looked at him and gave a shaky laugh with the echo of hysteria in it.

"What could I say? Tell them the truth? They'd think I was mad! Hadstock we must *know*! And if it is true we should stop it, or try, at least."

"Not we. I. You take the dog and go to your room and I'll investigate if that is your wish. I've been in a weak position—I'm not supposed even to enter the house. But if you ask me to see what is going on, I will; and if I can, I'll put a stop to it."

He'd do *that*! he thought viciously, whatever they were up to, even if it were—which he knew it was not—as innocent as sucking an orange. He'd take them by the scruffs of their necks and crack their silly heads together.

A glance at Linda informed him that the glorious moment must be postponed a little.

"I'll come back with you; you'd never manage him." He hauled on the makeshift leash. "Light your candle from my lantern; I'll leave it here and have both hands free."

They left the lantern by the cellar door; then Linda, carrying the candle, led the way back into the main part of the house and Hadstock hauled Simon, who fought every inch of the way, his claws scraping on the floor, his whole scruff pulled up to his ears by the straining collar.

Inside the sitting room Linda set down the candle and took

the belt's end in both hands. Simon immediately gave a plunging leap.

"You'll never hold him," said Hadstock, looking round. "Look, I'll tie him to the sofa leg. Then you lock the door behind me, and don't open it to anyone but me. I shall come back."

"Whatever Richard says? Promise. They'll be so very, *very* angry."

"That no longer matters. Don't worry. Just lock the door and wait, I shan't be long."

He twisted the belt around the sofa leg and buckled it firmly; stood up, took the candle, and went to the door. Linda followed.

Behind them there was a smart crack as Simon lunged and a leg of the sofa broke off. They turned and he catapulted past them, the sofa leg still held by the belt, banging from side to side as he ran.

Linda gave a loud cry and Hadstock swore.

"He'll be all right; the door was shut. I'll get him back. You stay here," he said; then as she showed signs of intending to go with him he gave her a slight push, snatched the key from inside the door, slipped out, and locked it behind him. Then he ran.

Simon was not in the passage, nor was the lantern; and the cellar door was standing wide open. The scent of incense mingled with a rank reek of burning came to meet Hadstock as he crossed the cellar. At its farthest end a stout new door also stood wide, its heavy padlock dangling uselessly. And beyond was the wide passage down which the bulls had gone to the altar.

In the temple itself smoke still billowed and swirled under the groined roof, but the fire had burned red and clear and the flames were steady on the thick, dark, evil-smelling candles. All the horrid paraphernalia of Mr. Mundford's rites were spread about and in the midst of them Richard Shelmadine lay on his side, his bloody hands still clutching his chest. At the very foot of the altar itself was Mr. Mundford, whom this time Simon had caught without his cravat.

Miss Parsons had waited and waited. The fog thinned out a little and the air seemed to grow colder. She shivered and shivered and her teeth rattled without ceasing. But she must wait because there was nothing else in the world to do, and nowhere to go. She had forgotten everything except that she must wait for Damask. She had been waiting now since the beginning of time and must wait on until its end. Slow cold centuries of the ice age went by.

Then there was life on the earth; something moved and there was light, a small, steady yellow eye, coming nearer and nearer. But it wasn't Damask; Miss Parsons broke into loud lamentations of disappointment when she saw who was so near, carrying the light. A very small Franciscan monk, a dwarf monk, hooded and robed with the skirts of his robe tucked up into his belt. Monks did tuck up their robes that way when they needed to move freely; Miss Parsons remembered reading about the militant Saxon monks who had tucked up their robes and gone into battle side by side with Harold's housecarls at Hastings. She was not surprised to see a monk on the Stone Bridge in the middle of the night, but she was most dreadfully disappointed.

"I'm waiting for Damask," she said, but the words came out all anyhow, what with the chattering of her teeth and her sobbing.

Inside the shadow of the hood the monk had a small white face and wide, sleepwalker's eyes. She could see them clearly because the monk had halted and reached out his hand and said:

"I am Damask." And it *was* Damask's voice; and the hand which now pushed its way under her rigid, shaking arm was Damask's hand . . . all most peculiar and confusing; but comforting, too. She brushed her hand against the coarse, rasping stuff of the grey robe . . . and was immediately enlightened. Poor Farm stuff! What on earth would they do next to these poor unfortunate girls? Steadying her chin with her hand, Miss Parsons made an effort to speak clearly. "Poor child," she said, "you're from the Poor Farm, are you not? You must come home with me. I will give you such pretty dresses!"

CHAPTER 18

MORNING BROKE OVER CLEVELY. THIN PATCHES OF FOG STILL clung here and there, but the sun was coming up wide and crimson over Layer Wood, bringing promise of a fine autumn day. Mrs. Clopton might have eyed it with bitterness, thinking, If only . . . Actually she spared it no glance, being far too busy organising hot water in the best brass cans and a stylish breakfast with three extra places. For the party had been a marked success; despite the fog the whole Thurlow Lamb family had driven out from Baildon, and towards the party's end the persistent fog and some remark about the trying drive back had emboldened Mrs. Clopton to suggest that they stay the night. Everything had worked out wonderfully well and young Mr. Thurlow Lamb had been most attentive to Ella!

Breakfast was also the concern at Fuller's. Sally had slept and waked feeling cheerful and well and ravenously hungry. She greeted with joy the laden tray which her mother-in-law, with a fond loving look, plumped down on the bed, bidding her eat hearty, for the newcomer was a lusty lad and would take a deal of feeding.

Downstairs again Mrs. Fuller said to Danny, "You'd hardly

believe it was such a touch-and-go job, would you? I feel almost as though I'd drempt it."

Matt Ashpole couldn't face his breakfast at all. His head was in two halves which kept parting and then coming together again with a sickening clash; all his bones were hollow and brittle; his tongue was thick with sour dust; he shook as though he had palsy and he was sicker than Mrs. Ashpole had been after her surfeit of chitterlings. But he was not unhappy and he lacked entirely the sense of remorse which is the usual accompaniment of his condition. In fact, discounting his physical woes, he was happy as a lark. It was damned good liquor; half a pint of it had made him drunk as a lord. He knew how to make it and he was learning how to handle it. Watered down, it would be grand, and it'd sell like hot cakes. Later on today, if he felt better, or if he did not, tomorrow, he'd go on his rounds and look out for more damaged barley and some old bottles, cheap; and all through the dirty winter days he'd just sit at home and work his still. The two halves of his head clanged together and he thought, There never was such a brew! One part liquor to four of water, I reckon. I'll make my fortune yet!

Hadstock hadn't breakfasted either. He was riding over to carry the news to Sir Edward Follesmark, who was the nearest Justice of the Peace, a friend of the Shelmadine family, and a man of sound good sense for all his eccentric ways. As he rode, Hadstock tested his story again and again. So far as he could see, it fitted together. One man stabbed in the chest, another with his throat torn out . . . what else, short of the truth, could be the explanation? And the truth was unthinkable, no one would believe it, and besides, Linda had said, "I did love him once and this is such a filthy way to die! Couldn't we . . . Hadstock, we *must* hide the truth."

And what was the truth exactly? Only one person on earth knew that. The girl to whom the yellow dress and the other clothes belonged; the girl who had run away, wearing her shoes and one of the grey robes to cover her nakedness; the girl who had left the door open for Simon. And, thought Hadstock, the secret was safe with her!

As it was, being locked away in some remote cell of her brain where even she would never find it again. She thought—

as she went about the task of caring for the now very sick woman—that she remembered everything perfectly clearly. She could have summed up the whole experience in very few words. Once upon a time she had been, or tried to be, a good Methodist, and because of that she had lost Danny and fainted and gone to that different world and chosen evil. Evil had led her to agree, happily, to take part in Mr. Mundford's experiment; he'd given her something to drink which had made her drunk, then he'd done something cruel and disgusting and she'd fainted, just as she had before, and gone to that different place again, and this time chosen good. Then she'd come round and was naked, but there was the grey hooded cloak to slip on quickly and she had put on her shoes. Neither Sir Richard nor Mr. Mundford had attempted to stop her and she had run. Along the passage it was easy, she could guide herself along the wall. Then she was lost until all at once the shape of a door was outlined in light and she'd gone towards it and opened it and there was a lantern on the floor as though someone had left it there purposely for her use. She'd picked it up, run along a passage, reached a door, opened it, and hurried as well as she could through the fog along the gravelled road. She had believed that she was a long way from Clevely and she had gone on believing that until she reached the lodge gates, which were . . . surely . . . they must be . . . the gates of the Manor. She realised then how Mr. Mundford had tricked her with his talk of a long drive and his driving round and round. . . .

She had got Miss Parsons to bed, with a hot brick at her feet and another in the small of her back and a mug of hot black currant tea to warm her inside, and although all the time she was trying to hold fast to the memory of that other place and the glimpse of truth which had been given her, it was fading steadily, just as the pattern on a fabric would fade after repeated washing and exposure to the sunlight.

(Despite all the precautions Miss Parsons' cold was worse in the morning and by midday she was breathing with a crackling sound, as though her chest were stuffed with brittle straw. Damask sent for the doctor, who, when it was all over, said that he had never, in all his life, seen more devoted, selfless nursing than that received by this patient. Mr. Turnbull, too, happening to pay a visit during this distressing time, was deeply impressed and reassured that in making the new will he had done the right thing. The poor girl hadn't even spared attention for her own appearance and her manner was . . . well, dedicated;

Mr. Turnbull disliked high-falutin expressions but that was the word—dedicated.)

Sir Edward, roused from his bed a little untimely, came down wearing his dressing gown and nightcap, which gave him a vulnerable look, so that Hadstock found himself breaking the news more gently than he had planned. Even so Sir Edward was profoundly shocked.

"I'll come back with you at once. What a catastrophe! Have you breakfasted?"

"I didn't feel like it."

"No, of course, naturally not." He knew a pang of self-reproach because his own appetite was unimpaired. Still, he reflected, he had positively disliked Mr. Mundford on the few occasions he had met him, and had not much cared for Shelmadine except just at first, when his warmth of feeling, he realised later, had been due to relief at finding him less black than he had been painted. Nevertheless, this was, of course, a shocking tragedy.

"Poor Lady Shelmadine," he said feelingly. "Poor lady! How is she taking it?"

"She is prostrate," Hadstock said truthfully.

"You look somewhat upset yourself," said Sir Edward, eyeing Hadstock's haggard, unshaven face and red-rimmed eyes. "I know what would do us both good," he went on kindly. He bounced over to the cluttered sideboard and routed about and at last produced a bottle of brandy and two glasses, one clean, one cloudy and smeared. He was rich and the house was full of servants eating their heads off, but he was the worst-served man in England. "I think we'd better take this up to my room and you can tell me more details while I get into my clothes. This dog, for instance," he began as he charged up the stairs, "was it naturally savage? Ever attacked anyone before?"

There was no point in hiding the truth and anyway every servant knew.

"Not naturally savage, but it had bitten Mr. Mundford earlier in the day; so Lady Shelmadine brought it over to my cottage and asked me to keep it while Mr. Mundford was at the Manor."

"And didn't you?"

"Yes. I left it locked in, but it broke out through the window."

"And where were you? Did you not go home last night?"

"No. There is a room above the stables which I use if I

have reason to be particularly early in the morning, or if the weather is bad. Last night was foggy." He was deeply grateful that he had established that habit, otherwise his presence might have given rise to questions.

"Yes, of course. Now there are some points . . . I was only just awake, you know, and of course vastly shocked. If you wouldn't mind recounting the whole thing again . . . And, I say, do drink that brandy, you look quite *grey*!" He drank himself and began to climb nimbly into his breeches. "Now, you heard the dog, you said . . ."

So once more, wondering how many times he would have to tell the tale before it was done with, Hadstock told how he had heard the dog, realised that it had escaped, dressed, lighted his lantern, and come down. "By that time the noise had ceased, but I went towards where I had last heard it, and hunted about and called. I saw the dog first, just on the edge of the park across the drive from the side door of the house. And there they were."

"Sir Richard stabbed and bleeding to death and Mr. Mundford bitten in the throat. What a very terrible thing! And what a mystery. What do you think happened, Hadstock?" Sir Edward struggled on his coat and buttoned it, his fingers skipping by long practice over the three places where buttons were missing.

"It's hardly for me to say, sir, is it?"

"To hell with modesty, man! This is an *inquest*! You found the bodies, saw how they lay. Who is better qualified to express an opinion? Wait a minute, I think I hear . . ." He went to the window, opened it, and poked out his head. "Brinkley! Hi, Brinkley! I want my horse. What? Yes, of course I mean *now*. The man's a fool," he said, closing the window. "Well now?"

"I can only think that Sir Richard and Mr. Mundford heard the dog and went out, that the dog renewed its attack on Mr. Mundford, who tried to defend himself, that Sir Richard tried to pull the dog away and was stabbed."

"With what?" asked Sir Edward sharply.

"Mr. Mundford had a carving knife in his hand. I think the gentlemen were just about to sit down to a late supper. Cards were laid out in the library, and a cold fowl, partially carved, was on the sideboard in the dining room."

Sir Edward tested this account, as Linda and Hadstock had done in the small hours, and found it acceptable.

"It might even be that Mr. Mundford, knowing the dog's

enmity, deliberately armed himself—with what a fatal result," he said musingly. "Well, I'm ready now." But outside the bed-room the good odour of eggs and bacon being fried for the servants' breakfast found its way up the back stairs. He paused and cocked his nose.

"You know, Hadstock, I still think we should have breakfast. By all accounts you've had a shocking night—and we've a heavy day ahead of us. I'm deeply shocked; old Sir Charles was my closest friend. I was at Clevely when we learned of *his* sad accident, you know. With Sir Richard I was not, of course, on such intimate terms, still it is a shock. But it must be faced and I think breakfast would help." He trotted into the dining room and pulled the bell rope vigorously. Then, just to show that his mind was still on the affair, he said, "That dog! The dog must be destroyed at once."

"I have already taken the responsibility for that, sir."

"Splendid. You seem to have kept your head and thought of everything. How very fortunate for poor Lady Shelmadine that you were at hand."

Hadstock's lips tightened and a kind of twitch deepened all the lines on one side of his face.

"Yes, the fog served some purpose," he said.

Sir Edward tugged again at the bell. As he did so, another explanation of the affair flashed into his head. Of Mundford he would believe anything, and once or twice he'd seen Shel-madine in a nasty temper. Suppose they'd quarrelled, perhaps over the dog, and Mundford had struck at Shelmadine and then the dog . . . But even trying that story over in his own mind made him recoil. Gentlemen attacking one another with carving knives in parks at night . . . no, no, that would never do. It had all the elements of a first-class scandal and in these revolu-tionary times that must be avoided. Sir Edward was looked upon as revolutionary himself; he was in favour of a fair wage for a fair day's work; on the Bench he was regarded as the poachers' friend because he could see what a temptation it was for a hungry man to "knock off one for the pot"; he was a ridiculously indulgent employer *but* he was a member of the upper class and loyal to his kind. No scandal, no betrayal at any price, he thought stoutly.

Even if there were evidence of a quarrel—which, thank God, there seemed not to be—one would have been bound to disregard it, if only for Lady Shelmadine's sake. Poor lady, the shock and the bereavement were quite enough, without any scandal. Accidental death in both cases and the whole thing hushed up as soon as possible.

"It'll be a nine-day wonder, I'm afraid," he said aloud. "We must try to see it through with as little fuss as possible—for Lady Shelmadine's sake."

"Yes, indeed," Hadstock said, and hoped he had not spoken too heartily.

PART V

AFTERNOON OF
AN AUTOCRAT

CHAPTER 19

SALLY AND MRS. FULLER WERE WAITING SUPPER FOR DANNY.
He still rode daily to and from Mr. Thurlow's office, for he had
not yet succeeded in hiring or buying any more land and anyway
they were under notice to quit the house again at Christmas.
It had been a shattering blow when, just before Michaelmas,
they had been given a quarter's notice. And for no reason. Mrs.
Fuller, too desperate to care whether she gave offence or not,
had asked straight out and the new Squire had said, "I'm not
giving reasons, I'm giving you notice!" His death, about a
month later, brought no hope. They'd been through all that
before; Sir Charles had given them notice and Sir Charles had
died and they'd hoped . . . but somewhere, obviously, records
were kept and Mrs. Fuller was certain that notices to quit were
written down before they were delivered, otherwise how would
anyone have known that Sir Charles had given Steve notice
that afternoon?

Danny had said, "There's a curse on us. Seems we aren't
meant to live in Clevely." He'd talked of selling Cobbler's
Corner and all his bullocks and the horse and the furniture and
going somewhere far afield—America even. And Mrs. Fuller
had cried and said she couldn't face another move. So then the
hunt for land, with or without a house, had become frantic. So

far it had been fruitless. But tonight, with the mid-December wind howling about the house, the dumplings gently bumping against the lid of the pot, the babies both asleep, Mrs. Fuller and Sally allowed themselves just a little hope as they worked away at a quilt. Tonight, on his way home, Danny had gone to call on Martha Bowyer.

Martha had, in the end, fenced the land that was her heritage. To do that and pay her share of the commissioners' expenses she had been obliged to sell everything else she possessed, every bit of stock, old Clem's plough and wagon and tools, every stick of furniture in the house, and even the gold ear-bobs which her grandmother had left her. And there she was with her neatly fenced barren acres, with not so much as a chicken to run over them, and her snug clod house without so much as a stool in it. She'd left them just as they were and gone away one morning, walking to Nettleton to catch the coach, with all the portable goods that she possessed tied up in one of Clem's red handkerchiefs. That had been in June. Then, two days ago, she had appeared again, carrying the same bundle, and had gone to her little farm and lighted a fire, borrowed a scythe from the Wellmans, and cut down the nettles and docks about the house, and when darkness fell, had gone and hired a room at the Black Horse. The news spread about the village, accompanied by the obvious explanation—she was tidying up the place preparatory to selling it. So tonight Danny had gone to make her a bid.

It was no good; they knew that before they saw him. He'd have shouted as he rode into the yard. He came quietly, and when he dismounted his footsteps were as heavy and springless as those of the old, cheap horse. Sally got up quickly and ran to the door. "I'll see to it you get into the warm," she said as she joined him. It was her delight to wait upon him now.

"No, you go in, Sal. It's going to snow."

"I'll help," she said. "You didn't get it, did you?"

"No," he said shortly, adding after a moment, "you'd never guess why!"

"Why?" Her interest was without a tinge of disappointment, Clevely or anywhere else in the world all one to her so long as Danny was there.

"I'll tell you inside. I can't go through it twice."

They busied themselves with the horse, closed the stable door, and crossed the yard.

"Did she ask too much?" Mrs. Fuller asked in a flat voice, barely looking up from dishing the dumplings.

"No. She's going to be married."

"What? Martha Bowyer! She must be fifty and more like a cart horse than a woman," cried Mrs. Fuller.

"Maybe. Nevertheless, she's going to be married. And why do you think she's back in Clevely?"

"To sell her place, of course."

"No. This man she went to keep house for asked her to marry him on Sunday night; she said yes and left on Monday morning because it wouldn't be right for an engaged couple to be under the one roof. She said that, solemn as a judge; she did, truly!"

Danny leaned back in his chair and laughed; Sally joined in the laughter and so, after a moment's hesitation, did Mrs. Fuller.

"That beats all," she said. "But what about her place, Danny?"

"They're going to live there. The man has a bit of money, enough to stock the place anyway."

The last glint of amusement faded from Mrs. Fuller's eyes, leaving them cold and curiously empty.

"I see," she said. "Then there's only one glimmer of hope left. We'll hev to ask Lady Shelmadine to let us stay on."

Danny's spirits rushed downwards at this new proof of tenacity to a place; he said, a trifle sharply:

"You can't count on that! She'd be bound to stick to what he said—him dying so lately and the way he did!"

"I don't see it," said Mrs. Fuller, setting her mouth stubbornly. "I been through all that; your dad died sudden, but if he'd done something mean and cruel just afore he died—which he never would, as we all know—I'd of been only too glad to put it right. Look how she acted about the people on the Waste. She's doing right by them and she'd do right by us, if she realised. And if you're too backward to go and ask, then I will."

"I don't see the point of stopping on at Clevely, where I can't get my hands on any arable," Danny said. "How can I get on, buying all my winter feed at millers' prices and with nowhere to put my good muck? This way I'll be stuck in that old office till I die!" He looked sulky and attacked his dumplings as though they had done him an injury. Sally waited in vain for a word of praise.

It was then that a knock fell on the door. They all jumped at the sound. It was late for callers.

Danny rose and went to the door and opened it cautiously, gave an exclamation of surprise, and widened the aperture, the wind-whipped colour in his thin face deepening a little as he said:

"Hullo."

"Hullo, Danny," Damask said. "I wanted to ask you something."

"Oh, did you?" said Danny in a rough voice. "Well I once asked you something. Remember? Whatever you want with me the answer is the same as I got."

"Danny Fuller!" said his mother. "Step in, Damask. Come to the fire."

Quite apart from any consideration of civility for old times' sake, curiosity alone would have issued the invitation. Damask Greenway's clothes and demeanour had been the talk of the parish when she was just the old lady's companion, a sort of servant; heaven knew how she'd look and behave now that she was an heiress, all that big house and the land and the money left to her outright.

Save that the dress she wore was dead black, with a rough frieze cape of the same colour, the Damask who stepped into the Fullers' kitchen was much the same as the one who had once visited the house to be inspected and who had won Mrs. Fuller's approval. The cleanly washed, undecked face was the same, though a little thinner; the hair dragged back smoothly and dressed in hard-looking plaits was the same, and so was the manner, a little prim, a little nervous.

Sally said, "Hullo, Damask," in her usual careless friendly manner, and Damask returned the greeting just as she had always done in the past, civilly but stiffly.

Danny kicked the door shut and went back to his place at the table.

"You'll excuse us if we get on—supper's getting cold." He nodded to Sally to proceed with her meal.

"I don't wish to interrupt you," Damask said. "I can talk as you eat. It won't take long."

"Sit down, my dear, do, and have a bite," Mrs. Fuller said, throwing one curious glance at Damask and another, even more curious, at Danny. Never, never in all her days had she known Danny behave so rudely—even to a girl he had jilted. Surely if there was a grievance it was Damask's!

"No, thank you, Mrs. Fuller. I've had supper."

"Well, leastways, sit down."

Damask did so, her feet in their heavy plain shoes placed side by side, the skimpy folds of the ugly black dress falling primly, her hands folded in her lap, just the way Danny remembered. She turned her eyes on him, and that brought to mind the way she had looked at him on the night when he'd gone to ask about hiring some land—but this was the old look, grave and friendly, with something innocent about it; the look she had turned on him when she had said she couldn't walk out with anyone who swore or went into the Black Horse. And all at once he remembered the smell of her too, clean, soap-and-the-ghost-of-lavender smell. Through the piece of dumpling in his mouth he said gruffly:

"Well? What do you want?"

"I came to ask you whether you had all the land you wanted."

"Ha! Ha! Wouldn't you like to know?"

"Danny! What's got into you tonight? That's what I should like to know!" said Mrs. Fuller. "You'll have to excuse him, Damask. He's tired; and we've just had another disappointment. No, we ain't got any more; there don't seem to be no land in Clevely, more's the pity."

"There's mine," Damask said simply. "What isn't let, I mean. I thought if you still wanted some . . . I don't want it any more. Abel Shipton is still at Bridge Farm and the other tenants are keeping theirs, of course, but what Miss Parsons got out of the enclosure—you could have that, if you liked."

Danny choked on a piece of dumpling.

"Why, Damask, that'd be wonderful," said Mrs. Fuller, her face suddenly red and her eyes full of tears. "That's the best news! Of course we'd hev it and be thankful. Why, I never reckoned . . . I don't know how . . . Why, that'd be *wonderful*!"

Damask kept her eyes on Danny. The piece of dumpling slid down at last, but the effort had reddened his face still more and brought water to his eyes. When he spoke his voice was defiant.

"Hire or buy?" he asked.

"Which you like, Danny. If you have any money . . ."

"I've got the whole of twenty-five pounds which I went to offer Martha Bowyer tonight. And I've got my bullocks. What are you asking?"

"Twenty-five pounds would do very well."

"Not for all that! Why, Cobbler's Corner, poor damp place it is, cost me a pound an acre..."

"Twenty-five pounds will do very well. I'd rather sell than let it. I'm going away, you see, I don't want to be bothered with rent collecting. What land is still let, Father will see to and use the money for the chapel."

They stared at her in wonder and nobody spoke until the silence was embarrassing; then everyone spoke at once.

Danny said, "Well, I take it very kindly, Damask. If you're sure you know what you're doing."

Mrs. Fuller said, "I can't get over the wonder of it. Now all we hev to do is ask Lady Shelmadine about the house."

Sally said, "Where are you going, Damask?"

There was no need to reply to anyone. She stood up and said, "That's settled then. Mr. Turnbull will see to the papers, Danny. Good night. Good night, Mrs. Fuller. Good night, Sally."

She had gone before they had fully recovered from their astonishment. It was some moments before Danny broke through the jubilant exclamations to say, "Maybe I should've walked her home."

"If you did I'd of come too," said Sally, laughing.

"You know," said Mrs. Fuller, "I verily believe she've gone right back to be Methody again."

And that was true. As the other-world experience faded, she had found herself left with the little that she had not known before; there was nothing, really, that the stark, simple teaching of the Methodist faith did not cover. She had never heard of the Jesuit who said, "Give me a child until he is seven and after that you may do what you like with him," but she was a living proof of his theory's validity. She had tried to be good and had disliked the wages of virtue; she had tried to be bad and turned away in disgust from what was, after all, the thing to which badness led; she'd had experiences of an unusual kind, seen and heard and known things that there were no words for and she'd come back, in the end, to the things that there were words for... she was a lamb which had strayed from the fold, she was the brand plucked from the burning, she was the one from whom the seven devils had been cast out... It was all in the Bible.

Now she had set her house in order. Danny had the land to make amends for the wrong she had done him and his family; Amos would have his chapel; she had even arranged that Julie should have her tea and her medicine and the creature comforts which she—being a weak member—craved. The Dower House was sold. (Fred Clopton had bought it as a wedding present for his daughter Ella, who was marrying young Thurlow Lamb at Easter. "After all, Fred," Mrs. Clopton had said, "we must do our part, and it's cheap and it'll make an impressive present. And if Danny Fuller can ride in and out every day, surely Bertie could manage it in a gig. And I could keep my eye on Ella.")

Damask was free now. And she knew where she was going. To Georgia, where Wesley himself had once worked amongst the slaves and the convicts. That was logical; Captain Parsons had made his money in the slave trade. Damask had read "Papa's journal" while she sat by Miss Parsons' deathbed. And if half of what he wrote was true, no people on all the face of the earth were more in need of the one thing which she could give them, the absolute assurance that this world was just a passing shadow show, a sort of dark tunnel through which the spirit must pass, blinded by its physical eyes, deafened by its physical ears, made stupid by its bone-caged limited mind. Slaves, whose physical life was a misery, would welcome the truth . . . the one thing all her experiences had taught her.

She thought of her mission as she crossed the Stone Bridge. The snow which Danny had predicted was falling, large crisp flakes, slanting down the wind's current. The ground was whitening, but the river ran dark. She thought, What I *knew* then, both those times, is like the snow on the water, swallowed up and gone; but it was real and it is still part of me. And it was not of the slightest importance that she had forgotten so much, or had such difficulty in putting it into words—it was all in the Bible. Christ, who knew everything, had had the same difficulty—that was why He had spoken in parables.

CHAPTER 20

ON CHRISTMAS EVE OF THE YEAR 1797, LADY SHELMADINE
set out to make a tour of her village and carry Christmas presents
to the cottages on the Waste.

It was the first time she had visited the village and the third
time she had left the Manor since the night of All Hallows'.
The two earlier outings had been shopping expeditions, and on
those occasions such villagers as caught a glimpse of the pale,
black-clad figure in the carriage had bobbed or twitched their
forelocks and remarked how ill she looked, Lady Shelmadine-
pore-lady. The sympathy would have been genuine enough,
even unleavened by gratitude, for it was a tribute to the reserve
and fortitude with which she had behaved in the past that she
should now be so deeply pitied in her bereavement; and alongside this irony ran another, for Sir Richard, unpopular as he
had been, had died, it was believed, in a manner not far from
heroic, attempting to preserve his friend from the attack of a
savage dog. Matt Ashpole's was the solitary voice raised in
Simon's defence. "If that was a savage dog I'm a Dutchman,"
he said. "Take my owd Ripper now, nicer owd bitch never
wagged tail, but if somebody went and upset her she'd hev his
leg off as soon as look at him. And something or somebody
went and upset that other pore creature."

It was regarded as natural enough that Linda should suffer a breakdown in health. Poor women, as Mrs. Palfrey pointed out, when they lost their man, lost their breadwinner and had to pull themselves together and get out and earn something. This statement was received gravely, nobody remarking that it did more justice to Mrs. Palfrey's loyalty than to her logic.

"And thass a pity," she added, "that there ain't a young 'un or two. Nothing like young 'uns to take your mind off."

In speaking this, Mrs. Palfrey expressed, with indisputable authority, the general opinion of the county; it was, everyone agreed, a great pity that there was no heir; there was not even a relative to inherit the title, which would thus, after almost two centuries, fall into abeyance. It was strange and sad to think that there would be no more Shelmadines at Clevely Manor.

The sympathy of the village people, especially that of the Waste dwellers, who had troubles enough of their own, might soon have waned; but early in December something happened to fan it into flame again. Hadstock carried to the Waste the incredible, wonderful news that Lady Shelmadine was returning, in the form of allotments, all that part of the common land which had fallen to Sir Richard's share in the recent enclosure. And to make certain that the hovels and the acres would never again be divorced, Mr. Turnbull was preparing deeds of gift.

Mrs. Palfrey and several others who had watched with dry, stony eyes while the fences went up, saw them come down with tears of relief and joy and wonder, and Matt Ashpole established for himself, in one moment and by the simple practice of that self-praise deplored by the copybooks, a reputation for infallibility which lasted his lifetime.

"There y'are," he cried, "what did I tell you, I said all along she was on our side, pore lady. And why? Because I went along and put the case to her prop'ly. But for *me* she'd never hev known we was ill done by. Thass me you got to thank, owd Matt Ashpole, what everybody laughed at and said was running his blood to water in a lost cause. I trust you're thankful."

They were thankful; to Lady Shelmadine-pore-lady, who had given them back the land; to Mr. Hadstock, who had brought the news; to Mr. Turnbull, who was writing the papers; to Matt, who claimed credit for it all. Naturally no one was thankful to Damask Greenway because no one knew that she had had a hand in the business; and had they known, and the way in which that hand had served them, it would have been their bounden duty to see that she was hanged outside Baildon Gaol, with her skirts, in the interest of common decency, tied about her knees. But nobody knew, and Damask celebrated that Christmas by being uncommonly seasick just out from Bristol, passing with exemplary fortitude and patience this first sample of the tests and trials that awaited her.

Matt Ashpole, his taste for leading deputations thus whetted, was all for leading another, this time to express the gratitude of the cottagers. He tactfully approached Mr. Hadstock about it and the bailiff said he thought it would be contrary to her ladyship's wish, but he would mention it. Secretly he hoped that Linda would consent to receive Matt and whomever he chose to bring with him; even so slight a contact with the outer world might serve to rouse her from her apathy. But she shrank away from the idea and Matt, thus robbed of his deputation, began to concoct another plan.

Hadstock was not the only person to be concerned about Linda. Lady Fennel, who had ridden over and taken charge of everything on the morning after the tragedy, was by the beginning of December openly speaking of the danger of decline.

"She always was a poor spiritless creature. I've seen women like that before. No hold on life, that's the trouble. The loss of a baby is enough to topple them into the grave, leave alone a husband. Short of giving her a good shaking, I don't know what to try next to rouse her."

She had tried many things: extended an invitation for a prolonged visit to Ockley; suggested that Linda should have one of the family from Didsborough Rectory to stay at the Manor; suggested that Linda should go and stay at the Rectory; endeavoured to entice her out in the carriage; offered to accompany her on walks; spoken bracingly about the responsibilities which sooner or later Linda must shoulder; she had coaxed and scolded and exhorted. Once—and she must have been despairing to have attempted anything so clean out of character—she had tried to apply religious consolation, with its promise of eventual reunion with loved ones. "Not my line of country at all," she told Sir Evelyn. "Did it so badly that the poor girl went into hysterics!" She went on to say that she verily believed that Linda would stay moping in the house until she died.

Hadstock was not far from the same conclusion, when, midway through December, a chance remark of his seemed to touch some hidden spring of energy and interest.

"I hate to bother you with this, and I'll see to it if you just tell me what you wish. What about the Christmas doles this year?"

The Christmas doles at Clevely had been instituted by some bygone Squire as a means of exercising charity and preserving discipline. Every cottager and small tenant who had been civil, industrious, and law-abiding throughout the year received, on Christmas Eve, visible evidence of his Squire's approval. Sir Charles had left a long list, a muddle of amendments and additions and cancellations, though it was not up to date since he relied upon his memory and knowledge of the village. On the Christmas after his death Sir Edward Follesmark had good-naturedly made himself responsible for the doles, and the Routs at Wood Farm were surprised to receive a wooden doll with red-painted cheeks and a box of bright marbles. The Wood Farm item on the list—written heaven knew how long ago—read, "Children only—boy, girl." Mrs. Rout had made the presents useful by passing them on, but Captain Rout missed the bottle of choice port which he, the Rector, and at one time Fred Clopton had been accustomed to receive. Fred, when he fell from grace, had been firmly crossed off.

In 1796 Richard had studied the list and said, "Outdated nonsense! However, for this year, while they're feeling sore about enclosure, the cottagers should have something. Do the best you can with this." He had given Linda a couple of sovereigns, which she spent as thriftily as possible, aware all the time that her gifts, however well chosen and nicely packed, compared very ill with the "14 lbs. prime beef," "12 yards red flannel," "half load logs" with which, if the list were to be believed, the old Squire had booned his virtuous poor.

It was with some thought of making amends for last year's parsimony that she roused herself, wrote out a list of her own, told Hadstock to send a bullock to the butcher, and herself ventured out to shop in Baildon. Like everyone else who has always been short of money and then suddenly has a pocketful, she found shopping delightful; one trip was not enough; she made another and indulged in an orgy of spending. She provided something of solid value for every poor person and something really "Christmassy" for the children. Then the Christmas spirit nudged her conscience with regard to the Rectory family; this year she had intended to send her brother Arthur a really handsome money present—but was that enough? Arthur had been very kind, offered to send Constance, his eldest daughter, to keep her company, offered to come himself if her affairs needed supervision, invited her to stay at the Rectory if she felt in need of a change. She decided suddenly to invite the whole family to spend Christmas at Clevely. She sent the money with the invitation, so that Arthur could hire someone to take the Christmas services for him, and could pay the coach fares.

The Liddiard family had arrived on the day before Christmas Eve, which was the day of the Baildon Christmas Market, and Matt Ashpole had happened to see them alight from the coach and go swarming to the two carriages sent from Clevely to meet them.

"There looked to be a round dozen, and call me a liar if there was one better fed or better shod than Spitty's here."

Nobody called him a liar; he was infallible.

The elder children of the family had helped to carry out the parcels to the hooded gig in which Hadstock was to drive Linda to the Waste. The lumps of prime beef and the logs had been dispatched by Hadstock the previous day and Linda had, with some reluctance, been persuaded into delivering the gifts of flannel, tea, sugar, sweets, and toys herself. Hadstock had been curiously insistent upon that and she had agreed on condition that he went with her.

Now as the cheerful children, crammed to bursting with food, drew back on to the steps, at the top of which their father smiling and their mother with an expressionless face stood to watch the departure, Linda suffered an onset of shyness, and a recurrence of the feeling of utter helplessness which had held her immobile during the last weeks.

"I can't go," she said, and half turned towards the door, became conscious of all the watching eyes. They were all—with the possible exception of Mrs. Liddiard's—friendly eyes, the children already loved this kind, generous aunt, but they looked, at that moment, inimical. She turned back to where Hadstock waited. "You take the things for me, please, and give them my good wishes. I'm afraid they'll try to thank me—and I only gave them back what had been filched from them. I couldn't bear it."

Hadstock spoke with some urgency, unaware that he sounded brusque. "You must come. I promised them when I headed off the deputation. They'll be so disappointed."

"Oh well, if you think I should," she said helplessly. As though sensing that her leaden limbs made movement difficult, he came and half lifted her into the gig, tucked the rug around her, and then climbed in on the other side, nodded to the boy who held the horse's head, and gathered up the reins. The gig rattled away at a smart pace.

"There! You heard that?" said Mrs. Liddiard. "What did I tell you? 'You *must* come. *I* promised . . . *I* headed off the deputation.' He's got the whip hand there and no mistake. I knew yesterday, from the way she introduced him."

The words pierced the pleasant torpor induced in her husband by an unusually large meal, the sight of his children's happiness, the joy of reunion with his sister, and the reflection that *this* year Christmas would not confront him with the task of carving one goose into eleven more or less equal portions.

"He was here, you know," he said mildly, "at the time of the tragedy. Women suddenly bereaved do tend very much to turn and cling to the man who happens to be nearest. I have often noticed that in the course of my professional visits."

"A clergyman's quite different. And Linda is weak. The way they went trailing about the world when Sir Richard fell out with his father proves that. Any woman with a grain of sense would have settled up that silly little quarrel before you could say 'knife.' I know I should. She just drifted along and she's drifting now. Before you leave, Arthur, you must have a talk to her, otherwise you'll wake up one fine morning and find that your lady sister is plain Mrs. Hadstock!"

Mrs. Liddiard had other plans for her sister-in-law. She hoped very much that she would take "a fancy" to one of the children: Mark, who was delicate and such a worry; or Paul, whose wolfish appetite was noticeable even in that family of hearty eaters. With either of them their mother could gladly dispense.

Hadstock said with false joviality, "You've got a fine lot of parcels here."

"Well . . . they've all had a hard year. Besides, who knows where we shall all be by next Christmas."

He shot her a glance and then said lightly:

"It is to be hoped for Clevely's sake that you will be here, and still in generous mood! Look . . . if you really don't feel up to facing them, you needn't. It was just that they wanted to see you—they're simple, you know, and they are so grateful, as indeed they have reason to be. And I thought it would do you good to see how pleased they are."

"At getting back what was their own! I sent for Mr. Turnbull, you know, as soon as I decently could and he showed me something they'd got together and written; it said the land was theirs 'in the eyes of God and by right of custom.' Wasn't that touching?"

"That'd be Amos Greenway's phrase; he's got the gift of the gab. Look, we're just coming up to his chapel now. He displays a new text every fortnight. Let's see what he thinks a suitable Christmas message."

Amos had not been blind to the fact that many of his neighbours had celebrated their good fortune by becoming intoxicated. (Actually Matt, in a burst of generosity and self-congratulation, had given away the produce of one whole brewing, and the Waste dwellers who had been through a period of forced abstinence had developed some alarming symptoms.) The board on the front of the chapel still held out the promise of the building's completion; a promise soon to be fulfilled since Damask had provided money for proper draining of the site, proper laying of foundations; but the boards on the sides struck a sombre note. WINE IS A MOCKER, it said downstream, and upstream, STRONG DRINK IS RAGING. From the gig it was necessary to turn one's head in order to read the third board's message, and Hadstock was disproportionately relieved to see that Linda did so turn her head.

"Not precisely in the festive spirit," he commented, "but mild compared with some of Amos' efforts."

Linda had turned her head in the other direction, looking sideways and backward at the column of smoke which rose over the trees which screened Fuller's farmhouse from the highroad.

"Did you do anything about Mrs. Fuller?" she asked.

"I did. I said they could stay. You said, when I asked you, that you didn't care one way or the other, and young Fuller had got hold of some land so I thought . . ."

"Oh yes, you were right. I shouldn't have said I didn't care. It was just that at the time . . . I couldn't even *think*."

"Probably I shouldn't have bothered you."

They crossed the Stone Bridge and reached the first of the cottages, where there was no one at home. In the second Bert Sadler's old father, purblind and very deaf, came to the door. He seemed disinclined to embarrass anyone by effusive thanks; he grunted as he felt the weight of the parcel and said "Eh" when wished a Happy Christmas. Then, having closed the door and fumbled his way back to his chair, he opened the parcel and very much enjoyed the sweets intended for the children.

The third cottage had been Widow Hayward's. During its few months of emptiness it had collapsed in upon itself and was now a heap of clods, with nettles and dead willow herb growing out of the crevices and its sunken roof covered with grass. Linda said, "It's strange, isn't it, I've noticed before, however rickety they are, they don't fall down while they're lived in; the moment they're empty they do."

"The ceilings rest on the people's heads and the pressure of bodies inside keeps the walls upright," Hadstock said, and was rewarded by a smile.

In the fourth cottage a cheerful, toothless old woman was in charge of several children.

"Mrs. Gardiner?" Linda asked.

"Thass me, my lady." She took her parcel and fingered it avidly.

"Flannel! Oh, thank you, my lady, I'm sure. I did sorely miss the flannel last year and the year afore. Wish you a Happy Christmas, my lady, and many many more to come; and God bless you indeed for your kindness to the poor."

Every other cottage was deserted, to Linda's delight.

"Is it safe to leave the parcels on the doorsteps?"

"Oh yes. Nobody will be far away." He sounded, Linda thought, a little uneasy; and she noticed that as they went towards the last cottage—the cobbler's—he was holding the reins so tightly that his knuckles showed white against the weathered skin of his hands.

He halted the gig by Amos' door; nobody was at home there, but from somewhere came a murmur of voices, muted into a beelike buzz.

"I'd have prepared you," Hadstock said quickly and guiltily, "but then you'd have thought it was an ordeal. It won't be . . . and it was all their idea . . . they wanted to please you."

As he spoke he had slipped his hand under her elbow and walked her round the corner of Amos' house. There on the patch of ground which had been Julie's garden, then part of the enclosed field, and was now the beginning of the new allotments was gathered every inhabitant of the Waste capable of standing upright for half an hour, excepting Amos, who had gone to Nettleton for the Christmas Eve service.

They were not, perhaps, a very creditable gathering; ragged, ill-shod, undernourished; most of the women dragged down by hard work and childbearing, many, like Mrs. Palfrey, heavily pregnant; but just for the moment a kind of brightness shone on them; the dullest face wore a look of excitement and expectancy.

They were drawn up in an orderly semicircle, and in the centre of it, a little way in front, stood Matt Ashpole in his moleskin breeches and ragged coat, but cleanly shaven and wearing a new neckcloth patterned with yellow and black horseshoes on a red ground. He held on a leash an animal which almost anywhere else on the face of the earth would have drawn a crowd that was neither orderly nor quiet. It was a huge white dog whose thick close pelt had been clipped short over his haunches and in certain other places, and in others left long; there was a sort of shawl of fur cover over his shoulders, cuffs on his ankles, a ball on the tip of his tail, and a pow, tied with a bow of bright pink ribbon, on top of his head. No dog so ridiculously tricked out, no dog in the least like this dog had ever before been seen in Suffolk. Even Linda for a moment...

This was, Hadstock knew, the moment of greatest danger. He called out in a taut voice:

"Hang on to him, Ashpole. Let her ladyship go to him first."

Fortunately sheer incredulity held Simon in check for the second or two that mattered. He sniffed at the black shirt, looked upwards... It was!

"Look out," said Hadstock. "He'll muddy her ladyship's dress. Here, let me have him and you make your speech!" He took the leash from Matt's hand and quietly proceeded to half throttle the dog.

"But he've took to you, your ladyship," said Matt happily, "and we hope you'll take to him." That was not how the speech should have started. He cleared his throat and began again.

"My lady, all of us what you see here assembled was wishful you should know that we ain't blind to what you hev done for us. We wanted to give you a token of our gratitude and our esteem. We got a dog because I happened to say to Mr. Hadstock I wished my owd bitch had had pups so you could hev one of them, but he said he knew a dog, the very latest fashion. Mr. Hadstock said I weren't to keep you standing about in the cold, so I'll wish you, from all of us, the compliments of the season so far as possible and say God bless you, your ladyship, and thanks for giving us back the Waste."

Everybody agreed that Matt had spoken out like a man and though Lady Shelmadine-pore-lady didn't say anything except "Thank you, all of you, thank you very much indeed," the broken voice in which she said it and the real tears that came into her eyes showed her sincerity.

"And I was right, wasn't I, to say no cheering," said Matt later, glaring at those who had suggested it. "'Twouldn't hev been seemly. And mark you, I never said 'Happy Christmas.' 'Compliments of the season,' I said as being more suitable in the circumstances. I trust you marked that."

"One thing you did wrong, Matt," said Bert Sadler boldly. "You said bitch; you never ought to hev said that, not in front of Lady Shelmadine-pore-lady!" Matt was not, at this stage, going to admit that the word had slipped out.

"Why, you iggerunt lump, you, don't you reckon I thought that all out aforehand? Couldn't very well say 'lady dog' could I, when I was talking to a lady!"

"Anyway," said Mrs. Palfrey, "that don't matter. She was pleased and the dog and a houseful of young 'uns'll cheer her up, pore lady."

Mrs. Palfrey walked heavily towards the Gardiners' cottage, where she had left her two youngest. She was herself very happy. There was a great lump of beef on her food shelf, they'd all have a good Christmas dinner. And they'd got back their potato patch. By Good Friday this latest young 'un would be born—and if it was a girl it would be named Linda—and Mrs. Palfrey would be free to get on with her digging. How she would dig!

The big white dog sat in the gig between Hadstock and Linda. Her arm lay round his neck and every now and then he turned his head, shot out his tongue, and licked her face or ear with an ecstatic shiver.

"Well," Hadstock said, breaking silence, "that's over. I admit to moments of grave anxiety, but it seemed the only way."

"How did you manage it?" Her voice was still inclined to shake and her eyes kept brimming and spilling tears.

"As Ashpole said. He said he reckoned you'd been main fond of your dog and missed it and he wished he had one to give you. He's pretty shrewd, he said he reckoned it might be some time before you felt like getting one for yourself. So then I said I knew where there was a dog for sale, cheap; a real French poodle, grown a bit too big. You must remember that his name is Beau, and if he shows any signs of resuming old habits he must be checked at once. I'm sorry he had to be made such a figure of fun. But it seemed to me that any big white dog *might* be open to suspicion. I'd been racking my brains for some way of getting him back for you."

She sat very still, with that last sentence ringing in her ears. And Hadstock was silent too, regarding with some dismay the gap which this one short outing had made in the protective fence of formality which had reared itself between them since the night of Richard's death. On that night when he broke the news to her she had clung to him weeping and he had held her and comforted her, even kissed her, as though she were a frightened, overwrought child; they had truly been alone then. But almost immediately she had spoken about her old love for Richard, about the necessity for concealment; the world had asserted itself, and there they were concocting the story with which to deceive it. Since the morning when he had ridden off to fetch Sir Edward, they had hardly been alone at all; Linda had been ill, Lady Fennel and other well-meaning females had been in attendance, and the few times when he had been in her presence had been devoted to talk of affairs; she had been apathetic and he businesslike. Something had fallen over their relationship, as a thin, tinkling, transparent sheath of ice will form over a tree when a night frost follows a day of rain.

There were times when Hadstock caught himself wishing that he had arrived in the subterranean temple before the blow was struck. Then, at least, he had something to offer—a refuge, however humble, from horror and disgust; but whenever his thoughts tended that way, he remembered that moment when he had tried to plan a future for them both, and how unsatisfactory his plans had been. He was realist enough to see that the situation had been an impossible one from the very first.

He was staring that sombre realisation in the face once more when Linda moved her hand from the dog's neck and laid it on his arm.

"I do love you, you know," she said. "This probably isn't the time or the place, and perhaps I shouldn't speak first, but I do love you and I don't see why I should go on pretending—not when we're by ourselves."

He shot her a startled glance and then looked away; but he moved his hand so that hers lay in it, curved like a shell. He gave it a swift crunching pressure and then laid it back on the dog's neck.

"That's the trouble. People never are by themselves. There's always the world to be reckoned with. I love you. You know that. But being in love isn't an end in itself, however much the poets may pretend that it is."

"It's something to begin with. Enough to make me feel that nothing else matters so long as we are together."

"Being together means marriage," said Hadstock bluntly, "and that involves several other things. Mild scandal for one. 'Imagine Lady Shelmadine marrying her *bailiff*!' Social ostracism as a result. I'm used to that, but I should hate it for you. Also—we might as well face it—I don't think I should fit into the role of kept man with much grace."

The bitterness of his voice shocked her but she said lightly, "I can't imagine anyone who would do it worse. You're much too masterful and set in your ways."

He did not answer, nor turn his head. He sat slightly hunched, the reins slack in his fingers, his craggy profile blocked in against the gathering dusk.

She thought about the little she knew of his history, and realised that his whole life had been one long affront to his pride, blow after blow falling on the same sensitive spot and this last the heaviest of all. A vast aching pity, like a physical pain, set fangs in her flesh; she could have assuaged it by putting her arms about him and dragging that proud, humbled head down to her breast. But that, she knew, was not the way. A line from a poem read long ago began to chant in her mind. "Eyeless in Gaza, at the mill with slaves," Arrogant Samson brought low could not be comforted by pity . . .

"That night," she said, "if it hadn't ended as it did, I was going to ask you to take me away, to let me cook and mend for you. Would you have taken me?"

"I think you know the answer to that. But the cases aren't comparable."

She saw suddenly that pity was misplaced. He had taken his blows and survived; had preserved his integrity and his pride and was, even now, master of the situation.

It was she who was reduced to pleading.

With the skill of long practice she began to put forward her pleas.

CHAPTER 21

ON AN OCTOBER EVENING IN THE YEAR 1798, MATT ASHPOLE drove home from Baildon Market in a mood of such high good humour that his piggy little eyes glistened and his leathery lips stretched every now and then into a grin.

The old horse, when it reached the Waste, slowed down and prepared to turn, as usual, but Matt flapped the rein and said,

"Giddup Gyp. Step or two further tonight."

The ironshod wheels rattled hollowly over the Stone Bridge, but just beyond the sound of Matt's passing was momentarily engulfed by the sound of the singing which rang out from Amos' chapel.

Faith had been justified. Amos had proved the truth of all the texts and all the proverbs; he *had* trusted in the Lord and the Lord *had* provided; he had tried and tried again and he had at last succeeded. There stood the chapel on its properly drained site, its ugly walls of Peterborough brick firmly set on sound foundations. Amos had his chapel and, what is more, he had a congregation.

He would have stared in mild, puzzled reproach at anyone who suggested that his methods of filling his pews smacked of the same autocratic spirit as had once made Sir Charles withdraw his custom from a Methodist, but there would have been some truth in the charge. Damask had left Amos custodian of several hired acres and Amos had lost no time in making clear to the tenants that it would be in their interests to "turn chapel." He suffered no pang of conscience over that; in fact, his conscience would have rebuked him had he done otherwise; it said in the Bible "*Compel* them to come in." Besides, Damask had left those lands for the good of the chapel, and she and anybody with a bit of sense in their heads must know that a chapel needed not merely funds, but members for its "good."

So on this Wednesday evening the midweek service was well attended, and at the moment when Matt Ashpole jogged past, the congregation was endeavouring to dispel the chill engendered by one of Amos' long extempore prayers by a lusty rendering of Charles Wesley's hymn, "Soldiers of Christ arise and put your armour on." Even Mrs. Shipton was singing heartily, for Amos was now, to all intents and purposes, her landlord.

Matt grinned as he passed the chapel. He was all for everybody enjoying himself after his fashion, and unless by some most unfortunate chance he had been forestalled he was about to enjoy himself hugely.

He knew where he would find those he called "the chaps." The papers which Mr. Turnbull had been all this time preparing had been delivered that very morning; Amos had read one out, valiantly tackling phrases like "in perpetuity" and "their heirs and assignees." Tonight, Matt guessed shrewdly, all the Waste dwellers were feeling like property owners, and though they might be no better off, in cash, than they had been last night, they'd all be down at the old Black Horse celebrating.

There was no need to rein in at the inn; Gyp, smart as he was, had never mastered the fact that a feud existed between his master and Mrs. Sam Jarvey. Several times in the past this stupidity had resulted in a sharp blow; but tonight, when the old horse halted by the inn door, Matt said in a pleased voice:

"Right y'are! Smart owd nag!" And he climbed down from the cart, reached into his pocket, and produced a small, wizened apple which the old horse, hungering for his supper, accepted with such slobbering gratitude that Matt entered the inn rubbing his hand on his moleskin breeches.

He had not set foot in the inn since the night when he had left in umbrage because Mrs. Sam had objected to his language, but he entered boldly, with a loud, "Good evening, all." And they were all there, as he had expected; Shad Jarvey, Bert

Sadler, Matt Juby, Tom Gardiner, all his neighbours, even Spitty Palfrey was there; and of course there were also the more regular customers, Strong 'Un the smith, old Ricky Wellman, Bert Crabtree, and the comparative stranger who was always known as Mr. Martha Bowyer, although presumably he had a name of his own.

The Waste dwellers returned Matt's greeting with a heartiness which owed something to embarrassment; they felt that by gathering in the inn they were showing disloyalty to Matt, whose homemade liquor had so often comforted them in what they thought of as the bad old times. Still, there was no denying that, cheap and potent as Matt's brew was, it was capable of producing some astonishing effects; Shad Jarvey had once sobered up and found that his legs had no feeling in them, and another time Tom Gardiner had waked up blind as a bat. Also, with something to celebrate, they felt an instinctive need for communal drinking and there was nowhere on the Waste large enough to hold them all in any sort of comfort.

Uneasy under his eye, surprised by his arrival, they blundered over one another to ask what he would drink. He apparently bore them no grudge; he said genially:

"Thanks, Shad, thanks, Bert, thanks, all; we'll hev one together in a minnit but I'll start meself off. I fare a bit fancy tonight. . . ." He turned towards the bar—untended at the moment because Sam Jarvey was fetching a fresh log for the fire and Mrs. Sam, hearing the car arrive and mistaking the driver's identity, had darted upstairs to put on a more becoming cap— and said loudly, "The service here ain't what it was!" Mrs. Sam was just in time to catch the words; the sauciness of them and his presence, bold as brass after all these months, made her "Well, fancy seeing you, Matt Ashpole," extremely acidulous.

"Well, leastways you recognised me," he said cheerfully, "and that show I ain't got all that much fatter!" He shot a sly wink at the company; Mrs. Sam, since her accident about a year ago, had become less active and grown very buxom indeed. Her face reddened.

"Did you come here to be recognised or take a proper drink for once? Whadda you want then?"

"Fust of all—do you hev sich a thing, Mrs. Sam—I want a little brandy. Not too little! Time I downed that, all them mugs'll be emptied and then we'll fill 'em up. All here," said

Matt, including in his glance the regular customers as well as his neighbours, "is heving a drink on me tonight."

"You còme into a fortune or something?" asked Mrs. Sam, handing him his brandy with an expression Lucrezia Borgia would have taken great pains to disguise; it said, so plainly, Here you are and I hope it poisons you!

"Not eggsactly. Got a bit of news though!" He took the glass and said, "Good luck, all," in an ordinary way, but he was mentally holding his breath. Now was the moment when anyone else who had heard, or guessed, would speak up and spoil his lovely surprise. Licking his lips, he looked in the direction of Jim Jarvey the lodgekeeper; he'd be the one to know if anybody did.

Nobody spoke the dashing words; they were all looking at him, waiting for him to reveal his bit of news. Mrs. Sam, after a second or two, said crossly, "I s'pose you mean you got your papers, like all the rest of 'em. I don't call that *news*. You all knew last December that her ladyship had took pity on you. The papers only show she kept her promise, and to tell you the truth, Matt Ashpole, and all the rest of you, I don't think that look well to make sich a fuss about getting the papers. That look as though you didn't trust Lady Shelmadine-pore-lady to keep her word, not till you saw it in writing."

"And *that* just look as though you bin missing us ever since last December," said Matt, with a shrewdness few of his hearers fully appreciated. "Point was, missus, we worn't no better off then. Couldn't afford your prices, could we, boys, not till we'd dug out taters and got things going again. Them papers ain't news, as you say, but I reckon they brung us here tonight and thass a stroke of luck, because I hev got a bit of news. Well, thass warmed me up a bit, though I've had better in my day. Now, chaps, name what you fancy and don't be shy, all of you, I mean, not just us what got papers to fuss about. Hullo, Sam, just in time; chuck on that log and come and join us. I got news to tell you and then we'll drink a toast."

A dark suspicion stirred in Mrs. Sam's mind. This was a trick. Matt Ashpole hadn't been inside the door for nigh on two years and the Waste dwellers had come rarely and never in full force . . . she'd be willing to bet that this sudden invasion, this pretence to be celebrating and bringing news and treating, everybody, was all part of an elaborate plot. When it came to paying, that cheeky rascal would turn out his pockets and have no money, and trust Sam, soft fool that he was, not to make a row. She knew Sam was a soft fool because months ago when she'd heard that Matt was making and selling liquor, she'd wanted to take action against him and Sam had said, "Oh, let be. He's only selling cheap poison to them that'll starve to death anyway."

She said now, "You're making very free with your brandy and drinks for all; if you don't mind, I'd like to see the colour of your money."

"You shall, missus, you shall." He dived into his pocket and produced a guinea. "There y'are! Bite it if you like. A proper gentleman give me that, the same time as he give me the news *and* the office to spread it, you might say, when I met him in Baildon Market this very afternoon."

Actually the guinea was one of two, for the gentleman had been generous as well as proper; but Matt Ashpole knew as well as anybody how to make one coin do the work of two. The other one could stay snug in his pocket until he found a way of making it breed.

Mrs. Sam took the guinea and said in rather a defeated way, "Well then . . . ?" And she and Sam took the somewhat confused orders. And all the time the frustrated master of ceremonies, leader of deputations, foreteller of events who lurked behind the rough exterior of the huckster Matt Ashpole stood and gloated while the artist who stood at the back of them all carefully prepared the scene and the words.

All the mugs of the humble, the glasses of the more ambitious were charged at last. Sam Jarvey, who was a weak fool in the reckoning of the one who knew him best, had chosen to drink the ale of the majority; Mrs. Sam, still suspecting a trick, had thought, All right, and poured herself half a pint of her favourite port wine into a pewter tankard; you might as well be hanged for a sheep as a lamb . . . yet the guinea seemed all right.

"Well now," Matt said, smugly aware that he had everyone's attention, "this here'll be news to *you* though, mark you, I worn't all that astounded meself, being foresighted, as you all know!" He paused to allow anyone who wished to express agreement by a grunt to do so, and Mrs. Sam took advantage of the pause to say:

"That ain't news, we all know you're foresighted; so's a fox!"

"The gentleman what give me that guinea and the news and the office to spread it, you might almost say—'You being a sorta unofficial town crier, Ashpole,' he says to me—was Mr. Hadstock; and what he tell me is that he's gorn to be married." He was so skilfully concealing his narrative art that they failed to perceive it.

"Is that all?" asked Mrs. Sam in a disappointed tone, and an anonymous voice muttered, "More fool him!"

"The lady what is going to be Mrs. Hadstock," Matt went on with the triumphant joy of a conjurer producing the rabbit from an empty hat, "is known to you all and I reckon you'll drink to their health and happiness then more hearty when I tell you who 'tis. Thass our own lady, Lady Shelmadine!"

Any but a Suffolk man born and bred would have been disappointed by the reception of this announcement, but Matt knew his audience; their very silence was eloquent, and so was the way in which they stood there holding their mugs, waiting for him to propose the toast. Leisurely and fulsomely he proceeded to do so.

ABOUT THE AUTHOR

Norah Lofts is one of the most respected writers of women's historical fiction. She and her husband lived in a 250-year-old manor house in Bury St. Edmunds, Suffolk, England until her recent death. Over the years Ms. Lofts wrote numerous historical novels which have sold millions of copies in the United States.

14   TAF-58